Praise for the [

The

'Intelligent and pacy thriller … a taut keenly observed tale of revenge, perseverance and the struggle against injustice.' (Paula Hawkins)

'A stunning debut from an exciting new addition to the world of crime fiction.' (Stephen Booth)

Cold Dawn

'Stylish, authoritative crime writing from someone who knows … vivid and gripping.' (Oliver Harris)

Cold Summer

'A police procedural so action-packed it reads like a thriller – with a Nepalese twist.' (Dr Andy Martin, *Reacher Said Nothing: Lee Child and the Making of Make Me*)

'Ellson hits the spot with *Cold Summer*. This pacy and intriguing thriller is not to be missed. Pull up the drawbridge and settle in. Castle is back!' (Keith Wright, the Inspector Stark series)

'A gripping series.' (Samantha Brownley, UK Crime Book Club)

Base Line

'Gallops along to a gripping climax. A cracking read.' (Zoe Sharp)

'A gripping and complex story with characters to root for. Completely authentic from the first page.' (Sarah Ward)

James Ellson was a police officer for fifteen years, starting in London and finishing as a detective inspector at Moss Side in Manchester. When he left the police he started writing, and his debut novel *The Trail* was published in 2020.

Both *The Trail* and *Cold Dawn* were longlisted for the Boardman Tasker Award. *Cold Summer* concludes the Nepal trilogy, and *Base Line* is the fourth book in the DCI Castle series.

Rockburn is the first in a new series.

Born in Surrey, James now lives on a smallholding in the Peak District, which includes bees and an orchard.

facebook.com/james.ellson.98
www.jamesellson.com

ROCKBURN

James Ellson

Cambium

First edition, 2025

Cambium Press
All rights reserved

A CIP record for this book is available from the British Library

ISBN 978-1-7394421-8-7 (paperback)
ISBN 978-1-7394421-9-4 (ebook)

Printed in Great Britain by Clays Ltd, Elcograf S.p.A

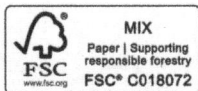

MIX
Paper | Supporting
responsible forestry
FSC
www.fsc.org   FSC® C018072

1 3 5 7 9 8 6 4 2

1

Rockburn rode around the back of the working men's club in West Manchester and parked the panther next to Flack's three-wheeler. Light and hubbub spilled from the club's rear windows. He locked a heavy chain through the wheels and hoped the full moon was a good omen. If he won the quarter-final, then maybe his life wasn't a total fuck-up. He unbuckled a pannier, took out his match arrows and a small towel, and walked inside.

The bar was as busy as a cross-channel ferry. A line of tape cordoned off the playing area and round tables had been arranged alongside. The seats mostly taken, the tabletops strewn with glasses and jugs of beer. The room was hot and smelt of fried onions. He was pleased he'd practised with the heating turned up.

Flack stood by himself at the bar. He was a big man, too big for two wheels. He wore a leather jacket with looping chains. His auburn ponytail reached his belt. Rockburn ordered Flack another beer, and a coke for himself.

'Anyone phoned?'

Rockburn shook his head. Passing Flack his pint, he rolled the cold coke bottle across the back of his neck.

Flack gulped down the beer. 'You're nervous.' Grinning like

a crazed Viking, the leader of the Demons Motorcycle Club set the empty glass on the bar. 'Someone'll call.'

Rockburn drank some coke. Maybe his phone would never ring. If he won, the prize money would cover his rent for another month. If he lost *and* the phone didn't ring, then he'd try the pubs and clubs.

The commentator blew through a microphone. 'Good evening.' His voice boomed. 'Tonight we have the quarterfinal of the North West Cup. Home lad Dave Dave Cummins against –' The commentator paused to allow a cheer to subside. 'Against another Manchester player – former cop Rockburn.' The booing was drowned out by Flack's throaty roar. Rockburn's sole supporter cleared a half-circle, his ponytail sailing up, and glared at the home crowd. 'Standard PDC rules. Five hundred and one, best of eleven legs. Darts please, gentlemen.'

Flack gripped Rockburn's shoulder, whispered a sweet nothing.

Rockburn walked over to the referee and Cummins. His opponent was wearing an England football shirt stretched over a molehill stomach. The ref was dressed in black and wore silver bands on his sleeves.

Rockburn shook his opponent's hand. Cummins' pudgy fingers were sweaty, his hand like a leaky tin of mackerel. The ref tossed a coin. Rockburn called and lost.

'Quiet, please.'

Cummins lined up. He wiggled his backside to the noisy delight of his supporters. He threw one hundred and forty, to another huge cheer.

Rockburn's turn. He back-and-forthed. Threw a twenty. Another twenty. A third.

Dave Dave scored one hundred.

Rockburn: twenty-six.

Cummins: one hundred and forty.

Rockburn: twenty-two. Someone cat-called.

'Quiet, please.'

Cummins: sixty.

Rockburn: forty-five. It was better, but not much. He'd be home before the chip shop closed if it continued.

'Dave Dave needs sixty-one to win the first leg.'

Cummins wiggled his backside, the crowd hooted. He threw an eleven. A ten. He threw double twenty to checkout.

Rockburn lost the next leg, and the next one. He won the fourth, lost the fifth, won the sixth. Two behind at the interval. He bought Flack two pints of beer, then went for a piss. The bone-coloured moon glowered through the frosted window.

The commentator boomed, the scoreboard ticked down, the referee marked a pocketbook with a small pencil. The crowd jeered and caterwauled and stood up and down on chairs and tables as part of a Mexican wave. The players reached five legs apiece and the second interval. Rockburn stood outside with Flack who smoked half a foul-smelling cigar while he kneaded Rockburn's shoulders and clicked out his fingers. They checked on their motorbikes, and stared at the shadows stretching across the car park.

Flack said nothing which was unusual.

The deciding game began, Rockburn leading as he'd won the previous leg. One hundred, his standard opening. Cummins equalled it. The room quietened.

Rockburn reached a potential checkout. He needed one hundred and five. Flack raised an arm and gripped his bicep. Rockburn wiped his darts on the towel. The crowd booed and whistled. An egg was thrown.

'Quiet, please.'

Rockburn stood at the oche. He threw triple twenty. He threw a five. He needed double top to checkout. Everyone in the room knew. It would temporarily solve his rent problem, give him some breathing space.

He licked the tip, then raised the dart, drew it back. Aimed, drew it back a second time. An image from his last case flickered across the board. A seven-year-old girl tied to a rusty pipe, gagged and naked from the waist down. He spilled the dart. It slipped from his hand and landed in the plastic mat halfway to the board.

'He doesn't want it, he doesn't want it,' chanted a bank of Cummins' supporters.

Rockburn walked back with his head down. A small light in his tunnel of gloom almost extinguished.

Dave Dave stepped up and pretended to throw a dart left-handed. The crowd roared. A man lined up against Flack until he was pulled away. Flack downed his beer and winked at Rockburn.

Cummins threw a seven, then double twenty.

Checkout.

The room erupted, Flack turned over a table. Rockburn stared at the board. Feeling hot and lightheaded, he sleeved his darts, folded his towel. He thanked the ref and dragged Flack out to the bikes.

'The beer was off,' said Flack.

Rockburn rode back to his garret in Templeside, the moon gleaming like a sheriff's badge. Stars winked at him as if they were asking questions.

He locked the panther to the fire escape in the backyard, and walked through the alley to the street. Next to the front door were three plaques in storey order: *Flack's Tattoos, RCS Holdings, Rockburn Investigations*. He buzzed in and climbed the stairs. In the morning he'd start phoning recruitment agencies.

As he unlocked the door, he saw again the young girl bound to the pipe. Heard her screams. Felt her terror. Wondered if it would be his last ever case, and the following week he'd be stacking shelves or making deliveries.

His mobile rang.

Salvation?

2

Rockburn scrabbled in his pockets.

'Hello.'

No answer. He'd missed them, or they'd not held on. He stabbed at the screen to call back but heard only the engaged tone. A mobile number he didn't recognise.

He shut the door. Home – until things got better, or worse. One long narrow room which served both as a living and a working space. At one end there was a tiny kitchen and a cupboard with a shower. A dartboard hung at the other. In-between, a sofa and a desk. He slept on the sofa and intended to work at the desk. It was cheap, and thank God, not in the slightest detail cheerful.

He phoned again, the line connecting, ringing and ringing and ringing.

A few minutes later he tried a third time, then gave up. There was nothing else he could do. If he'd still been in the Job he would have traced the call, and if it had been registered, obtained the address and the owner's details, and used them to cross-check the police intelligence databases. It was surprising how often a scenario emerged. Now, however, he had nothing. Probably someone trying to persuade him to switch utility provider – but it *could* have been his first client. He yanked the darts out of the board, stepped back to the oche he'd chalked across the worn carpet, and thumped them home.

Music from the wine bar blared. He looked out of the window. A line of parked minicabs, the drivers standing alongside one car, smoking and wisecracking. The chippie was still open and the smell of rough cooking oil wafted up. Elsa or another former colleague might do him a favour on the phone number, but the request seemed too minor to waste.

He'd bought a plaque for the front door, printed two thousand business cards and hand delivered over half to local residents and firms. Haggled for insurance. Rockburn Investigations was going to perish before it had even begun.

He grabbed a bottle of beer and slumped down on the sofa. Taking a swig he wondered what Flack wasn't telling him. He ate a handful of cornflakes from an open packet. The final part of his police disciplinary – a decision on his pension – was in a few days' time. He ate another handful. Contemplated a different match result, a different tribunal decision, a different life.

An ambulance wailed past, phantasmal flicker bounding across the walls like the northern lights.

Twelve hours later, his phone rang again.

He threw down a biking magazine. 'Rockburn.'

'Fenwick Street.' A young woman's voice. 'Please, Mr Rockburn.' She sounded Asian, Chinese or Thai maybe.

The line went dead.

Phone number the same as before. He prodded it, waited, but again there was no answer. He looked out of the window, thinking it was possible the caller was outside, hoping to meet nearby but not wanting to be spotted entering his stairwell. The pavements were busy and traffic queued at a zebra crossing. A man standing in a cherry picker was mending a streetlight. No woman caught his attention.

In the kitchen he downed a glass of water. Like his one chair, the glass was also from the bar, and pinching them had helped distinguish what he'd done before and what he was doing – trying to do – now. Fenwick Street sounded familiar. He tapped on his phone, located it near the Universities.

Rockburn pulled on his leathers and jogged down the metal fire escape to the panther. The motorbike was a leaving present to himself, something good to have come from it. A 1000 cc red and silver superbike, faster than a cheetah, punchy as a bear. The rip of the engine still gave him pleasure, as if he'd designed the water-cooled, double overhead camshaft, four-cylinder engine himself. He pulled out into the Manchester traffic.

Ditchwater clouds filled the sky, and a mist of precipitation hung in the yellow air. The industrial revolution still lingered, despite all the glass-panelled office skyscrapers and blocks of riverside flats. He opened up the throttle and eased past the cars as if they were stationary.

Parking the bike two streets away, and carrying his helmet and holding a clipboard, he walked the short blocks to Fenwick Street. He passed a restaurant set in a basement, two chefs smoking on the steps, and a shop selling gym supplements.

As he crossed Upton Street, he called the cops and made a false report of a man beating a woman with a dog lead. A violent domestic incident, and high priority in Job-speak. In his new undertaking, police could be knights in shining armour or pains in the balls. The situation at Fenwick Street was still to be assessed, but it might be useful to have them close. But not too close.

At Fenwick he pretended to consult his clipboard.

A dark blue car with thick tyres turned into the street.

Three up, south-east Asian males in their thirties or forties.

Rockburn studied his clipboard as the car cruised past. Like hyenas, the men surveilled all round, alert for any scavenging opportunity. Or maybe they were after girls, or just looking for trouble. Or they were on a mission, and the reason he'd been dragged to Fenwick Street. Possible, too, he was the target. Plenty of his old – and not so old – cases with cons who bore a grudge. Smith A; the Stringer family; Carpolski; and the most recent, the Kingman brothers, Pete and Bobby.

Rockburn's stomach filled with butterflies. Being confronted and assaulted would not be unusual. But it was always better to be forewarned, and wary, than surprised and end up on the losing side.

Sirens sounded in the distance.

At the end of the road, the blue hatchback screeched across the junction and accelerated out of sight.

Rockburn walked down the pavement, glancing occasionally at his clipboard as if he was looking for an address. A high-vis roadcrew were digging up the opposite pavement, and a coned path led down the carriageway. A mini digger stood idle next to an empty skip. Fluorescent jackets were a favourite disguise but the digger would have been an expensive prop. Pedestrians meandered. At the end of the road stood a post box, and a bus stop with people waiting. Halfway along, shops started. Dark windows above.

Rockburn kept walking. The sirens strengthened. Boys and girls in blue, a kids' game, but one he'd been more than happy with before the Kingman case.

At the end of the road, the blue hatchback bumped up the kerb, and two of the Asian men decamped. Taking a pavement each, they headed up Fenwick Street towards Rockburn.

He considered his options. Watching from inside a shop would put him in a corner. He crossed a side-street, and glanced back. No taxi he could hail. He passed an alley, but like the cab, running was avoiding the issue, an issue he was meant to be investigating.

For Rockburn, investigation was a grand word – despite its reputation for poking into sleazy corners, bracing ne'er do wells, for playing dirty. Private investigation was an important, even honourable job. It wasn't painting a client's house, or serving them beer, or fixing their car. It was sorting their problems, kickstarting their life, improving their wellbeing. Failure often meant a lifetime of unhappiness. Investigation was a job where he couldn't shirk his responsibilities.

The man from the car on Rockburn's pavement was the width of a football pitch away, and closing. His pal opposite was keeping level. They were large men and moved heavily, like warring apes. Their jackets bulged, either with muscle or weaponry, or both.

Rockburn stepped out into the road, weaved diagonally through the traffic, and at the same time, fitted a knuckleduster onto his right hand. Not used it before, but in the Job he would have had a baton, and a radio to summon assistance. In his new role, he roamed, cogitated, batted alone.

Less paperwork, though.

He straddled the white line as the Asian men drew level. Covered the knuckleduster with his left hand. His stomach butterflies now flapping birds.

Let his left hand drop.

Drew back his right –

The two Asian men passed him.

A van with protruding carpet rolls trundled past, followed by a bus. Rockburn hopped up onto the far pavement and slipped the knuckleduster into a pocket.

A confrontation had been avoided – maybe – but he was

still no closer to why he'd been summoned there. He considered following the men from the car, but decided to continue to the end of the street. His stomach calmed. He felt like a blind man playing poker, but with an unknown pot and a trio of twitchy onlookers.

He'd almost reached the end of the road, and nothing had caught his attention. The blue car had driven away, and no one was waiting to meet him. No damsel requiring his assistance, no altercation, no disturbance. Which only left a set-up as the explanation for the call.

No client meant no money. He kicked a stone at an empty bus stop. It struck the reinforced plastic with a satisfying thud. As he neared, he checked the street behind him. The Asian men from the car had also disappeared.

Something remained in the shelter. The bombing of the Arndale and 7/7 meant he, like most police officers, had dealt with dozens of suspicious packages. He could make another call.

He glanced inside.

Underneath the end seat sat a boy about ten or eleven years old. His arms hugged his drawn-up legs and his forehead rested on his knees. He wore jeans and a black top with a hood covering his head. His skin was light brown.

Rockburn walked in. A child wasn't what he was expecting, but it was clear the boy needed help. The image of Pricha Kuri tied to the pipe in the Kingman case returned.

He squatted down. 'Are you okay?'

The boy shook his head.

Rockburn glanced up the street, and back at the boy. 'Are you waiting for someone?'

The boy's eyes were red-rimmed and his face thin. He was clutching a card. *Rockburn Investigations. Former detective. Reasonable rates.*

'That's me,' said Rockburn, pointing at the card. 'I'm an investigator. A bit like a policeman.'

The boy stared, unblinking. Not a stare of incomprehension, but of shock, maybe fear.

'Understand? Police?' Rockburn thumped his chest. 'Me.'

A pause, then a tight nod.

'Normally,' said Rockburn, 'I'd tell you never to go anywhere with a stranger, but –' He glanced up the street a second time. The blue car had reappeared and the two Asian hyenas were climbing aboard. He felt like a water diviner whose rods were twitching.

'Can you run?'

The boy nodded.

Halfway down the road, the blue hatchback pulled out from the kerb and accelerated along the centre of the carriageway. Cars hooted, and cones from the in-road walkway buckled and fell.

'Come on,' said Rockburn, standing up.

Ditching the clipboard and his helmet, he grabbed the boy's hand and yanked him to his feet. He started running, and half-dragging the boy. They turned the corner, around the barred windows of a convenience shop.

'Bit faster,' whispered Rockburn. 'Don't want them to catch us.' The boy began to swing his other arm. Rockburn half-pulled him past a butcher's with glistening pig carcasses hanging in the window, and ducked into an alley. One he'd been down before. Bags of rubbish lined one wall and it stank of urine. He headed towards an oblong of a tiny side-street.

The boy slipped and fell.

Rockburn hauled him up, continued running and pulling. Wondered if he might need to carry him.

As he neared the side-street, the blue car filled the oblong. Doors were flung open, and two of the passengers climbed out. Rockburn checked behind. Another large Asian man blocked the view of the street.

The boy looked up at Rockburn, his mouth agape and his eyes pulled back into their ruddy sockets.

3

Rockburn halted outside a peeling green door in an otherwise blank wall. Sandblasted graffiti was still visible.

In front of them, there was a triumphant shout, and behind them, the chasing man slowed to a walk.

Holding the boy close, Rockburn hammered on the wood.

No response.

There wasn't a handle so he tried his shoulder, but the door was sturdy as an oak tree. Against Job protocol, Rockburn had recommended the security firm who'd installed it. He released the boy, backed up and charged.

The door didn't even shudder. He kicked opposite the hinges, tried another shoulder-barge. The boy screamed at the advancing thug.

Suddenly the door opened inwards – stopped halfway. The boy ceased yelling. Rockburn hauled him inside, and a woman all in black and wearing a veil shoved the door shut. She locked it and slid home the bolts. She pushed back a steel frame and locked that too.

Half a dozen heavy blows struck the door.

Angry voices.

'Come,' said the woman. Rockburn followed, guiding the boy in front of him with a hand. The boy pushed it off.

She led them through a dark passage which smelt of cooking and spices. It was a comforting smell, making Rockburn think of his early childhood, before the time the sitter had opened the front door to two police officers, a man and a woman holding their hats, their belts bristling with equipment. The officers' visit which seemed to last all night and into the next day imbued the Job with a sort of magic which he'd wanted to be part of and had never really lost.

Clothes hung from pegs. A rack of sandals. Two low stacks of boxes with labels showing saucepans.

The passage continued, past flights of stairs going up and a set of stone steps descending to a dark basement.

'How are you, Leila?' said Rockburn. She'd told him her name meant born at night.

'We're okay. There've been no more problems.' She kept walking, her dress trailing. Rockburn could hear her children running about and laughing. A door slamming.

Using the communal passage, they walked through three or four dwellings at the back of the shops. Another difference between being a PI and a detective was that in the Job, there'd always been backup.

They reached the end of the passage, and another door. More sandals. Coats on a stand, and a shelf of crocheted hats. Behind the door were the sounds of traffic and people.

Leila produced a key from within her dress and unlocked it. Pushed it open. Steps led down to a wide pavement thick with people, and a busy street. Opposite was a greengrocer's with a pavement display of fruit and veg.

'Go with God.'

'Thank you,' said Rockburn.

Leila put a finger to her lips, and shut the door.

Two drummed principles for detective work in respect of victims. Treat them how you would want your own family

15

treated. And, today's victims are tomorrow's witnesses and informants. Leila's kids had been bullied at school and her husband's shop robbed at gunpoint. Rockburn had arrested and charged two brothers for the robbery, ensured their shop as well as their home had its security improved, and persuaded a family liaison officer on light duties to engage with the school.

Subconsciously, he still thought of himself as a detective. He hustled the boy across the road and into the back of a waiting taxi. Handing over a few coins to a lad wearing an apron, he grabbed a banana and an apple from the boxes of fruit, and climbed in beside the boy. He made him squeeze down into the footwell and gave instructions to the driver. They set off. Rockburn looked behind, and ahead, but couldn't see the blue car or their pursuers.

The car smelt of a sweet tobacco. Religious inscriptions adorned the back of the seats and an ornate cross dangled from the rearview mirror.

He opened a window. The cool unclean air of Manchester drifted into the back cocooning him and the boy, and for a moment Rockburn felt like they were being embalmed, and it calmed him. But not the boy. The boy was shaking and whispering to himself.

'We're okay now,' said Rockburn. He stretched out a hand. The boy thought for a moment, then took it. Rockburn squeezed. 'It's going to be alright.'

The boy nodded, but his eyes told a different story. Rockburn wondered whether the woman on the phone had left him in the bus stop. And if so, where she was and why the Asian men were chasing them. First, he would take the boy somewhere safe – not to the nearest police station; the pursuers might expect that; Hocking's? – then start working on the answers. The pursuit would have been caught on CCTV, and give opportunities for facial recognition or number plate enhancement. Maybe, he would pull in that favour.

'You hungry?'

The boy nodded.

Rockburn passed him the fruit. The boy unzipped the banana and ate it in large mouthfuls, cheeks bulging.

The driver turned on the radio. Wailing music blared out and he mumbled along. Although an obese man, the driver warbled in a high-pitched tone. The handle of a baseball bat protruded from under his seat.

The boy started on the apple, rocking back and forth, his hood fallen down. Bloodshot eyes; humming to himself. His jeans were clean but worn, his trainers scuffed. He had a buzzcut, and cigarette burns on the back of his neck. Rockburn knew from experience how painful they were. Vowed he'd find out who was responsible.

'I'm Rockburn by the way,' he whispered. He waited, but the boy didn't take the hint. 'Rock as in stone, burn as in fire. You understand?'

The boy nodded.

The driver turned off the radio.

'What shall I call you?'

'My name is Quang.'

'How old are you, Quang?'

'Ten.'

'How old do you think I am?'

The first hint of a smile.

'Forty?'

Rockburn dummied a punch at Quang. The boy swayed back, another half-smile briefly appearing. 'Thirty-one.' He looked older, Rockburn knew it. Like the boy, he'd been through a lot.

The cab stopped at a traffic light. Rockburn glanced at the car behind, then at the motorbike alongside. Reminded him he'd left the panther behind. Not only that, but he'd dumped his helmet in their escape. No question but he'd have to go back tonight for his bike – the panther was family. The lights changed, and the cab pulled forward.

They drove past a secondary school, older pupils spilling out of the gates and rough-housing along the pavement. Boys with weird haircuts and girls with short skirts. A car hire forecourt, a garage, a tower block called *Nelson*.

Quang finished the apple, and began to suck and chew on the banana skin. Wishing he'd taken more fruit, Rockburn opened the window wider. He turned to the boy.

'Where are your parents, Quang?'

The boy shrugged. 'I don't have.'

'Who left you in the bus stop?' Rockburn had wanted to say *abandoned*, and when he did catch up with the person responsible, his language would be less select.

'Mina.'

'Who's Min—'

The driver's mobile flashed, the driver pressed a button, and a voice boomed in a language Rockburn didn't recognise. The driver checked in the rearview mirror and spoke briefly on the phone. He ended the call and checked in the mirror again. He winked, his face writhing like a bag of snakes.

'Pull over,' said Rockburn, leaning forward. He wasn't sure, but waiting to be sure might be fatal. 'I'll explain later,' he whispered to the boy.

The driver ignored the instruction. Rockburn tapped him on the shoulder. 'Stop, anywhere here.'

'No understand.'

Stop was a basic English word, written on road signs and the road itself. Rockburn reached around the front seat and gripped the driver in a headlock. 'Does that help?'

Gasping and muttering in a foreign language, the driver braked. The cab veered to the pavement. Cars behind honked and overtook.

Tyres scraping the curb, the car stopped. Rockburn nodded at the door, and the boy scrambled out. Using one arm to control the driver, Rockburn reached forward for the car key. Releasing him, he climbed out of the cab.

Quang began to walk away, hands covering his ears. He looked as confused as a lost child at a pop concert. Rockburn ran after him, put a hand on his shoulder. Wanted to hug him. 'It will be alright.' He didn't promise; he never promised.

'How about chips later?'

Slowly, the boy nodded.

But there was no time to talk further – the driver had climbed out of the cab, and was demanding his key. Later there would be time for talking, for questions and explanations and counselling. And for chips.

'Come on, Quang,' said Rockburn. He tossed the key down a grid and grabbed the boy's hand. Behind him, the driver was shouting on his phone.

Half-pulling the boy, Rockburn ran down the pavement and into a housing estate. He took a series of alleys and emerged at an entrance to Little Park – where Sal sold coffee and wraps of hash. The two of them slowed to a walk and entered. Every few days Rockburn jogged around it and beat himself up in the jungle gym. It was a mile from his flophouse.

He stopped at the shop. There were benches and a stand of trees around a dark pond with a family of overfed ducks. The shop consisted of a graffiti-covered green trailer with heavy bars on all the openings. A stinking Portaloo stood to one side, and an empty wheelie bin lay on the ground. Litter was scattered around the scrappy piece of hardstanding.

'Okay, Sal?'

The girl, who looked about twelve, nodded, and shifted her baby to the other hip. Rockburn hoped she'd avoided the gear while she was pregnant, but without much conviction. She looked the boy up and down, then turned to Rockburn. 'Ta with that form.'

'My cut's ten per cent.'

Sal chin-jerked, but her face remained passive.

Rockburn ordered a can of coke, sandwiches, and flapjacks. Sal busied with the order, her baby cooing as if it had been born in a palace. She brewed him a coffee, and Rockburn left her the change from a twenty. One day he'd make her smile, but not today.

Rockburn and Quang sat either side of a wooden table, damp and algae ridden. They sat like father and son. The boy took off his hoodie and laid it on the table, then ate with concentration and speed. Both sandwiches, one of the flapjacks, and after raising an eyebrow and receiving a nod, the second one.

'Sorry she doesn't do chips,' said Rockburn.

'Okay,' said the boy. Drinking from the can, he developed hiccups.

'Hold your nose, and drink backwards,' said Rockburn. He took the can and demonstrated.

Quang tried.

Rockburn sipped his coffee, watching the boy and behind him the pond. Ripples ran back and forth, racing and playing games. A breeze rustled the last leaves on the trees, and a kaleidoscope of patterns reflected on the dull water.

He looked out over the park, turning a full circle, from their entrance at the rear of the housing estate, the north-west gate, along the paths to the two southern gates, and back following Lose River to the north-east gate. Half a dozen young teenagers were playing football, and a couple of lone dogwalkers wandered through isolated trees and alongside the river.

'Quang, I need to ask you a few more questions. Are you okay with that?' He wanted to ask about their pursuers, the cigarette burns on the boy's neck, his relationship to Mina, and where the hell she was.

The boy shrugged. Hiccupped. Another hint of a smile.

'You like football?'

Another shrug. Another hiccup.

'What team do you support?'

'Song Lamb '

'Never heard of them. Any good?'

The boy began scraping up the sticky residue and stray porridge oats from the flapjack wrappers. He turned and looked all around the park.

Rockburn surveilled with his mini telescope. The teenagers across the park had finished their game and were mooching towards them.

'Your English is very good, Quang. Did you learn it at school?'

The boy shook his head. 'In the factory – in China.'

Rockburn moved the scope from his eye. Chinese factories were well-known start points for trafficking from Asia.

He nodded. 'And who's Mina?'

'My aunt.'

'Where is she?'

The boy crushed the empty can, shrugged. 'Want to go –' he said, standing up and looking around.

Rockburn pointed, and the boy walked over to the Portaloo. He balled the wrappers, waited until the door banged shut, then lifted the boy's hoodie and swept the pockets and lining.

He found a map of Manchester, a piece of paper with *Detective Sergeant Paul Rockburn* written in marker pen, and sewn into the collar, five twenty-pound notes. A story for the boy's presence in the bus stop was beginning to suggest itself. The boy was likely to be an illegal migrant, possibly trafficked. Had escaped with Mina, and at some point the two of them had come across Rockburn's name. The whereabouts – and safety – of Mina, now his secondary concern.

The boy his primary.

The footballers arrived at the shop and queued noisily. Two of them kicked the ball across the concrete, the others bantered with Sal, the girl giving as good as she got.

Rockburn folded up the banknotes and checked the park. The dark pond with its hoard of shopping trolleys and traffic cones, the stand of trees, the empty football pitch, the pathways, the oily river. The four entrances.

He looked through his scope.

Approaching from the housing estate was a large Asian man, the same one as earlier. The southern gates were deserted, but the north-east entrance, the access for the grasscutters, was also busy.

One Asian man unhooked the pedestrian entrance and walked through, two more climbed the locked five bar gate. After a quick discussion, they started heading towards the shop.

The level of interest in the boy, which was both organised and sustained, worried Rockburn. No one cared about a single runaway migrant – even two runaways. It suggested Quang and his aunt Mina had seriously annoyed someone.

He considered their options. Quang could hide in the shop. He could mingle with the footballers. Or he could squeeze into the wheelie bin and Rockburn could trundle him away. The first would put Sal in danger, the second would endanger the boys, and both would dilute control of the situation. The Asian men were approaching the shop in a pincer movement, but weren't moving fast. Coupled with their bulkiness, it meant they were unlikely to be fit. Outrunning them gave a fourth option.

The young footballers paid and mooched off toward the pond. If questioned there was a chance they hadn't even noticed the boy. Most people were as observant as trees.

Rockburn dragged the wheelie bin over to the Portaloo. Surprise, distraction, disguise were his favourite weapons.

'Quang?'

The cubicle opened and Quang stepped out. He looked pale, and tired. Strike out running away. The boy looked beyond Rockburn into the expanse of the park, then at the wheelie bin. He shook his head.

'You've got no choice, Quang. *We've* got no choice.' Rockburn nodded towards the Asian men approaching from two directions. Already, they were much closer.

Quang backed up to the Portaloo.

'It won't be for long, I promise.' One promise he could keep.

The boy's hand hovered on the door handle of the Portaloo. Neither option seemed attractive.

'Come on, please!'

Quang shook his head, opened the door.

'I'll get you a Mars Bar from Sal if you get in.'

The boy held up two fingers.

'Two Mars Bars, done,' said Rockburn, tipping the bin on its back.

Quang sat, and legs first, squeezed inside. Rockburn eased the bin upright, aware Sal was watching from the shop counter. She was rocking the baby on her hip, and clucking softly. An innocent noise which didn't belong in the scruffy park or in the unfolding situation.

Rockburn passed Quang the money he'd taken from the boy's jacket. 'Talk about it later.' He flipped over the lid. It banged shut, restarting the world and making the baby cry.

Sal set her infant in its buggy and walked over.

'Trouble?' Her voice lost in the wailing.

Rockburn surveyed the park. It would only be minutes before the Asian men arrived.

'Maybe. You might want to lock up. But before you do, can I get a couple of Mars Bars?'

She blew a raspberry. Thirty seconds later, she threw him a

checked jacket worn by road crews and a padded hat with earflaps. She could have opened a thrift shop with the stuff people left behind. Rockburn put them on, knowing he looked like a crazy. Then again, all the bin men he knew were a tad unhinged. Sal handed him a roll of black bin liners, and a litter-picker. He could have kissed her.

'Want to ask you a thing,' said Sal, passing the chocolate bars.

Rockburn slipped them under the lid of the wheelie bin. 'Can it keep?'

She nodded, suddenly looking young and shy.

Rockburn set off, hauling the bin towards the south-west gate, next to the signboard. The hat smelt of petrol. The small wheels rolled noisily, catching every stone. But the Asian men didn't change direction, and were still heading for the shop.

For a moment Rockburn thought about going back. He'd not anticipated feeling torn, and he would have to hope Sal played young and dumb, and not get riled. The marginally better option was to keep going – returning would risk harm to Sal and her baby *and* Quang.

Halfway to the exit, he stopped at a bench and an overflowing park bin. He hefted out the liner, tied a knot and flipped open the lid of the wheelie bin. The boy sat in a heap, chocolate around his mouth, and looked wretched as a beaten dog.

'Sorry,' said Rockburn. He dropped the bag of refuse onto the boy and spread it across. The boy didn't murmur. He closed the lid. If they were stopped, it might fool them, it might not. He ripped off another sack, and relined the park bin.

The three Asian men had reached the pond and the shop. The largest male was in charge; he had jet black hair tied into a ponytail. Rockburn wouldn't forget him. The three men started gesticulating at Sal.

Feeling even worse, he set off again. He wanted to speed up but held back. Being in disguise was like playing an extra in a film: a moment's relaxation would ruin the deception.

Fifty metres from the exit. Two women with pushchairs stood next to the signboard.

A shout rose from the shop.

Rockburn didn't look back, but he knew it was them, and knew it was him they were shouting at.

Forty metres.

He just needed to maintain his speed and his demeanour, avoid confirming their suspicion. He picked up a discarded beer can and squeezed it under the lid of the wheelie bin.

Thirty metres.

The women pushed their buggies towards him. He swerved onto the grass, the wheels of the bin cutting down into the turf. He passed them moved back onto the path.

Ten metres.

Rockburn reached the exit alley. Tall fences on both sides screened it from the neighbouring houses and from the park.

He tipped the bin onto its back wheels and started running. The heavy load kept wanting to pull upright, kept yanking his pulling arm backwards. The alley turned onto a road of terraced houses. He turned right and hauled like a husky train along the pavement. He passed cheap boxy dwellings with tiny gardens at the front, and garages and refuse collection at the back. An idea formed.

After ten houses there was a driveway to the rear. He veered off the pavement and followed it to the back of the terrace. A service road ran behind There was a caged area with fifty wheelie bins. Rockburn shunted his bin into the cage, and manoeuvred half a dozen others so the hidden boy was surrounded. He opened the lid.

Lifted out the sack of rubbish.

'Quiet as a mouse, Quang. One hour, then I'll be back.'

The boy didn't look up.

'Okay?'

Still, the boy didn't move or speak. Rockburn felt sorry for him, sorry for his nightmare. He felt guilty, as if a conspiracy of all adults was responsible. 'Quang, I need to know you're okay. I mean, not okay okay, but okay. You understand?'

Slowly, the boy looked up at Rockburn. 'Quiet like mouse. Understand.' He spoke with the gravity of a village elder.

Rockburn raised a thumb. He spread the bag of rubbish back over the boy, and lowered the lid. He opened it again. 'Hey, Quang, you're a very brave lad. Brave as a lion.' He growled, closed it. He'd make it up to him – something more than kind words.

And even better than chips.

4

Rockburn took a jinking course of backstreets and alleys to the nearest bus route. He turned the jacket inside out and dumped the hat. He knew it was a risk to leave Quang, but alone Rockburn was almost invisible, whereas a man with a boy was something people might remember if questioned.

He jogged up the road until he heard the whine of a bus, and after a ten-minute ride, disembarked opposite a motorbike dealership. A warehouse-sized building with a glitzy showroom of other men's dreams. Normally, he could have spent a week there.

As he crossed the road, a long black car with a crest drove past. The mayor's car, a glint of silver chain in the back.

Rockburn offered a sham salute, and the car hooted in reply.

In the showroom, he bought two helmets and a reversible snood, then caught a second bus back to Fenwick Street.

Climbed out wearing a black and white checked snood around his neck. The pattern of a finishing flag – yet he felt he'd hardly started. He had no idea why the Asians were pursuing the boy. No idea of the whereabouts of Mina.

He entered the café opposite the bus stop and queued at the counter. The smell of brewing coffee filled the air. In front of him, there was a group of builders, and at the tables, lone office-workers and women with children.

While he waited, Rockburn alternated checking on the bus stop and searching the internet on his phone. *Song Lamb, football team*. Not Lamb, but Lam: Song Lam Nghe An, a Vietnamese club in Hanoi, Nghe An province. They'd won ten major titles, and were named after the Lam River.

The builders took their mugs and paper bags, and from a waitress with a watery-blonde flick of hair, Rockburn ordered coffee, water, and a chicken baguette *to go*.

He looked outside: the bus stop was still deserted, and no south-east Asian – Vietnamese? – males cruised. No woman loitered nearby.

The waitress set down his order and issued a half-smile. She reminded him of an eighties popstar, pretty and troubled. But he doubted she'd be there if he came back a week later.

'Did you see anyone leave a young boy in the bus stop opposite?'

The waitress shook her head. 'Sorry.'

The coffee was bitter as a witch's kiss. He added cold water, gulped a couple of mouthfuls, stashed the baguette in a pocket. Quang was waiting in a dark smelly refuse bin. The boy would be petrified.

Rockburn gulped more coffee.

Thirty seconds, then he'd go. He looked up the name Quang – in Vietnamese it meant *clear*. Only one thing was clear, the boy was being hunted. He was likely to have travelled from Vietnam. Living conditions were poor in much of the country, and people were seeking a better life in Europe. Along with everyone else.

Time to go. He drained the coffee, chewing on the dregs as he strode to the door.

The waitress was serving another customer. She glanced over at him and mouthed, *Do I know you?*

Maybe he would come back. He left a card on the table.

Rockburn shoved out into the afternoon. A stiff breeze blew rubbish down the pavement and a spatter of rain fell.

He jogged to the corner, and the two blocks back to the panther. If he lost her, he didn't know what he'd do. He released the chunky padlock and wiped raindrops from the seat and handlebars. He rolled down the snood and pulled on a new helmet. The motorbike was definitely female, all sleek lines and hidden power.

'*I'm coming, Quang.*'

He mounted up, and feeling like royalty, purred through the backstreets. Ripped along the main roads.

Fifteen minutes later he turned down the street where he'd left the boy. The row of houses was loud in its quietness. He parked at the cage of wheelie bins and walked inside the wire. The bin he'd trundled through the park stood where he'd left it.

He lifted the lid.

Empty.

5

There was a beer can in the bottom, but there was no sack of rubbish and no Quang. Rockburn slammed the lid back down.

The image of Pricha Kuri attached to the pipe appeared before him. The young girl sat in her own soil, crying and pulling pathetically on her shackle.

Rockburn raised the lid and crashed it down again.

The criminal justice system had acted too slowly for Pricha and a hundred others like her. The system didn't prioritise, and never committed the resources so it could act quickly enough. *Proactively*. Enquiries, finger-pointing, recommendations, always took place after the event. Children were collateral in an adult world of greed and laziness and stupidity.

A panel of the wire cage rattled.

Rockburn stepped closer, his senses on full alert, and ready for action. Someone was hiding in a bush. Friend or foe?

The boy.

Thank, God.

Quang emerged from a bank of thick rhododendron and crouched outside the wire enclosure. The boy tapped his watch.

Rockburn couldn't help but grin and waggle his thumb. Quang hadn't given up and had shown good initiative. The boy mirrored the gesture and grinned back. Rockburn checked all around, up and down the service road, and at the windows of the overlooking houses. No one was watching – at least, no one he could see. He beckoned Quang closer.

'I think you not come back.'

'You don't know me,' said Rockburn. He handed the boy a helmet. 'But you did the right thing, well done. Do you fancy a ride?'

Nodding slowly, Quang looked as if he'd been chosen to press the button controlling the lights to start a grand prix. The boy felt the give of the leather seat, admired the dials and forest of switches on the dash. He climbed up and crouched down as if he was racing.

'Before we go,' said Rockburn, 'I need to ask you one more question. Why did Mina leave you in the bus stop?'

Quang leant forward and toggled a switch. Toggled it back. The boy's finger hovered above another button.

'I wouldn't press that if I was you, it's the ejector seat. You understand, like a catapult?' Rockburn did his best to mime a rider being fired upwards.

Quang smirked, then tried to hide it. He seemed to be weighing things up.

'If I'm going to help her – help both of you – I need to know.'

There was a pause before the boy spoke. 'There are men who help us come England. Mina give lot money. But men want more.'

It appeared that Rockburn had been right about trafficking, but even so, the persistence of the pursuing men seemed disproportionate.

A car drove past the end of the service road. Rockburn heard it stop, then the whine of the reverse. A blue car turned into the road – began heading towards them. *The* blue car. The traffickers, if that's who they were, hadn't given up.

Rockburn pulled on his helmet and climbed onto the bike in front of the boy. He turned to help him with his helmet and showed him how to grip his jacket, then started the panther. The motorbike snarled and settled into a deep growl. The boy nestled closer.

The noise of the bike reflected Rockburn's mood. Quang was being hunted by a group of men, which was unfair and unjust in any reckoning. He felt angry and protective, as if the boy was *his* nephew.

'Hold on tight, Quang.'

Rockburn pulled away, accelerating quickly in the opposite direction.

A second car slewed across the opposite end of the service road and stopped. Rockburn braked hard, and U-turned.

Headed back towards the blue car, Quang clinging on behind him. The blue car reached the driveway to the front of the houses, blocking off their only escape route. There wasn't enough room on either side to slip by. Rockburn U-turned again, and headed back towards the second car which was preventing their getaway. The service road was bordered by walls and fences, and offered no lateral escape. He could hear the blue car following, could feel Quang gripping tighter as if the boy sensed Rockburn's fear that he might fall off the bike.

He spotted a gate in a fence.

Slowed.

And U-turned a third time, a difficult manoeuvre in the restricted space and with a passenger. The blue car was closing. Twenty car-lengths.

Darting forward, Rockburn skidded the bike round sideways to face the gate. Hoped it wasn't an old entrance the residents had bricked up after a burglary. Advice he'd have given.

Ten car-lengths.

The wooden gate looked flimsy enough, but litter clogged its base and it didn't show signs of use. They had little choice. He half-turned, shouted: 'Hang on.'

The boy tightened his grip.

Five.

Quang screamed.

Rockburn squeezed the throttle, and the three of them surged forwards, Rockburn snatching a glance at the sneering men through the car windscreen.

The front wheel of the panther smashed through the gate, pieces of splintered wood catching Rockburn's helmet and ripping at his leathers as the rest of the bike followed.

They entered a rectangular yard with two patches of scrubby grass and a pathway leading to an enclosed ginnel between the two terraced houses. Heading for the dark tunnel, Rockburn took a diagonal line across the scrub, past an empty rabbit hutch and a headless gnome still holding a fishing rod. He glanced round to see a figure in the gateway.

Turned forwards, switched on the headlight, and for two or three very long seconds, feared gunshots.

He slowed in the ginnel, the headlight showing another barrier at the end. Real fishing rods this time, and a broom, clattered behind them. A tackle box fell and smashed. Above their heads, thumping dance music. In for one gate, in for two. He increased the revs and they burst through the second wooden barrier.

Emerged on a short path leading via a couple of shallow steps to the road. The panther clunked down and Rockburn curved the bike round.

Accelerated.

He could feel the boy holding on, the slight pressure down his back. But Quang was quiet, dumbstruck maybe.

At the corner, two children on bicycles stopped to watch. Tossing away pieces of gate panel, Rockburn careered out into the carriageway and turned in a wide arc. In a wing mirror, he caught the boy flicking a wave at his peers. Maybe not.

They took off. Used only streets with bollards and back roads to leave the city. Lefts, rights, short bursts of acceleration and heavy braking. Grey clouds barrelled overhead. They passed a group of teenagers comparing knives, and three men goading their pitbulls to fight. Finally, they met the ring road, and after heading south for three junctions, the motorbike roaring like a blast furnace, Rockburn turned east toward the hills.

Slowly, the past and the future concertinaed flat, leaving nothing but the present: the wind rushing in his face, the engine's throaty hum, the smell of burning fuel and rubber, and the feel of the hot bike between his thighs.

He stopped in a layby. Leaving the engine running, he turned around and raised his visor.

'You okay?'

The boy nodded. His eyes were watery, his face waxy as polish.

They rode on, following narrow lanes flanked by crab apple trees and fields of sheep. The occasional smallholding offered free-range eggs and firewood for sale. Farm vehicles and cyclists patrolled the roads.

The countryside predated the city, and was innocent, and filled with hope. It made Rockburn melancholic, and reflective. The city, in contrast, was dirty, polluted, and besmirched by humans. A dark place filled with conflict and anguish. A place with little hope. He tried to forget the city, and instead wallow in his roots and imagine a life with Hocking. It was always the same, and the reason he rarely came.

But, he needed a favour.

He pulled into the old mining village where he'd spent his childhood, before and after the two police officers had knocked at his door. His great grandfather had also died in an accident –

underground, his grandfather one of the last people to work in a lead mine. Rockburn remembered his gnarled hands and hacking cough. Remembered too, his grandmother's gentle scowling at the blackened clothes and body of her husband.

They puttered through the tight roads, passing a dark squat church and a defunct post office. At the back of the village, a road dropped down to a river, then rose steeply and flattened. There was a farm entrance and a row of tiny cottages. A tyre still hung from a lone sycamore at the side of the end house. His grandfather had strung it up for him. Rockburn had been the boy's age, and mad keen on shooting squirrels and searching for mushrooms.

He parked and switched off the engine. Took off his helmet, dismounted. Steam rose from his damp collar. He felt stiff as a cowboy.

Quang climbed down, and Rockburn helped him unclip his helmet. The boy didn't hang it on the bike, but kept hold of it like a favourite toy.

The front door of his parents' house, his grandparents' house, his entire childhood, opened. The crack in the front step still there.

Hocking stood on the threshold. She was a small woman; freckly with short sandy hair. She was wearing a light-green gilet with multiple pockets like a big game hunter. Flecks of different coloured paint down the front. They'd both liked walking in the hills on his days off, and she'd loved riding on the back of his motorbike; had tolerated the darts.

'Sorry to drop in, Hocking.' It had been one of the things they'd argued about. If he wanted to be called by his surname, then so did she.

Rockburn pushed through the gate and walked up to her. He kissed the top of her head. She smelt of baking.

'Who's this?'

'This,' said Rockburn, turning round, 'is Quang.'

The boy stood at the gate, hugging his helmet.

'Do you like ginger cake, Quang?'

The boy shrugged.

She turned and headed back inside. 'Come in, I'm not the devil, whatever he says.'

Rockburn ushered the boy after her, but stood on the threshold looking round. He'd carved his initials in the sycamore tree, roasted chestnuts in the firepit in the corner. Daydreamed of joining Special Forces or becoming a helicopter pilot or the type of police who knocked on doors with important messages. Uniform was a pre-requisite.

He stared at the road leading to the village. He'd walked it every school day for five years, knew every undulation, every tree. When his parents were killed in a train derailment, his grandparents had been appointed guardians for him and his younger brother Simon and were bequeathed his parents' house. They moved in, everyone deciding the less upheaval the better for Rockburn and his brother, whom he'd not seen since Simon had run away at seventeen. They'd slept in the same bedrooms, and had bunked off from school to build dams and climb trees without censure.

He kicked up the stand on his motorbike and wheeled it around the back of Hocking's neighbour Mrs Gregory. At least there, it wouldn't get covered in chicken shit. The old woman's patio was being re-laid, tools everywhere. She waved at him through the kitchen window.

He entered the house via the rear of the integral garage. Paw prints ran across the bonnet of Hocking's car. Inside, the house looked the same as when the two of them had lived there. It always surprised him, how an artist who painted profusely and with painstaking attention to detail couldn't see the scuffed walls.

He detoured into the cramped front room, the table piled with art magazines and books. The chairs were stacked in a corner and cardboard boxes lined a wall. He walked to the windows and looked out. The road was clear.

Hocking entered.

Rockburn turned, but her attention was already taken by the cover of one of the books. She picked it up, and showed it to him. 'Incredible how she's done that.'

Rockburn turned back to the window. The road was still clear. He couldn't even hear a vehicle. Only a helicopter, buzzing in the distance.

'Quang's in the kitchen – eating. He's hungry as a carthorse.' She put the book down and stepped closer. 'Who is he?' A whisper. 'And why've you brought him here?'

'I don't know much. I'm hoping he's attached to a client or clients who haven't introduced themselves yet.'

'What about the police, or social services?'

Rockburn made a face. 'I can do a better job.'

'You mean, you need the money.'

Rockburn said nothing. He wanted – needed – a favour. He picked up a small charcoal drawing of a horse. 'This is good.'

Hocking scowled and picked up another book. 'She's good on charcoal, page twenty-five I think.' She started turning pages. 'Oh, you're not interested.' She slapped the book shut.

'You could teach Quang to draw, and he could look after the chickens.' Rockburn paused. 'A couple of days. Three at most. You do—'

'I know, I know, I owe you.' Hocking walked over to the door. 'I'm going to see how he's doing.' She walked out.

Seconds later, she was back. 'He's not in the kitchen.'

Rockburn felt his heart miss a beat. He ran past her to doublecheck. In the kitchen he opened the backdoor and stepped out into the garden. Half a dozen white chickens wandered around. Next door, his bike stood quiet and ready as a fire engine. Shame it couldn't speak.

'Quang?'

There was no reply.

'Quang!'

A helicopter – *who were they?*

Rockburn searched the rest of the downstairs: the living room, the WC. As a child he'd liked to hide, liked to tease people. He checked the room where Hocking painted. A low easel stood in the window and large canvases hung from the walls. More were stacked in the corner.

He ran up the stairs two at a time, pushed open the door of the spare bedroom. More of Hocking's artwork adorned the walls. Quang lay asleep on the bed, an arm round the new motorcycle helmet, his trainers cast on the floor.

Rockburn carefully retrieved the helmet, and padded back down the stairs to the painting room. The picture on the easel was an old mineshaft against a carved-out hill. Above it was a violent purple sky with looming thunderclouds.

'You can have it if you'd like,' said Hocking over his shoulder. Her breath, her closeness, her smell brought it all back.

Rockburn rode back to the city without the picture and without the boy.

6

Rockburn parked the panther underneath the fire escape at the rear of his block. The city throbbed with constructive and destructive energy. He started up the steps, rips of blue-grey sky showing through the grooves of the metal ladder. Tobacco smoke drifted down.

Flack stood on the first landing. The tattooist wore a black t-shirt and black jeans with a studded belt. Tattoos covered his arms and neck. He smoked thin French cigars which he said showed he was an egalitarian.

'A woman's been here asking for you.'

Rockburn stopped climbing, and waited for the clanging to dissipate. *Mina?*

'Did she leave her name?'

Flack puffed on his cigar and shook his head. The ball of smoke drifted out like the retort from a flintlock.

'She didn't.'

'Young, old, what?'

'Young, foreign. Looked like a lap dancer.'

'Did she leave a message?'

'Do I look like I've got shorthand?' He pinched and straightened the end of the cigar as carefully as if he was a surgeon, then took another puff.

Rockburn squeezed past and continued upwards.

'Not your telephone receptionist either,' shouted Flack. He sounded wheezy. 'Had a call from the darts people. Said they wanted to talk to you but didn't have your number.'

'What did they want?'

Flack scowled and coughed clouds of cigar smoke. 'Sweet mother of Magdalene.'

After entering via the fire exit, Rockburn stripped off his leathers and grabbed a bottle of beer. He drank half. Then unpicked the darts from the board, stood behind the oche and sent the first two. Twenty. Five. He wiped his hands on his trousers.

Third dart, wanted it to be a bullseye.

He licked the tip. Every player needed a touch of flair, of showmanship, one signature dart, otherwise no one would bother watching. The big players, at least. He aimed, unsure whether he wanted to become one. He back-and-forthed the dart, once, twice, three times –

And fired.

It landed dead centre, the black hole of the darts board. Perhaps he did.

At his desk he flipped open his laptop and selected the CCTV app. It showed two cameras, one on the fire escape and one outside his office door. The first showed Flack still standing there, smoking and tapping the metal rail. The second showed a deserted stairwell. He dug into the history. At 14.20 a woman knocked on his door. She was young, south-east Asian and wore western clothes and a small rucksack on her back. She waited, knocked again, waited. Then she went down the stairs and out of sight.

Rockburn rewound and zoomed in. The woman's raven-black hair was tied behind her head. Her eyes were bloodshot, her skin ashen. She wore no jewellery, only a cheap plastic watch.

The boy's aunt Mina?

He put bread in the toaster. Then researched Vietnamese migrants. Two routes into the UK, the first known as the VIP route on an aircraft using a false passport, and the second, far cheaper option, in the back of a lorry.

From Vietnam, migrants travelled overland to China where they worked for six to eighteen months to pay for their onward journey – Quang had mentioned a factory. From China to a Russian holding centre, and a wait of a month or two for an ongoing group to gather and set off. Routes varied, but most crossed into Belarus or the Baltic States, then Poland, Germany, and into a country with a port. Usually France, but sometimes Belgium. Migrants would stay with Vietnamese people at every stage. Finally, there would be the sea crossing to Britain, some migrants choosing an inflatable boat, others continuing in the back of another lorry. Usually, they would be let out close to an English port, drivers keen to get rid of them, but sometimes motorway service stations up north. Again, migrants would seek out the Vietnamese community to help and harbour. Delays, hunger, sickness, danger and violence beset every journey.

The toast popped.

A few of the migrants were caught and deported. The luckier ended up working – in nail bars, fast-food restaurants, petrol stations, mini-marts and barber shops; the unluckier were trafficked and sold to pimps and brothel-owners. Every year, the numbers were increasing.

He swigged his beer, buttered the toast.

Travelling in the back of a lorry, maybe for several weeks, even months, would explain Quang's skinniness. Rockburn ate the toast, hoping the boy was decimating Hocking's kitchen cupboards.

He finished the bottle, and unplucked his arrows. There'd be another competition, and he'd be better prepared. He decided to practise checkouts. High scoring looked impressive and felt good, but checkouts won games.

He'd mentioned it once to DI Jackson, who'd compared darts to golf – drive for pleasure, putt for profit. When Rockburn had told him golf was an old man's game, his boss had said darts was only played by slobs and thugs.

Rockburn disagreed, arguing it needed finesse and good mental arithmetic, a touch of élan. He licked a tip, then worked the three best, double twenty, sixteen, and nine. Hitting only a single on the first dart still allowed a checkout on the second, and even the third if repeating the mistake on ten or eight.

20, 10, double 5.

Jackson had been an uninspiring line manager, but had surprised Rockburn with the warmth of his testimonial at the internal enquiry.

> Detective Sergeant Rockburn has worked for me for three years during which time he has taken no sick leave and worked at short notice and long hours without complaint. A first-class detective, he can be trusted with the most sensitive enquiries. I have no doubt that in respect of this particular incident, he is telling the truth.

Rockburn had sent Jackson a bottle of the finest single malt, despite it not making an iota of difference. He'd lost his job, and been given a reference which confirmed he'd turned up at work for ten years, three hundred and thirty-eight days. He'd also been forced to sell the house – the house he'd been brought up in, which, following Simon's lengthy absence, had been given solely to him – to pay the legal fees for his trial.

He threw double 16.

Then 9, 3, double 3. He was on form. Some people walked

the dog, or walked round the golf course, some just walked. But he worked through his moods on his bike, and did his thinking throwing arrows.

He whipped the darts into the board, automatically noting the scores and feeling disappointed despite the frenzied action. 20, 5, 7.

After clearing his table and turning on the lamp, he pulled on plastic gloves. From a drawer he took out a bottle of charcoal powder, brushes, and a roll of tape. He dusted the outside of the boy's helmet with powder and stared with a magnifying glass. Several sets of prints showed. Some would be his, but some would be Quang's. Maybe one or two would belong to an assistant from the motorbike showroom. He pressed down sections of tape on the prints, peeled them away and stuck them to small sheets of clear plastic. He'd watched scenes of crimes officers do it countless times and it wasn't so hard.

Turning the helmet over, he held it closer to the light. Using tweezers, he plucked out half a dozen of the boy's black hairs and slipped them in a sealable plastic bag.

He switched off the light, pulled on a new pair of gloves and took the fingerprint kit into the hallway. He dusted the wooden banister where the female caller had taken hold. Several sets of overlapping prints gleamed. It was an outside chance, but he might get lucky.

He went back inside, locked the door and checked the windows. The fire escape was clear, the street held no persons or vehicles of interest. The old language remained, some of the tactics. Being in charge was a positive, but he was penniless, had only the one case and no guarantee of getting paid.

Grabbing another beer, he sat and waited. Picked at his fingers, chewed a nail as he tried to dredge up the registration of the blue car.

Outside, the light turned greyer. Rainfall tapped the windows. Darkness and sirens enveloped the city.

He finished the beer, threw some darts.

The plate ended 6FXR.

It was something.

7

Quang is being chased along a beach by lean black dogs. Rockburn sprints along a parallel path at the top of the beach, but an electric fence keeps him back. Each time he veers seaward he feels a jolt across his thighs. Waves are piling in, white frothy water running up the sand and drawing back. The boy turns into the sea, stumbles, falls, and disappears under a breaker.

Rockburn woke.

3.20 am.

He unzipped his sleeping bag. Stood. Shuffled to the window and peered out, his damp body making him shiver. A grimy half-light held the city. In the distance, the sound of a lorry braking heavily. Nearby, a couple arguing. The boy hadn't mentioned dogs.

Had he?

In the shadow of the fire escape something moved. He observed but it didn't move again, until finally, his rods started playing tricks and the shadows all began moving. He opened the window and tried again but it was no clearer. The panther lived in the backyard under the fire escape. He slipped on jeans and a pair of boots, unlocked the exit door, and walked down the metal stairs to investigate.

The yard was used by local residents and businesses. About fifty parking spaces. Access was from a service road at the rear, and an alley led to the high street and the front door of their block.

The metal clanged.

He stopped at the foot of the steps. The air was cold. A car he couldn't see drove down the street. *The blue car?*

Slowly, the uneasy quiet of a sleeping city returned. His night vision improved. The yard appeared deserted.

He checked on the bikes: the panther; Flack's three-wheeler; and the tattooist's spare, the diabolical Kawasaki. In the dim light, they appeared fine. The locks were secure, the tyres firm, the bodywork unblemished.

Rockburn returned to his sleeping bag but couldn't sleep, staring at the dark smudges on the ceiling until, hours later, a beeping bin lorry stopped, and bins clanked and clattered.

He phoned Hocking. 'Everything okay?'

'Why wouldn't it be?'

'There are a group of south-east Asian men looking for the boy. I don't know who they are, or what they want.'

'You're telling me now?' Each word reverberated with anger. If the two of them had been in the same room, Hocking would have thrown something. She was an artist and had a creative's temperament. Mood swings, bursts of frenetic energy, sometimes anger, interlaced with periods of self-doubt bordering desperation. Then again, she had a point.

'I'm the only person who knows Quang's staying with you, so you don't need to worry. How is he?'

'He's fine,' Hocking said slowly. 'Yesterday we pumped up the tyres on your old bicycle, and this morning he's been riding up and down.'

'Has he said anything?'

'I printed out a map of Vietnam, and he pointed out Hanoi

where he was born. And Hai Phong province which borders the South China Sea, where he was living.'

'How did he get here?'

'He won't talk about it – can't or won't. His English seems very good, but I don't want to push him.'

'Keep him close. And if you see anything sus, phone me.'

'You know I'm only doing this because.'

The phone line cleared. She was underselling herself; Hocking would have housed the boy without him doing her a favour, albeit a big one. She was a keeper, as his grandmother would have said. What his gran would have said knowing he'd lost her would not have been poetic.

He checked for messages, then the CCTV. No sign of the boy's aunt. He went out for milk and bread and cornflakes. Walked up and down the street, assessing the parked cars. He walked around the block. Checked the backyard and his bike. The fire escape glistered with dew. He saw no one, no blue car, no Asian hood, no Mina.

He, together with Hocking, could only safeguard the boy for a week or two, the boy's aunt must know that.

Rockburn phoned a former colleague and arranged to meet by a canal bridge. When Elsa asked why, he said he had something for her.

Before heading out. he researched Hai Phong province on his laptop. Vietnam meant three things to him: the war, the boat people, and migration to Europe and the UK. He refreshed his memory. The war between the Chinese-backed north and the south ended in 1975, American sponsorship of the latter ending two years earlier. The country was soon reunified under communist rule. There followed a mass exodus of its people, many by boat.

He pulled up a current map. Eight regions were subdivided

into a total of fifty-eight provinces. The Red River Delta region included Hai Phong, a poor – even relatively – rice-growing area. A quick search of news websites showed it had become a source of migrants to the UK.

He checked his phone but still there were no messages from Mina. Even if she showed up, if she had no money and no other clients appeared, then he would have to get a proper job.

His finances were a mess. His savings were gone, he was in debt on his credit cards, a month in arrears on rent for the flat. Perhaps he had been foolish to sell his grandparents' house to pay his legal fees, but Hocking had wanted to buy it, and selling it to her below market-price was a way of finishing their troubled relationship amicably. Also a way of keeping the house, if not in the family, then with a friend.

He ate a cheese sandwich and threw some carpentry darts. Doubles: 5, 20, and 1. He developed a Goldilocks problem, hitting the double next to the one he wanted.

Aiming for double 5, he hit double 12 twice and double top. He tried again. Same again. The harder he tried the worse he threw: 20, 5, double 12. He was too tense, too stiff, and his breathing jerky. He did fifty press-ups, fifty sit-ups, and tried again. Still aiming for double 5, he threw double 20, then buried the darts in the drawer of a kitchen cabinet.

The priority was to find Mina, and worry about everything else, including the darts, later. Without a means of contacting her, there were two ways forward: elicit a detailed story from Quang, or identify the boy and reverse-engineer a hypothesis. Jackson's favourite concept.

Grabbing a handful of cornflakes, he headed out.

The car park nearest the canal bridge was deserted. Rockburn switched off the panther's engine. There was a footpath sign and space for two or three cars. He was a few minutes early.

He walked the short section of roadway to Bridge 19. The lane crossed a shaded section of canal with tall trees on both sides. He looked around, but there was no sign of Elsa, and no messages. He walked down the cobbled ramp to the water. An identical ramp led down to the path on the far side.

An Asian lad on a moped crossed slowly over the bridge, heading away from the car park. He looked left and right, and puttered off.

There was a wooden bench next to the bridge, and a scattering of nitrous oxide canisters. The water was dark, olive-coloured, and covered with amorphous shadows. Rockburn read the plaque. The roving bridge allowed a horse to cross the canal when the towpath changed sides.

A man wearing a tie-dyed t-shirt jogged past, a small terrier trotting beside him.

Rockburn read the signboard. The Peak Forest Canal opened in 1800, linking east Manchester to Derbyshire. It was constructed to carry limestone from the Peak District quarries, but gradually declined as the railway network expanded.

The Asian lad buzzed back, looking only in Rockburn's direction. He stopped on the bridge, and remaining seated, leant an elbow on the parapet. He rested his chin on his hand and stared along the canal.

Perhaps the boy had come to get high. Or perhaps he had theft of an expensive motorbike on his mind. The boy was south-east Asian, like the men in the blue car. He stared into the middle distance, possibly only contemplating whether the stuff between his toes really was cheese. But possibly not.

Rockburn pretended to answer his phone. He turned and walked back towards the bridge, speaking loudly and gesticulating as if he was arguing about an unpaid invoice. He kept the boy in his peripheral vision.

The boy didn't stir. Cool as a northern pike.

Rockburn wanted to speak to the boy, but if his premonition was right and he walked up the ramp, the lad would whistle or skedaddle.

He kept up a stream of heated gibberish. The boy watched him walk closer and into the tunnel under the bridge. As he disappeared from view he ended the call with a loud expletive. If the boy was a lookout, then he would cross the bridge and look down, expecting Rockburn to emerge. If Rockburn about turned and exited the direction he'd entered from, the lad would know something was up. Either way, he would be no closer to bracing him.

He pocketed the phone and looked around. He needed a 1-2-3 checkout. The damp ground under the bridge was littered with cigarette butts, and two or three football-sized boulders. More boulders on the far side. He glanced up at the architecture of the bridge. Rusting ironwork stuck out of the stones. A girder with an H cross-section ran across the water.

First dart. He gripped the girder and raised his feet off the ground. Monkeyed out across the water, the rusty steel biting into his palms. Halfway. He paused, grimaced, wiped his hands. Continued hand over hand.

At the far bank he dropped down onto the damp path. Second dart: he picked up a boulder and shot-putted it into the water.

If the kid had a smidgeon of curiosity, he would scoot down to investigate. And if he was up to no good and had anything about him, he would do it on the far side so he wouldn't get caught. Rockburn would be waiting.

He heard the buzz of movement.

On the nearest ramp, a second tell-tale screech.

Rockburn snuck out the back of the tunnel, away from the ramp, and peered up at the side of the bridge. More rusting ironwork – not enough to surmount the parapet but enough to climb above the tunnel. He grabbed a dog's slobber stick and shinned up.

Clinging to the ironwork, he strained to hear the moped's wheels in the damp ground, the buzz of movement. He heard the moped move back and forth. Stop, move again.

The front wheel appeared.

Dart three. Rockburn dropped down and shoved the stick in the spokes. Checkout: he'd wanted to speak to the boy and now he could.

The boy half-climbed, half-fell off the moped. It fell on top of him. He shoved it away, stared up at Rockburn. 'No drug.'

The rider wasn't as young as Rockburn had first thought. Early twenties, maybe. English not his first language. No registration plate on the moped.

'Why were you watching me?'

'Not watching.'

'You got any identification?'

The young man shook his head.

'Get up.'

The rider began to stand, and as he did so, threw something into the water.

It hit the water with a splash, floated long enough for Rockburn to see it was a mobile phone, then sank. He grabbed the man's arm and twisted him against the weeping tunnel side. He patted him down. Rizla papers, matches, two half-cigarettes. A thumbnail of weed in a twist of clingfilm. A small knife strapped to the bottom of his leg.

'Start talking.'

'I not understand.'

'Why are you following me?'

'Rockburn!'

He looked up to see Elsa at the top of the ramp. She was a

keen young detective at Templeside CID, black, the first police officer in her family. A red blouse poked out from her dark suit. She walked down, her city shoes clipping on the cobbles.

8

A uniformed police officer waited while the suspect slid into the back of a patrol car. The PC climbed in alongside, the door slammed, and the car drove away. Blue lights flickering, a solitary burst of sirens.

Rockburn returned with Elsa to the bridge to collect the moped. When he'd been in the Job they'd once had a kiss and a clinch after a leaving party. She'd been drinking creamy cocktails and he remembered her sweet-smelling breath. The next day he took her for a ride on his bike, her arms tight around his waist.

'I think he was following me,' said Rockburn. Somewhere in the water's grimy depths rested the boy's phone. It might provide an answer, and it might not. He looked along the line of the canal to where it turned a corner. A yellow canoe appeared.

'Why?'

'Why was he following me, or why do I think that?'

Elsa smiled. 'How are Rockburn Investigations?'

'Singular. One case, one employee.'

The canoeist slid silently under the bridge, leaving an arrow of wash which flattened to nothing.

They walked back toward the car park, Rockburn wheeling the moped. He told Elsa about the telephone call, and Quang, and the Asian men who'd pursued them.

'You think the man I've just arrested might be connected?'

'Maybe.'

'Where's the boy now?'

'Staying with a friend.'

'I'll have to report it,' said Elsa, 'You know the rules.'

'Who knew you were meeting me at the canal?'

She looked across at him. 'That's quite an insinuation.'

'No one knew I was coming here except you.'

Elsa sighed. 'I signed out in the daybook.' Which meant everyone in Templeside CID could have known.

They reached the car park. Rockburn's motorbike lay on its side, slumped like a poached rhino. Leaning the moped against a post, he hauled his bike upright and found scratches on the fuel tank and engine cover. He opened a pannier. To his surprise, the bag with Quang's fingerprints and hairs was still there. He held it out to Elsa. 'Can you do these?'

The detective pulled a face. 'When you said you had something for me, I thought you meant information, not a bag of exhibits from your latest case. Sorry, your *only* case.'

Rockburn dropped the bag.

She caught it.

'Thanks. One more thing.' Elsa raised her eyebrows. 'Can you do a search for a dark blue hatchback with a registration which ends 6FXR?'

'I'm not promising anything.' She climbed into an unmarked police car and lowered the window a couple of inches. 'I'll never forget that bike ride.' She pulled forward, and with tyres flicking up gravel, pulled out of the car park.

Rockburn remembered Elsa's fingers working under his clothing and her fingernails digging into his midribs, and for a few seconds, reflected on what could have been.

He glanced around at the dark trees, loud in their silence. The suspect had turned up at the canal bridge by chance, or by following Rockburn, or through a leak at the police station. He didn't believe in chance which meant two things. One, they didn't know where he'd taken Quang, and the boy, therefore, was safe. Two, he needed to recover the discarded phone.

Rockburn rode back to his garret but not directly. He circled roundabouts until he felt dizzy, rode the wrong way up a one-way street, twisted through two sets of rat-run bollards. It was rush-hour, the traffic heavy and drivers bad-tempered. Grey clouds scudded overhead, mirroring the frantic activity on the ground.

After an hour he locked his bike to the fire escape, confident he hadn't been followed. He showered and ate a bowl of cornflakes and a banana. One of his five a month.

He threw some darts. a practice routine called Frustration. Score eighty plus with the first two darts, and if successful, attempt to hit double one with the third. Manage that, and throw again but ending with a double two, and so on. The idea was to recreate the high pressure on throwing a double because it took most amateur players several attempts to score more than eighty. Lots of traipsing up and down the rubber mat having scored less than eighty.

He threw 20, 20, walked along the mat and collected his two darts.

He flipped 20, triple 5, tramped up the mat, pulled out the pair of darts.

Triple 5, triple 1, trekked, gathered.

Triple 20, 5. Plodded. plucked.

He threw 20, triple 20. He checked his front foot was touching the oche, he wriggled his throwing shoulder, he breathed out. Licked the dart tip, glanced at the crowd. He let his body settle, breathed in, and threw.

1.

Gave up.

He thought through the sequence of events again. He hadn't been followed back from the canal bridge to his flophouse. Correction: if he had been followed, it was by helicopter which seemed as unlikely as him finishing a game of Frustration in under an hour. But just because he wasn't followed away from the canal didn't mean he wasn't followed *to* the canal. He thought he'd seen something – someone? – in the yard when he couldn't sleep.

He hefted the darts into the board, opened the door to the fire escape, and clanged down to the backyard.

He unlocked the panniers on the panther and checked inside. Felt and looked underneath. Nothing. He checked the mudguards, feeling up inside with his fingers. Again, nothing. He stood back and asked himself where he would hide it. Unscrew and remove a cover or a fairing and nestle it inside. He clanged back up the steps of the fire escape, two at a time. Dug out his tackle box of tools and lugged it back down.

Starting on the right-hand side of the bike he removed the lower fairing, then the side cowl. No alien object inside. He replaced the covers and re-tightened their bolts. He removed the clutch cover but found only the clutch. Screwed it back down, moved to the front of the bike. He took off the cowl – and bolted it back in place. The left side of the bike: lower fairing, side cowl. Nothing.

Perhaps he was wrong.

A waft of smoke made him glance up. Flack leant on the rail of the first-floor landing, puffing on a cigar.

Rockburn unbolted the large padded front seat and checked the cavity underneath, a perfect hiding place. He lifted out the crumpled pack of cigarettes – useful when befriending rough sleepers – and a pair of plastic gloves bundled up with a rag. Moved the balaclava, the telescopic pair of bolt croppers, and the bottle of emergency tyre sealant. His gear, nothing missing or added. He put it all back and bolted the seat in place, and removed the smaller rear seat. The void contained a compact first aid kit and a couple of multitools. The items he was expecting.

Unbolting the rear fairing, he found what he was looking for – a small black box the size of a deck of cards. It was held in place by a magnet and on the side were three small lights, one red and two orange. He could dismantle it, or crush it with a brick. He could attach it to a dustcart or a minicab and send them on a dance of the sugar plum fairy.

A shame the panther couldn't talk – or fight back. He rocked back on his heels, and held it up to Flack.

'GPS.'

'You want me to ride it out of town?'

Rockburn shook his head. He replaced the tracker in the cavity and bolted down the fairing. Now, they would follow him only when and where he wanted.

He cleaned the grime from the fuel tank and engine cover, then added scrapes of filler to the scratches and wiped them smooth. He felt differently about the machine, less friend and ally, more of a double agent. While the filler dried, he did twenty pull-ups from the bottom landing on the fire escape.

His phone rang.

'Bit embarrassing this.' said Elsa.

Rockburn waited.

'The suspect from the canal escaped from the back of the police car on the way back to the nick. The door was opened in a traffic jam, and he jumped out. They must have been followed. The lad in the back was a probationer but it shouldn't have happened. I'm sorry. Should have gone in a van, but we're stretched. Only a bit of cannabis.'

And a knife, and possibly responsible for offences against the boy and his aunt – trafficking, attempted kidnap. Harassment at the very least.

'Anything from the moped?'

'Gone by the time the van did get there.'

Rockburn took a breath, decided not to mention the tracker. The police cock-up gave him a small advantage in bargaining with Elsa. 'So—'

'I'll sort out the checks you wanted.'

He ended the call, made another – a former colleague in the dive unit. Recovering the phone had become a priority. At least working alone, he had only himself to blame for mistakes.

Dan had opted for specialisation over promotion and policework. His hobby was his job which made him dull but happy.

'Rockburn! How's being a private eye?'

'Up and down.' Still waiting for the up. 'Dan, if I said I've just dropped my phone in a canal, what are the chances you could find it?'

'Is there much flow?'

'Water looks stationary.'

'Probably not the case, but that would help. Then it all depends how long we spend looking. Two days and we could find it, a week and we should. But there're no guarantees, and even if we do, the phone's unlikely to be usable. Even data recovery is tricky.'

'Can you come now?'

'No way, *José* – not unless an MP or the mayor's been murdered. Next week, maybe.'

Rockburn hung up, cranked out fifteen more pull-ups. He could borrow some gear from Dan. Sixteen. Tomorrow. Seventeen. Tomorrow, he'd return to the canal to search for the phone, then ride out to check on the boy.

He dropped down, and using fine sandpaper, worked the scratch lines on the panther smooth. He wiped them clean and added beads of red polish. Rubbed them with a cloth, then added a layer of wax. Buffed the fuel tank until the marks had vanished and he could see his face. He buffed every cowl and fairing, cleaned every tube and duct, polished every light and every lever. He stood back. The panther gleamed in conspiracy at its stowaway.

His phone rang.

Mina?

9

He snatched it up.

'You're in luck, Rockburn. Had a cancellation for tomorrow.'

Not the call he'd have preferred but beggars and all that. He arranged to meet Dan at the canal, but he would need to borrow Flack's Kawasaki.

He went inside, knocked on the tattooist's door.

No reply.

He banged again.

But Flack had finished for the day, and would with near certainty be entrenched in the Arch, Demons MC's drinking den. Phoning him after hours as effective as sending a smoke signal.

The following morning, Rockburn got up late.

Still no reply downstairs. He wondered if he'd have to call a cab in order to meet Dan.

He microwaved the previous evening's takeaway, then threw for an hour. No call from Mina. Outside, leaves spilled down from the tree at the back of the yard and collected in eddies alongside the fat tyres of the panther.

Music suddenly throbbed.

He padded down again, past a cemetery-quiet RCS Holdings,

and rapped on Flack's door. Heavy metal pounded inside. The tattooist had once tried to teach him the differences between thrash, power, black, nu, but had got annoyed when Rockburn, had asked for earplugs. He pushed open the door.

Inside was a small waiting area which reeked of cigar smoke. Two chairs faced a simple wooden counter. A jacket hung on the back of one of the chairs, and a scruffy handbag sat underneath. Posters of tattoos covered the wall above the counter, and in the centre hung a framed certificate of competence. At the back of the room, a sliding frosted-glass partition stood half-open. It revealed part of a couch and Flack, his back to Rockburn, sitting on a swivel chair and working on the shoulder of a prone woman.

The tattooist turned and slid the partition aside. He turned down the music. 'Have a gander, Rockburn, Linh won't mind.'

The small woman on the couch waved assent.

Rockburn walked up to the partition. Flack wheeled away, gold earrings dangling, and his buzzing tattoo tool held up in front of him like a pistol. He wore a bandana over his head and surgical gloves. Linh wore a gown which left her arm exposed.

A stand directed a bright white light onto her shoulder. The black outline of a tattoo showed an ancient warrior on a charging horse, the soldier wielding a long bamboo rod against an enemy mob.

'Two minutes, Linh.' Flack downed his tool on a metal tray. He followed Rockburn into the reception area, sliding the door shut behind him.

'She's south-east Asian,' said Rockburn. 'Possibly Vietnamese.'

'Who is?'

'The woman on your couch. *Linh.*'

'So?'

'I told you, I was followed by a carload of south-east Asians.'

61

Rockburn continued in a whisper: 'Who were trying to snatch the boy – Quang – who's Vietnamese. And I was followed again yesterday, by another one on a moped.'

Flack peeled off his bandana and scratched the back of his head.

'How long have you known her?'

'She's a walk-in.'

'Exactly.'

Flack retied the bandana. 'You can't go suspecting every Asian of being involved. It's a coincidence – most of my customers aren't white.'

The tattooist had a point. In addition, the suspects had all been male. 'Alright, but humour me – don't mention the boy.'

'Okay, okay.' Flack slid open the partition door. 'Now fuck off, I've got a business to run, even if you don't.'

'Can I borrow your spare bike?'

'No. The Kawasaki needs an oil change.' Flack slammed the glass door shut, and seconds later, the sound of heavy metal strengthened.

Rockburn walked across the reception area toward the door. Past the chairs and the coat and bag. Maybe the ethnicity of Flack's customer was only a coincidence, but the tracking device was a real concern. And the boy was petrified. Glancing at the closed partition, he backed up. He couldn't not have a quick look in her possessions.

He lifted the coat from the back of the chair and patted it down. The pockets were empty except for tissues and a couple of buttons. He draped it back and glanced at the frosted door of the studio. At the amorphous shape of Flack, working on the tattoo of the ancient warrior. He turned back. The posters above the counter showed the most popular designs for women were hearts, birds, signs of the zodiac, and heavenly bodies. Glancing again at the glass door, he swung the handbag up onto the counter.

He pulled a large picture-book of tattoos closer and opened a page at random. Werewolves, zombies, creatures of the night stared out at him.

The handbag was traditional black leather with a silver-coloured clasp. The corners were worn and there were scratches across the leather. He clicked it open, the noise louder than he expected. The music in the tattooing room stopped. He looked up, his pulse racing as if he'd misjudged an overtake. He could hear voices and laughing. The fuzzy image of Flack moved off his chair and the heavy music resumed. It sounded like the same song. Flack sat back down.

Rockburn pulled open the bag. It smelt of almonds, and he pulled out a half-eaten packet of the candied nuts. There was a pair of leather gloves. A packet of tissues. Sunglasses. A dogeared comic book in a foreign language. He turned a few pages. Less cartoon, more adult graphic novel. The action showed villages and soldiers on horseback, an execution. Badly printed. He snapped photos on his phone. He pulled out a simple purse which contained a wad of pristine notes, four or five hundred pounds, and a few coins. Condoms. No identification which was unusual and increased his unease. He delved again. Three pairs of blue disposable gloves, the type used by police and hospital staff. He took more photos, then checked the tattooing room. The woman still prone, Flack still leant over her.

Rockburn looked at the items on the counter and hefted the bag. Felt the bag's lining. He prised up the base, a stiff piece of leather like the sole of a shoe. He unzipped a pocket and pulled out a CS canister.

He looked up. The two of them in the tattoo studio as before. He took a photo of the canister. He could seize it, but the woman would know he'd rumbled her. If he left it, he would be leaving a weapon that might be used against him or his clients, and missing out on a forensic opportunity. In any case, if they had one weapon, they were likely to have others. He was getting ahead of himself – the canister didn't prove Flack's customer was working with or for the Asians in the blue car. When he'd been in the Job, it wasn't unusual to find a section five firearm during a stop and search. Linh might not even know it was illegal to carry one. If he left it, she might still suspect he'd been through her bag.

He slipped the canister into his pocket. Then refitted the liner and replaced the items in the bag.

Glancing again at the partition, he walked around the counter and opened a drawer. Pens and pencils, a letter and an assortment of keys. He opened the drawer wider – the Kawasaki key nestled at the back. He picked it up, twiddled it, pushed it into his pocket alongside the canister. His eyes straying to the letter, he read, *Chestnut Road Medical Centre, Urgent.*

The tattooist's phone rang.

Rockburn jogged back around the counter, swung the handbag down on the floor and toe-punted it under the chair. He turned a page of the picture-book. Macabre sad-faced clowns, one with green cheeks and albino eyes. Next to him, the phone kept ringing. He turned another page. In the studio the music was lowered. A page of electric guitars.

The sliding door opened. 'You still here.'

Rockburn nodded, turned again. Ghosts, ghouls, and goblins. Pointed ears, red eyes, rotten teeth. One holding a flaming torch, another a pitchfork.

'Hello,' said Flack on the phone. A pause. 'Next Thursday at three?' The tattooist flopped down the receiver and made a note on a pad covered in thick doodles.

Rockburn glanced up to meet Flack's stare. 'Amazing stuff in here.'

'Uh-huh.'

Rockburn turned over. 'Yeah.' Gravestones, gravediggers,

headstones. The grim reaper. A guillotine. Bats flying across a translucent moon.

'You thinking of getting one?'

'Maybe.' Not unless he was press-ganged. The Job stereotype persisted: the more tattoos, the more unpredictable in the custody suite.

Flack returned to the studio and slid the door shut. There was the sound of voices, and the pounding music restarted.

Rockburn stared at the picture-book's centre spread. A seated muscled man with the tattoo of a woman's face covering most of his back. She was young, beautiful, heavily made-up, staring out obliquely. There was a red spot, a shell or a small sun on her forehead. Her hair intricately drawn in red and green whorls.

He closed the scrapbook and straightened it on the counter. Peered through the frosted door into the studio at the industrious shape of Flack, and listened for a few seconds to the heavy throb of the music.

Then walked back round the counter, opened the top drawer and took out the letter. He read it twice, put it back. As he squeezed the drawer shut, the partition slid open.

Flack filled the doorway.

The size of a doorman, the presence of a silverback gorilla, the mindset of a cage fighter. Hands like shovels, fists like lead weights. They'd rough-housed a few times, but never fought in earnest.

Always a first time.

'Course you can borrow the Kawasaki, I'll do the oil change another time. Key's in the top drawer.'

Bubbles rose on the surface of the canal. The water near-black, stationary, a slick of grime and detritus along one side. The top of Dan's ladder hung down from the edge, and his bag of equipment lay open on the bank. He'd said he would surface after thirty minutes, change tanks, and dive again.

Rockburn's job to safeguard his friend's kit and make him a brew. He hoped the young Asian suspect had spent ages trying to remove the handcuffs. Wondered whether he was connected to the blue hatchback. Whether he'd searched for the phone at the same time as collecting the moped. Always the same with leads – follow enough, and one would reveal the answer.

The bubbles moved back and forth near the bridge.

The minutes ticked by –

Approached the half hour –

When, like a shark fin, a scuba tank broke the water's surface. The mask and breathing tube followed. Dan swam towards the ladder, a gripped hand held up in triumph. Treading water, he pulled down his mask.

'Found it, just lying there. It does happen every now and then.'

Rockburn helped him up the ladder, and exchanged the retrieved phone for a brew. Dan stepped out of his flippers, tugged off his wetsuit. Rubbed his limbs and hair with a towel. Rockburn dried the phone with kitchen roll, took it apart and tamped the battery and insides. He wrapped the parts in a fresh piece and put them in an open Ziplock bag and into his small rucksack. He pulled out a bottle of spiced rum and passed it over.

'Thanks,' said Dan, sounding like he didn't mean it.

Rockburn picked up his rucksack and the oxygen tank, Dan the rest of his kit, and together, they walked back to the parking. His former colleague stashed his gear in the back of a Land Rover Discovery equipped with a roof rack and a snorkel.

Dan shut the rear door, turned. 'If this is going to be a thing, Rockburn, then needs to be more than a bottle. Cost more than that in petrol and to fill the tank.'

'I thought—'

'Yeah, this one's on the house. But your business, my business.'

His former colleague drove away, and Rockburn climbed onto the Kawasaki. The cost irrelevant: a lead was a lead was a lead.

10

Rockburn pulled into the twenty-minute parking at Stockport train station, and dismounted from the juddery Kawasaki. No trainee to take the rescued phone to the technical department which would unlock and interrogate it, and produce a smart report. No technical department. He trotted down the steps to a phone concession in the booking hall. The door was propped open. Signage outside shouted great deals and a stand held dozens of garish phone covers. He stepped inside.

No other customers. The tiny interior filled with cabinets of phones and equipment. A fridge by the door. Behind the counter, shelves of boxed handsets, and a sales assistant scrolling his phone.

Noonan.

The assistant looked up, and Rockburn held his stare for a couple of seconds before placing the Ziplock bag on the counter. 'I wondered what you can do with this. The SIM's locked, and I need it unlocking.'

Noonan pushed out his bottom lip, nodded.

He took the items out of the bag, threw away the paper towels, turned the pieces over on the counter. He fitted them back together, tapped on the screen. He took the phone apart again, removed the SIM, and slotted it into a second phone, tapped again. Noonan sighed, pushed out his bottom lip. 'Phone's knackered, SIM's probably okay. Fifty quid to unlock it.'

As a detective, Rockburn had either made requests in-house or shown his warrant card; occasionally his badge and a warrant. Either way, there was no discussion. Being a PI was very different, and he was beginning to realise every request was going to involve horse trading.

'Thirty.'

Noonan shook his head.

'Thirty and repeat business.'

The assistant paused, pushed out his lip. Rockburn wanted to shove him back against the wall. Finally, Noonan nodded. The assistant attached a lead to the second phone and plugged it into a laptop, partially hidden under the counter.

Rockburn wondered how much it would cost to purchase the software to be able to do it himself. Cut out the middleman. Realised he was running a business, couldn't only concentrate on investigation. And he'd need to employ someone – if he remained solvent.

'I'm in.'

'What's on it?'

'Not much.'

'What?'

'One stored number, ending 378.'

Noonan wrote two numbers on a scrap of paper, passed it across. He unplugged the phone, removed the retrieved SIM, placed it on the counter with the damaged handset. 'The number ending 085 is the SIM's.'

Rockburn tore the paper in half, wrote briefly, and pushed across an IOU.

Outside, he tapped the 378 number into his own phone, and

walking back up the steps to the Kawasaki, listened to the ringing tone.

The phone connected.

'Hello,' said Rockburn.

He could hear someone breathing.

Then:

Nothing.

One step forward, one step back, investigation didn't change.

Intending to check on Quang and Hocking, Rockburn rode the Kawasaki out of the city. The ride was bouncy as a trampoline, but it was better than being followed on the panther.

To make certain he wasn't being shadowed, he jumped a set of red lights and detoured through a line of bollards into an industrial estate. At a petrol station he wandered around the shop looking for something for the boy. Settled on a bag of marshmallows, and at the till added a pack of Flack's diabolical cigars, a copy of *Better Darts*, two packs of sandwiches, and a wrap of flowers.

Leaving the streetlights behind he headed up a steep rise into the hills. The bike vibrated and whined. As he swung round a switchback he glanced down to check no one was following. At the top he pulled into a viewpoint and looked back at the city. The castellated skyline, the yellow bubble of light. Who were they, and why did they want the boy? Where was his client? The city asked the questions and he hoped, by allowing him to breathe, the country would provide the answers.

At the house, he parked at the front and knocked. As a child he'd liked kicking a football in the front garden with his brother, and building a camp in the corner next to the rhodo-dendron. Would still enjoy a kickabout with Simon – they'd fought like most siblings but were essentially made from the same cloth – for better or worse. Rockburn wondered what his brother was doing, whether he was even still alive.

He walked over to a front window but couldn't see anyone inside. He walked around the back and tried the door. It was locked.

Hocking's face appeared at the window. Rockburn breathed out, and heard a key in the lock.

'It's only you.'

He handed her the flowers. 'Any problems?'

Hocking shook her head. 'Not the ones you mean. He's had a couple of nightmares, cries out in the night.'

'Has he said anything?'

'Nothing.' Hocking shouted upstairs. 'It's okay, Quang, it's Rockburn.'

They waited like strangers in the kitchen. Hocking offered him tea, and he asked how she was. He watched her put the flowers in a vase. 'I really appreciate you looking after him.'

Quang burst into the room. He looked around, went out again. Rockburn followed him into the hall where the boy had sat on the stairs. He wasn't surprised – traumatised children behaved unpredictably.

'You want to go for a ride?' he said gently.

Without looking up, Quang nodded.

'You okay?'

The boy nodded again, faster.

They rode for thirty minutes across the moors. Early on, Rockburn pulled over and turned around. They lifted their visors, the boy's eyes shimmering with excitement. They went on, passing isolated cottages and a windy pub with an empty car park. They saw a bounding hare and disturbed a pheasant nestled into a verge. Rockburn kept to the minor roads and his speed low. Once or twice, he looked round again. The boy was a natural bike-rider, and although it made no sense, Rockburn felt a burn of pride.

They reached the gate and the track to the foot of the climb. The boy jumped down and removed the chain to let them pass. Rockburn gave him a thumbs-up as he wheeled the bike through. The track was rough and potholed, and Rockburn weaved slowly along. Once, they dismounted and pushed. The studded tyres of Flack's Kawasaki did their job.

Rockburn was pleased he'd bought cigars for Flack. Not only did he feel bad for taking the key prematurely, he couldn't unknow what he knew. His own problems added to by Flack's. The definition of a friend.

The track ended at a locked gate. They dismounted and Rockburn wheeled the bike into a thicket. The boy scraped mud spatter from the fairings and felt the warmth of the engine. Leaving their helmets on the seat, they walked a short distance along a path to the foot of a craggy bluff.

It rose steeply in rocky steps but in-between there were flatter sections. The boy went first, using his hands to clamber up. The air cooled and their breathing deepened. They reached the first tricky problem. Two large smooth boulders with a narrow crack between and no obvious hand or foot placements. Rockburn showed the boy how to jam his fist in the crack and use it to work the flats of his feet up the smooth rock.

They scrambled on. The gritstone rocks were rough and satisfying to the touch. The second difficult problem. A huge steep slab. Climbing onto it was straightforward but it then required a confident approach to move up. Some people remained on their hands and knees. The boy climbed up and stopped, glanced back.

Rockburn waited. A bird of prey hovered far above them.

The boy took a step upwards. He took another step, spreading his arms wide to give balance. He kept going, and when he reached the end, looked back. Raised his thumb.

An hour passed. They stopped for a breather at the foot of the last and trickiest problem. Looked out over the undulating hills. It rained a lot so the hills were green, even in November. Cause and effect was the essence of the country. Little made sense in the city.

Quang inspected the final boulder problem. Two large blocks which held a chockstone five feet off the ground. The boy pulled up on the chockstone and tried to run his feet on one of the boulders but they weren't close enough. He hung from the chockstone and tried to flip his feet up and over.

Rockburn waited. He felt the coarse rock and wondered how old it was. What animals had lived then.

The boy shook his head.

Rockburn made a stirrup with his hands. Quang placed a muddy boot on Rockburn's fingers, grabbed the chockstone and heaved himself up and over. Rockburn's turn. He was tall enough to reach a hold the boy couldn't. He hauled himself up and over, the boy pulling on his jacket. He belly-flopped over the chockstone, and they lay in a heap together.

'Well done,' said Rockburn.

Quang grinned like a boy should at his age.

They scrambled up the final rocky slope to a small copse of trees at the summit. There were the remains of a fire and a log to sit on. Rockburn found a silver birch and tore away strips of bark while the boy gathered kindling. He built a small fire and they collected more wood.

The burning kindling snapped and spat and smelt like all wood fires since the beginning of time.

They ate the sandwiches, and took it in turns to lay thicker branches across the flames. Quang set fire to the sandwich wrappers which curled and melted, and released a noxious smell which the boy inhaled, then coughed until there were tears in his eyes.

The fire died down and the daylight seeped away.

Wishing he was a magician, Rockburn pulled the packet of marshmallows out of his pocket. He showed the boy how to whittle a green stick. Rockburn balanced his skewer on a Y-shaped branch jammed into the ground. The boy held his, impatiently twiddling it over the glowing embers.

The boy blew on the sweet and dabbed it with a finger. He ripped it off the stick and ate it. He speared another.

'Are you okay at the house with Hocking?'

Nodding, Quang tasted the marshmallow. Rockburn offered him the bag. The boy ate one cold while he turned the one toasting. 'Where's Mina?'

'I don't know,' said Rockburn.

'Is she okay?'

Rockburn inspected his marshmallow. He didn't want to lie, but didn't want to tell the boy what he thought was true – that she was in great danger. 'I'm going to find her, and if I can, help her.'

The boy nodded, and set up another marshmallow.

'How did you and Mina get to England?'

Quang stared into the fire. 'Long journey – more six month.' He tested the marshmallow on the stick.

'You mentioned a factory where you learnt English.'

Quang nodded. 'In China. We are in clothe factory in China for three month. Hard work, make clothe from seven in morning 'til eight in evening, sometime get beaten for not work hard. Man comes factory, and we okay to leave.'

'Who was he, this man?'

The boy shrugged.

'Vietnamese?'

'I think, yes.'

74

'Go on.'

'We travel in lorry to Russia, and wait in very big and very old building for forty-three days. We counting. Rain in roof, rats during night. Many people sick, some die. We leave building, walk for one month through forest, head east to Europe. To France country. I always cold, always hungry. Mina give me her food, her coat.'

'I'll find her,' said Rockburn.

The boy fingered his marshmallow, picked off a piece and ate it. He nodded.

Rockburn removed his stick from the fire and ate the blackened mess. 'Your turn for a question.'

'Why can no see in dark?'

Rockburn tried the marshmallow, trying not to smile. 'We can, just not as well. Our eyes are made of cones in the centre and are surrounded by rods. Cones can detect colour, but rods can't. Rods are also less sensitive – less good, you understand?'

Quang nodded.

'So, one tip for seeing better in the dark is not to stare at an object but to look to the side of it.'

The boy nodded, and ate another marshmallow. 'You turn.'

'Tell me about where you lived in Vietnam.'

The boy licked a marshmallow. 'I live Hai Phong – in Hong River Delta. *Hong* mean red. Lots, very lots people live there. Everyone grow rice. In England, you grow rice? I not see.'

'It's too cold at night, even in summer.'

'Hocking your girlfriend?'

Rockburn grinned. 'Used to be.'

'What happen?'

'It wasn't to be.'

'How know?'

'We knew.'

But had they? Had *he*? Could he not have lived a different

life, a life with Hocking in the country. Was investigating bad men's actions and counteractions what he wanted to spend his time doing, or what the city had indoctrinated him to want to do?

He heard rustling in the scrub and surveilled around. The gloom was thickening, and the temperature dropping. He'd cooled down after the climb which meant the boy would be cold.

'*Why* did you and Mina come to the UK?'

The boy shivered. 'Lot words.'

Rockburn razed the embers and led the boy through the back of the copse to the top of the descent slope. The grassy hill was an easy gradient and they jogged down to warm up, then retraced their steps along the path to the locked gate and the Kawasaki.

At the house, Rockburn parked on the road. Quang raced up the path, and Rockburn followed, past stacked bags of peat and chipping from a garden centre.

The boy rang the doorbell. An absurd noise in the country gloaming.

Rockburn handed the boy the half-empty packet of marshmallows. The gloom encased the row of houses, and for a moment he felt they were the only people left on the planet. He asked Quang again about Mina.

'We come England, two reason. One reason, go school, not grow rice. Two reason, you no understand.'

Hocking opened the front door and a shaft of light spilled out. She smelt of wine and perfume, and inside music was playing softly.

The boy walked in, leaving Rockburn alone with Hocking. The chilly air embraced them. They could try again. She lived in a house and a place he loved.

'I'd thought once,' said Rockburn, 'me and you—'

'So did I for a while, but you were always working. I wanted more of you, a life together – in the country.'

'That's being in the job.'

'You could have left the police, got a different job.'

The same argument, over and over.

Hocking toyed with the door, pushing it back and forth a couple of inches. She'd wanted to live an increasingly hippy lifestyle, to get up late, and sketch and paint with a glass of wine never far away. To grow vegetables, keep a few chickens and take a stall at farmers' markets and country fairs.

'It's too late now, anyway.'

'Why's that?'

'It's complicated.' She paused, listened. 'It wasn't only your job, the hours, worrying about you.'

'What, then?'

A voice from upstairs.

'Quang's calling. I should go.'

Rockburn pecked her cheek, and she shut the door.

In the distance a pair of headlights roamed. They too then disappeared. One day he'd be ready. But not yet. The country was both an antiseptic and an antidote to the dark places, but the city gave him purpose. And he still had work to do.

On the ride home Rockburn stopped at the same viewpoint as before. Manchester sat smug and insatiable in its radioactive glow. He'd been wrong earlier. The city asked the questions *and* provided the answers. Who was chasing the boy, and why.

Leads were few. The 378 number on the discarded phone. Forensics from Rockburn's banister, from Quang's motorbike helmet, and from the CS canister he'd taken from Flack's client Linh. The part registration plate on the blue car. He phoned Elsa and left a message.

He stared again at the sprawling conurbation. Traffic

hooted, raced, snarled. Sirens started up, fell silent. Overhead, a helicopter roved with a searchlight.

Like a moth to a lamp, Rockburn mounted Flack's bike.

He'd start with the alley where he'd fled with the boy. Check for physical clues, witnesses, and speak to Leila.

11

The entrance to the alley was full of rubbish. Soggy newspapers, a vacuum cleaner missing its hose, and a burnt-out saucepan with the putrid remains of the last meal. Sacks of masonry, bags of clothes. Cans, bottles, pizza boxes. Choked and choking, the city bred self-interest and indifference – *Not in my backyard. Not my problem. Who you looking at?* – antisocial behaviour and criminality.

Rockburn paused before entering the alley. Approaching him on the pavement was an emaciated girl pushing a buggy.

'You okay, Sal – what happened in the park?'

She looked embarrassed. 'I'm fine.' In the buggy, her sleeping baby looked angelic, no idea of the life ahead. 'You escaped,' said Sal, a glint in her eye. 'Is that boy okay?'

'Yeah, he's doing alright. Thanks for your help, I owe you. Didn't you mention something in Little Park?'

'Nah, don't worry.'

'Is it money?'

She shook her head, took a deep breath. 'You know how posh kids have a godparent, looks out for them and stuff?'

Rockburn nodded.

'I was wondering if you –' She glanced at her baby.

Him – a godfather. Rockburn pictured Vito Corleone

smoking a cigar and toying with a decision about the family business. 'I'd be honoured.' He took out his wallet.

'I didn't mean.'

'I know. Would you prefer a gift later?'

She took the money and walked away pushing the buggy.

Hoping she wouldn't spend it on drugs, Rockburn entered the alley. He stepped over the papers and retraced his steps from three days earlier when he'd escaped with Quang. The boy and his aunt had come to the UK for two reasons: for Quang to go to school which made sense, and a second reason which the boy had said Rockburn wouldn't understand. Mina was pregnant? A family feud?

Glancing back over his shoulder, he banged on a door. No answer. He moved aside a traffic cone, rapped on a fire exit – again no response. When he reached the peeling green door, he knocked a third time, and waited, pondering whether to wear a suit for the final session of his police disciplinary which was scheduled for four pm. He glanced at his watch.

Bolts were drawn back and the door opened a crack, revealing a vertical sliver of a veiled woman – Leila.

Rockburn held up a tin of foil-wrapped biscuits. 'I wanted to say thank you for the other day.'

She nodded faintly.

'Not just thank you,' said Rockburn. He could smell cooking – spices he didn't recognise. 'I'm now a private investigator.' He slipped a business card into the crack.

The door opened halfway. She stood in the opening and took the biscuits. 'My children will like them. It's kind of you.'

'The boy I was with, do you know him – his name's Quang?'

Leila checked up and down the alley. She was tall, her long robe giving a graceful appearance as if she hovered rather than stood. Rockburn followed her gaze, but apart from the rubbish heaped at both ends, the alley was deserted.

'Come in a moment.'

Rockburn stepped inside and Leila closed the door.

'I'm sorry, I don't know the boy.' She read his card. 'I know you do this now. So do my carriers. I – we – help people arriving here. We watch out for them, give them a little money, steer them in the right direction. I was told about the boy and his aunt. And I did what I could.'

'Where is the boy's aunt?'

'I don't know.' She reached for the door handle. 'You must go, you are putting us both in danger.'

'Danger from who?'

Leila didn't answer.

'Please,' said Rockburn. 'Do you know Mina?'

Leila shook her head. 'I'm sorry.' She opened the door, peered out.

'What about a young woman, maybe also Vietnamese, called Linh?'

Rockburn looked up and down the alley. 'I'm trying to help the boy, and his aunt. Have you any idea who's following them?' The woman shook her head, the folds of her robe gently brushing the wall. 'Hold on.'

She shut the door again.

'Wait here.'

Rockburn heard muffled voices, then silence. He decided he'd wear a suit to the disciplinary, give them no easy excuse. Checked his watch – he still had an hour.

A minute or two later, Leila reappeared, and handed him a photo. 'One of my carriers found this.'

'Can I speak to them?'

'No, I'm afraid it's not possible. Please, go now.' She opened the door and Rockburn stepped out into the alley.

The door clunked shut and the bolts were drawn across. Rockburn examined the photo. It showed Quang and the woman on Rockburn's CCTV – according to Quang, his aunt. The two of them were huddled together in the corner of a walk-in freezing compartment, possibly in a lorry container, but he couldn't be certain. They looked cold and petrified.

He walked back down the alley, slaloming through the refuse and smelling decay, but feeling a sense of lightness. Leila was a woman who was making a difference, a woman who would be talked about for years to come, and maybe, just maybe, would fade into legend.

12

'Please sit down, Mr Rockburn.'

In a police setting the absence of his rank stung, but he kept his face blank. He'd worn a suit, and to begin with at least, he'd play their game. Still in his head, the image of Quang and his aunt cowering in the freezer. Pale, thin, terrified.

'Thank you.'

He sat, feeling peculiar to be wearing one of his old work suits. His better one, reserved for paperwork days and Crown Court appearances. His fighting suit, which he'd worn most of the time, had been rejected by two charity shops so he'd cut it up for motorbike rags.

In front of him sat the five members of the tribunal who would decide on his pension. If at least four of them found in his favour, he'd get a sixtieth of a sergeant's salary for each year of service when he reached sixty. Which wasn't much but it was something, and a vestige of recognition for a decade of grafting at North Manchester. The divisional head of human resources sat in the centre, flanked by two chief superintendents, and two lay persons, a vicar and a former FTSE 100 director. Three women, including the chair, two persons of colour and one in a wheelchair. The police always led the way for equality.

Loud modern art brightened the walls of the fifth-floor

meeting room at headquarters. They looked splashy and obvious, and Hocking would have taken the piss. The panel sat behind a row of desks. One table was marooned in front of them, empty except for a jug of water and an upturned glass. Rockburn poured out a measure.

Behind the panel members were large windows with open blinds. The cavernous sky was pale blue, empty and beguiling.

'Before we start,' said Superintendent Cantlebury, 'are you quite sure, Mr Rockburn, you don't want someone here with you? A solicitor, or your Fed rep.'

'Quite sure.' Flack had offered to come but Rockburn declined, fearing the tattooist might receive unnecessary scrutiny. A whiff of cannabis might lead to a search, even arrest, and confuse the issue he was meant to be assisting. Rockburn could no longer afford a lawyer, and he wasn't a member of the Federation – he detested their fat cat building, their inflated salaries and luxury cars.

'We will start then,' said the chair, 'with a summary of the facts.' Deborah Foxton put on her glasses which had a blue tint and dangled on a chain. Heads of HR, thought Rockburn, all looked the same. Foxton was in her fifties and plain as a shovel. She was single, childless, and kept a cat called Humpty Dumpty. The cat's name was the most interesting thing about her. She'd made her career her life. Rockburn sipped the water. He could talk: unless the panther was included, he didn't even have a pet.

The head of HR looked left and right along her colleagues, and receiving small nods, glanced down at her file. The ancient vicar wore his dog-collar, the FTSE director a silver trouser suit. She was a millionaire, and a household name after floating her first company of retractable dog-leads. The two police officers wore uniform. Rockburn didn't know Cantlebury, but he knew Williams. Washerwoman Williams was the more polite of her nicknames.

'Eighteen months ago, on Friday the fifth of April, Mr Rockburn – then Detective Sergeant Rockburn – attended Redville Warehouse in Moston following a lead on a people trafficking case. DS Rockburn was alone and didn't request backup or indeed even inform the control room. There is no CCTV or witness corroboration, but according to Mr Rockburn, he entered the premises unobserved and found an observation point. From there he watched the auction of a seven-year-old girl – child X – who'd been trafficked from Asia, possibly Thailand. The sellers were a Glasgow OCG, the buyers a dark web collective from Chesterfield and Barnsley. Leroy Jones, an NCS nominal, was the fixer and also present.'

Rockburn stared out of the window into the expanse of blue sky. In the distance he could see a small plane. The girl – Pricha, not unlike a younger version of Quang – had been tied to a piece of piping like a dog and gagged with a strip of masking tape. She wore only shoes and a t-shirt. She sat, bawling, in a pool of urine. In the hidey-hole behind a door, Rockburn had felt ashamed of his gender, of his species, and a surging heat –

Sitting there, in the headquarters meeting room like a tailor's dummy, Rockburn felt it again, a fire coursing through him. He filled his glass and drained it.

He wondered if it was possible that Leroy Jones had also arranged Quang's sale in Manchester, and the Glasgow OCG the acquisition at Clydebank. The modern slave trade. The Asian posse in the blue car didn't look like Scottish hardmen but could have been local hires. Flack's customer, the Vietnamese woman Linh, could simply be a coincidence.

Foxton glanced across at him.

If it had been her child, her nephew, her friend's child?

It was always the cases involving children which had got to him in the Job. Nothing had changed. Children were blameless by definition. Like motorbikes. No excuse for a chattering gearbox, failing brakes, a clunky clutch, and seeing or hearing a poorly maintained machine always stirred his blood. Buy a bloody manual, learn the art of maintenance!

'Mr Rockburn – in his own words – *saw red and waded in.* In the resulting fray, two of the buyers were assaulted, their injuries amounting to actual bodily harm. Both men were arrested by uniform before they left the scene. Leroy Jones was arrested by Mr Rockburn and is currently awaiting trial. One of the Glasgow OCG escaped, but Robert Kingman was found unconscious at the foot of three flights of metal steps. He has suffered life-changing injuries.'

The Glasgow criminal had broken his neck and would spend the rest of his life in a wheelchair – and mostly in jail. The public and Rockburn's colleagues were sympathetic but the Independent Office for Police Conduct hadn't liked it. So despite being hailed a hero in the popular press, Rockburn had been charged.

Foxton turned over the page. 'At the subsequent criminal trial Mr Rockburn was found not guilty for the attempted murder of Robert Kingman. Following the trial there was an internal enquiry which made seventeen recommendations, including Mr Rockburn being required to resign.' Foxton paused to look left and right. 'Any questions so far?'

Rockburn wanted to scream. She hadn't even mentioned the victim. 'How is Pricha?' said Rockburn, squeezing the arms of his chair.

Foxton scowled and shuffled her papers without conviction. 'I don't have that information. Child X was placed in the care of social services and that's all I can tell you.'

Rockburn gripped until his knuckles were white. Foxton was worse than the washerwoman.

'Today,' continued the chair, 'we are solely considering Mr Rockburn's police pension. As such the panel needs to decide two things: one, whether he has brought the police service into disrepute, and two, whether it is fair he receives such a bounty from the state.' She glanced left and right, then straight ahead. 'Anything to say, Mr Rockburn?'

He looked along the line of panel members. The elderly vicar, sitting askew in his wheelchair, his face serious. Then Cantlebury, avoiding Rockburn's stare by pretending to make a note. Foxton, wiping her glasses. Superintendent Wendy Williams, also known as Willy in the locker-room after once being caught there. She, too, would not be an ally, he was sure. His only hope was the outliers, the disinterested vicar and the FTSE director in her silver suit, Pat McDuggan.

'Have you watched the videos showing what they did to Pricha?'

'I don't think—'

'You don't think what – that it's relevant? It's the founding stone, the centre, the *point* of the whole case.' Rockburn stood up. 'If any of you had watched even five minutes of the video – there are nine of them – then you would not only know exactly how Pricha is today, but you would have started with a minute's silence or worn black armbands or pinned pink ribbons to your chests. Something – anything – to signal your compassion and your inclusion in the human race.'

'Mr Rockburn!'

He glared along the line of faces, feeling adrenalin surge through his body.

'That is enough. Now, please wait outside.'

The corridor was wide and airless. He walked along to the toilets, and pushed open the door. He ran a basin of cold water and submerged his head. Later he might go swimming. He wanted to immerse his whole body in cold water, swim lengths submerged, visit another world. He ripped out some paper towels and mopped his face. There was no hope for his pension and he might as well leave.

He waited.

After thirty-five minutes, Cantlebury ushered Rockburn back into the meeting room. The chief superintendent smelt of extra strong mints. Two uniformed police officers – Foxton's blackshirts – now stood at the back of the room.

Rockburn sat when he was invited, and took up his earlier posture. His hands gripped the seat arms and his eyes roamed.

'The panel has carefully considered all the material in this case, and has now reached a decision – by a majority of four to one. Mr Rockburn, you will not be receiving a police pension.' Foxton took off her glasses and put them inside a case. She snapped it shut.

'Has even one of you watched a video?'

Foxton nodded at the officers behind Rockburn. Their boots clip-clopped towards him.

Rockburn stood, shook his head, looked along the line of dull faces a last time and walked out. He felt as numb as if he'd ridden the auto routes to Gibraltar in one piece.

In the car park the panther waited patiently and without judgement. Rockburn took off his tie and hauled on his salt-stained leathers. Their familiar sweaty smell calmed him. He replaced his shoes with his boots, and stashed the garb in a pannier. He pulled on his helmet.

The old vicar wheeled along the pavement. He stopped opposite Rockburn and looked across. 'These people, son, will burn in hell.'

Rockburn tightened the helmet strap, and gave the faintest of nods. He mounted the bike. The vicar sat watching him.

'Who do you mean?'

'All of 'em, son. All of 'em.'

Rockburn fired the ignition, the sound as sweet as ripe figs. Hoping the man of God was right, he puttered to the gate, and judging the rising barrier to millimetre perfection, ducked down and shot out onto the street. He gunned away from police head-quarters trying to blank the flickering images of Pricha.

He kept riding, too angry to stop. Headed for Whitby, a route he knew like the layout of a dartboard. Kept his head down, and his speed up. The panther warmed to the task, and as the miles passed, the two of them fused in a missile of energy and focus.

Two hours and five minutes later, they drew up on the front. Rockburn stripped naked and ran into the sea, dived into the waves. He swam until he was cold and exhausted, dressed, pitched up at the chuntering chip van. Bought coffee and a fish supper, and consumed them leaning against the panther, and staring out to sea. The sea was like the country, a place of recovery, a better place.

But the city was where the answers lay. He threw his trash, mounted up, and headed back. Time to stand with Leila, time to make a difference.

13

Elsa phoned early the next morning. The hairs and fingerprints from the helmet Quang had worn did not match anyone on police or border force databases – the boy hadn't been arrested or processed for any crime in the UK, and immigration didn't know about him. Which took Rockburn no further: the boy might be an illegal migrant, he might not. However, the detective had seven possible vehicles in Manchester for the part registration. Names and addresses but no associated intel.

'Thanks,' said Rockburn feeling buoyed. The list was a potential springboard to some answers. 'Do you want to go out later for something to eat? I know a place.' He needed to move on from Hocking.

'Where's the boy? You need to tell me, Rockburn.'

'I already did, he's with a friend, someone I trust. I wasn't going to mention it, Elsa, but it was your lot who allowed a possible suspect to escape.' He paused. 'So is that a yes about grabbing a bite? A ride too.' He could take her to the chip van on the front at Whitby.

'No.'

After a cold shower he ate a couple of rounds of buttered toast, threw a few darts, then headed out on the Kawasaki. He wasn't in the semifinal anyway. Leroy Jones and the Kingman brothers felt like a flight of fancy, so if Mina didn't turn up, the blue car was his best substantive lead.

The city throbbed and caterwauled, people and vehicles in constant flux. Seemingly, everyone had an origin and a destination, and a sense of purpose. Everyone belonged. All day the city cried, but all day the city lied.

The first address was in Stockport, an end-of-terrace with a caravan in the front garden. Already, it seemed unlikely. Three or four kids sitting across their BMX bikes were gathered on a corner. There was no sign of a dark blue hatchback.

Rockburn left his bike and helmet two streets over. He brushed down his suit trousers – his better suit, his only suit, for tribunals and for fighting – and picked up a leather wallet file, checked his greased hair in a car window.

Standing on the step he could hear vacuuming and smell fried onions. White sheets and pillowcases hung on a clothesline at the side. He knocked. The noise of the vacuum stopped, and the door was answered by an Asian woman wearing a black abaya.

'It's your lucky day.' Rockburn smiled and tamped down his hair. 'My name's Jim Spencer and I work for a law firm special-ising in compensation following a car accident. If I could see your car I could give you an estimate.'

'You're too late. It was scrapped three weeks ago.' She shut the door. One of the BMXers threw a stone which skittered down the path towards him. He threw it back. As he walked back to his bike, stones rained down around him. They were children, barely teenagers. One in three would be arrested before they were twenty.

Rockburn rode on to the second address in Stretford. The Kawasaki was still juddery as a pneumatic drill and he was glad he hadn't eaten more than toast.

Number 53 Wood Road was a large semi-detached house

with front windows in need of painting. Two vans and three cars including a dark blue hatchback were jammed into the drive. Spare tyres had been used to make a border with the next house. A young boy appeared at an upstairs window.

The door was opened by a man wearing shorts and a Union Jack t-shirt. Fetid air spilled out. Rockburn took half a step back.

'Whatever it is, we don't want it.' The door slammed.

He checked his list. Knocking on doors was old-fashioned policework but without the Job's intelligence databases, he didn't have a choice.

He rode further into Manchester, past Old Trafford cricket ground and into Salford. He jinked through small streets and stopped opposite a primary school at a three-storey block of flats. He took off his helmet, slicked down his hair, and prepared his patter. He couldn't see the car. He climbed the stairs to the second floor and walked along the balcony. Classical music blared from the first flat and a tv from the second. A cat sat on a welcome mat outside the third flat. He rang the bell.

He rang it again for the count of ten.

The door was opened by an old man wearing a dressing gown. 'I was on the fecking bog.' The accent thick Irish, and hoarse as a town-crier.

'Mr O'Brien?'

The old man nodded.

'Do you own a car, a blue hatchback?'

'Gave it to my eejit nephew. Lives in Newtonmore wherever the feck that is.'

'Is he Irish?'

The old man cackled, then bent in a fit of coughing. 'He ain't fecking Japanese.' Finally he straightened, hoiked and spat over the balcony wall. 'You ain't blessed, are you, fella?' He pushed the door to.

The cat purred.

Rockburn rode back to a drive-thru he'd passed. He ordered a burger and chips and a large coffee and sat on the kerb in the staff parking area. While he ate he scrolled through the photos he'd taken at Flack's. The CS canister which he'd bagged and stashed in his office, the foreign comic book which he'd put back. He'd meant to ask Quang about it. He finished the chips and tried to copy the words from the front cover into the search engine. Some of the letters had no English equivalent and his searches produced no meaningful hits. The burger was cold but he hardly noticed.

He wondered if he'd chosen the wrong lead to follow up. The blue car was a substantive lead to the Asian pursuers, Flack's customer more tenuous. But should he have waited and followed her? He stood and balled the paper bags. He needed a trainee investigator, despite not being able to pay himself yet alone any staff. Someone he could trust. If Simon ever turned up, and regardless of what he'd done, what he was accused of doing, maybe he'd ask him.

He jammed the refuse in a bin, mounted up. Three of Elsa's list of blue cars down, four to go.

The next address was in Bolton, a terraced house opposite a cemetery. He felt sick after the cement-mixer ride, but grabbed his wallet file and plodded on. Two reindeer hauling Father Christmas in a sleigh sat on the roof and last year's tree stood in a bucket outside the front window. He rang the bell.

A middle-aged Asian man opened the door. He wore a suit without a tie.

'Yes, sir? How can I help you, sir?'

'Name's Jim Spencer. I work in insurance, specifically compensation for accidents. Do you own a dark blue hatchback?'

'Yes, sir. Well, I own it and insure it. My son drives it.'

'Does he live here?'

'Sometimes, sir. He's a student in Cambridge, studying medicine. Do you have children, sir?'

Rockburn shook his head. He thought of Quang and the rocky scramble and the marshmallows. Maybe one day.

'You should. My son's going to be a doctor, sir. Look after my wife and me, let me read the paper and drink tea.'

'Cambridge?'

'Yes, sir. Corpus Christi College.'

The man opened the door wider to reveal a wall of framed pictures. In the centre a Corpus Christi matriculation photo.

Rockburn walked back to his bike. Criminal investigation was part science and part art. Feel, gut, instinct. He was feeling sick again and not just from the fairground-induced sensation of riding the Kawasaki. He felt sick because he wasn't making any headway, and might have to get a normal job like every other Tom, Dick, and Jim frigging Spencer.

He consulted the list and rode onto the next address. On the ring road the bike whined into a headwind. He turned off at Denton and stopped in a layby to look at a map on his phone. Over the roundabout, third right, behind a supermarket.

A young girl opened the door. Her clothes were dirty, her face taut. She wore no shoes and her feet were swollen.

'Is your mum or dad at home?'

The girl shook her head.

'Who's looking after you?'

'Katy.'

'Can you ask Katy to come to the door?'

The girl returned and held out a teddy bear missing an eye.

He phoned it in and waited for uniform to arrive. Rummaging through his pockets to find something for the girl, he found half the apple pie from the drive-thru. Offered it to the girl. He sat on the doorstep, and while she ate, told her the story of Cinderella. 'Again,' said the girl when he'd finished.

He rode away after checking with a neighbour. The current occupants had lived there for a month, and didn't own a car. Dad

94

was in prison, Mum worked long hours in a processing plant. Five down, two to go. But that wouldn't be the end of it. The dark blue hatch could have come from further afield, Blackburn or Liverpool, or even from down south. It could be on false plates. He pulled over and tossed a coin, let fate have its say. Heads, he'd continue, tails he'd ride back and concentrate on Flack's client Linh.

Heads.

Like the Moors Murders, there would never be an end to it.

The penultimate address was in Glossop on the high street, next to an undertaker. A terraced house with the lights on. No one answered to heavy banging. No sign of the blue car on the street. Rockburn went round the back. A service road contained dustbins and an old mattress but no cars.

His phone rang.

'Rockburn,' said Flack. 'She's back.'

14

The door to Flack's Tattoos stood ajar and rock music spilled out. Rockburn pushed the door wider and stepped inside.

'Upstairs,' shouted Flack from the studio. 'She didn't want to wait in here.'

Rockburn climbed the stairs two at a time. RCS Holdings was dark as a tomb. Oblongs of light pushed through the stairwell's filthy windows and sat obliquely on the worn carpet. His heart thumped.

A small Asian woman sat on the floor outside his door. Her legs were drawn up and she hugged her knees. Propped up next to her was a small rucksack. She wore black pumps and a coat with a hood. She looked up. Long black hair, a pale face and dark eyes. The same woman as in the photo Leila had shown him. The same woman as on his CCTV.

'Rockburn?'

'Mina?'

The woman nodded and closed her eyes. She took a deep breath, opened them again.

The street door opened and the sound of traffic rushed up the stairs. Voices crackled at the foot of the stairwell.

Mina jumped up. Rockburn put a finger to his lips, unlocked his door and pushed it open. She grabbed her rucksack and entered. He pulled the door to and stepped back to the top of the stairwell. He looked down.

No one.

He descended a couple of steps, still looking down the central shaft. He reached the oblongs of light, and RCS Holdings. The street door slammed and the traffic clamour ceased. He jogged all the way down and yanked open the door.

Looked up and down.

No one he could see of any interest.

Flack's door still stood ajar, rock music piling out.

Rockburn closed the street door and stepped inside the tattoo parlour. 'Flack, did you just open the front door?'

The tattooist walked out of his treatment room. He wore a leather waistcoat, a red and black bandana. He shook his head.

Rockburn climbed back up the stairs, stopping to peer into the dark recesses of RCS Holdings. One internal door stood open, but he couldn't remember whether it had been open the last time he'd glanced inside. He walked up to the second floor, shut and locked his door behind him.

Mina stood by the window, peering out. She was holding a small wooden-handled knife.

'Anything?' said Rockburn.

Mina shook her head. She folded the knife and put it in a pocket.

Rockburn checked the shower room and opened the big cupboard in the kitchenette. He looked out onto the fire escape and checked the exit door was bolted.

Taking down the bottle of brandy, he poured out two doubles. Handed one to Mina. She took the drink and moved from the window to the sofa. She sat, took a sip, grimaced.

Rockburn pulled over his desk chair. If he had ten questions, he had a hundred. He felt like a foster parent, a social worker, and a police detective. He was a private investigator. He didn't know what he was, but needed to be paid to do it.

'Are you okay?'

Mina nodded. 'How is Quang?'

'The boy's fine. He told me you're his aunt.'

'Yes.' She took another sip of brandy. 'But feel like mother. His mother father dead. I look after him seven year. His grandfather fought in Vietnam War. Quang no brothers or sisters. He is special boy.'

Rockburn stood up. 'Of course he is.' He didn't feel like brandy. He went to the window and looked out. An Asian man wearing a leather jacket exited the bookmaker's, and hurried away. Rockburn walked over to the kitchenette and grabbed a handful of cornflakes.

Mina stared at him. 'Where is Quang?'

'He's safe – with a friend of mine, out of the city.' Rockburn took another handful of cereal and sat back down. 'I went to see him yesterday. He eats like a coalminer.'

Mina tried to smile. 'I like see him.'

'I'll take you.'

'Thank you,' she said, nodding. 'We travel half a year. Food sometime difficult.'

'Quang told me you paid a lot of money to come here. He told me about working in a clothing factory in China. And then travelling to Russia and hiding in a warehouse with other migrants for forty-three days.'

'He talk a lot.'

'I ask a lot.'

Mina again tried to smile. 'Quang was counting the days but me too. I spent all my saving on journey, pay men to get us Europe.'

'Where did you go from Russia?'

'We walk through huge forest for one month and finally get Europe. Man in charge drive us south France, pay border guards. In Toulouse we stay in safe house. We wait and wait and wait.

Then new man comes with lorry, we hide in back, and he drive us to England over sea. We drive north, stop in service station. A minibus come, and we go Glasgow. There were seven of us – young women, all under twenty-one – and Quang. We were taken to a very high house, not allowed leave. Forced to work, three or four men a day, more Friday and weekend.'

Rockburn nodded. It was a familiar story – not a story, a reality – for many women and girls from Eastern Europe and beyond. 'How did you escape?'

'Quang was beaten if I did not do what they said with who they said. They stub cigarettes on back of his neck. Once, he forced watch me.' Mina looked away. 'I want die. So, next Saturday when most men watch football, we climb out of window and onto roof. We run.'

Rockburn wanted to hit something. *Somebody*. To ride hard all day and night.

'They come looking and next day we spotted.'

'What happened?'

Mina put her hand to her mouth and shuddered. Rockburn thought she was going to be sick. He fetched a bucket, paper towels, a glass of water.

She took a sip.

'You can tell me later,' said Rockburn. 'Tell me now what you want from me.'

Mina unbuttoned her coat. Underneath she wore a long black cardigan. She was even thinner than the boy. She glanced around the room, at the dartboard, the clothes rail with seven shirts, two large sports bags heaped with clothes. The overflowing toolbox. A heap of leathers, three motorcycle helmets. The table with his laptop, and underneath, a box of paperwork.

She picked at her nails. 'We saw you in old newspaper in Glasgow. You solve big migrant case. Rescue young girl. Get her papers, new life.' She shook her head. 'We no papers. Newspaper headline, *Hero Cop Saves Migrant Girl*. I remember your name, and we came to Manchester to find you. I asked in shops and one woman gave me your card.'

The investment and two weeks of foot slog *had* been worth it.

She stared at him with large dark eyes.

He walked to the window. The street was quiet. A few pedestrians, three or four cars. A boy waited at a bus-stop, flicking a fluorescent yo-yo up and down. No blue hatchback, no posse of Asian hoods.

He turned back to face her.

'I'm no longer a police officer, Mina, and I'm really sorry, but I don't think I can help you. I can't get you a visa. You should go to a solicitor, or the police. I can take you there.' Rockburn sighed. It wasn't what he wanted to say to his first potential client.

'No trust police. In Vietnam police lazy, in China they racist. In Russia they want sex in return for even small thing. All police same Eastern Europe, large ugly men with big sticks who stay warm by beat people. In France police not listen, in Scotland I go police, but they too busy.'

Rockburn stood up, walked over to the dartboard and plucked out the darts. He walked back to the oche. He wanted to help her; both her and the boy.

He threw a dart. A five.

Riding back from door-knocking the list of dark blue hatchbacks he'd realised a few straightforward cases would kick-start his new business – an employee theft or a cheating husband. Quick, easy money, paid in advance. But they weren't the cases he was interested in. Mina and Quang's plight was.

He aimed and threw again. A one. The biggest difference between his old job and his new one was that in the police it didn't matter whether he spent the shift doing the crossword or working his arse off, he still got paid.

He threw the third dart – another five. He wasn't going to pay the bills by winning darts competitions. Still, he'd take the case for nothing. Sort out his finances later.

There was a knock on the door.

Mina started, thrust a hand in her pocket. Rockburn put a finger to his lips, thinking of places she could hide. The kitchen cupboard; the roof.

'Rockburn,' shouted Flack. 'Everything okay?'

'It's fine. See you tomorrow.' He looked over at Mina. 'The tattooist from downstairs. Flack might look like the devil's handmaiden, but he's a good guy.'

She nodded. 'I have trust you, Rockburn.' She stood and took off her coat. 'And I can pay you.'

Rockburn thrust out a hand.

'No!'

'It's okay,' said Mina, slipping off a shoe. She removed the inner sole, felt inside, pulled out a small plastic bag and threw it over to him.

Rockburn poured the contents onto his hand. He fingered them across his palm, the brilliant glassy surfaces catching the light. Diamonds, or crystals which looked like diamonds.

'From a grateful Russian man.' A glimmer in her eye.

'Are they real?' If they were, he could help her and Quang *and* get paid. He wondered what she'd done to get hold of them, hoped it was only theft. 'I'll find out. There's a pawn shop at the end of the street – I'll only be gone ten minutes.' He shuffled the jewels back into the plastic wrap and put it in his wallet. He bent to his box of paperwork and pulled out a sheet headed *Terms of Service*. 'While I'm gone, can you complete this?'

She nodded. 'Understan'.'

Feeling the hot bulge of his wallet, he walked over to the door. 'When I get back, I'll need answers to two questions: who's following you and Quang, and why?'

Mina walked over to the window, hand back in her pocket. 'Don't open the door.'

Rockburn locked it behind him. He jogged down the stairs, pretending to throw darts. Treble top, treble top, this is sensational darts from the ex-bobbie Rockburn. Treble top, he does it again. One hundred and eighty!

He jumped down the final three stairs, landing with a bang.

S R Jones, the owner of the pawn shop, was a small fat man with a bald head. He kept a pencil behind his ear and wrote in small capital letters in an old-fashioned triplicate book. One copy for the customer, one attached to the pawned object, and one left in the book. Receipt AA211 already sat in Rockburn's wallet, fifty pounds for his electric guitar. He'd dreamt of being in a band but there'd been no time in the police to practise. Now he had time, but no money – and no guitar.

Jones tipped Mina's packet of jewels onto a small wooden tray lined with dark green baize cloth like a miniature snooker table. He nudged them apart with his pencil, umming and ahhing like a sewing machine. From a drawer he took out a pair of tweezers and a magnifying glass. He bent closer an Anglepoise lamp.

The bell clanged with the entrance of two more customers. Teenagers, hands in pockets, eyes everywhere. *Both Asian.* Rockburn stiffened. The two lads loitered near the gaming consoles and phone handsets. They wanted a private word with the proprietor, and would wait.

Jones held up a jewel in the tweezers and turned it around. He stared through the glass. Held up another. He examined every crystalline piece, then switched off the lights and tidied away his equipment.

'People bring in old trainers, would you believe.' His voice was low and monotone.

Rockburn glanced over at the waiting duo. One held a

book-sized lump under his jacket. He turned back to the counter. 'So?' he said, quietly.

Murmuring to himself, Jones made a few pencil calculations. He looked up. 'Seven thousand. Less two hundred pounds a month, three month minimum. Collect any time before then. Six thousand, four hundred. I can't give you cash, but I can phone up. Now if you like?'

The broker's loan was five per cent of the overall value, making the diamonds worth a hundred and forty thousand pounds. Not enough to retire on, but enough to try – hard – to get them back.

Rockburn nodded, and while he waited signed the triplicate book. Behind him, the two youths had moved from the consoles to the display of power tools. Drills, drivers, saws, all goods stolen in van and garage burglaries. As a trainee detective at North Manchester, he'd run an operation on a pawn shop, arresting half a dozen burglars and recovering property from over fifty crimes. Nevertheless, he wondered if pawning was their real intention.

'All done,' said Jones. 'Do you want to check your account?'

Rockburn shook his head, swept up the receipt and exited. He wanted to get back, to check on Mina and start afresh on his first case.

The sky seemed brighter, the pedestrians chatter more upbeat. Two men were unloading shiny new bicycles from a lorry. His fledgling business now had more than business cards and headed notepaper with terms of service – it had a client and cashflow. One day he'd have separate premises and a coat stand.

The external door to the block was jammed open with a half-brick. He swore at Flack – today of all days – and looked up and down the street, but couldn't see him. The tattooist knew the sensitivity of his case. He pushed the brick inside with his foot, made sure the door clicked shut and climbed the stairs, thinking he might treat himself to a shave in a barber's and a new set of tungsten steel-tipped darts.

As Rockburn passed RCS Holdings he saw a flash of light inside. He backed up and looked in through the door's glass panel. It was dark and he raised a hand to lessen the glow of the hall light. The premises remained dark, and it felt like looking into an old tv screen.

He resumed climbing the stairs, keen to quiz Mina and find out who was pursuing her and the boy.

The lock on his door was smashed, the deadbolt and latch assembly hanging out of the splintered doorframe. On the door, the cylinder sat askew and below it were a line of compressed wood and boot marks. Slivers of wood and paint chippings dotted the floor.

He pushed it open.

'Mina?'

There was no answer. He stepped into the large room. The Vietnamese woman lay on the sofa. He walked closer. 'Mina?'

Her head was slanted to one side, and looked uncomfortable, as if she'd fallen asleep when very drunk. She didn't answer. He walked closer. The sofa had been moved a few inches back, revealing spots of blood. Mina looked ashen, and slightly blue in the lips. Her neck was bleeding – from a fine cut. Rockburn shook her arm. Her chest was still. He put a finger to her bloody neck, but he was too late.

He stood up. Kicked the wall. If he hadn't rushed out to the pawnbroker's she'd still be alive.

Or they'd both be dead.

15

Police vehicles filled the yard behind Rockburn's block. A young police constable clutching a logbook stood at the front, and a second at the foot of the fire escape. Flack sat with a detective in one of the cars, giving a statement. The windscreen was slowly steaming up.

Rockburn leant against the wall near his motorbike. Through the window of his flat, he could see white-suited forensic officers moving about. Aeroplanes circled overhead and the city squawked and spat as if nothing had happened.

Elsa walked towards him, talking on her mobile. She stopped in front of him, pocketed the phone. She wore a red waistcoat, black trousers, looked like a backing singer in a band.

'I've been told to bring you in.'

Templeside custody suite smelt of curry and was busy as a beach in summer. Rockburn was led straight down the hall to a cell where he was processed by two trainee detectives. He wasn't in handcuffs, but still felt a flutter in his chest.

His hair was combed into a paper bag by the taller of the two, a plug-eared officer called Griff. He was patted down and his wallet and keys placed on a plastic tray. After the search, they would be itemised on the custody record, which meant he had to

act. Discovery of the pawn ticket tucked inside his wallet would only confuse things.

The two officers talked about a fishing competition. Jason, the smaller PC, told Rockburn to strip. He took off his shoes and clothes, and Griff handed him a white suit and black plimsolls. Rockburn pulled on the suit but dallied with the shoes. He sat next to the tray on the bench, began to pick at his feet. Jason's uncle was the fishing club secretary and had promised him a good pitch. Yabbering on as they sealed each item in a separate paper bag, they were cackhanded with the tape, and impatient, both working rather than taking it in turns. Rockburn stood up, knocking the tray onto the floor. His wallet spilt open.

'Sorry.' He bent down, shielding the wallet from the officers and in one quick move, plucked the ticket, slipping it between his fingers.

'Sit down!' said Griff.

Rockburn sat and watched while the officer picked up his valuables and the tray. When the trainees were busy again, he pulled on the plimsolls and swallowed the receipt.

After all the exhibits had been sealed and labelled, the two PCs handed Rockburn back to Elsa who led him into the main hall of the custody suite. He felt like a relay baton. There was a queue waiting to be booked in.

Officers from a public order serial were guarding a huge long-haired man, naked to the waist and covered in sweat. A young solicitor sat on a bench with his client. The lawyer sat with crossed legs looking serious while the pimply goose-white teenager picked his nose. Prisoners shouted at each other in the juvenile cells. A radio was playing pop music. Behind the counter the two custody sergeants sat on raised seats like kings of the jungle.

Rockburn had seen it all before, a thousand times. But this time there was one key difference: he couldn't leave when he felt like it.

The long-haired man was dragged away to be searched in a cell. Rockburn moved up to the counter, Elsa hovering beside him. A hint of perfume about her.

'Name?' said the young custody sergeant. Blond hair which she kept curling back behind her ears, and an array of coloured pens in her top pocket. Fast-track – he'd stake the diamonds on it.

'Rockburn.'

She looked up. 'Were you once—'

He stared back, expressionless.

She glanced across at her colleague, a tubby man with short greasy hair. He followed her eyes, then nodded and smirked. The sergeant stood and retreated to a back room where he picked up the phone. He seemed familiar. Older, fatter. Russell Scarisbrick from training school, thick as clay. He'd been kept back a class.

'First name?'

'Paul.'

'And what do you do?' The custody officer paused. 'Now.'

The question hurt, and the delayed kicker made it worse. He wondered if it always would, or whether, ten cases on – fifty cases, a hundred? – he would once again feel pride in what he did. 'Investigator.'

The custody sergeant raised her eyebrows, the keys of her computer clacking away. She could touch-type.

'Elsa?'

'Murder, Sarge.'

'Grounds?' The sergeant stopped typing, and waited, as if there was a decision on his detention to be made.

'Young woman found strangled to death in Rockburn's flat. He says he doesn't know who she is or why she was there.'

The sergeant clacked away. 'You know the form, Mr Rockburn. Solicitor? Phone call?'

Behind him waited the jailer, mouth open, staring into the middle distance, as if rapt. Rockburn remembered his own jailer postings. The only things prisoners ever wanted were the sausage and egg breakfast and the butterscotch whip. Each time – three of them – Rockburn had lived for six weeks on identical-tasting pots of curry, stew, and shepherd's pie.

He shook his head and watched the jailer write his name on the whiteboard. *Murder, Rockburn.* The jailer put down the marker pen and jigged to the song on the radio. He caught Rockburn's eye and turned away.

'Doctor, then,' said the smiley sergeant.

Elsa signalled to Griff and Jason waiting nearby, and the two trainees escorted Rockburn to the doctor's room. Jason said he'd caught a carp weighing thirteen pounds. Griff didn't believe him. Mr Ansari arrived carrying a briefcase. He was a tiny man with a pot belly and terrible breath. His white vest showed through his shirt. He clipped and swabbed Rockburn's fingernails. Rockburn peeled the suit to his waist and the doctor examined his arms for injuries and marks. Some chafing and bruising on his fingers from the scrambling with Quang. The doctor observed Rockburn's face and noted the bloodshot eyes and misshapen nose. He sketched the six-inch scar across his forearm, caused by Leroy Jones's knife.

He pulled the suit back up and sat down.

'You okay, doctor?' said Jason.

Mr Ansari raised a thumb, and the two officers went out, closing the door.

'I have a form, see.'

Rockburn nodded. He'd read hundreds of them, and occasionally gleaned something interesting. Drug or gambling addictions, phobias, beliefs, a terminal illness.

'Do you feel well, Mr Rockburn?'

'Yes.'

'Are you taking any medication?'

'No.'

'Do you have any mental health concerns?'

Rockburn scowled.

'A Home Office study shows eighty-eight per cent of people arrested have something seriously troubling them.'

'I've been arrested for murder.'

'Are you being uncooperative, Mr Rockburn?'

'No.'

'Do you ever get angry?'

'Sometimes.'

'Violent?'

'Does anyone say yes to that question?'

'If I show you this picture, what do you see?'

'A river by a bridge, a duck with a line of trailing ducklings. Pollution, the climate crisis. Sunday dinner, mint sauce – that's a joke by the way. Vegetarianism, veganism. Obedience, imitation. Brotherhood, siblinghood, honour. Family. Life, danger, death. Survival of the fittest. Heaven, hell. The point, the big fat fucking point. What are we all doing here?'

'Good, good, you're not a stupid man, Mr Rockburn.' The doctor scrawled notes on his pad and continued into the margin. He stopped writing and looked up. 'Would you describe yourself as hopeful?'

'Yes, and no. Realistic.'

'What are you looking forward to?'

'What do you think? Sorry, doctor, enough.'

The two trainee detectives were waiting outside. Jason's girlfriend Lisa was buying him a telescopic fishing rod for his birthday. Griff shot Rockburn a look, then escorted him to the tabs and dabs room. He took a DNA sample, fingerprints. He told Rockburn that he'd slept with Lisa on his last rest day. He took mugshots, front, side and back. The two officers were incompetent, their own friendship a sham, and yet the Job employed them. And had sacked *him*.

Life was unfair. He knew that, knew he had to move on. Find a new way to live, to make sense of his time on the planet.

He'd found a way.

Rockburn saw the image of Pricha Kuri shackled to the pipe. Then, Quang and his aunt cowering in the freezer. Mina bleeding out. He wondered how he was going to tell the boy about his aunt who'd mothered him since he was five years old. By the time Quang was a teenager, he would have suffered more than most people in their lifetime.

Rockburn sat on the stone bench in cell twelve. The thin blue mat was sticky and cold. Obscene graffiti scarred the walls and floor. There were no windows. Hubbub from the hall slowly faded. The flutter in his chest returned, and he picked at his fingers.

The CCTV outside his door had shown one suspect wearing dark clothing and a bandana. Of slight build, but probably male. Short – shorter, and smaller, than the men who'd chased him and Quang through Little Park. Possibly the young male on the moped at the canal. Which raised the question, were the men in the blue hatchback, the arrested man, and Mina's killer all part of the same gang? Or two groups: the owner of the diamonds, or people working on their behalf; and the traffickers.

Rockburn paced round his cell. He couldn't investigate if he remained in custody. There was insufficient evidence to charge him, surely. But if he was charged, he wouldn't get bail. At least nine months before a trial. Redville Warehouse would no doubt be included in the case papers. Mandatory life sentence, out in fifteen. First offence, no sexual interference. Unless there had been? He closed his eyes. The flutter became a thump, repetitive, like someone descending a never-ending flight of wooden stairs.

The wicket crashed down.

A passport photo of the custody sergeant's face and blond hair. 'Need you to sign this.' She pushed a clipboard through the wicket.

He scribbled his name, squeezed it back through.

She paused with her hand on the wicket. 'For what it's worth, I don't think you should have been cast. I signed the petition, made sure my whole team did. I followed it in the papers. If I was having a problem on the street, the last person I'd want to see is me. Job doesn't know its arse from its elbow.'

The custody sergeant eased up the wicket.

Rockburn stared at the opposite wall, considered using his one permissible phone call to contact the mayor, the only politician he had time for. The mayor's reputation had been founded on demanding a public enquiry for a chemical leak into a river causing a dozen deaths, and cemented by implementing cheap public transport. He didn't know the mayor well, although he sometimes felt he did, but the two of them had met a few years earlier.

Half an hour later the wicket reopened. Elsa pushed through a cup of tea and a Kit Kat. Behind her, there was singing and shouting. 'Half a stag party's been arrested for commandeering a bus.'

'Thanks,' said Rockburn. He glanced at his watch. He didn't feel hungry, yet he hadn't eaten all day. Definitely didn't want a shepherd's pie.

Elsa remained at the open hatch.

'You can probably guess why I'm here?'

Rockburn nodded.

She looked him in the eyes. 'Are we okay?'

He stared back. 'We are.'

The wicket closed and her footsteps on the concrete floor receded. He knew she was worried about the vehicle checks she shouldn't have authorised. It gave him an advantage. But she knew he was harbouring the boy which levelled the playing field. Rocking back and forward on the stone plinth, he worked on a story for the recorded interview, and decided, if he was charged, to call the mayor.

16

DS Mackay indicated Rockburn take the seat across the table. The detective was mid-forties and appeared to be dressed for a special occasion. His hair was cropped, his ivory shirt pressed, and his tie pulled tight. While Elsa set up the recording, Mackay glanced through his notes. He wore a glittering analogue watch with a bracelet-style strap. If it was real, it would be worth thousands – too much for someone on a sergeant's salary.

'Are you going to talk, laddie?' said Mackay, who spoke with a Scottish burr.

'I've got nothing to hide.'

There was a bottle of water and a column of plastic cups on the table. The wood marked with salt rings and scratched graffiti. The room smelt like an old car.

'Okay,' said Elsa, sitting down alongside her colleague.

'You know how this works, laddie. We'll start with a first account, go back and forward a bit, then hit you with what we've got.'

'I got up, ate some toast, threw darts for an hour or so. Borrowed my neighbour's motorbike and went out middayish.' Rockburn glanced at his cheap digital watch. 'Eight hours ago.' It seemed like a week.

'Your neighbour the tattooist?'

'Flack,' said Rockburn.

'Go on.'

'I rode out towards Sheffield, parked in a quarry and watched the rock climbers.' The key to lying was to stick as close as possible to the truth, and he'd ridden to the quarry dozens of times. Stopped there to tinker with his bike. 'Flack phoned me to say my client had turned up. So I rode back. She was waiting at the top of the stairs, outside my door. We went inside. She told me her name was Mina. She was very thin, and shaky, clearly in shock. I gave her some brandy. She said she'd read about me in a newspaper. Said she was hungry. I didn't have much in, so I went out to buy something. When I got back, the door was busted open and she was dead.'

'That's it?'

'That's it.'

'Did you buy any food?'

'I did.' Rockburn paused. 'Two lots of prawn fried rice, spring rolls, and crackers from the takeaway one street over.' His regular order.

'Looks like she'd know one end of a chopstick from another.'

Elsa took a deep breath and poured a cup of water. Rockburn half-expected her to throw it over Mackay.

'Which quarry?'

'Stone Mill.'

'Know any of the climbers?'

'No.'

'Elsa?'

She murmured, as if in deep thought. 'How did you pay for the food?'

'Cash.'

'Did you stop for petrol?'

'No.'

'How much brandy did the two of you drink?'

'I poured two big measures, she drank hers,, I left mine.'

Elsa gave a small shake of the head. Mackay unfastened his watchstrap and refastened it. 'The tox reports will show if you're lying. Moving on, or in fact backwards.' He paused to smile at his joke. 'How's business?'

'Okay.'

'Many clients?'

'Still early days.'

'*Any* clients?'

'Mina was one.'

'And what did she want you to do for her?'

Rockburn glanced at Elsa who stared directly back. He was only partly reassured. 'I don't know. She never got round to telling me. I went out for food, and well, that was it. My CCTV shows the suspect – so I'm not sure why you've even arrested me.'

'You've got motive.'

'Go on.'

'All in good time.' Mackay poured a cup of water. 'Your CCTV shows someone in dark clothing at your front door.'

'Reaching up to the camera to disable it.'

'Do you recognise them?'

'They're not dissimilar to the male who was arrested at the canal, but then escaped from a police car on the way back to custody.'

Mackay scowled.

Rockburn glanced at Elsa, who was glaring at him. She took off her jacket. Their unspoken deal to remain quiet at breaking point. He wondered if she'd told Mackay about the boy.

'How's your bank account, laddie?'

'Could be better.'

'You're overdrawn and in debt on three credit cards. You owe two months' rent and have no clients. You need money.'

'Most people do.'

'You seriously injured a man by pushing him down a set of stairs with a chair, at least that's what you said you did. The jury believed you, but an internal enquiry led by an ACC didn't and you were kicked out of the Job. I know whose judgement I'd trust. You're prone to bursts of temper and violence.'

'Robert Kingman had just indecently assaulted a seven-year-old girl. He was off his head on a cocktail of speed and ketamine, and wielding a kitchen knife.'

Mackay held Rockburn's stare. 'Did you find Mina attractive?'

'That's cheap.'

Mackay stared at Rockburn. He cracked open his watchstrap, clicked it shut. 'Let's back up to your version of events. The takeaway on the next street over. We went there. No CCTV, they speak very little English, most people pay cash. No memory or paper record of your visit.'

Rockburn shrugged, glanced at Elsa.

'Where's the food you bought?'

'I left it in the stairwell when I saw the broken lock. Maybe the uniforms ate it.'

'Maybe it never existed.'

'You don't really think I did it. We could pool resources. You want to find out who killed her, and so do I.'

'Enough jockeying around, laddie.' The detective sergeant took a small exhibit bag from inside his jacket and laid it on the table. 'There's a pawnbroker's near the takeaway you mentioned. This is a page from their receipts book. It records you obtaining a loan for some diamonds – diamonds which we've seized and hold here in the police station. Worth a few bob too.'

Rockburn was tempted to mention Mackay's watch but resisted. 'So?'

'You don't deny it's your transaction?'

'No.'

'Let me put a wee scenario to you, Rockburn. You got Mina drunk, and when she was in the bathroom you searched her bag and found the diamonds. She caught you, and you killed her.'

There was a knock on the door. Elsa stood, walked over. Opened the door enough for Rockburn to recognise Scarisbrick. The two of them whispered, then Elsa turned to Mackay. 'Sarge, something's come up.'

Mackay stood. 'Don't go anywhere, laddie.'

Elsa stopped the recording, and Mackay left the room, shutting the door behind him. She sat down. Drained her cup of water.

'I suppose you think I'm in your debt?'

Rockburn shrugged. 'You don't share that view?'

She refilled the cup, shook her head. Forcing a smile, she glanced at the door. Seemed nervous.

'He's new. Transferred from Scotland – Glasgow. He was suspected of being in the pocket of one of the gangs up there. Nothing was proved, but no one wanted to work with him so he requested a move. They were only too happy to let him go.'

'Glasgow?'

Elsa nodded.

Rockburn fell silent. Mina had travelled down from Glasgow. When he'd been booked in, Scarisbrick had made a phone call. To Mackay? Was Mackay a bad apple? Mackay *and* Scarisbrick both bad apples? He tried to tease it out . . . Mackay is on the take from a trafficking gang in Glasgow and asked to transfer to Manchester to give them a foothold there. Mackay is tasked by the gang. He befriends a custody sergeant or two and asks them – in return for a few quid – to notify him of interesting arrests. It worked as a hypothesis but needed testing. He would speak nicely to his training school friend Scarisbrick.

And what about Bobby Kingman's even nuttier brother Pete? Pete Kingman had been in the witness gallery when Rockburn had been found not guilty for the attempted murder of his brother, and again when Robert had been sentenced to a paltry five years. Both times Pete Kingman had been escorted out of the courtroom, shouting he would take revenge on Rockburn. The Glasgow-based Kingman OCG no doubt had connections to one or two corrupt police officers.

Including Mackay and / or Scarisbrick?

Rockburn was about to work it through again when the door opened and the Scottish detective entered. He was holding a statement form.

'Seems like your friend the tattooist heard someone enter your block – a few minutes after you left for the pawnbroker. He heard them go up the stairs and ten minutes later run back down again. You returned another twenty minutes later. He's very precise with his timings is our Mr Flack. He has more form than the Kray twins, and would be shredded in court. However, the Can't Prosecute for Sweets outfit are accepting your alibi. For now.'

He turned to Elsa. 'You can book him back in.'

The door slammed.

Elsa raised her eyebrows.

'You didn't tell him about the boy?'

'I did – I had to, but he didn't believe me – thought you'd made it up. I will have to take it further, though. I know you want to safeguard the boy, but we have a legal duty of care. I could lose my job. So could he.'

A church clock chimed eleven when Rockburn was bailed. It was a big favour from Elsa, and a significant risk. Maybe she felt responsible for the suspect escaping from custody, maybe she wanted to keep Rockburn onside following the unlawful vehicle checks, but whatever the reason it allowed him to keep working.

He walked stiffly down the station steps and out into the foggy darkness. Dull yellow light seeped from windows and a dead streetlight buzzed. Mackay's apparent disbelief in the boy increased his suspicion of the sergeant from Glasgow.

A single headlamp cleaved the gloom.

Sat astride his three-wheeled motorbike, Flack looked like a giant king of the hobgoblins. He wore his horned helmet, and his flaming hair reached halfway down the back of his studded leather jacket. He smelt of cigar smoke and engine oil.

The tattooist threw Rockburn a helmet and fired up the bike. The exhaust had no silencer, the roar loud and throaty. Rockburn climbed up behind him. The big man turned and bared his crenulated teeth.

'You need a drink with the boys.'

They lurched forward, bumped out onto the road, and accelerated into the dastard darkness.

Demons MC's preferred boozer was squeezed into a railway arch. Bikes were lined up outside. There was one small door which forced both of them to duck their heads. Inside, it was warm and smelt of wet dog. The windows were blacked with heavy insulation. The door was guarded by Fat Man stroking a pit bull. His tractor tyre belly flopped out from under a dirty white t-shirt. Small groups of men, including Flack's deputy Max wearing his commando-style woollen hat, and one or two hefty women sat at round tables.

Flack headed to the bar, the tattooist greeting people with a growl and shakes of his raised forearm which made the chains on his jacket rattle.

Rockburn sat on a barrel in the corner.

The coal fire glowed.

Flack set down two pints of swampy-looking beer, then returned to the bar. He came back with shots of whisky and a plate of what looked like florets of cauliflower. Grey speckled, as if it had been sitting at the greengrocer's too long. He wheeled over a second barrel and sat.

Rockburn held up his pint in acknowledgement of the pillion ride and the police statement. He drank, the beer tasting pungent and leaving a fiery peppercorn aftertaste. Flack downed half his drink and sank the chaser. He pushed the plate over.

'We call this dibble brains.'

Rockburn picked up a floret. Scarisbrick's brain maybe, but he was less sure about Mackay. The Scotsman was a detective, a sergeant, the same position he had held formerly. Suddenly he was aware of everyone in the room watching him, the fat man at the door, the lanky barman, and the groups of leather-clad bikers. He put the morsel in his mouth and chewed slowly. It was cold, and tasted like soggy cauliflower although he knew it wasn't.

Flack threw his head back and guffawed. As the room followed his lead, the tattooist grabbed a handful of florets and dropped them into his mouth like sweets.

'Pig's brain. Delicacy in this arch.'

Rockburn drank, set down his pint, leant closer. 'You know you can be sent to prison for making a false statement?'

Flack shrugged. 'Weren't false.' The tattooist turned away and coughed without mercy. He turned back, his eyes bloodshot. 'I heard 'im. Up and down. Kicking myself now.'

Which made two of them.

Fat Man heaped up the fire, the flames flickering and reflecting on his pensive face.

Flack picked up another chunk of greying slippery brain. 'Something else came back to me though. My walk-in, she asked who you were, and when I told her you worked upstairs and investigated stuff, she asked if you looked for missing children. At the time I thought it was about her – every client has a sob story – but now I wonder if it was about you.'

'What did you tell her?'

'Said you'd do anything, and I gave her one of your cards.'

'She was packing a canister of CS.'

Flack turned and coughed heavily. He turned back, wiping his mouth with his cuff. 'So?'

'It's possible she's connected – a scout sent to sniff out the boy.'

Rockburn stared into his murky beer while Flack finished the plate of brain. If there was a chance the walk-in was connected, he needed to ask another favour from Elsa.

Flack licked his fingers, drained his glass. Rockburn bought refills and settled the tab with part of the loan against the diamonds. Two more bikers entered the den and wandered over to the bar.

The tattooist lit a cigar. 'What next?'

Rockburn twiddled a beer mat. The Arch's rotten air and camaraderie, the rare bar snack, and the alcohol made him feel like getting pissed. Darts always helped him think. He pretended to hold an imaginary arrow, rocked back and forth, threw. He lined up a second dart, licked the tip.

'You up for a rat trap?'

Flack drained his beer and glanced over at the nearby table crowded with glasses. He poured dregs from several into his tankard. Stood up, downed it.

'Is the pope Catholic?'

17

In the shadow of the fire escape Rockburn unbolted the rear fairing on the panther and removed the tracker. He opened the electricity meter cupboard and set it on the shelf next to an empty coke can. He closed the door, bolted the fairing back in place. Zipped up his jacket, pulled on his helmet. He kicked up the stand and pressed the ignition. The noise was sweet as a skylark and true as a hammer. He puttered through the yard, revved the engine, and shot out into the traffic.

A pickup braked hard, its driver pumping the horn.

Rockburn raised an arm and accelerated down the centreline. He was a free man, and heading for the hills. And he'd left the juddery Kawasaki languishing in the cowshed. It sat on blocks, partway through an oil change and service.

At the county boundary he took off his helmet and bungeed it to the rack behind him. He shook out his hair, grown long – one of the advantages of no longer being in the Job. He could smell the heat of the engine and feel its latent, throbbing power. In the distance ashen clouds shrouded the summits. He put on dark glasses, adjusted the black armband on his sleeve, and rode towards them. God's own outrider.

*

Quang was in the back garden near the hedge. He'd found an old spade and the wheelbarrow, and was digging a hole and shifting the earth away in the barrow.

Rockburn walked over, his leathers squeaking. He pushed up his glasses. The hole was four feet deep, and revealed the entrance to a tunnel facing the hedge. The boy filthy as a hippo.

Rockburn crouched. 'You okay?'

Quang nodded.

'Where are you tunnelling to?'

The boy shrugged.

'You want a ride on the bike?'

'Yes!'

Hocking emerged from the house. She was wearing her painting gilet, a blob of green paint on the end of her nose – as if someone had dabbed it there. They watched the boy working in the hole. On his knees Quang hacked away at the tunnel face, then scooped the stony earth into a bucket. The boy stood and hefted the bucket onto the lawn. Climbed up and emptied the bucket into the barrow.

Hocking put a hand on Quang's shoulder and whispered in his ear. The boy glanced over at Rockburn and jogged back to the house.

'He helps out. Looks after the chickens, moves my canvases around. Trailed around the supermarket with me.'

'Has he said anything?'

'Not much, I've told him he can. But there's something on his mind, he's not sleeping. I hear him humming to himself.'

'Hocking,' said Rockburn, glancing towards the house. 'I've got some awful news. His aunt's been murdered.'

'Oh my God.' She clamped a hand over her mouth.

Rockburn put an arm on her shoulder, and lowering his voice, told her what had happened. He held her for a moment, then slowly let go.

The chickens wandered around, the ground bare where they'd worn away the grass. An egg lay in a flowerbed.

'I'll tell Quang on the ride.'

A young woman with short blond hair stepped out from the house. She wore a pink fluffy jumper and faded denims. She walked closer. Scarring ran from the corner of her mouth down her neck. Pretty even so; young and pretty.

'Is this him?'

Hocking's freckled face flared. 'This is my friend Sarah-Jane; she's sitting for me.'

'Heard a lot about you, Rockburn.' She looked at him with her head cocked slightly to one side – the scar hidden.

He'd heard nothing about her.

'I thought I'd do some baking later, Rebecca, with Quang. Teach him how to make rockbuns.' She looked at Rockburn, raised an eyebrow. A veiled mixture of amusement and challenge. Maybe, wariness too.

'Perfect,' he said, nodding.

She walked back into the house.

Rockburn took a deep breath. He was shellshocked. He felt hollow. *Pierced.*

'You never said anything.'

'You were always working. I wanted a different life – a different *way of life*.'

In the kitchen, there was a clattering of pans. He and Hocking glanced towards the house. Rockburn could hear Sarah-Jane talking to Quang.

'What about children?'

'They're still possible. She's really good with him.'

Maybe it explained everything, or maybe it explained nothing. But he was clear about one thing: he would have to find someone else to ride pillion, to climb the zig-zags, to scream down through the valleys. To eat chips at biker watering holes, and at the end of the day, to sit on the back porch drinking beer, staring out into the twilight, slapping at the midges and counting the stars.

'I still can't believe it,' said Hocking, 'about the boy's aunt.'

Rockburn nodded.

He'd started a new business and had his first investigation to progress. A bike to ride. Darts to throw. A life. *His life.*

When the boy had cleaned up, they rode out to a burger caravan Rockburn knew. It sat at a roundabout and served truckers and bikers. There was a mound of old tarmac, a stack of railway sleepers and a ditch full of litter. A rich smell of frying. Old tyre-treads lay along the verge. Sheep filed across a nearby field.

Rockburn bought burgers and chips, coffee, a soft drink for the boy. The caravan was busy, the talk of gear ratios and speed cameras and the numpty in number ten. Road boys liked their politics as much as their meat. The picnic table was deserted. Rockburn had never seen it occupied. The two of them sat on the table, their feet on a bench.

'I've got some bad news about your aunt. Some very bad news.'

The boy nodded, took another bite of his burger. He chewed slowly, tapping his feet on the bench.

'Mina is –' Rockburn screwed up his burger wrapper and chucked it into the bin. He waited for a cement lorry to drive past. 'There's no easy way to tell you, Quang, but your aunt's dead. Someone killed her. I don't know who, but I want to find out. I will find out.' He put a hand on the boy's shoulder. 'I'm very sorry. I know she was more like a mum to you.'

Quang put down the remainder of his burger, his eyes filling with tears. 'Mina look after me.' He jumped down from the table and walked over to the ditch.

Rockburn flipped the lid on the coffee and drank a mouthful. It was hot and bitter. He adjusted the armband on his sleeve.

One thing at a time. Elicit the boy's story. Work out who murdered Mina. The rest would follow.

Quang fished beer cans out of a ditch, and filled them with the smelly brown water. The boy walked back and forth to the field placing five of the cans on top of fenceposts. He jumped back over the ditch and collected a handful of stones from the verges. Sat on the picnic table next to Rockburn and dumped the stones between them.

The sheep began to file back across the field.

'I need to show you something,' said Rockburn. He took out his phone and began to scroll through the photos he'd taken at Flack's, looking for the graphic novel in a foreign language.

A black four-wheel drive with tinted windows pulled into the layby. A rear window was open an inch and unfamiliar music blared out. A fiddler dominated, then a woman singing. Traditional music – folk music. Rockburn looked across at his bike, knowing he could outgun the car. He pocketed his phone.

The car shunted backwards, towards the bike and the picnic table. It stopped a few metres away, but no one climbed out. If they knocked his bike over, he'd need an alternative plan and he looked around for a weapon. He spied an iron bar attached to a lump of concrete lying five or six metres away. It would be no half-measure.

A wing mirror on the car moved around and stilled. The fiddler took over from the woman.

A police car drove past.

The window of the four-wheel drive buzzed halfway down and a strew of fast-food wrappers pushed out. The window closed and the car screeched out into the road, tyres spinning. It accelerated away in the opposite direction to the patrol car, to jeers from the customers at the caravan.

Rockburn drank more of the bitter coffee and tried to settle. The boy ate a few of the remaining chips and shuffled the stones he'd collected. He seemed unperturbed by the four-wheel drive. A wrapper dumped out of the car blew across the layby.

'You see this?' said Rockburn fingering his armband. 'This is for Mina. I wondered if you want to wear one?' The boy nodded. 'You know what it means?'

'We sad.'

'It does. We are sad. It is also a mark of respect for her, that we think she was a good person.'

'Even if she kill someone?'

Rockburn sipped his coffee slowly, calmly, carefully. But his head was spinning: he wanted to interrogate Quang, ask him a hundred and one questions, but before he did he had to answer the boy's question. 'That depends on why she killed them.'

Rockburn pulled a second armband from a pocket and handed it to Quang. The boy slipped it over his coat and up his arm, and straightened the material so it sat true.

'They try take me. And she pushed man in front of bus.'

'What man?'

Shaking his head, the boy picked up a couple of stones.

'Where were they trying to take you?'

'Home.'

'To Vietnam?'

The boy nodded, clinking the stones between his hands.

'Why?'

The boy shrugged and hurled a stone at the beer can targets. It missed. 'Your turn, Rockburn.'

He thought about what Quang had said. If the traffickers took the boy, they could use him as a bargaining chip against his family. But he'd said his parents were no longer alive. And, if the boy's information was correct, they wanted to return him to Vietnam where his value would surely be less.

'The big black car which drove off, Quang, was playing music. Was it Vietnamese?'

The boy pulled at Rockburn's sleeve. 'Come on.' He passed him a stone.

Rockburn thought back to his own childhood. His grandfather never let him – or Simon – win at anything, not cards or checkers, or running up a hill, or names of trees starting with the letter B. Later on, not an arm-wrestle or an argument about the electoral franchise. Not until he'd been given a dartboard one Christmas, did he start beating his grandfather. Were the two of them stronger for it, more resilient to the world? If he let Quang win too easily, the boy would feel cheated. But if the boy lost, it might worsen his melancholy. Five beer cans, someone had to win.

Rockburn slid off the table. He felt the heft of the stone, and threw. He knew about throwing, aiming. A can toppled and crashed into the scrub.

The boy jumped off the table. He selected a large stone and threw. A second can fell backwards and disappeared noisily in the undergrowth. They threw more stones. A van pulled into the layby and two men in spattered overalls climbed out. One chucked a stone, but it missed and the two men joined the scrum in front of the caravan.

The boy's turn. He chucked a lump of concrete which hit a fencepost, wobbling it enough for the can to fall. Rockburn threw again, fast and flat, and the penultimate can fell into the scrub. Two each.

Denise walked over. She'd managed the caravan for as long as Rockburn had been a customer but never seemed to age. She was overweight with a face like a bean bag. Her dyed black hair was stuffed into a cap and her ears were full of rings. She wore a leather apron and short sleeves which revealed the snake tattoos winding around her arms. Flack's handiwork.

'Someone's been here asking about you.' She glanced back towards the caravan.

'When?'

'Two days ago, maybe three.'

'White?'

She shook her head. 'Asian. Three of them, one stayed in the car. Blue, that's all I can remember. Didn't buy anything, neither.' She glanced over at the boy. 'Who's this little lad?' She reached out towards him.

Quang retreated behind Rockburn.

Denise cackled. 'Yours?' She laughed again. 'I see'd your little game.' She picked up a half-brick and hurled. The final can cartwheeled into the undergrowth, and she walked away.

'If you see them again, Denise.' She turned. 'Can you take a reg? A photo even. And phone me.'

She nodded, blew him a kiss.

On the way back to Hocking's Rockburn backtracked a couple of times, and stopped in a driveway for ten minutes to check they weren't being followed. Waiting with Quang on his ex-girlfriend's doorstep, Rockburn felt like an estranged father.

'Take me climb again,' said Quang.

'Sure,' said Rockburn, tamping the boy's hair which was tufty from the helmet.

The door opened.

'You're back,' said Hocking. She ushered the boy inside and watched him take off his trainers and run upstairs. 'How is he?'

'Sad, angry, confused. He doesn't know what to feel. It'll take time – lots of time and lots of love.'

Hocking glanced over her shoulder, then took a half-step closer. 'Are we safe here, Rockburn? His aunt was murdered.'

'No one knows he's here.'

Hocking nodded. Behind her, there was a crash of saucepans from the kitchen. She retreated the half-step and began to push the door.

'Did you tell your friend about me?' said Rockburn, keen to change the subject.

'What do you think?'

The door closed, and Rockburn returned to his bike. He mounted up and pulled on his helmet. Quang appeared at a window and Rockburn raised a hand. The boy waved back and disappeared from view. Quang was having a tough time but at least he was eating – he'd even put on a little weight, and he liked digging his tunnel. The mirroring of Quang's fantasy world with reality was not lost on Rockburn. He was no psychotherapist, but it seemed clear Quang's subconscious was telling the boy to escape.

But from who and why was still unclear. The boy either didn't know, or wasn't ready to reveal it.

His mobile rang.

'Mr Rockburn?'

'Yes.'

'It's Geoffrey Crowther, secretary of the North West Cup. I've got some bad news, well good news for you.' He cleared his throat. 'Mixed news. David Cummins has died – heart attack, poor sod – but we've spoken to his family, and they're keen for the competition to continue. So according to the rulebook, Section 34a, subsection 3, the losing player in the previous round is deemed to have won. That's you. You're in the semifinal. It's on Thursday. I take it you're not busy?'

'I'll be there.'

Rockburn fisted the air and fired up the motorcycle, drinking in the heady roar and engine bouquet.

18

Pondering the revelation from the boy, Rockburn wheeled out the three bikes from under the fire escape. He lined them up against the wall. Flack's Kawasaki, which if he'd been in charge of a firing squad, would have been shot. The tattooist's three-wheeler, large and sloppy as a boat – although he wouldn't tell the big man even if he was drunk. And the panther, a meaty machine which looked good enough for a catwalk yet accelerated like Blue Bird.

It seemed that whoever had killed Mina wanted the boy too. For them to be people traffickers didn't make financial sense, but if Mina had killed one of them, then maybe it was personal – and worth travelling down from Glasgow, and tracking Mina and Quang around like foxhounds. Eventually, he would have to inform social services about the boy, but for now the fewer people who knew of his whereabouts, the better.

Traffic and pedestrians flashed past at the street end of the alley. Ditchwater clouds swept the sky, but over to the east there was a hint of brightness and no rain was forecast. They needed dry roads for a rat trap.

He sprayed the bikes with a hose, scrubbed the tyres clean. He sponged the bodywork free of grime and used a chamois to wipe them down. Applied elbow grease until his darting bicep ached.

As he worked he kept glancing along the alley, but the pedestrians kept moving and the traffic didn't stop.

Pausing to sit on the metal steps of the fire escape, he searched the internet on his phone. Fatal accidents involving a bus in Glasgow in the last three months. He tried different words and different combinations, but produced no hits. Seven deaths on the roads but none involving a bus. Pushing someone under a bus would have been headline news. It wasn't there. Which meant either, the traffickers had covered it up or the police had suppressed the incident, or Quang was lying. Mackay might know, but Rockburn didn't trust him.

He could ask Elsa.

An alternative was DCI Castle, who ran the special investigation unit at South Manchester. Castle had dealt with a couple of high-profile cases involving foreign nationals, had a reputation for leftfield thinking, and was true as a plumbline. An option, Rockburn thought, to keep in reserve.

If he'd still been in the Job, he could have trawled all the police databases. He could try the hospitals, but it would take all morning.

The boy had no reason to lie. Perhaps the man hadn't died, and had been hauled away by his friends. The bus was empty and the driver not keen to be subject to a police investigation. Perhaps he'd been drinking. So many ifs and buts and maybes. The nature of policework. But he was now a private investigator – and the work three times harder.

He cracked on. Oiled the chains and waxed the chrome covers and fairings. A final buff made the bikes gleam like showroom exhibits.

Footsteps clinked on the fire escape. A match hissed and cigar smoke drifted down, the smell like burnt toast.

Rockburn looked up at Flack leaning on the rail. He extracted the packet of cigars he'd been carrying round in his jacket pocket and lobbed them up.

'Busy?'

Flack blew out a cloud of smoke. 'Two lovebirds in a few minutes' time. She wants a heart with his initials, and he wants a sawn-off with her name on the barrel.'

Rockburn's client – his *only* client – had been murdered before she could tell him what she'd wanted, but was hoping whoever it concerned would soon tell him about her.

'Anyone else?'

Flack knocked a lump of ash from the cigar. 'Be free at noon.'

While he waited, Rockburn replaced the GPS tracker in the fairing of his motorbike, then practised his darts. The semifinal was only three days away, and held the potential of prize money and a shot at the five-grand winner's cheque. Winning the competition would keep him in cornflakes and bog paper until a second client turned up.

He practised using a routine called 121. Nine darts to checkout from 121, and if successful, move on to 122, then 123. A failure at any point meant a return to 121, and honed mental arithmetic as well as recreating the pressure of a match. He reached 127 but struggled to concentrate. Kept thinking about the boy's admission about Mina, who she'd killed and why, and the day ahead, visualising how he – and Flack – would extract the story from whoever they caught in the trap.

Crowther phoned again.

'One thing I forgot to mention, Rockburn. Section 34a, subsection 8, states the prize money from the quarterfinal should be given to you. It's only a small amount, but can I confirm your address?'

'Buy some flowers for Dave's funeral, wish him peaceful darting, and send the rest to his family.'

At noon, Rockburn pushed open the door of Flack's tattoo parlour. He shut it behind him, and flipped over the closed sign.

133

The metalhead music in Flack's studio stopped throbbing and the glass door opened. Flack appeared, wearing leather trousers and a grimy white vest, and carrying his horned helmet. Grinning manically, the red-eyed tattooist held out a wrap.

Rockburn shook his head. A speeding partner wasn't ideal – they both needed to be able to act and react quickly but at least the tattooist was used to it.

They swapped helmets and riding jackets. Rockburn held the tattooist's up and admired the artwork on the back, a flaxen-haired Viking wearing a long-horned helmet and wielding a burning club. Dozens more behind him, leaping out of longboats, the gleam of the full moon reflecting on the water. One sleeve had been patched where Flack had skidded off on a Demons MC ride on New Year's Day. Rockburn had tagged along, and helped drag the Kawasaki and the big man out of the ditch.

He zipped up the jacket which felt cavernous, despite his extra layers. He swept up his hair and tied it with a band.

Flack tried to squeeze into Rockburn's jacket but couldn't pull the zip. He took off his vest and tried again. His chest revealed a tattoo of Jesus nailed to the cross. Wearing a crown of thorns and a loincloth. Blood spatters down his body. Under his feet kneeled three disciples.

Flack caught him staring.

'I didn't know you were—'

'Neither did I. It was the only bit of me left, and I was saving it for something special. I wasn't looking, but then a fortnight ago I came across this. It was like it was meant to be.'

The tattooist ducked behind the counter and rummaged around. Finally, he pulled out a plain leather jacket, similar to Rockburn's. He replaced his vest and put on the jacket. Patted his ample chest.

'So?'

'You ride out on the panther,' said Rockburn. 'Hopefully the people who killed Mina will be alert to its movement, and thinking you're me, start to follow. I'll be waiting on the trans-Pennine road. You ride past, I identify the tracking car, and start to follow *them*. You lead them into the housing estate in Sheffield where your clubmates live. They will be forced to follow on foot, you signal your mates, and we confront them.'

Flack fiddled on black fingerless gloves, then clenched his hand.

They bumped fists.

'You want to say a prayer, now?'

Flack lunged forward, throwing his arm around Rockburn's head and raising his hand as he pushed his elbow out. Intending for a headlock. Rockburn's self-defence training kicked in. He thrust his arms upwards and sideways, a movement which the instructor had promised, if executed early enough and with enough power, would break any headlock or stranglehold.

It worked. Rockburn dummied left then smacked Flack's left ear with his right hand. He stepped back to the counter and picked up Flack's horned helmet. He put it on, tucked his hair up inside, and passed his own plain black helmet to the tattooist.

Flack pulled it onto his head and dropped the visor, and Rockburn fitted dark glasses. They looked at each other. Their identities would confuse people in the Demons, at least initially.

In the yard, they fitted padded gauntlets. Squeaked and clinked across the rough concrete towards their waiting steeds, like knights of the damned. Flack mounted up and started the panther's ignition. He glanced at Rockburn, nodded, and roared out of the yard.

The trap was set.

Rockburn rode the juddery Kawasaki out of the city and followed the route across the moors to Sheffield. Sheep dotted the fields, and squat stone houses sat at the end of potholed tracks. The sky was grey, still, enormous.

He slowed through a small village with a pub and a school. Puttered past an allotment with sheds and a ragged scarecrow. He saw no one. He was close to the plague village and remembered going there once on a school trip.

Bored of the museum, and having seen a Harley Davidson in the car park, Rockburn had gone outside and climbed up and sat on the long seat. He stretched for the handlebars and swayed his body from side to side as he went round the corners, leaned his neck back as he surged down the straights. Mrs Elton had spotted him and banished him to the minibus. She'd made him write a letter of apology and in front of class 2B, hand it to the owners and say he was sorry.

He climbed higher, via a succession of switchbacks. Bleak moorland stretched out on both sides of the road. A lorry blew past him, the driver giving him a toot.

Three-quarters of the way across the moor he reached a crossroads with a pub and a small hotel. He turned off, and rode several hundred metres past the pub. Pulled over in the entrance to a field, next to a footpath sign and a stile.

He opened a pannier on the Kawasaki and removed his own jacket and spare lid. He took off Flack's horned helmet which made him stand out like an anorexic at a darts competition. Opening the second pannier he took out a screwdriver and a different number plate and swapped it for the original. He unzipped Flack's jacket and took it off together with the extra layers. Wrapped up the original plate, and stowed it along with the tattooist's gear in the panniers. Finally, he pulled on his leather jacket and felt like himself again.

At least, the person he was trying to become – not the police detective he'd once been more than happy being. He and Quang were in this – his first case, whatever it was – together.

He remounted the Kawasaki and zipped back to the pub car park. It gave a good view of the road back to Manchester, and in the opposite direction, the road to Sheffield. Half a kilometre both ways. He manoeuvred so the bike stood on the Sheffield side of a van and was shielded from the road by a wall and a tree. He turned off the ignition and dismounted. Red berries hung from the tree, and the ground was slippery underneath.

The plan was for Flack to run an errand in Manchester to allow Rockburn to get into position, then head out along the trans-Pennine. He kept his spare helmet on.

There were half a dozen vehicles in the car park and lights shone from the windows in the pub. He could hear a jukebox playing, and people laughing.

A Land Rover with a trailer of sheep drove past. The sheep peered out of slots in the sides, their eyes like polished conkers. The vehicle creaked and groaned but the animals were silent.

For a moment, he wished he was a smoker. He threw an imaginary dart. Picked a berry off the tree and sniffed it. He squeezed it into a paste, then flicked it away, leaving a brown stain on his fingers.

A car went past, the faces of two children on the back seat lit up by the glow of screens attached to the front seats. The engine noise receded, and the car turned a corner and disappeared from view. The road was quiet. The jukebox changed records.

The people who'd trafficked Quang and his cousin, and killed Mina, had had ample time to visit and threaten Rockburn. They hadn't, which suggested they wanted to snatch or kill the boy without a second confrontation. Confrontations were messy and unpredictable and invariably attracted the attention of the authorities. But why they would want them both dead remained unclear – if their motive was revenge for Mina pushing one of them under a bus, then they were expending a large amount of time and expense to obtain it. Revenge for a family member, maybe.

On the other side of the road stood an old icehouse. A stone structure with a domed roof, about the size of a garage. Likely to have stored ice for the pub when it was a staging post for journeys across the moor. The fifty-mile journey from Manchester to Sheffield would once have taken two days.

Pop music still blared.

Then he heard it:

The throaty snarl of the panther.

After a few seconds, Flack came into sight.

The bike held a perfect line, just to the left of the centre of the road and avoiding the slight undulation of the painted flashes. But Flack's body position was all wrong: too upright, too big, too rigid.

The tattooist screamed past.

Rockburn gave no sign of recognition – they'd agreed no signals. Flack sped down the road to Sheffield, leant stiffly into the corner, and was gone. The roar receded and the sound of the jukebox returned.

Rockburn waited. The speed limit was fifty and Flack was riding at sixty to avoid suspicion. The suspects could simply be tracking on a phone or computer, but Rockburn's sense – his hope – was they wouldn't wait. If he was right, the tracking vehicle would appear within a minute or two and stand out because of the lack of traffic and alternative roads.

After a minute, Rockburn tapped ash from an invisible cigarette. He threw a dart. Broke a twig from the tree, plucked off the berries, and one by one flicked them away. Threw another dart.

Two minutes.

A motorbike came into view from the Manchester direction.

Rockburn had been hoping for the blue hatchback, and hadn't been expecting a motorbike. Far more versatile for U-turns and abrupt, discreet parking, and for negotiating bollards and alleys and one-way streets, a bike made sense in an urban area. But was just as exposed as a car in a rural one.

There was nothing else on the road. The motorbike had to be the tracking vehicle.

It shot past.

A mid-range city machine, versatile, good for commuting and short trips. No pillion passenger. The rider was slight, and wore black leathers and helmet. Rockburn noted the number plate but expected it to be false.

Two minutes. The bike reached the bend in the road and disappeared.

Rockburn mounted up, pressed the ignition. He moved forward to the exit of the car park. Two minutes thirty.

He curved out onto the road and accelerated. Following without a tracker, he had to rely on a combination of line of sight and knowing where Flack was heading. Knew he'd risk showing out if he followed the tracking bike too closely or for too long. Three or four miles would take them into the suburbs of Sheffield where he would be concealed by the city's traffic. That was the plan.

Rockburn reached the first bend, and began the long descent into Sheffield. He curved left and right, but still couldn't see the target bike. He sped up.

He knew he was at a considerable disadvantage to the tracking bike which could stay a kilometre or more behind Flack, and remain as good as invisible. In contrast, Rockburn had to keep the tracking bike in view, but at the same time hang back as far as possible to avoid detection.

He rode past a golf course and a rugby club. A car pulled out from a side road and headed out to the moor. Still no sign of the target.

His heart beat faster. The sergeant of the crime squad at North Manchester, a former soldier, had said at every briefing, no plan survives contact with the enemy. The sergeant had always been right.

And this time was no different: the target had disappeared.

19

Rockburn reached the thirty miles per hour sign and streetlights. The first row of houses and a petrol station with a small shop. More shops, an undertaker. He looked further ahead but couldn't see the target bike.

He rode on.

Straight over a roundabout, towards a DIY store and a supermarket. Houses on both sides of the road, a constant stream of traffic. Curved round to the left, back to the right. A triple-fronted premises displaying lawnmowers and leaf blowers. Who bought a leaf blower?

He crossed another roundabout, and passed a precinct of shops with a barber's and a curryhouse. Open 'til late. Two small boys were tugging a woman towards the door. A whiff of spices percolated his visor.

He spotted the target bike: a hundred metres ahead, caught by a red traffic light at a pedestrian crossing.

He slowed.

Changed down two gears.

The lights changed to green and the target bike started off.

Rockburn moved up to ten car lengths, then matched its pace. He began to think about the end game. Flack was heading for the tower-blocks of the Ashmead Estate where he would park and walk into its maze-like interior. Anyone wanting to see which one of the four hundred and fifty front doors the tattooist visited would have no choice but to leave their vehicle and follow on foot.

The two cars in front braked suddenly to a stop. The first flashed its lights at a coal lorry which reversed out into the road. A man climbed down from the lorry's cab and held up traffic in the oncoming lane. He was sooty and stooped. Vehicles began to queue.

The target bike was getting away. He remembered his crime squad sergeant's catchphrase for the hundreth time.

He paddled the bike between the two cars in front and bumped it up the kerb and onto the pavement. An old man hugged closer to the building line. Rockburn puttered forward. The driver of the coal lorry curled his fingers, shook them.

Rockburn bumped the bike down onto the road and accelerated away. He couldn't see his target. He reached a roundabout and turned towards the city centre. Traffic was heavy and queuing at a traffic light.

The target bike was waiting in the front row. Rockburn slowed, breathed out. Somewhere ahead was Flack. The Ashmead Estate was on the far side of Sheffield.

The lights changed, the road widening into a dual carriageway with a central reservation. Keeping the target in sight, he followed through the one-way system, their progress slow and intermittent through numerous sets of traffic lights. The motor-cyclist was a skilled, observant rider who avoided the bus lanes and stopped in good time at the signals. Despite tracking Flack, or maybe *because* he was tracking him and leaving nothing to chance.

Rockburn followed the bike's exit toward the eastern suburbs. It passed a police car, as did Rockburn twenty seconds later. Drug-dealers and drink-drivers drove cautiously because they didn't want to be pulled over by the police. A minor road traffic offence was the patrol officer's excuse to look for more serious crime. The bike rider didn't want to be stopped and searched. A firearm would explain why. Rockburn cursed himself. He hadn't thought it through, yes, this could be a recce, but it could also be the hit itself. Which meant Flack was at serious risk of getting hurt.

He swerved into a bus-stop and stopped. He pulled off a gauntlet, extricated his phone and called Flack. Straight to voicemail. It wasn't surprising. Even if the tattooist wasn't wearing earplugs, the road noise would drown the ring of his phone. And even if Flack heard it, he might ignore it – they'd not discussed using phones.

He tried again.

Nothing.

As he was shoving the phone away, the police car he'd seen pulled into the bus-stop. An officer climbed out and indicated he should wait.

Rockburn clenched and unclenched his hand to try to exorcise his irritation. If he didn't remain calm, he would be significantly delayed, the plan would disintegrate, and Flack could be injured – or worse.

The officer approached.

Rockburn took off his helmet.

'You know this is a bus-stop.' The officer was young, his light-blue eyes clear and alert. He stood with his hands resting on the equipment on his belt.

'Sorry.'

'Is this your bike?'

Rockburn breathed slowly. He couldn't even clench his fingers because it would be a giveaway. Anyone who answered no was asking to be questioned further. Likewise, anyone who hesitated. The problem was the false number plate which meant he had to allay suspicion almost immediately. The only answer was to lie.

'Yes.'

The officer bent his head to his radio. 'Delta Mike, Sierra Three, vehicle check.' He glanced up at Rockburn. 'What's your name, sir?'

Behind the officer, on the far side of the road, was a dry cleaners called Johnson.

'John. John Ashmead.'

'Date of birth?'

'Third February 1986.' The drycleaners was offering three pieces for the price of two.

The officer looked across. 'How old are you, sir?'

'Thirty-two,' said Rockburn. Knew he had to stay close to the truth and be ready for check questions. His address would follow, and he chose a house near where he'd arrested Pat Fiennes, known as the Northern Stranger. He knew the area well after a week of house-to-house enquiries and would be able to answer any follow-up questions. The officer relayed the details, and stood waiting for an answer. His blue eyes restless.

'Won't take long, sir.' The officer was tapping the radio. Humming, thinking, weighing things up.

Rockburn created more of a legend. The bike wasn't registered to him because he'd just bought it. A man he'd met in the pub. If asked, he'd describe Fiennes.

'Just a minute or two.'

Rockburn didn't have a minute, let alone two. Flack was relying on him. The Kawasaki was only two metres away. He could shove the officer, jump on, skedaddle.

Lining up the ignition key in his fingers, he bent his legs – ever – so – slightly. The PC should have taken his keys. A small mistake but gave Rockburn a way out – if the stop turned pear-shaped.

Braced –

'Sierra Three,' spat the constable's radio, 'we've got a central station alarm at the jewellers on Grove Street, can you attend?'

The officer glanced back at his colleague in the police car. The headlights flashed. 'Yes, show November Three.' He took his hand from the radio. 'Your lucky day, sir.'

The patrol car U-turned and screeched away with its lights flashing. Rockburn mounted up and pulled onto the road, accelerating hard and jumping the first set of lights. Hoped he wasn't too late.

At the Ashmead, he slowed and headed into the estate. Past a playground and a small scruffy park. Low-rise blocks of flats in every direction. Between the blocks were landscaped parking areas with rows of cars and vans. He stopped by some railings and dismounted. Took off his helmet and pulled up his hood.

Scanning around, he walked to the nearest block. Outside the front entrance at the top of a set of steps two teenagers sat on their skateboards. They were a couple of years older than Quang. Three storeys of flats were piled above them.

'Have you seen a motorbike ride up, last ten minutes or so?'

'Information has a value.' The boy who'd spoken stood up. He wore a dark green hoodie. Bumfluff covered his top lip. He winked at his friend who rolled back and forward on his board.

'How much?'

'Five pounds.'

'One.'

'Two.'

Rockburn fiddled coins from a pocket and tossed one at the boy. 'The other one when you've told me.'

'A motorbike parked over there, near the shop.' He pointed. 'You can't see it from down there.'

Rockburn walked up the steps and looked to where the boy was pointing. It was the panther, standing in a line of motorbikes outside a convenience shop, but there was no sign of Flack.

'Did you see where the rider went?'

'Through the arch. Big man. Strong man.' The boy flexed his bicep.

Rockburn heard a motorbike enter the estate as he tossed over a second pound coin.

It was the tracking bike. Somehow, he'd beaten it to the estate. He stilled. 'Show me what you can do on your skateboards.'

'Entertainment has a value.'

A second boy laughed and spat into a litter-strewn flowerbed.

Rockburn leant on the handrail of the steps and tried to disappear into the scene with the boys. The target parked at the other end of the line of bikes, and dismounted. Looked about. The rider was short and although he appeared stocky, leathers made anyone look like they worked out.

'Buskers entertain without knowing they'll be paid.' Rockburn glanced back at the entrance to the estate. He and Flack shouldn't have a problem overpowering the target if he wasn't armed *and* didn't have any backup.

'Buskers are losers,' said the first boy.

A silver-coloured car entered the estate, two white men in the front, a third in the back. Rockburn surveilled the lines of parked vehicles. No sign of a dark blue hatchback or a vehicle with Asian occupants.

The target stopped a woman with a pushchair who'd walked out from underneath the arch leading to the next courtyard. The woman turned and pointed. The target nodded, said something, and bent down to his bike. The woman pushed her buggy forward.

'How about,' said Rockburn, 'you give me back the pound coins, and I'll give you a fiver. Then the two of you show me a couple of tricks.'

The target stood and finished zipping up his jacket. Had he stashed something? A cosh? A firearm? The target hurried off towards the arch.

The second boy stood and flipped up his board. 'Go on, Jermaine.'

Jermaine considered the coins in his hand. Rockburn could see the boy calculating: he was in charge, not the other boy.

'Okay,' said Jermaine. He tossed over the coins.

Rockburn caught and pocketed them. The target had disappeared through the archway. He tip-tapped down the steps and started running. 'Guile has a value,' he shouted back over his shoulder.

He ran to the archway, and peered into the alley but there was no sign of the target. It led to a second large courtyard with more short-rise blocks and lines of parked vehicles. He counted to five and walked through. Ducking behind a white van, he used the windows of the cab to look around the courtyard.

About half the size of a football field, it contained four short-rise blocks at compass points. A fenced and landscaped garden with benches in the middle. Half a dozen battered trees.

He spotted the target, heading towards the block on the left. Moving out from the van, he jinked forward, keeping the cars as cover. He stopped behind another van, and used its rear window to look out through the windscreen.

The target was pressing all the buttons on the entrance panel. A tinny voice spoke. The target replied and the door buzzed. He pulled it open. Entered, and as he did so, unzipped his jacket and removed something black and shiny.

Rockburn wiped the misted glass on the van. When he looked again, the target had shoved the object in a pocket or under his waistband. The block door pulled shut.

Rockburn emerged from behind the van and sprinted towards the block. *Foxglove*, according to the sign on the patch of razed grass. He ran past a skip, stopped and backed up. He overturned a window panel and spotted the very stained lid of an old jam pan. It wasn't body armour, but it might cause a deflection.

The heavy block door wouldn't budge. Like the suspect, he pressed multiple buttons.

Finally, it buzzed.

He yanked it open. Stale air wafted out. In front of him were two lift doors, and beyond them, a corridor with a staircase halfway along. A raft of notices and signs in the entrance hall. *No Ball Games, Quiet After 9 PM, If You Smell Smoke* –

He could hear voices in one of the flats. The smell of boiled greens seeped out from the nearest door.

One of the lifts was taped out of service. The other sat at the top. If he was Flack, he'd have taken the stairwell. If he was the target, likewise, whether or not he'd seen Flack. He gripped the handle of the pan lid and jogged to the foot of the stairs. Pushed open the door and entered the gloomy staircase. The door pulled to. He could hear footsteps padding up. He hit the light switch and a bulb broke the shadow.

Rockburn had no choice but to follow. He'd got Flack into this dead end, and even if he couldn't see a way out, he had to try.

He started up the concrete steps, listening and looking upwards.

'Flack!' His voice echoed around the stairwell. 'They might be armed.' He bashed the lid of the pan against the handrail.

On the first landing he peered up the central column. The lights popped and darkness prevailed.

Someone above him hit another light switch, and the lights returned.

'Rockburn!' Flack's voice. 'I'm on the fifth, heading down.'

'Don't,' shouted Rockburn. 'I think he's got a gun.' He ran upwards, keeping his back to the outer wall and looking up.

'Fourth floor,' shouted Flack.

'Second,' shouted Rockburn.

They met on the third. The door out of the stairwell and leading to the flats was still pulling shut.

Rockburn yanked it open. Unless the lift had stopped on the third, the target would have nowhere to go. They would have him cornered.

He might try forcing open a flat door, or *shooting his way out.*

Squares of light from high windows. A broken chair, and further down, someone waiting outside the lifts.

The target, still wearing his motorcycle helmet.

'Police,' shouted Rockburn, instinctively. Six months earlier, it wouldn't have been a lie.

The target stepped into a lift and pressed a button.

Rockburn sprinted forward with the pan lid and jammed it in the closing door. Forced his way inside, trying not to think of the consequences. If he could identify the target, it would help to shed light on everything. Who'd killed Mina, and who was pursuing Quang. It would help clear Rockburn's name, especially if a weapon or forensic links to Mina's murder were found. It wouldn't help his financial situation, but life was no fairy tale.

Wondering why the target hadn't fired his weapon, he charged across the lift and shoved the target up against the side.

Knife?

He yanked back an arm and applied pressure. The target was slighter, weaker than he'd expected, and struggled only briefly.

'Arm out to the side,' said Rockburn, 'nice and slow.'

The target did as instructed.

Rockburn patted him down, but the padded leathers made a thorough search difficult. He worked his hand around and pulled down the jacket's central zip. He felt inside for a weapon.

Instead he found –

Bazookas.

Rockburn finished the search – he was a professional – and stepped back. Behind him, Flack had appeared and was holding the lift doors. Sweat was running down his jowly face.

'Take off your helmet,' said Rockburn.

The target turned slowly and pulled it off. Holding it in one hand, Elsa ran her other through her hair.

20

Rockburn threw the lid of the jam pan into the corner of the lift where it clattered to silence. Flack released his pressure on the doors and stepped inside. The doors closed with a clunk, and the three of them descended. Holding her motorcycle helmet in front of her, Elsa looked furious – with Rockburn, and no doubt with herself.

'She's police.'

Flack nodded. 'Arrested you.'

Rockburn pretended to read the alarm instructions behind Elsa's shoulder. The tracker hidden in his bike was a hardware store model, not police kit.

The lift bumped down and the doors opened. Three men were waiting. Rockburn recognised them from the car which had pulled into the estate.

'You okay, Ells?' said a bald-headed man holding a police radio.

She nodded.

Outside the block, the two boys with skateboards were taking it in turns to slide down a metal rail bordering trampled bushes. Their boards bumped and crashed. The three officers, one a customer of Flack, walked away with the tattooist towards the arch and the first courtyard.

Rockburn jogged after them. Swapped the panther key for the Kawasaki's with Flack. No way was he riding back on that juddery contraption.

He waited to talk to Elsa while she gave crime prevention advice to an elderly couple on the ground floor who'd left their window open.

The two young skateboarders rolled closer. They were practising a stunt which involved weighting the end of the board and jumping in the air, the board flipping over and rotating 180 degrees.

'Not bad,' said Rockburn. He walked over and gave them each a five-pound note. It was penance for a wasted day. Looking surprised they slouched away before he could change his mind.

Elsa finished up with the elderly couple, and walked over, her leathers squeaking.

'Where's the boy?'

'The fewer people who know the better.'

'We're the police.'

Rockburn shrugged. He'd been a believer once, but he'd served enough time to know the Job leaked like an exhaust pipe.

'Are you still interested in dinner?'

He nodded slowly. She would try to probe him, but as long as he knew she was trying, it didn't matter. And it would be a chance to probe her.

'I'm renting a houseboat at Heston Basin – it's called *Vixen*.'

Rockburn rode like a trust fund brat back through Sheffield. Jumped traffic lights, revved the engine, raced a modified Astra with skirts and a spoiler. The panther wasn't built for the city and they caught each other's mood. Both man and machine were destined for a better existence than trotting about and snarling at the other animals.

Immediately they passed the last streetlight, they felt better. He fired up to the moor, the bike purring and Rockburn humming along. He glanced across at the pub, caught a snatch of tinny pop music, and pressed ahead. He hadn't told Flack about the false number plate on the Kawasaki. A carton of cigars wouldn't be enough if a traffic car stopped and arrested the tattooist.

Fields flew past on both sides. Abandoned farm equipment sat in corners, the dark and lethal shapes piercing the skyline.

He wondered if the traffickers would give up and return to Glasgow. It was possible they'd be deterred by the involvement of the police – having killed Mina, decide to escape while they could. But without understanding their motivation, it was impossible to know. Revenge for a relation or associate pushed under a bus, and / or recovery of the diamonds.

Descending from the moor, working the angles on the switchbacks, Rockburn also pondered the tracker. It was strange the crime squad unit had used such a basic device. He leant one way, leant the other. The technique couldn't be taught, the only way to learn was to practise, to feel the curves. And to slide off occasionally.

In the zone, now. He and the panther were one – seamless – leaning over together, straightening, leaning back. They knew each other like brothers or best friends, like father and son. They perceived when the other wasn't feeling well and needed a checkup, or some tlc – oil or beer or a rubdown. Rockburn had sensed an impurity, a foreign body – the tracker – in their midst.

Leaning into the next bend –

An idea popped.

Entering the outskirts of the city, he stopped at Killer Servicing and asked the mechanic tinkering in the maintenance pit if he could borrow a set of tools.

Dave peered out from the underside of a VW Beetle. He wore a baseball cap backwards and his face was filthy. His eyes like white gobstoppers.

'Sure.' He removed his hat, scratched his head and refitted it. 'Choose a corner. You might have to move stuff.' He ducked his head back under the car.

The garage was crammed with vehicles and spare parts. Racks of tyres lined a side wall and the day's deliveries were piled up at the entrance doors. A dented Mercedes sat in the first bay and a van and a moped in the second. The maintenance pit occupied the third bay. A talk show blared out from overhead speakers.

Rockburn wheeled the panther between the vehicles to the back. On one side, a spotty teenager was balancing a tyre on a machine. Opposite, behind the Mercedes, stood trolleys of tools. A door propped open by a lead weight led to a small office with shelves of paperwork and a computer on a desk. Dave's infamous coffee machine sat on a table by the door. Rockburn set his bike on the stand and leaving one trolley, wheeled the others further back.

On the radio, a debate about immigration. Ten migrants had been found dead in a lorry in a motorway service station.

Rockburn stared at the panther. Sensed something still wasn't right. She stared back, unimpressed. *Do something.*

He'd already searched her once and doubted he'd missed anything.

But still.

He started by unscrewing the panniers. Searched both and stacked them to the side. He unscrewed and unbolted the cowls and the fairings. Removed the small black box he'd found previously and set it down by the bumper of the Merc. A cheap GPS tracker which anyone could buy.

On the radio, a local politician was extolling the virtues of immigration. Filling vital gaps in the labour force; nurses, doctors and farm workers; a greater cultural richness; freedom of movement.

Rockburn unscrewed the seat and looked underneath. The leather was pristine, and the underside not tampered with.

He rocked back on his haunches and stared at the bike. No spare room in the clutch. He wondered about the lights and the light housings. He switched them on, pressed the ignition and tried the brake light. They all worked. No dead space.

'Taking our jobs,' shouted the spotty lad at the radio.

Rockburn stood up and walked into the back, yanked out the plug. His head was jammed with the chatter.

'Oy.'

Ignoring him, Rockburn returned to the panther. He observed the bike from the back to the front. Not enough room in the hugger or the swingarm. Impossible in the tyre or the brakes, ditto on the front. The fuel tank was a large space but the opening narrow and the tank unsuitable. Which left the engine block and the twin set of exhaust housing. He examined the engine but there were no nooks or crannies large enough, and no superfluous parts. He unbolted the exhaust pipes and checked the cavities. They stank of spent fuel but were devoid of foreign bodies.

He was stumped. In the Job he'd been trained to search. Nothing could be hidden as long as the searching was slow and methodical. No one worked for more than fifty minutes before taking a ten-minute break.

He stared at the panther.

Help me here.

Dave walked over, wiping his hands on a rag. 'Heard you're in the semifinal of the North West Cup?'

'Day after tomorrow,' said Rockburn, still staring at his bike.

'Want me to have a go?'

Rockburn nodded, stepped away.

The mechanic threw the rag onto a workbench, rummaged in the toolbox and set to work.

Rockburn wondered if coffee would give him a new perspective. Deciding to risk Dave's machine, he walked into the office, positioned a mug, pressed a switch and stood back. Black liquid fired out from a nozzle. At least half remained in the beaker. He sipped the coffee which was thick as tar, then drained the black sludge. It tasted like tar and would sit in his stomach like tar. A coronary seemed more likely than a fresh outlook.

'Rockburn.'

He walked back into the workshop.

'Is this what you're looking for?'

Rockburn nodded slowly.

'Behind one of the rear shocks.'

A small black box half the size of the first tracker.

Police kit.

Dave – Killer Dave, although there was no better bike mechanic – placed the small box on the ground next to the first tracker. He stood up and winked.

Two trackers.

Which explained why the police had followed Flack, but not why the traffickers hadn't. Maybe they'd been spooked by Elsa following on the motorbike. Maybe they had a scanner and knew the police were running an operation. Maybe they'd been tipped off. Maybe they'd had a breakdown or overslept. Maybe, a hundred reasons.

He hefted the weight holding the office door open and lugged it over to the trackers. The door booted shut.

The spotty teenager stopped work and turned to watch.

Rockburn replaced the everyday GPS tracker back inside the rear fairing and secured the bolts. He picked up the weight, held it square above the police tracker, and let go.

He lifted the weight off. The box was squashed sideways and

broken. He gathered all the bits and dumped them in the oil drum used for rubbish.

'Music?' said the spotty lad.

Rockburn nodded. 'Anything, just play it loud.'

21

Showered and shaved and wearing his best shirt, Rockburn rode the panther to the Heston basin. A dozen barges nestled alongside each other. Smoke drifted from two or three chimneys. The air carried a faint smell of waste, the water peaty brown. He walked along the bank, checking the names and avoiding the mooring stakes. On the roofs of the boats were sacks of coal and firewood, bicycles, tubs of dead flowers. An upturned wheelbarrow.

Vixen was the last boat. It was a deep red, the name written in gold paint. He'd assumed they were all old, but it looked new. Classical music and pale lamplight seeped out around the hatch. He knocked.

'It's open.'

He pulled it across and stooped. Entered the galley, where everything was half-size: a small kettle, a two-ring hob, a tiny sink. He felt like Gulliver.

'Through here.'

Keeping a hand on the ceiling, he pushed open another door.

There was a table screwed to the floor and benches on both sides, and further down, two long seats with cushions facing each other. Shelves and small cupboards everywhere.

'Welcome,' said Elsa. She sat on one of the padded long seats.

She put her book down. She wore a low-cut purple top and short black skirt.

'I brought you wine and chocolates.' Rockburn put them on the table. It had a rim to stop things sliding off. He wondered about the sleeping quarters, the size of the bed, the proximity of the ceiling. It felt like camping.

Elsa pointed at the seat opposite her.

He sat down. The seat uncomfortable as it looked.

'Beer?'

She fetched two bottles from a pullout box in the galley and stepped the two metres back. There would be no secrets on a barge.

'You were more difficult to read in interview,' said Elsa.

Rockburn held up his beer. 'Cheers.' They knocked bottles and he drank. 'Well.' He took another swig. 'Feels quite restrictive, difficult to express yourself. Maybe I'd get used to it.'

Elsa smiled. She opened a bag of peanuts and tipped them into a bowl. 'You mean, it's small and smells a bit.' She ate a couple of peanuts. 'A friend at work saw it advertised and I needed somewhere quickly. It's cheap, and the sound of lapping water together with the gentle rocking motion is soothing after a long day. I won't be here forever.'

Rockburn ate a clutch of nuts. Glanced around. Shelves with rims, like the table. Half a dozen books, a box of tissues. Framed photos; her family, he assumed. He sipped his beer.

'Do you have friends at work?'

'Define friend,' said Elsa.

The barge suddenly lurched up and down while a motorboat chugged past. The undulations decreased as the sound faded. Outside he could hear people riding around on mopeds. Teenagers, horsing about.

'Would lend you their motorbike.'

Elsa laughed. She crossed her legs. 'Anything else?'

'Someone you could go to if you're in trouble. You trust them. You trust them not to tell whoever they agree not to tell. Even if they're subjected to thumbscrews.'

'Flack?' said Elsa. She sipped her drink.

Rockburn nodded. 'Your go.'

'Sends you a card on your birthday. Would lend you money. Would risk smoke inhalation to save you from a burning building – or conveyance.'

Rockburn chuckled. It was a police joke – under the 1968 Theft Act, conveyance included barges. He grabbed a few more nuts. There was no sign of dinner, the galley devoid of food except for a bowl of over-ripe bananas and a packet of blueberries.

He drained his beer.

Elsa finished her drink. 'Are you hungry? I'm not much of a cook, and there's not much of a kitchen, so I thought I'd order a takeaway.'

He nodded. 'Fine.' He drained his beer and stood cautiously. 'Phone call.' Hand palming the ceiling, he made his way to the hatch and climbed out.

It was dark and cold, and the moon was rising. Steam rose from vents on the barges. A man was waiting for his dog on the towpath. No sight or sound of the youngsters and their mopeds.

Rockburn phoned Hocking.

'Have you made any progress?'

'Yes and no.'

'I'm shit scared.'

'I know, I'm sorry, it won't be for too much longer. How's Quang?'

'Spends hours digging. His tunnel reached the hedge and he's started shoring it up with wood I found in the garage. He's been telling me about his grandfather who fought in the Vietnam War. He was a sniper in the Vietcong and operated mainly underground, via a network of tunnels. Interesting to hear it from the other side.'

'Has he said anything more about what's happened since he came to the UK?'

'I'm afraid not. I keep thinking he will.'

'Can I speak to him?'

He heard her calling the boy over.

'Hello, Rockburn.'

'I hear you've almost dug a tunnel to Australia.'

'Digging helps me no think.'

'I'll come and see you tomorrow.'

'Please take me ride.'

'Sure.'

'I like lot.'

Rockburn held the phone, waiting for Hocking to return. The boy had something about him – a maturity far greater than his years. But more than that: a sense of peacefulness, and a poise. He'd said people thought he was special. Maybe, Rockburn thought, they were right.

Hocking came back. 'They were talking about a darts competition on the radio. You never said.'

'You hate darts.'

Rockburn pocketed the phone, and walked over to a tree for a piss. He was yet to see the bathroom in Elsa's boat, but it could only be cramped. He wondered whether it drained into the canal and explained the pong.

Elsa was opening his bottle of wine in the galley. He squeezed past and sat back on the sofa. He half-wondered if it was a trap, arrest him for drink-driving to ratchet up the pressure.

'Not for me, I need to ride back.'

She sat down, holding a large glass and handing him a second beer. 'I don't police my friends.' She tasted the wine, nodded. 'How's Quang?'

'He's okay.'

'You can't look after him forever.'

Rockburn put the bottle down on the galley floor. 'I was wondering—'

'Were you?' She sipped her drink, looked across at him, eyes sparkling with make up or alcohol or intent. Or all three – a fatal combo.

'If you'd get this fingerprinted.' From an inside pocket he removed the bagged CS canister. 'Seized it from one of Flack's customers.'

'You mean you stole it,' said Elsa, taking the exhibit. 'You lost your powers of search and seizure.' She paused. 'You think he—'

'She.'

'She – one of the traffickers, possibly one of Mina's killers – would risk showing out?'

'Maybe.' Rockburn paused. 'Also—'

'Also?' said Elsa, raising her eyebrows.

He knew he was pushing it, and flirting aside, wondered what she was after. 'Can you run Peter Kingman through the system? I want to pay him a visit, make sure he's not behind all this. He holds me responsible for his brother.'

'Isn't this a bit involved for the Kingmans?'

'Maybe.'

'They're more plastic bag over head, roll up in carpet, bury under new house.'

'Still, seems a big coincidence—'

'Pizza,' shouted a delivery driver from the towpath.

Stooping, Rockburn padded across to the hatch and climbed out. A skinny youth handed him the box and hurried back to his scooter. Rockburn looked up and down the path, lingered over the shadows. He saw no one else, could hear only water trickling into the canal. He ducked back inside.

The pizza was pepperoni, extra large. Hot. Better than camping.

He asked Elsa why she joined the police, and after she'd answered, she asked him the same question. He finished his half of the pizza and wiped his fingers on sheets of kitchen roll. She offered him the remaining slices. He'd joined the police because everyone expected him to, even if they didn't want him to. Elsa had joined because nobody had. She asked how he was finding being a private investigator.

He thought for a moment. Less admin, and he didn't have to answer to a boss, but he had few resources, and so far, earnt no money. But he was doing the same thing, and wanted the same thing – answers. As a cop, he'd found them, but as a PI, he was still looking.

'Ask me again in a few weeks.'

She watched him start on the final slice. 'We'd really like to speak to Quang. The boy's likely to have vital information for the investigation into Mina's murder, and you'll be exonerated far more quickly.'

'Quang's not saying much,' said Rockburn, his mouth full.

'We've got people who can talk to him; you know that.'

'The CS canister might yield something.' He wiped his hands as he finished chewing and threw the sheets of kitchen roll inside the pizza box. 'And you must have other leads.'

Elsa hesitated. She tidied the box away and filled the kettle.

Rockburn guessed at her dilemma: unlike a normal informant, he wanted information, not money. So their informant–handler relationship was more equal. Like an international negotiation on trade talks, the two of them had to keep talking, had to keep tickling each other along, exchanging titbits. Otherwise, if there was no talking, no exchange of information, then neither of them benefited. The trick was to give things which held little value, and if that tactic proved fruitless, to give less than you were given.

'Not many, and nothing substantive. Your flat was clean –

apart from Mina's, only your prints and DNA. Little sign of a struggle, some very faint defensive injuries, minor bruising. She was chloroformed and a wire – metal – noose used to strangle her. No sign of the noose. No intelligence from the community in Manchester or in Glasgow. No witnesses, a few seconds of CCTV. We're scratching. The wire noose is the only thing we've got to go on. It's an unusual MO.'

'How unusual?'

'Very.' She paused and Rockburn waited. If he'd still been in the Job, he'd have searched the MO database on the PNC, and he hoped Elsa had – and was going to tell him. He raised his eyebrows, willed her to speak.

'As a weapon in non-domestic cases, a noose is unusual. Occasionally, it's used as a method of torture, but in professional murders like the hit on Mina it's rare as the DCI buying a round. A wire noose made of metal – confirmed from contact traces by the CSI – even more so.'

'The chief super buying a round?'

Elsa smiled, nodded. 'There was a case a couple of years ago in Bradford, where a rabbit snare was used to kill a drugs rival. The killer's inside and will be for a long time so it's not him. And I couldn't find any other recent cases in the UK. Plastic noose, yes – fishing line is a favourite, but not using a metal wire.'

'What about intel from the Border Force, or internationally – Interpol?'

She shook her head. 'I've sent the request, but got nothing back so far. That's why we're keen to talk to the boy.'

The kettle whistled.

'Do you want to see the rest of the barge? Then I'll make coffee.'

Rockburn held back a smile. Unlike a trade negotiation which was professional, their relationship was personal. Affairs were commonplace between spies as they tried to lure their opposite number into leaking information. One-on-one negotiations were tense, high-staked, unpredictable affairs. They were erotic, and often sexual. And his body was telling him it was interested.

The bathroom was tiny. A shower with a wraparound door and a nozzle at the height of his sternum. A tiny stained-glass porthole with the image of a mermaid. One electric toothbrush, one wash kit on the back of the door. The bedroom was at the end. A door with louvers opened to reveal a decent-sized bed with a red duvet the colour of the boat. Large heart-shaped pillows and reading spotlights on flexible rods.

They drank coffee, and Rockburn asked about Elsa's family. Her parents lived in Burnley, her brother was a teacher in Salford. She described a disastrous family Christmas where her brother had smoked cannabis with their parents.

'Did you?'

'Didn't inhale.'

They laughed together. Rockburn liked her. Was waiting for her to make a move. At the same time wondering if she was waiting for him. Times were changing –

Elsa walked out with him to the panther. The autumn moon shone through denuded trees and reflected on the water. Water lapped softly against the boats.

Rockburn sat on the bike, and Elsa bent to peck him on the cheek. 'Have you ever slept on a boat?'

He hadn't. He fiddled with the straps on his helmet, knowing he was leaving with more information than he'd disclosed. If he stayed, the balance might change.

22

Rockburn sat at his laptop and worked on the information divulged by Elsa. A noose was often known as a garrotte, and made from wire, cord, plastic, or cloth: guitar strings, piano wire, fishing line, telephone wire. Since the Second World War it had been commonly used by soldiers as a silent method of executing sentries. Two sticks controlled a length of wire which was placed over an enemy's head and whipped back.

Quick, silent, deadly.

He looked up the government stats on strangulation, not disbelieving Elsa, but wanting more detail. Homicides averaged seven to eight hundred a year in the UK. The most common weapon was a knife, and shootings only accounted for about thirty deaths. The number of homicides by strangulation was similar, but most were domestic cases with a known suspect.

However, research over the previous decade showed the noose was used far more frequently, in so-called 'rough sex'. Victim groups had campaigned – successfully – for a new offence of non-fatal strangulation, but despite the new law, they believed it was still hugely underreported.

Rockburn scrolled down the search engine returns and skimmed page after page, but was unable to find a more detailed breakdown of strangulation homicides. Maybe it didn't matter.

The official stats supported what Elsa had told him: in non-domestic cases, the use of a noose as a murder weapon was rare, and the use of a metal noose rarer still.

He wolfed a handful of cornflakes.

And searched again.

The garrotte's history ran further back than the Second World War. It was used as a method of execution in Rome, and in Spain and Italy in the Middle Ages. Often reserved for the ruling classes, and victims included an Inca emperor and priests. Became a common assassin's weapon and used in eighteenth-century India by roving bands of robbers known as the Thuggee cult. They used a yellow cloth with a knot in the middle to crush the larynx.

He ate more cornflakes. Other proponents of the garrotte were special forces and guerrilla troops, including the French Foreign Legion, and the Viet Cong in the Vietnam War.

He stopped chewing.

Poured the cornflakes in his hand back into the cereal bowl.

Quang's grandfather had been a member of the Viet Cong.

He played with the cornflakes in the bowl. Quang and Mina were Vietnamese, and someone – the traffickers – wanted to take the boy back to Vietnam, and his aunt dead. The traffickers were Asian, possibly Vietnamese. They'd killed Mina using an unusual method for twenty-first century Britain. Unless they were elite soldiers, or had specific knowledge of a slice of history. Or they'd done a lot of research and chosen the garrotte on its merits.

Rockburn flicked back and forth through the internet pages, followed the links, reversed back through them. He went over everything but no matter how hard he tried, he couldn't develop Elsa's information into a solid, cold, forge-tempered lead.

He stood up.

Unbolted the door to the fire escape and stepped outside. In the yard below, Flack was collecting litter in a bucket. The yard was full of it. Plastic bottles and cans, polystyrene takeout trays, rips of plastic sheeting. It swirled around and gathered in the corners like leaves in a garden.

He clattered down the steps, wanting to talk to the tattooist. If he couldn't develop a new lead, he would have to reprise an old one.

Flack emptied a bucketful into an open wheelie bin. He wore a sheepskin coat which smelt of cigar smoke.

'I don't want people to think I didn't care.'

The tattooist wheeled the bin back to the service road at the rear of the yard. A brush leant against the wall. Rockburn followed. A man in a flat cap was walking his boxer dog. The animal stopped and sniffed the bin.

Man and dog walked further down the dark narrow road.

'Maybe I should've had a dog.'

'What about all the biking, the Demons' trips up north and abroad?'

The tattooist set down the bucket and took hold of the brush. 'A dog and a different life. Maybe I should've run a dog kennels and planted some trees. Every man should plant a few trees.' He swept the far corner of the yard. Soft drink cans rusted with age, sweet wrappings without their cheery veneer.

'It's not too late.'

'Isn't it? I don't know the first thing about trees, which species would grow well, where, and whether they need staking or a special kind of compost.'

'You provide a service to people. You've got lots of customers, you're good at it.'

'But not good enough for you, Rockburn?'

Flack had him.

He had thought about it. Most times he entered the tattoo studio, but he didn't like the permanence, the brazen identification. A tattoo seemed like a sheep-tag or a prisoner number stamped across the forehead. It was a reason for people to remember you. He didn't want to be remembered for what he looked like, but for what he did.

Flack stopped sweeping, leant over the handle of the brush and coughed brutally. He hoiked, spat, coughed again. He straightened like an old man. 'Have you ever wondered, Rockburn, how we got into all this?'

'You mean how the Earth has just the right thickness of atmosphere, is just the right distance from the sun, has a combination of gravity and stable rotation which keeps us here and gives night and day? And on top of that, the two journeys undertaken by hundreds of millions of sperm to impregnate our mother's eggs were won by the only two sperm which would produce you and me?'

'No, I don't mean that. Fuck.' The tattooist swept the pile of rubbish into the bucket, kicking in pieces which missed. Emptied it into the wheelie bin and swung the lid shut.

'You mean the rat trap?' Rockburn felt uneasy. He'd coopted Flack without explaining the consequences. Legal, sub-legal, physical. The Job had multi-page risk assessments, reams of health and safety standing orders. If Rockburn Investigations was to survive its first year, it would need more than headed notepaper.

Flack cleaned the bristles by brushing the wall. Mud flicked around. They walked back towards the fire escape. Rockburn heard the whine of a moped on the service road.

The tattooist turned to face him. 'I mean me, Rockburn. Wearing these clothes, looking like this.' He grabbed the ragged lapels of the sheepskin coat, then flicked the tendrils of his long greasy hair. 'And doing what I do, tracing patterns from a pamphlet and colouring-in.' He surveyed the yard. 'I mean I know *how* I got into it. At school I only really liked art and I spent most lessons drawing – or doodling. Pencil drawings mainly, cartoon characters, vehicles, especially jeeps and futuristic motorbikes with spikes on their tyres and a row of headlights. I was quite good at light and shade, and I began sketching some of my classmates. This led to me doing caricatures of some of the teachers, and earning a few quid. The history teacher Mr Sampson even bought a couple, swore me to secrecy. In the fifth year my best mate Jimmy Jagger, he's dead now, broke his arm jumping out of a window. I drew on his plaster cast, and he liked it so much, he asked me to draw on his good arm. I suppose that was the turning point. I left school, did a couple of courses and never looked back. Only now, I am. What I suppose I mean is *why*. *Why* did I become me?'

'There's probably no answering it. Maybe Nietzsche could, or Marx.'

'What do you know about Nietzsche?'

A beermat would be plenty of room. Rockburn wondered whether the doctor's letter had brought on the tattooist's angst. His friend was seriously ill, but didn't know Rockburn knew. He felt guilty even asking Flack for help, but he had no other leads. The two of them should at least talk about the illness; that was what friends did, and he'd only just confirmed to Elsa that Flack was a friend. But first he had to confess to nosing through his friend's stuff. Maybe, he thought, now was as good a time as any.

He was about to speak –

When the gate opened and a moped nosed into the yard. The rider looked around, hesitated, and wheeled further inside. He tapped a phone, looked over his shoulder, then up at the windows of the surrounding buildings. Spotting Rockburn and Flack, he buzzed closer.

'Delivery for Quang Tran.'

Rockburn shook his head. 'No one by that name in this block.' He couldn't see a parcel. The moped didn't have panniers and the rider carried no shoulder-bag. The helmet was black with a tinted visor. 'What's the address?'

'Rockburn Investigations.'

'That's me.'

'Quang Tran must make sign. He has more address, I can take?'

'There is no Quang Tran.'

The rider glanced across at Flack who gripped the broom with both hands as if he was a highlander about to swing at an infantry charge. The rider looked back at Rockburn. Then flicked the throttle and shot off towards the alley, his feet still hanging down.

'Flack!' shouted Rockburn.

The tattooist hurled the broom. It missed the back wheel of the moped and skidded across the yard. The moped disappeared into the alley, and the two of them ran after it.

When they emerged onto the street, the moped was already turning at the crossroads, and the two of them drew up, Flack coughing and spluttering.

'Are you okay?'

'Course I'm okay.' The tattooist sucked in a mouthful of air like a surfacing pearl diver. 'What was all that about?'

'I don't know,' said Rockburn. 'Listen, Flack, I want to run the rat trap a second time.'

The tattooist leant back against the wall, still breathing heavily. 'Leave it with me.' He took another deep breath. 'Over the years we've had one or two problems in the Demons which we've had to take care of.' He paused again to breathe. 'We know what we're about.'

'Soon as,' said Rockburn. Hoped he did too.

The tattooist nodded. 'I'll speak to a few of the boys tonight, and tomorrow we'll go catch ourselves a Christmas turkey.'

23

Rockburn had the morning to kill.

Flack was at the doc's and unavailable for a rerun of the rat trap until lunchtime at the earliest. When Rockburn had told him the plan, the tattooist had promised two dozen bikers from the club, and said there'd have been more if it hadn't been a weekday.

He laid out his two sets of match darts on a baize cloth. Both were made of tungsten. He unscrewed the shafts and set them aside. He checked the tips retracted smoothly from each barrel. Points which withdrew slightly on impact virtually eliminated bounce-outs. He wiped the ridged grips and patted them dry. Thin barrels to allow for a tight grouping. Extra coarse to prevent slippage. He wiped the shafts and checked the flights.

After screwing the darts together he felt the different hefts. Against Dave Cummins, he'd used twenty-five-gram barrels – and lost. Twenty-eights would help to counter his nervousness in the opening rounds.

Darts like most repetitive sport – snooker, golf, shooting – was about two things: practice, and performing under pressure.

He sat cross-legged on the floor and closed his eyes. Sitting up straight, he made circles with his thumbs and first fingers and rested his hands on his knees. He breathed deeply through his nose, counting to seven, then exhaled, consciously expelling the air from his stomach, his lower lungs, his upper lungs, again to the count of seven.

Outside, traffic battled along the street. A bus humming past, cars and vans stopping, starting, a cyclist with a bell. A scooter whined along like an annoying child. He breathed in – and out. In – and out.

After five minutes, he'd had enough. He researched Redeye Reynard on his laptop. Various theories why Reynard was called Redeye: he was born in Redcar; he'd been poked in the eye as a child; he drank too much homebrew; he'd prodded himself with a dart after losing a game on which he'd bet his house. Reynard had been a North West Cup finalist for three successive years, winning twice. He was proficient in consistent heavy scores and checkouts. Only one weakness according to *Darts Weekly*. As long as he was two or three legs clear, Reynard would throw like a top top professional. But if the score was even or he was losing, he would fall apart. Carpentry darts, low scores, and haphazard attempts to checkout. His dodgy eye swelled up with the pressure according to *Darts W*.

Rockburn opened up another tab and entered *Viet Cong*.

Infamous for their effective guerrilla warfare: skilled proponents of defensive infantry tactics, especially traps and tunnels. Their favourites were *punji* sticks, sharpened points hidden in camouflaged pits; cartridge traps, triggered bullets hidden like mines; snake pits; and booby traps, explosives hidden in flags and other VC memorabilia. Known also to use the garrotte.

Known also to use the garrotte – an unusual MO for modern Britain. If the traffickers were Vietnamese – *if* – maybe they'd travelled from Vietnam to search for Mina and Quang. Found them in Glasgow, and followed them to Manchester. But why, if what Quang had said was true, did they want to take the boy *back*?

He poured a bowl of cornflakes and ate a handful. His analysis was stuck like a blocked carburettor.

He returned to musing on the semifinal against Redeye Reynard. Best of three sets, which meant all he had to do, all anyone had to do, was win two sets. It seemed simple. Darts wasn't rocket science.

Winning the semi would pay for two months' rent and additional marketing for his floundering PI business. It was difficult to know where to advertise. Hiring a private investigator was not an impulsive action, but the final resort. Maybe a journal for solicitors or in the back pages of *Private Eye*. He grabbed more cornflakes from the packet.

To settle his roiling stomach, he decided to play 101. Six darts to finish from 101. It was possible in only two darts by ending on a bullseye, but more usually attempted in three, and achieved in five or six. It gave lots of practice on the big trebles and throwing at all parts of the board. It helped make the choice of finish instinctive, Rockburn for example always choosing five, twenty, double top when needing sixty-five. Despite the alternative, starting with treble nineteen, giving two attempts to checkout. For him it was the statistical play. At the same time, 101 built the preferred finish into muscle memory. The result, as for a golfer on the eighteenth green or a marksman with one bullet left, was for matchplay to be automatic, ingrained, unthinking whatever the external factors. Crowd noise, lighting, temperature. Internal factors were the wild cards.

He wiped down a section of blackboard and chalked up 101. Underneath he would record his scores.

He started off. 20, 5, 1. He collected his darts. 20, 20, double top. Easy as a rolling stoppie. He chalked a six on the board.

20, 12, 20. He plucked out the darts and worked the maths. Forty-nine to checkout, so nineteen, double top. He hit nineteen. He saw Redeye Reynard grinning like a fox in the henhouse. He threw in no man's land. He threw a carpentry dart. He collected his spears. He closed his eyes, took a deep breath, counted for seven, exhaled for seven. He kissed a point, then threw 20, 10, double 5. He chalked up a nine.

He played on. 7, 12, 5, 6, 8, 6, 4, 11, 8, 8, 8. He was reassured, surprised, annoyed, and ultimately disappointed. He wasn't ready or he wasn't good enough.

A motorbike fired up in the yard. The noise rose and fell as the engine revved. Like the sound of the call to prayer for a Muslim, or church bells for a Christian, the guttural thunderous roar stirred his core, caressed his soul, eased thinking about tomorrow. He opened the window.

Flack sat astride the panther, and glancing up, raised his fist.

Rockburn slammed the window down. Rat Trap Mark II was GO.

The wind swept slate-grey clouds across the sky and made the roadside trees shimmy and shake. It was cold and the wind chill made it feel arctic. Rockburn puttered into the pub car park on the trans-Pennine. He manoeuvred the Kawasaki into the same place as before, under the tree with red berries. He stashed Flack's Viking helmet in a pannier, and switched number plates.

Lunchtime trade spilled out of the pub. A fat sales rep after stopping for a pie and a pint and twenty minutes on the quizzie. A white-haired Daimler driver and a woman half his age wearing cowboy boots and driving an old runaround. They hugged but didn't kiss. The jukebox piped out a tired Christmas carol. It was still only November.

Rockburn looked up the road towards Manchester, and down the road towards Sheffield. No sight or sound of any motorbikes. He again wondered why the traffickers had not followed the panther the first time, and only Elsa caught in the trap. Possible Mackay had tipped them off. Possible they were spooked by police units – albeit unmarked vehicles – following Elsa. Hoped it was a case of second time lucky.

A container lorry with an aerodynamic hood on the cab rumbled past. Followed by a minibus carrying grammar school boys wearing red blazers. In the back window, hands held up a cardboard sign. *Honk if you **** and drive*

Rockburn took out a lighter and thumbed the wheel. The flame sprung to attention. He checked it twice more, both times the flare leaping readily into existence.

Putting it away, he wondered if he should have brought a spare, or matches. He worked down from 101, calculating the sequence he'd use to checkout. Eighty-one could be played in two ways. One, double top, double top. Or triple nineteen which was harder, but gave two chances to checkout with double twelve. He was unsure, needed to conduct a trial, but the match against Redeye was only a day away.

The buzz of multiple motorbikes pierced the air. Arriving from the direction of Manchester, and at a canter.

The first came into view. More followed quickly. They rode in an arrowhead across the width of the road. Black shiny helmets like beads atop suits of black leather and machines of silvery steel.

A car heading in the opposite direction slowed as it drove to meet them. In a well-practised move, the bikers in the wrong lane merged into the correct one. They were a club, not a gang, Flack had once assured him. It didn't matter: they looked the part.

The car passed them and the bikes fanned out.

They shot past Rockburn, a noisy black and silver blur. A dozen or fifteen. Punters looked out of the pub, and three young boys ran out into the car park to watch.

Fifteen minutes to wait. He tried more checkout sequences, but couldn't concentrate. He checked the lighter. He snapped off a twig of berries and flicked them away.

The three boys climbed a tree at the side of the pub, two descending when a man came out of the pub and climbed into a car. The third boy refused to climb down, and the car drove away towards Sheffield.

Another motorbike. It came into view from Manchester, but wasn't Flack. It wasn't the panther. The sound was similar, but less raw. Less hungry.

The car returned to collect the boy who'd climbed down and sat crying by the car park entrance.

Rockburn heard the keening of the panther. Around the bend appeared Flack, riding as he always did. Like a garage door on a bike, square-shouldered, upright. A bluff to the wind. Rockburn took a litre bottle of petrol from a pannier and shoved it down the front of his jacket. He pressed the ignition on the Kawasaki and mounted. He walked the bike forward to the exit.

Flack thumped past.

The traffickers hadn't followed the first time, and there was no knowing whether they would follow the second.

Rockburn crossed himself and said a few words of prayer. He wasn't a religious man. He wasn't a superstitious man. But for Quang's sake, he needed it to work. For both of them.

He checked his watch.

Sighed.

He'd set the hare running and couldn't do any more: a tracking vehicle would or wouldn't appear.

The jukebox started up.

'Come on!'

He heard a car.

It rounded the bend from Manchester. A blue car. It moved closer. The blue hatchback.

Rockburn glanced back down the road but no vehicle followed. It was too early. The rearguard of motorbikes from Demons MC which were sweeping would be a minute or so back.

The blue hatch drove by, heading for Sheffield. Two Asian men in the front, one in the back. Rockburn made a mental note of the number plate.

Rat Trap Mark II was on.

One thousand, two thousand, three thousand. He pushed the Kawasaki forward onto the road, arced around, and took off. Bent down into a streamlined position and accelerated hard, pinging up through the gears. He kept the perfect line on the deep first corner, and accelerated as it straightened out. He gunned it along the straight. Riding the Kawasaki was like crossing a never-ending cattle-grid, but it was tuned to fuck.

The hatch came into view.

Rockburn pressed forward, knowing the tricky part was still to come. He curved left and right, and caught the hatch on the next straight. He screamed past, avoiding even a glance into the car. Rounding a corner, he reached the entrance to the rugby club and the golf course. Figures on a distant green.

Flack and the panther had disappeared around the next corner.

Rockburn braked to a standstill, curved round and drove back to the corner. Thirty seconds was his estimate for how long he had.

He dismounted, pointed the Kawasaki diagonally across the road and pushed it over. He took out the bottle of petrol and sloshed it over the bike. No other vehicles – all were being held back by the two groups of Demons MC bikers. He stepped back, took out the lighter. A moment of panic as he realised he needed a taper to throw at the fuel-soaked bike. He felt in his pockets and pulled out a serviette from the pizza with Elsa. Perhaps he should have stayed.

He lit the serviette and hesitated. A bike felt like family, even the juddery Kawasaki. He threw the flaring serviette. There was a whoosh as the flames ran over the machine. He ran down the road and lay down. Arranged his body so it looked like he'd slipped off the bike and skidded along the carriageway.

The bike exploded, metal and glass flung in all directions. Rockburn closed his eyes but could feel the heat.

He waited. Setting the bike on fire was essential, he'd finally convinced Flack. Not because Rockburn didn't detest the Kawasaki but anything less might not convince the occupants of the hatch it was a genuine accident. They still might not stop.

A car pulled up.

Rockburn stared out through slitted eyes. The blue hatch.

The driver's door opened, and a large Asian man with a ponytail climbed out. Rockburn recognised him from the chase across the park where Sal had her kiosk. The driver was arguing with the men in the car, and speaking in a language Rockburn didn't recognise. The driver walked forward, towards the burning bike and Rockburn. The two passengers climbed out of the car.

Rockburn heard the thrum of motorbikes, dozens of them.

The hatch driver bent down to Rockburn. He scowled and stood up. Swore and shouted to the men at the car. Ran back towards them.

Two phalanxes of motorbikes drew up to the scene. One stopped at Rockburn's spreadeagled body. The second directly behind the hatch. Stony-faced men and one or two women, some in pairs, astride throbbing machines. Harleys, BMWs, a Yamaha, a Ducati with fat exhausts, a Honda with a chair seat and a windshield, kit bikes, bastardised bikes with extended handlebars and modified suspension. Red, silver, black, every hue and cry. Gleaming with excess and power, and promising only one thing: anarchy.

Grey smoke rose from the Kawasaki.

Rockburn stood up. The noise of the bikes was intense, more than a noise, a thing, a heavy fog which lay down and suffocated.

Half a dozen bikers dismounted and approached the blue car. The driver shook his head at his goons and opened his palms in surrender.

Flack rode up on the panther, followed by a tow-truck with a winch. Men piled out of the truck. Flack gave instructions, and spoke into a walkie-talkie. The three Asian men were patted down and frogmarched away towards the rugby club. One biker grabbed a fire extinguisher from the tow-truck and sprayed the Kawasaki with foam.

A ramp was hauled out from the truck. The Kawasaki was righted and wheeled up onto the back. Flack rescued his horned helmet. The bike was tied down. The road swept and the blackened fragments shovelled into a sack. The sack, shovel, fire extinguisher all stashed in the back of the tow-truck. The truck drove away, heading to Sheffield, then back to Manchester. In twos and threes, half the bikers rode away. The remainder rode into the entrance of the rugby club.

Rockburn checked up and down. Only Flack sitting astride the panther remained. The carriage was clear, except for a black stain left by the burning bike and blobs of brown foam. He nodded at the tattooist.

Flack coughed viciously, spat, then held up the walkie-talkie. 'Release the roadblocks.'

Rockburn climbed up behind Flack on the back of the panther, and they followed the others into the rugby club. The tattooist smelt like a battlefield.

24

Potholes riddled the track to the rugby club. It wound through a copse of fir trees and emerged into a car park. Beyond was a large playing field with two rugby pitches, and a practice area. Between them stood the clubhouse and an access road which led around the back. On the far side of the pitches was a small stand for supporters.

Flack rode the panther to the end of the car park. Riding pillion and hating it, Rockburn scanned around for the others but couldn't see them. The gate to the access road was open and they rode through. On one side behind the clubhouse were scrummage machines, tackle bags, columns of cones, and on the other, rotting pallets, a heap of sand, and two green dumpsters. The tattooist curved the bike round to the rear of the supporters' stand.

Parked in a line stood a dozen gleaming motorbikes, and at the end, the blue hatchback. The three Asian men sat on the ground at the side of the car, and the bikers stood around them in a horseshoe. Rockburn recognised Fat Man and one or two others from the Demons.

The tattooist stopped, and the two of them dismounted. The weak sun was sinking behind the copse of trees, and beams of gold were striking the tops. The branches and trunks black as the devil.

At the far end of the training area, a groundsman was working. The Manchester–Sheffield road was out of sight, and apart from the man tending a bonfire, the rugby club was deserted.

'Max has a key for the gate,' said Flack, nodding at his deputy. 'He plays prop for the reserves. We come here sometimes if there's club business to sort out – an internal spat or preparing for a rumble with the Red Angels – and in the summer we have a barbeque. Invite a stripper with Union Jack tassels on her whirligigs.' The tattooist pointed at the back of the tiered stand. 'I thought over there would do.'

Underneath the web of scaffold bars supporting the seating was a cavernous space. A tractor and grass cutting equipment stood at the end, but it was mainly empty. The concrete floor dusty and dotted with clumps of dry grass.

'We'll start with the one in charge,' said Rockburn.

Flack whispered to the posse of bikers. One of them set two plastic chairs ten feet apart in the middle of the floor. Two others escorted the man who'd approached Rockburn on the road to one of the chairs. They pushed him down onto the seat.

'They've all been searched, the car too,' said Max, handing Rockburn a plastic bag. 'They must expect to be pulled by the cops. No wallets or paperwork, no identification. A bit of gear but nothing heavy – baseball bats, rope, tape. Three or four blankets. In the bag are three mobile phones.'

Unable to wait, Rockburn took out his mobile and tried the 378 number stored on the SIM card he'd recovered from the canal. The phones in the bag didn't flicker, his call diverted straight to a universal voicemail. New burners knowing one had been compromised? Not the jigsaw piece he'd been hoping for. Needed more from the interview.

Much more.

Two bikers grabbed a table from a stack, folded out the legs and manoeuvred it to the side. Fat Man placed items on top. Duct tape, a hammer and a box of nails, a cordless drill with a bit in the chuck.

Rockburn plonked down the bag of phones. He was starting to feel uneasy. His specialism was eliciting answers, not forcing them out.

Flack walked over and spoke in his ear. His breath smelt of stale beer and cigar smoke. 'Think of me as your stage manager.' The tattooist grinned. 'But you're writing the script.' He returned to the posse of bikers. The audience.

The two traffickers by the car fell silent. Stared at their leader on the chair. Perspiration glazed his forehead.

Rockburn sat on the second seat. He hadn't written the script, hadn't rehearsed.

Improv, then.

Max jumped onto his motorbike and fired the ignition. He revved the engine, the sound a frenzied and peculiar music. Music to accompany climbing out of trenches, jumping off a landing craft, parachuting from an aeroplane.

The noise cut.

The bikers waited. Flack waited. The traffickers waited.

Rockburn picked at the calluses on his fingers. Silence was his usual weapon.

The man on the chair was in his fifties and well dressed. He wore expensive pointed leather shoes, and a cream jacket with a crest on the cuffs. Trousers with a crease. Long black hair pulled back into a ponytail, and a bulging stomach from too much fast food and a sedentary life.

He watched Rockburn assessing him. Glanced at the array of aids on the table, wiped his brow with a tissue, then closed his eyes.

Five minutes passed. Two minutes was a long time, everyone knew that. Five minutes was ten times longer.

The trafficker opened his eyes. 'Have you a cigarette?' Perfect English.

Rockburn glanced back at Flack.

'I'll check,' said the tattooist, doubling over. He muttered to the other bikers for a few seconds, coughed and spat. 'We ain't.'

Rockburn stared at the man on the chair. He was playing a game, and Flack was playing his own version.

'The boy's got cigarette burns on his neck.'

'Maybe he didn't do as he was told.'

Rockburn stood up, walked round his chair, sat down again. He stared at the trafficker. Without the qualifying word, he might not have been able to control himself. It was where it had all gone wrong in the Job.

'Name?'

'You can call me Zafira – Mr Zafira.'

The trafficker could ask for anything, could say anything – or nothing. Rockburn might humour the name but not the title.

The afterglow of the sun reached through the trees. The day was almost done, and the temperature was dropping.

'What do you want, Zafira?'

'You are not a stupid man, Mr Rockburn. You know what we want.'

Two crows tossed up from the trees. They flew around, looping and jinking. They flew in silence. One moment diving, the next climbing. Chasing each other or being chased. Squabbling or fighting. They clashed in mid-air, or they seemed to clash. One fell a couple of metres, then bucked and pulled up to resume the jousting if they were rivals. The dogfight if they were enemies.

'The boy?'

'We don't want *him*. We want what's in his possession.'

'And what is in his possession?'

'Come now, Mr Rockburn.'

The pair of crows returned with a third crow, and their antics in the gloaming continued. Swooping, banking, soaring. Bombing down, pulling up, stopping abruptly and showing their claws. Two chased one, then one chased two. The same two or a different pairing? The original two or only one of them? The third bird changed everything. Were the birds on the same side with the same aim, or on different sides with the same aim, or on different sides with different aims? Even with three birds, the permutations were numerous.

'Why did you kill Mirza?'

Zafira tutted. 'We didn't kill her. Dead bodies attract the police and that's the last thing we want.'

'Was it because she pushed one of your men under a bus?' Men wasn't the right word. They were cowardly killers of a tiny woman alone in a foreign country.

'I don't know what you're talking about. A bus, you say?' Zafira pursed his lips and shook his saggy cheeks. Beads of sweat on his forehead.

Rockburn didn't know whether to believe him. So polite, so unusual. A new tactic to him. Maybe he'd try one. He stood up, walked over to the table, picked up the hammer. Passed it from hand to hand, set it down again.

Walked back towards Zafira.

He pulled out his phone, snapped a head and shoulders photo, and two more of his associates. He would show them to Quang, and make sure. Ask him about the cigarette burns.

Zafira scoffed. 'You don't seem sure, Mr Rockburn. The drill and the hammer are perhaps not for you.'

Flack walked forward to the edge of the stand. 'Do you want me to do it?'

Rockburn shook his head. 'Need more light.'

Flack walked back, pressed a switch. The striplight under the stand flickered and blew. He grunted orders. Half a dozen motorbikes were shunted back and forth and lined up to face into the stand. Headlights were turned on, their beams blazing at Zafira.

The trafficker shielded his face.

Outside it was dark, the crows and the trees only a memory. An occasional vehicle thrummed past on the trans-Pennine. The smell of the bonfire still lingered.

Finally, the headlights were dipped.

Zafira dropped his hand.

Rockburn stood behind the chair, put his hands on the top. 'I can only keep them off for so long.' He paused. 'Tell me, if you didn't kill Mina, who the hell did?'

Zafira took off his jacket. His shirt soaked with sweat. 'Are you a religious man, Mr Rockburn?'

'No.'

'Well, we are at least alike in that. But you do understand I'm sure the power of religion. What it drives men – and women – to do, and not to do. Abstain from food for weeks at a time, take a vow of silence, set themselves alight. Kill, maim, and torture sometimes great numbers of people in the name of faith.'

'What are you saying?'

'I'm saying we're not like that, we're driven by the power of the dollar. We have more in common with the mafia than with the fundamentalists.'

'You're saying fundamentalists killed Mina.'

'I'm not saying that, I'm saying if we didn't kill her, then someone else did. That's all I'm saying.'

Zafira sounded convincing, but Rockburn wanted to be sure. He nodded at Flack.

The tattooist walked over to the table and picked up the drill. He tightened the chuck with the key and pressed the trigger. Revved it as if he was throttling a motorbike. He set the drill down. He rummaged in the box of nails and took out a masonry nail. A steel nail in the shape of a sawblade and strong enough to batter into brick. Positioning it on the table between his thumb and forefinger, Flack tapped it with the hammer, then walloped it home.

Zafira remained still, his face impassive.

The tattooist walked over to him, walked behind him. Zafira swivelled in his chair, looking up left and right. Two bikers trundled over, held the trafficker's arms. Flack tapped Zafira on the head. A light tap. Then harder.

'Okay,' said Rockburn.

'You sure?'

Rockburn let the moment dance –

before nodding.

'For now.'

The tattooist threw the hammer back on the table, and walked back to the line of glaring motorbikes, his boys trailing.

A truck klaxon blew on the road. The noise was loud and abrasive, like a ship's foghorn warning against disaster.

Rockburn stared at the trafficker. 'Last chance.'

'Do you know what we do?' said Zafira. He wiped his face with a sleeve.

'You're people traffickers.'

'Nearly, but not quite. And there's nothing for nearlys, as you English like to say. We help people come to England. We're people movers. People smugglers if you must. But we don't sell the people we move, and we don't pimp them, or use them in any other way.'

'You charge exorbitant fees which they can't escape from.'

'Our service is a good one, a very good one.'

'I spoke to Mina before she was killed,' said Rockburn. 'She told me she'd paid a lot of money to get to the UK with the boy. But they were kept locked up in a tenement in Glasgow, and she was beaten and forced into prostitution. She feared for the life of the boy. So she escaped.'

'She's lying. She stole something that wasn't hers, and we're here to get it back. The boy must have it. Once we have it, we'll disappear, like how do you say, like a puff of cigarette.'

'Like a puff of smoke.'

'A puff of smoke. So, Mr Rockburn, do you have the diamonds?'

Flack revved the drill.

'Mina said she got them from a Russian man. Implied they were a gift.'

Zafira scoffed. 'Everyone lies, Mr Rockburn. You as old policeman must know that.'

Rockburn thumped the top of the chair. He still felt police. Zafira was right – everyone did lie. *Everyone.* The trickier assessment was separating the lies from the truth. The whole truth and nothing but the truth. Zafira not only polite but had remained confident and consistent under pressure.

'You can drill out my ears and eyes, and hammer a hundred nails into my body, and I won't tell you anything different. I might say everything that comes into my head but I can't *tell* you anything different.'

Rockburn glanced at the row of motorbike spotlights. He sensed what it would be like to be on a stage with everyone watching, waiting. But on a stage, his lines would be written, rehearsed, honed. Now he had a decision to make. Lives depended on it, maybe his own life. Stories had existed since the beginning of time, and were as slippery as eels. Facts were cold, hard, true, like masonry nails.

'And if I give them to you?'

'We're only interested in the boy because of the diamonds. Return them to us, and we'll leave the boy alone.'

'Forty-eight hours, meet us back here. The three of you – no one else. I will give you the diamonds.'

Zafira stood, wiped his hand, offered it.

Rockburn shook, despite himself.

'Let them go, Flack.'

The tattooist hoiked, spat.

Rockburn walked over to the table. He was playing for time, the risk not releasing the three men, but in two days' time, handing Zafira one hundred and forty thousand pounds' worth of diamonds and *hoping* they would disappear like his puff of cigarette. Disappear *and* leave the boy alone.

He picked up the drill, revved it over and over.

25

A stinking, pearl-grey fog smothered the city. An overnight factory fire was still smoking and particles were floating down like volcanic ash.

Rockburn sat on the panther outside a deserted pub – the Clarion Call. He was polishing the wing mirrors and cleaning the dash while watching the front door of the house opposite. Sergeant Scarisbrick lived in a semi with an integral garage. In the open porch a hanging basket devoid of life swung in the breeze. The custody sergeant liked to boast he could work a late shift and make last orders at the Clarion.

The door opened and Scarisbrick stepped out for early turn. A scrawny cat ran along a fence, leapt down and disappeared into the shrubbery. Dressed in half-blues, the custody sergeant was eating a piece of toast. He aimed a key fob at the garage door and returned inside. Revealed: an estate car with a bollard-shaped dent in the rear.

Rockburn pushed off his helmet and walked over, his leathers squeaking, and his boots crunching on the gravel. Not being in possession of the diamonds complicated things.

Scarisbrick reappeared holding an insulated mug. At training school he'd been disciplined for failing to display a tax disc on his car. Stupid, even if he wasn't corrupt.

'What do you want, Rockburn?'

'Is Mackay bent?'

A spidery smile crept over Scarisbrick's face. 'Does he like boys, do you mean? No idea. Try holding his hand.'

Stupid and not funny. Rockburn unzipped his jacket to let out some heat. 'Corrupt. On the take. Why is he so interested in pinning the murder of my Vietnamese client on me?'

'You'll have to ask him. Now, exc—'

Rockburn jerked a shoulder.

Scarisbrick flinched, the side of his head hitting the hanging basket. 'I could get you done for harassment.' He rubbed his head. Stupid, not funny, and ignorant of the law – harassment required at least two acts to prove a course of conduct.

'Did you phone him when I was brought into the custody suite?'

'What if I did? Mackay's CID team are on the take this week. Now, can I get off to work? Some of us have a proper job.' Stepping sideways to avoid Rockburn, he strode off.

Rockburn let him go.

Then smacked the hanging basket and walked back to his motorbike, the basket screeching behind him like a tortured animal.

Rockburn threw darts at his board. He plucked them out, retreated to the oche and threw again. He wasn't keeping score, he wasn't playing Bob's 27, Frustration, or round the clock. He was just throwing darts. It was the way to get worse, he knew that. To get better, throwing needed to be focused and intent.

An investigation was always bitty, frustrating, mostly dull. Gathering and assessing scraps of information, fag butts of detail, snippets of gossip. Semi-facts, misleading facts, incorrect assertions. Assumptions. Untruths. Lies. All were assiduously typed into the HOLMES computer system, or without it, thrown into the brain of a former detective.

Bracing Scarisbrick had confirmed nothing. Finding Zafira had produced more questions than answers.

If Mina hadn't pushed one of the traffickers under a bus in Glasgow, why'd Quang said she had? Rockburn believed the boy, even if Mina had lied about how she'd obtained the diamonds. In addition to an aura of serenity, Quang had an air of truthfulness. Either way, it was a convenient explanation for Zafira to use for killing Mina, but he hadn't taken it. And if Zafira hadn't killed Mina, who had? He again wondered about Peter Kingman, or someone working for him. Maybe he thought Mina was his girlfriend.

He threw 20, 5, 1. Twenty-six, known as Bed and Breakfast. Yesteryear's price for a bed and breakfast, two shillings and sixpence.

Pondering the diamonds question he threw 20, 5, 20. Forty-five, known as Brimful of Asha after the pop song by Cornershop. The number referring to the speed of the record player, the lyrics to the cheery escapism of the Hindi movie industry. He threw double top, 12, 18. He was getting worse. Seventy, exile to Babylon. No one could argue darts wasn't a sport with cultural and historical associations.

He was getting nowhere so he slipped on gloves and emptied the bag of mobiles from Zafira's crew on his desk. He tried pressing a few buttons, but the phones were PIN-locked. He pulled off the gloves and called Elsa.

'I can't talk, Rockburn, I'm at work.'

'Quickly then – anything on Peter Kingman?'

'He's inside. Arrested ten days ago for assaulting a pub landlord who was cashing up for the night.'

'What about the CS canister?'

'A set of prints but no match on the database and no answer from our partners.' She paused. 'And if you're about to ask me to chase them up, how about a trade?'

Here we go again, Rockburn thought. Back to the farmers' market. 'If you sit up on SR Jones the pawnbroker for a week, I guarantee you'll see a couple of burglars.'

'I've got to go,' said Elsa. In the background Rockburn could hear her colleagues' banter.

'Last thing – I have in my possession a bag of burner phones from a trafficking operation. The owners might be responsible for killing Mina.'

'How did you get hold of it?'

'Will you submit them?'

'Drop the bag off. And—'

'What?'

'You owe me dinner.'

Rockburn pocketed his phone. Even he might be able to manage pizza. He grabbed a handful of cornflakes and his jacket and went out. A fallback plan had come to him.

The pawnbrokers was empty except for Jones and a young woman in tight black leggings. She fingered her hooped earrings as she spoke quietly to the proprietor. Rockburn knew her, the younger half of a mother and daughter shoplifting team. During his probation he'd arrested Evie and Pauline and searched their tenth-floor flat. Not the Aladdin's cave he'd expected, but cold and damp.

He worked his way closer, through racks of hanging clothes. Men's jackets and designer shirts. Shelves of women's shoes. He reached the end of the counter. The buggy was piled with boxes of perfume and aftershave. The seat belt hung down, a blanket and a doll dumped on the floor.

Rockburn picked up an old-fashioned brown leather case containing a pair of binoculars. He slipped them out. Heavy, 20 x 50 magnification, and like new. Quang, he thought, might like them, give him something to do when he was fed up with digging.

Evie unloaded batteries from her pockets onto the counter. She signed the triplicate book and money changed hands. Evie stacked the boxes on the floor. She plonked the blanket and the doll back in the pushchair, muttered under her breath. Jones laughed loudly and she cackled with him. Rockburn remembered her dirty good humour.

She turned to go.

Rockburn put the binoculars down and hugged into the women's shoes. They gave off a scent, a not unpleasant sweaty musk.

The bell clanged as Evie left, and Rockburn approached the counter.

Jones closed the triplicate book and moved it to a drawer. He swept the batteries into a box and set it on a chair behind him. An open tray of identical batteries sat on the counter, three for two pounds. The bald man looked over the top of his spectacles.

'You remember me?'

Jones nodded. 'If you're here to reclaim your property, you can't. The police have seized your diamonds. And I can't loan you any more money.'

Rockburn rearranged the batteries on the counter into a pyramid. Elsa hadn't thought to tell him. She'd thought *not* to tell him. 'Why not?'

'They told me not to. If I don't comply, they'll apply to shut me down.'

Rockburn toppled the pyramid and the batteries clattered to the counter and the floor.

'Hey!'

Rockburn walked back through the shop to the door and turned over the *Back In Ten Minutes* sign. He flicked the Yale and drew the bolts.

'What the hell do you think you're doing?'

Rockburn returned to the counter.

'I used to be police.'

'I know.'

'That girl, Evie. I recognised her. She's a professional thief and everything she brought you was stolen. Last time I was here, two young lads waited for me to leave so they could sell you some hot gear.'

'And?'

'How long have you been in business?'

'Seventeen years next month,' said Jones. 'I'll put my daughter through college, then I'm going to move to the sea. I've had enough of it round here. Takes me half an hour to lock up and set the alarms.'

'Life's hard, I get it. But right now we can do each other a favour.'

Jones took off his glasses and huffed on the lenses. He polished them with a cloth. 'I've been burgled three times, robbed twice, and assaulted half a dozen times. Few weeks pass without being spat at or threatened. And now you're blackmailing me. I'm going to the coast and I'm going to run a flower shop.'

The front door rattled as someone tried to enter.

Jones held up his hand and indicated five minutes. His eyes were puffy and red-rimmed. He put his glasses back on.

'You must have other diamonds?'

Jones shook his head. 'I've got plenty of bling, shiny baubles and chunky rings, but not the real thing. What you brought me was very unusual. I see plenty of jewellery: watches, necklaces, brooches, earrings. I get silver spoons and plates and cufflinks and tiepins. But very rarely diamonds, and nothing close to the value of the ones you showed me.'

'You played it pretty cool when I brought them in.'

'High-value items always bring trouble.'

'Could you get some?'

'I could make some calls – maybe I could get a few stones, but it would take several days, maybe a week.' Jones moved the box of batteries onto the floor and slumped down onto the chair. He pushed his glasses up and rubbed his eyes. 'And they wouldn't be as good.'

'Forget it,' said Rockburn. He only had two days and would have to think of something else. A fallback plan to his fallback plan. He fetched over the case with the binoculars. 'Just these, against my tab.'

Jones glanced up, scowled.

Holding the binoculars case, Rockburn walked to the shop door. He hauled the bolts across, flipped the sign and stepped outside.

Under a grainy yellow sky, the grey street was clamouring. One street in a thousand grey clamouring streets. The city was rotting, and he felt he was rotting with it.

26

Rockburn hightailed out of the city toward the country. He took a shortcut along the Cowley Road, passing the allotments. An assortment of ramshackle sheds dotted the site, and over a wooden fence, he could see a couple of people working. Tired-looking vehicles in the nearest layby matched the sheds and the gardeners. One exception: an orange VW Golf with a spoiler and an oversized engine. Anticipating future horse trading with Elsa, he whacked a U-turn and stopped in a side street.

Keeping his helmet on, Rockburn walked back to the gate of the allotments. The car belonged to Matthew Headley, a burglar he'd arrested frequently as a juvenile. His parents were both inside and it was his grandfather who'd turned up in the middle of the night to act as appropriate adult. The grandfather owned the allotment, and Rockburn had once searched his shed while Headley was in custody.

He peered over the fence at the strips of land, some grown wild, but most sprouting impressive arrays of knee-high greens. He opened the gate and walked inside, preparing to give a story of a lost delivery driver.

A huge polytunnel sat in the centre of the site, and behind it, the grandfather's allotment. Rockburn walked up to the tunnel and glanced inside. Finding it deserted, he entered, took off his helmet, and peered through a hole in the sheeting.

Headley, stripped to the waist and tensing his muscles like a bodybuilder, was posing for photos. He was holding a handgun. A teenage girl wearing next-to-nothing was pointing a phone and laughing. Headley was only recently out of prison but clearly wanted to go back.

Rockburn pulled on his helmet, and jogged back to the panther. If he'd still been in the Job, he'd have called for backup and taken Headley out. As it was, he'd have to make do with telling Elsa. He climbed back on the motorbike and slammed his visor down. Headed out to the country, hoping the ride would exorcise his frustration.

He needn't have worried. The panther ghosted up the hills and hugged into the curves. The air was cool and fresh and the hum of the engine as pure as a lute. His mind drifted, Headley soon replaced by Simon – Rockburn wondered if his brother would have liked riding; as teenagers, they'd watched races on the tv and gone to trials' events. Maybe *he did like* riding, and even then was sitting astride a throbbing machine. *Somewhere.*

Simon by Zafira. Substitute diamonds wouldn't have fooled the trafficker for long. Even if Zafira didn't realise immediately, someone would, and he would be back. Quang would remain in danger. Returning the boy to Vietnam wouldn't make him safe. The only option would be a new identity in the UK, or as a last resort, a new identity *and* a new country of residence. He was beginning to hope it wouldn't come to that.

The three of them sat in the front room with mugs of tea the colour of walnut, and doughnuts Rockburn had bought at a petrol station. A wood burner kicked out a heavy heat. Thick curtains, pictures on the wall, and shelves of books.

Hocking sat on the edge of her chair and kept glancing at the door as if she was expecting someone. The traffickers, or the girl? Quang tinkered on the floor with an ancient Meccano set which had belonged to Rockburn. For three or four years, Meccano had been his favourite toy. He'd built cars, forklift trucks, cranes, and hundreds of motorbikes. Some had working suspension and gears.

The boy fiddled a nut over a bolt, his face tight with concentration. Beside him, the half-eaten doughnut.

'How's he been?' whispered Rockburn.

'Quiet. Reflective. Thinking about his aunt, and the future. He's had a couple of nightmares, came into my bedroom once. But we read stories and he goes back to sleep. He wants to know what's going to happen to him, and practical stuff like where's he going to live. Whether he's going back to Vietnam.'

Rockburn licked jam from the plate, nodded. 'Anything else?'

He looked up to find Hocking watching him. He put the plate down, beginning to understand about the girl. He was oil-smeared and wind-chapped. His hands were calloused, his body scarred and pitted from fisticuff arrests and spilling from motorbikes. Sarah-Jane was as clean and sweet-smelling as soap. He played darts and drank beer. The girl liked art and classical music. Also bore a scar. Hocking possibly her saviour. She'd dressed *his* wounds before, picked him up. He was rough, tough, licked his plate. The girl . . . was a girl.

'Not really,' said Hocking, looking down at Quang. 'He's told me a bit about his extended family. He's got lots of cousins, other aunts and uncles. All in all, he seems okay here. He loves being outside and digging his tunnel. He's polite, helpful. Yesterday he washed up, and today he's dug and peeled potatoes.'

On the floor Quang studied the instructions, then rummaged in the box of pieces. He pulled out more metal strips, matched them with the paperwork and laid them out. Doublechecked the instructions and set to work.

'He asks a lot about you, when you're coming back, when he can have another ride on your motorbike.'

Rockburn slipped down onto the floor and picked up the instructions for the winch. He remembered building it twenty years earlier.

'Can you help?' said Quang, passing Rockburn a metal strip with a nut and bolt in the wrong place. Rockburn fitted the wrench. The bolt was tight with age. He applied more pressure and it gave. The boy smiled and took the pieces back.

'Thank you,' said Hocking.

'Thank you,' said Quang.

Rockburn felt goosebumps on the back of his neck. He couldn't explain it, or maybe he didn't want to.

Slowly, the winch took shape. Rockburn loosened the odd nut, explained instruction 7B which two decades earlier had also left him guessing. They both agreed it was wrong. Outside the day faded out. Rockburn put a log in the wood burner. He'd wanted to give Quang the binoculars, but hadn't wanted to break his concentration. The vague recollection of afternoons in his own childhood when nothing mattered except homework for the next day.

In the future maybe –

He took out his phone and pulled up the photos of Zafira and his two henchmen. 'Do you recognise any of these people, Quang? Did Mina push one of their friends under the bus?'

The boy scrolled back and forth, then shook his head. 'They big.'

'The man who Mina pushed under a bus was small?'

Quang nodded.

The winch was done. There was a metal basket which could be hauled across rivers, or ravines or canyons. Rockburn helped Quang move furniture so the basket was strung between the mantelpiece and the coffee table. The boy transported a shipment of drawing pins, raisins, and loose change from Rockburn's pocket. Grenades, vital food supplies, and priceless jewels. Together Rockburn and Quang made up a story of a village encircled by bandits, a sick people and their efforts to escape. The vital role of the winch.

Rockburn carried mugs and plates out to the kitchen and grabbed a beer from the fridge. Only so much tea he could drink.

He heard someone unlock the front door.

Grabbed a knife from the block, silently set down the bottle.

'It's me!'

Recognising Sarah-Jane's voice, Rockburn relaxed. Returned the knife, picked up the beer. Listened to the girl enter the next room, greet Hocking and Quang. Kisses, hugs, chit-chat on the winch, then whispers.

She came into the kitchen, shut the door behind her. 'He's a really nice lad.'

Rockburn leant back against the sink, wondered what was coming.

'I know what it's like to be chased, to be hounded, to be hated for who or what you are.' She perched on a chair, her scarred side away from him. Then straightened, as if correcting herself. 'I was on a Pride march.'

'Was anyone arrested?'

Sarah-Jane shook her head.

Lowered her voice. 'A group of us were chased by a far-right gang; black clothing, facemasks, you know the sort. I turned down an alley, was cornered by one of them, thought it was going to be worse.'

Rockburn gripped the bottle tighter.

'He was only young. I got the feeling he felt he had to do something, had to leave his mark, couldn't return without a tale. He threw the acid and legged it.'

201

'Do you want a beer?'

The girl stood. 'I'm not stopping. Just came home to change.'
She opened the door to the hall. 'Hocking means a lot to me.'
She nodded at him, walked out.

Home.

He heard her climbing the stairs. He drained the bottle,
picked at the label. Everyone had a story, and not many were
good. Still scraping when the front door slammed.

Hocking entered the kitchen. 'S-J said she told you.'

'She did, poor girl.'

'She's not a girl – she's a woman and so am I. Perhaps you
never understood that. You always treated me like one of your
mates.'

'Sorry.'

He set the bottle by the trash.

Stood up.

Unsure, but –

'I want to ask you something.'

'What?'

He was a hard man on the street and in the custody suite; not
as hard as some, but harder than most. But in his grandparents' old
house, and in front of his former girlfriend who he'd loved –

and probably still did –

he felt like putty.

'When you were with me, were you pretending?'

'Of course not. I liked you, wanted you, Paul, loved you even.
But I had other feelings too, have always had. And when I
thought about the future, I wanted something different.'

Rockburn pulled on his leather jacket which was scuffed and
battered like him. It was as if Hocking had told him she was
moving to the moon. He fetched the binoculars. 'I brought these
for Quang. Maybe give them to him tomorrow.' He zipped up
his jacket.

The boy zoomed into the kitchen. 'Can you come and see this?' Seeing Rockburn in his leathers, he backed up. 'More bandits have arrived.'

The boy walked up slowly to the two of them, put out a hand and tentatively touched Rockburn's waist. He knelt down and the boy hugged him.

Rockburn glanced across at Hocking, who was dabbing her eyes.

He could hear the oven clock ticking, the bird feeder knocking against the kitchen window. Outside, the pale moon was hauling itself up into a dark sky.

Rockburn rode back to the throbbing spangled city, and to his dark silent flat. He enjoyed the ride, but not as much as usual. The boy might have been mistaken, or Zafira might have other men working for him. He tried to remember how many had followed him and Quang in the park. Three or four, but he wasn't certain.

As he picked up his darts he realised he'd forgotten to show Quang the photos of the comic novel in the bag of Flack's tattoo customer. It was an excuse to ride back out to see the boy the following day. He threw a few volleys of henhouse darts.

He kept throwing, darts landing all over the lid. Someone had killed Mina, even if it wasn't Zafira.

The street door buzzed.

Rockburn walked over to the intercom. 'Yes?'

'It's Jim Mackay.' He paused. 'I'm here in a personal capacity – I'd like to hire you.'

Rockburn hurled the darts at the board from twenty-five feet. All three thudded home. Maybe bracing Scarisbrick had worked.

27

The detective sergeant walked into Rockburn's flat wearing the same suit as in the police interview. He pushed the door shut behind him. His hair was ruffled, his tie loose, and he looked tired. The city ground everyone down, good and bad regardless.

'*You* want to hire *me*?'

'I think my wife's having an affair.' Mackay swivelled his watch but didn't check the time. 'In fact I know she is. But I'd like to know who with, and I'd like some proof.' He adjusted his watch again. It was too obvious a tell. The DS was trying to appear embarrassed or nervous, but Rockburn thought more likely, he was lying.

'Why don't you ask a colleague, or follow her around yourself?'

'Option one is out of the question.' Mackay looked over Rockburn's shoulder, surveying the multipurpose room. 'I could tail her, but I might do something I later regret. I'd prefer a third party.'

'Why me?'

Mackay shrugged. 'I don't know any other private investigators. I could look one up but I'd have to research them. I've already checked you out.'

'She's here in Manchester?'

Mackay nodded. 'Her idea to move down, I didnae want to come.'

Rockburn desperately needed clients, anyone who could pay a deposit and had an objective which he understood and could be achieved in the UK. But he smelt a rat. Three rats. Mackay's story was different to what Elsa had told him – the sergeant's request to relocate, not his wife's. In addition, not only was it against the police conduct code to meet yet alone hire a suspect you were investigating, but most officers would do the job themselves. Rockburn sensed an opportunity but needed more time to assess his potential second client.

Plus the possible conflict of interest with his first one, and his own best interests. 'Do you want a beer?'

'I don't drink.'

'Do you play darts?'

Mackay glanced across at the dartboard. 'No, lad. I mean I can play. Had a board in the common room at school.' His eyes narrowed. 'I heard you play a bit, laddie.'

'I'll throw one dart to your three. Three hundred and one, you don't even have to checkout with a double.'

Mackay took off his jacket and tucked his tie between the shirt buttons. 'You're on.' He was keen all of a sudden. Too keen. Rockburn handed him a set of his old sticks. Mackay flapped his elbow, rolled his shoulder forward and back, and threw a couple of practice rounds. Every arrow scored.

Like every serious or semi-serious player, Rockburn knew the maths. Eighty-four per cent chance of hitting a single, nine per cent a double, six per cent for a treble. One per cent for the bulls. A single averaged 10.5, a double 21, a treble 31.5. Which for a random scoring throw averaged 12.9. Three darts scored just under 39 – on average. So, if Mackay was as unpractised as he said, he would take twenty-three darts – eight throws – to reach zero. A few darts less to reach the point where he could checkout and win.

Rockburn averaged 66 for three darts, 22 a dart. Which meant it would take him eleven or twelve throws to reach a position he could checkout. He'd put himself under pressure from the start. He knew that, wanting to test himself.

They started off. Mackay's style was laborious and pernickety. He swung each dart forward and back, his stance taut and concave. Rockburn threw a single. Mackay returned to the mat: thirty seconds of limbering-up, then a three-dart dilly-dally. Versus Rockburn's rock-up-and-launch. They counted for themselves, doing the mental arithmetic and chalking the scoreboard.

'Do you play darts with every new client?' said Mackay, having taken an early lead.

Rockburn addressed the board, and threw a twenty. 'Only ones I don't think are new clients.' He marked up his score.

Mackay took his time, adjusting his stance, wiping the darts. He was taking the game seriously, too seriously. Rockburn blamed his loss of rhythm on throwing singles. Mackay reached two hundred and one.

The detective sergeant walked to the line.

'Most darts players like to have a wager on the result,' said Rockburn. 'Heightens the tension, gives the heart an extra little flutter.'

'How much?' said Mackay. He stepped away from the throwing line.

'It doesn't have to be money. Could be an object or a favour.'

'Like what?'

'Anything.'

'Hah!' Mackay tapped his finger with the dart points. 'Okay,' he said slowly. 'If I win, you let me have a spin on your motorbike.'

The panther was like a younger sister. If she let Rockburn down, he would forgive her. He spoilt her, not because she needed enhancing, but because he loved her. Letting her go out without him was a rarity – rat traps one such exception – and if he did, only if it was dry and on the understanding she had to be back before dark.

'Okay,' said Rockburn. The pressure would be good training.

'And supposing I lose?' said Mackay.

'I want – need – my diamonds back.'

'*Your* diamonds?'

'My client's. And I'm sure you would want me to do everything I possibly can for my clients.'

'Ha!'

'The stats are on your side,' said Rockburn, offering his hand.

The detective hesitated but shook. Then turned to the board and sashayed. Threw 8, 17, 19. Forty-four, reaching ninety-seven. He was scoring well above average. Rockburn threw treble top, leaving him one hundred and twenty-seven. He was closing.

'What makes you think your wife's cheating?'

'She's taken a couple of phone calls in the garden. She bought me a new tie and had an expensive haircut with highlights. She's started humming.'

Rockburn threw his dart and turned to face the sergeant. 'Not even circumstantial. You know that.'

'I know my wife, laddie.'

'Sex?'

'Better than usual. She's trying. She's feeling guilty. I know her.'

They reached the checkout stage of the game. Mackay needed seventeen, Rockburn thirty-four, double seventeen.

Checking out was where matches were won and lost. Like putting in golf – anyone could drive a golf ball from the tee, but few people could putt well and consistently. Allegedly, the common golf adage, drive for pleasure and putt for profit, had been pinned up inside Jack Nicklaus' locker at his home club. In darts, it was easy to score, but difficult to checkout – even if, for beginners like Mackay, they didn't require a double. Score for cornflakes, checkout to pay the mortgage, Rockburn's adaption for darts.

Mackay threw an eight, shilly-shallied and threw a one. The detective dried his hand on his trousers. He needed eight but threw a twenty. Busted.

Rockburn took the stand, trying not to think about the semifinal – the match balanced, the final leg, a winning position. His hand steady as an anvil, he threw double seventeen and pictured himself can-canning around the room.

Mackay handed Rockburn his darts, the points encased by his fingers. 'Will you take my case?'

'I think the traffickers who killed Mina travelled down from Glasgow. You've recently transferred from there. I'm an investigator, I don't like coincidences.'

'I get it, but they are possible. I first suspected my wife was cheating when we lived up there; she's a sales rep, goes away a lot. I confronted her and we had a massive row. After a couple of months of wrangling she suggested we move to Manchester, and try again. But I think moving suited her – I think he lives here. If I was involved in something, I'd hardly ask you to follow my wife round.'

'Wouldn't you? This gives you a chance to see what I'm up to, snoop round my flat.' Rockburn put his visitor's darts into their leather wallet, and shoved them on top of the cabinet holding the dartboard.

'I will take your case,' said Rockburn.

Mackay nodded. 'Thanks.'

Rockburn trusted the detective as far as he could throw him. But having him as a client was an easy way to keep tabs. 'But as agreed – I won the darts – you'll take my property out of the store safe and return it to me. Tomorrow morning, midday at the latest.'

'Technically, they belong to Jones.'

'Return them to him, then.'

'If I get caught, I'll lose my job.'

'You know as well as I do, I didn't kill Mina. It's only a matter of time before you cancel my bail and return them.'

Mackay took out a notebook and wrote down a name, a date of birth and an address. He ripped out the page, and together with a photo, handed them over.

Rockburn showed him out.

The photo showed a small woman with mousey hair. She was on a boat trip somewhere cold. She wore a pink duvet jacket and was trying to smile. Like any undercover legend, Mackay's story was elaborate and involved checkable facts. The Scot wasn't a typical UC, but could still appear to be doing one thing while doing another.

Rockburn took a beer from the fridge. He flipped off the lid, and took a swig. Stared out at the deserted yard, and beyond it, into the blur of the darkening city. By midnight the next day, he could be in the darts final and Quang could be safe. Or he could have lost and Quang anything but.

28

Waking with a prehistoric hunger, Rockburn headed out to the local café. Man couldn't live on cornflakes alone. He could survive without fruit and vegetables, but he needed bacon and eggs, and ideally someone else to cook and wash up afterwards.

The waitress with watery-blonde hair was locking the front door. 'We've had a power cut,' she said, as he walked up. She wore a yellow top and a tight red skirt. She was a reason to eat in the café and nowhere else – power cuts excepted. He'd have to pick up supplies from Mr Patel's on the corner and do it himself.

'You were in before.' The waitress glanced at the café window, as if she was looking back in time. She fiddled a card from the pocket of her white apron. 'Rockburn – private eye.'

He nodded.

An engineer's van pulled up at the kerb.

'And you play darts.'

He did. 'You play?' he said, keeping a straight face.

The waitress smiled as she assessed him, and then laughed. She flicked her hair, laughed some more.

The engineer climbed out of the van, grabbed a toolbox from the back. Unlocking the café door, the waitress turned to Rockburn, seemed about to say something, then disappeared inside.

Thirty minutes later, supplies bought at Patel's, he was still thinking about her. Bacon hissed in the pan and smelt good enough to wake the dead. Rockburn cracked three eggs to the side. He glanced at his watch, looked out of the window, but there was no sign of his second client.

Smelling burning, he popped the toaster: the thick white slices both looked okay. One day he'd empty the crumbs in the bottom. He slathered each piece with butter and marshalled the bacon and eggs on top. He wiped two slices of bread around the pan and sat down to eat.

No missed calls, no messages. He wondered if Mackay had had second thoughts, or had never intended to honour his side of the wager.

Even, the sergeant had been caught.

The smell of smoke persisted while he ate. Blaming the factory fire and a change of wind direction, Rockburn scrolled through his phone. Only an hour to go and still nothing from Mackay. He wasn't going to start surveilling the detective's wife until the Scot had fulfilled his side of the deal.

He phoned Hocking. She was okay, the boy was okay. She passed over the phone. Hocking had found an old bird book and Quang had so far identified a chaffinch and a robin with a bad leg. Later he was going to dig more of his tunnel.

'How are you?'

Rockburn smiled. He looked at his watch. Still no word from Mackay. He wiped his plate with a slice of bread, stood up. With or without the diamonds he was still due to meet Zafira at the rugby club that afternoon.

Shouting erupted in the yard. The smell of burning had thickened, and outside the window, smoke billowed.

Rockburn looked down at the yard. A dumpster he'd not seen before was on fire in the centre. Flames were leaping up. A firework exploded, then another. Rockets whizzed out. Bangs, flashes, coloured trails of sparks. Passersby with phones at the ready were edging up the alley to have a look.

Rockburn ran down the stairs, shouting at Flack as he passed the tattooist's door. He ran along the street to the chicken shop. Their fire extinguisher had been stolen. He asked next door in the vaping outlet. The interior smelt of blackcurrant; the girl behind the counter stopped scrolling her phone. She had one.

He ran back to the yard through the crowded alley.

Wearing a black leather waistcoat, Flack stood in the yard. The tattooist held up a bucket at Rockburn who brandished the extinguisher. A screaming rocket buzzed out of the dumpster making them duck.

He pulled the pin on the extinguisher and walked round the dumpster spraying white foam. The flames died down. He kept spraying. Clouds of smoke rose.

As a fire engine clanged nearby, he noticed a second fire was burning.

Under the fire escape an effigy half the size of a door hung down from the underside of the metal ladder. He walked closer with the extinguisher. Flames rippled along the intricate construction of wires. Pieces of soaked cloth wound around the frame provided the flames with fuel. He sprayed foam and stepped back.

The smoke cleared to reveal a man on a horse. A soldier, an ancient warrior, bearing a lance. The horse was rearing up, its front hooves poised. It would have taken many hours to construct. He glanced across at the foam-smothered dumpster. The two fires had to be linked, but one was senseless, the other a sign – for him, or for someone else?

Flack walked up.

'Does that image look familiar?' He took a couple of photos.

'The tattoo I did a couple of days ago.' Coughing, Flack

turned away. He hoiked and spat. Kept coughing. 'The Asian walk-in,' said the tattooist in a chopped-up voice.

'You okay?'

'It's the smoke.'

A fire engine, lights flashing and bells pealing, arrived on the service road. The sirens died away. Three firefighters in yellow overalls climbed down and jogged through the gate. A marked police car pulled into the yard. Two uniformed officers climbed out of the front, followed by Mackay from the back.

Rockburn's hopes rose.

The firefighters assessed the dumpster, one giving a thumbs-up to their colleagues in the cab, then spoke to the police. The crowd began to disperse back down the alley to the street.

Mackay walked over.

'You're on bail, Rockburn. I'll have to report this.'

'What about—?'

Mackay glanced round at his colleagues. Whispered: 'Not possible this morning, but I'll try again.'

Cursing silently, Rockburn checked on the panther.

The paperwork took an age but finally he and Flack were done. Ash still floated around, and the air, his clothes and his breath all smelt of smoke.

He mounted up. He was going to be late for his meeting with Zafira.

'You okay to clear up?'

The tattooist winked, hefted the extinguisher, and sprayed a jet of foam toward the departing vehicles. Rockburn fired the ignition, pulled down his visor, and roared out of the yard.

29

The trans-Pennine cleaved a route through sodden moorland. Dark, silent birds perched on stone walls sagged and twisted with the rake of time. Scraggy sheep sheltered in the shadows.

Hunkered down, Rockburn lined up excuses for why he was late and didn't have the diamonds. He'd been robbed on the way to the rugby club, bike-jacked at a set of traffic lights. A contact – nameless Mackay – whom he'd entrusted with their safekeeping had let him down. He could even tell the truth, that the police had them in custody.

He began the descent from the moor into Sheffield. The air was warmer, dirtier. The panther felt his mood, throbbing a reassuring soundtrack to his raggedy thoughts.

He reached the sign for the rugby club. He turned down the track, stopped ten metres from the road, and waited.

Two or three cars flashed past the entrance.

Reassured no one had followed him, he wheeled his bike into a copse of fir trees. A few metres across the pine-needle floor, it was as dark as a grave. He kicked out the panther's stand and left his helmet on the seat. He ripped off a couple of low-hanging branches, and returning to the spot where he'd left the track, covered over his tyre-marks.

Pulling up his hood he headed back through the trees towards the rugby pitches and the buildings. Branches pulled at his clothing.

At the edge of the copse, he stopped and crouched behind a tree. Security lights edged the car park, the clubhouse and the stand. The pitches were invisible in the gloom. There was only one vehicle in the car park.

He took out his night scope, focused. The car was a dark-coloured hatchback, and the registration plate confirmed it was Zafira.

The cardinal rule of a face-to-face was to arrive first, recce the escape routes and the dead ground, and watch how the opposition set up. Where they placed their men and their vehicles, even whether they were bickering or in good humour.

Arriving second, his only option was to watch the traffickers for a few minutes and hope to glean something of significance.

The car sat near a pool of yellowy light from a security lamp. Two figures were in the front seats. No movement inside the car, no tell-tale glow from a cigarette. No snippets of conversation escaped through the crack in the driver's window.

He waited five minutes.

No movement. No voices.

Rockburn backed up into the solid dark of the trees, and stood. He picked his way through the brushwood to the end of the copse. The back of the clubhouse was lit by security lights and appeared deserted. He scanned around with the scope.

Leaving the cover of the copse, he ran forward to a lone tree at the edge of the car park. No one shouted, and the car doors didn't open.

He picked up a stone. Waited for a minute, then hurled it at the car. It struck the rear bumper. Still there was no reaction.

Moving out from behind the tree, he climbed over the barrier to the car park, and walked up to the back of the hatchback. The men inside were some of the most unobservant people on the planet or had fallen asleep.

He checked all around but there was no one. In the distance, a dog was barking. City lights of Sheffield leaked into the sky.

There was a third possibility. He knew that. He slipped on gloves, and sensing a trap, checked all round again. He rapped on the window behind the driver's door and drew back. He stepped forward and bent to the driver's window.

The driver sat slewed towards his door. The passenger a mirror image. The same men from two days earlier.

He opened the door.

The interior light flared:

The driver slumped down. Eyes unfocused, staring, a bead of blood running down his nose. Rockburn twisted the man's wrist and felt for a pulse. His skin felt warm. But would soon be cold.

Rockburn looked all round, his ticker thumping. The assailants wouldn't be too far away. He surveilled again with his night scope. Nothing held his attention. He walked around the car, opened the passenger door, felt the man's wrist.

Two dead traffickers.

No obvious injuries to either man. No blood, except for the trickle from the driver's nose. Rockburn bent down the passenger's shirt collar. Just above the Adam's apple a deep indentation circled the neck, brown in colour and flanked by narrow red staining. No raised imprint caused by hanging. A thin ligature, possibly a wire.

The dashboard was clear. Wedged between the front seats nestled a large box of toffee popcorn. Open, half-eaten. Sugary fragments littered the footwell. A Scottish newspaper lay on the backseat. Rockburn opened the glove compartment. Chocolate bars, crisps. He felt the passenger's pockets, and extricated a thin wallet. It held a black and white photo of an old couple sitting on a rock, a hundred and thirty-five pounds in cash including two Scottish banknotes. A plaster.

Rockburn shut the door, and looking all round, walked back

to the driver. A similar mark encircled his neck. He searched the man's pockets. No wallet. A packet of tissues, a button, two house keys. Rockburn checked the footwells and under the seats.

He checked the boot. A spade lay at the front. Behind it sat two holdalls, one blue, one brown and a supermarket carrier bag. The blue holdall contained boxes of forensic gloves, overshoes, suits. The brown, duct tape, rope, plasticuffs, a hood. The plastic bag, bottles of water, sandwiches, crisps, apples. The sandwiches were a few days old. He clicked the boot shut.

Kidnap kit. But no car keys, no phones, no identification. For the boy?

Or him?

He stilled, checked all around. He could hear his own breathing, could see his chest rise up and down – long may it continue.

He took half a dozen photos and hurried away.

The gate to the service road was padlocked. He climbed over, walked a few metres along the track before veering onto the practice field. He detoured around in a wide arc keeping well outside the reach of the security lights. The ground was muddy. At the edge of the practice area he continued curving round until he stood on the far side of the main pitch and the supporters' stand.

Under the tiered seating, where he'd spoken to Zafira the first time, the strip lights blazed. The tractor and grass-cutting equipment stood at the end. Silent witnesses. Two plastic chairs were set out in similar if not identical positions to forty-eight hours earlier. An Asian man sat on one seat, the second was empty. The man looked like Zafira. He wasn't moving.

Rockburn waited in the darkness.

A vehicle went past on the trans-Pennine, the engine noise rising, and fading away again. A siren wailed in the distance, then fell silent.

He moved forward, his senses taut. He looked around for a weapon, picked up a half-brick.

He reached the edge of the white light. No one challenged him, no one shouted, no one appeared. He walked forward, his boots crunching on the gritty concrete.

The man sat slumped back. Pressed trousers, pointed leather shoes, cream jacket. Zafira's shiny black hair was ruffled, his face blank and lifeless. One ear was bruised and swollen. Rockburn checked for a pulse, but there was none. Hearing a noise, he whirled around.

No one.

Blamed mice, or rats.

A thin purple groove marked Zafira's neck. Death by strangulation, the same as the two traffickers in the car. Rockburn patted him down but found nothing. No weapon, no phone, no identification. He stepped back.

There was a chalk drawing on the floor near Zafira's legs. It depicted a charging horseman brandishing a lance. The horse was rearing up to show the underside of its front hooves. The lance and the horse's eyes and hooves were shaded white. Rockburn snapped a couple of photos on his phone, then took some of the dead man and the ligature marks.

After a last look around, he retreated across the practice area towards the waiting panther. The lights of Sheffield beckoned.

30

The Black Dog was a tiny pub in one of its backstreets. It served local beer and traditional food, and hoped never to feature in an online guide. Flack said if he ever retired, he'd consider taking a part-time job. The windows were misted with condensation, and inside it was warm and smelt of the deep fat fryer. Half a dozen customers, one at the slot machine and the others at a table in the corner. The dartboard was unattended.

Rockburn bought a whisky and asked to borrow a set of arrows. He gripped his glass and circled the rust-coloured contents. No longer did he need the diamonds on the hurry up. They would be returned to him when he was eventually cleared for Mina's murder. He trusted the process – once, he *was* the process.

Rockburn downed the whisky. It bit the back of his throat, and fired his insides. Questions came at him like fiends.

He ordered another, walked over to the board. Lined up on the oche, decided on Round The Clock. A kid's game; the first game to teach Quang.

Threw 1, 18, 18.

Started again. Threw 1, 1.

Restarted. Threw 1, 18, 4. Better. Had the same people who'd killed Zafira and his henchmen, murdered Mina? It was the same MO and would explain why the boy hadn't recognised the photos of the traffickers on Rockburn's phone.

The barman brought the whisky. Rockburn drank it while he waited, handed back the glass. Resumed play. What did Zafira's killers want? Threw 13, 6, 6.

Back to the start. Threw 1, 18, 4. He collected the sticks, walked back. Threw 13, 6, 10. The horseman was key. Three times he'd seen it: Flack's customer, the burning effigy, and the chalk drawing on the stadium floor.

Kept throwing. Aware, the customers and the barman of the Black Dog were watching. He had no answers, and only one conclusion: the boy wasn't safe.

Nor was Hocking.

Outside, standing in the cold air, he phoned her. Told her to pack an overnight bag for her and Quang, to get into the car, and drive to Caiges. To leave immediately, to use the back roads. Flack and his boys would meet her there. They'd be safe in the midst of hundreds of people.

'What about after the match?'

'A hotel, maybe, just for a few days.'

'And then?'

'I'll work it out, but you need to leave – now.'

He phoned Flack, asked him to meet Hocking at Caiges, to safeguard Quang until after the match. To take a couple of the boys with him.

The tattooist began a reply, coughed to silence. Tried again. 'Got it,' he wheezed.

Rockburn pocketed the phone, returned into the saloon. Realised he was still holding two arrows.

He threw a 5.

Last throw of the darts. Double 20, always had to finish on a double.

He threw too high, landing in the gutter. Grabbing his helmet, he shoved out into the night. He wasn't ready for the semifinal, and he felt powerless to protect the boy.

31

The final two rounds of the North West Cup were always played at Caiges Academy. A hexagonal-shaped brick building on a roundabout north of the city. During the day it looked like a prison, but midway through the afternoon, the searchlights on the roof were switched on, and staff and fans began arriving. A venue predominantly for pop concerts and stand ups, Caiges offered standing room for a thousand or seating for five hundred. As a sport, darts felt like it should have the former, but Cup rules stated it must have the latter. The last comedian to appear at the Academy had wagged a mixture was too complex.

At six-thirty, a queue of darts fans ran across the front of the building and along the pavement for fifty metres. Doors opened at seven, the semifinal kicking off at eight. Marshalls walked back and forth along the line of supporters. A burger van had parked opposite and a steady trickle crossed back and forth across the road. The smell of frying onions, a hum of chatter.

Rockburn drifted up and down the surrounding backstreets but couldn't see anything untoward. No one parked up in a van, no one loitering. He returned to the front, lapped the roundabout and pulled up near a programme seller. Removed his helmet.

'Sal!'

She walked over to him, her baby in a papoose on her chest.

Wearing a tiny blue hat he stared out, eyes brighter than his mother's.

'How was the doc?'

'Prescription, you know. You want a programme?'

Rockburn paid with a twenty, refused his change. Sal looked down at her baby, stroked his head. 'I should know his name, now I'm his—'

'His name's Paul.'

Rockburn's heart flamed. He would make sure he went to school, help him avoid the traps that had snared his mother.

She leant over and pecked Rockburn on the cheek. 'Good luck.' She walked back to the line of punters. 'Programmes, programmes –'

Rockburn puttered forward.

Two-times winner Redeye Reynard was his opponent. He scored heavily and consistently, and checked out as if he was late for his daughter's wedding. One supposed weakness – wobbled if the score was tight. Rockburn was a newcomer, never having made the knockout stage of the competition. The bookies held him as a 10-1 outsider.

He showed his driving licence to a marshal. A lad with long ginger hair swept over to one side.

'You going to win?' The youth stroked his hair.

'What do you think?'

A wisp of a smile. 'No.' The youth turned and pointed. 'Parking's round the back, follow the signs.'

Rockburn throttled slowly past the queue, recognising no one apart from Sal. Halfway along, he turned the panther into a side-road and rode around the back of the Academy. He parked in a hatched area with the other bikes. Flack's three-wheeler stood at the end, and between them were five mopeds with similar registration plates. Reading number plates was a habit from the police which he couldn't drop.

He walked towards the entrance at the back of Caiges, past the rows of cars. Recognising the number plate of a small red runaround, he stopped and peered through a window. The binoculars he'd given Quang lay on the backseat.

After showing his licence twice more, Rockburn was allowed inside the Academy and shown to a reception room. There was a sofa and a low table with a fan of magazines – *Darts Illustrated, Bullseye, Playboy*. A tray of soft drinks and a packet of peanuts waited on the side. Warm air gushed in through a vent. He could hear a dull thump of pop music and the buzz of the crowd. He took off his jacket.

The room was too hot – his fingers already felt oily. He should limber up, swing his arms, throw some darts.

He phoned Hocking.

'You okay?'

'We got here.' She paused. 'Flack met us in the foyer, and has assigned a few of his mates. They're at the end of the row. Sarah-Jane's here too, sitting the other side of Quang.'

'The more eyes the better. How is he?'

'Can't sit still. He's so excited I don't think he's aware of anything wrong. Are you going to come and say hello?'

'Better I don't. It might put him – both of you – in danger.' It was possible he was being watched.

Hocking didn't reply immediately, Rockburn hearing only the voice of an excited crowd in the background.

Finally:

'What about afterwards?'

'Stay behind, I'll come and find you.' He pulled out his phone, scrolled through the images, forwarded a couple to her. 'I've just sent you photos of a book I want Quang to have a look at.' He waited, listening to more crowd noise, boozy cheers for Redeye Reynard, not a single shout for him.

'Hello, Rockburn.' Quang's voice, high pitched, tentative.

The boy had sensed something was wrong, but was trying not to show it.

'Hello, Quang.' In different circumstances, he'd have been buoyed by the boy and Hocking's presence. As it was, he was as apprehensive as them.

'You win?'

'I hope.'

'Me too.'

'Thank you. The photos of the book I sent to Hocking – can you read what it says on the cover?'

'Easy. It say The Red Village.'

'Vietnamese?'

'Yes!'

Hocking returned on the line. 'Anything else?' Her tone concerned but trying not to be. Rockburn knew her better than anyone, but still there were things about her he hadn't known. He would never have guessed about the girl.

'Look after him.' He paused, took a deep breath. 'Both of you.'

He set down the phone, picked up a bottle of water. Drank, clicked out his greasy fingers. Knew he shouldn't have drunk the whisky. Standing up, he mechanically turned a few pages of *Bullseye*, but his senses remained with Quang and Hocking, and the boy's unknown pursuers.

The comic book was Vietnamese; Mina had been killed with a metal noose, a weapon favoured by the Viet Cong. The link made him wonder if Quang and Mina had been followed from Vietnam, despite their protracted journey. The boy had said he was special, but not mentioned a reason. A Vietnamese prince? A king, even. Rockburn needed to ask Quang, but face to face so he could coax the boy into telling.

He wasn't sure if Vietnam even had a royal dynasty. He picked up his phone, tapped the internet, began to search.

There was a knock on the door.

Flack walked in. 'I've spoken to Hocking, told a couple of the boys to watch her. The rest are in a boozer, but they're coming.' The tattooist started coughing, took out a red bandana to cover his mouth. It sounded painful. 'Are you ready?'

'Not really.' He opened the packet of peanuts, ate a handful. 'I can't go and see them because whoever killed Zafira might be watching me.' He kicked a peanut across the carpet. 'You should probably stay away from them too – you're more distinctive than the Kraken.'

The tattooist dummied a punch, shook out his long hair, grinned with gaping teeth.

They knocked fists, and Flack left.

Rockburn pocketed the peanuts to give to Quang later. He washed his hands and dried the fingers individually. They were capable of expressions of camaraderie; also finesse, precision, delicacy, of art and lifesaving surgery. Equally, they were capable of V-signs; also of bluntness, massive force, repetition, of cruelty and life-taking savagery.

The domed hall throbbed with pop music and was as hot as a greenhouse. At the centre of the stage spotlights focused on the playing area, and at the front two large screens showed close-ups of the dartboard. A table with a jug of water and two chairs stood to the side.

Rockburn necked a glass of water and surveyed the crowd. Half of them were standing up, some on their seats. Flack and his boys including Fat Man sat halfway down to one side. Banners revealed fanatical support for Redeye. He couldn't see Hocking or Quang.

He phoned her, then Flack, but neither answered. He sent them both a message.

Felt a heavy stone in his stomach. Maybe he shouldn't play.

More people were entering, and Rockburn kept looking. He

spotted the new waitress with blonde hair from the café. As she checked her ticket she was overtaken by a surge of spectators, and when he looked again, she was gone. He thought he'd seen her. It felt like a good omen. Flack would know. The tattooist knew about omens.

Rockburn felt nervous, his mind flickering: the waitress – Flack – Hocking and Sarah-Jane – Quang.

He imagined a candle.

Concentrated on the flame.

The white core, the peace of church, the heat of civilisation. Purity. Silence.

Double top.

The first dart . . .

The music faded, and a commentator wearing black tie lolloped onto the stage. He told a couple of jokes and introduced the players. Rockburn was hardly listening. The lights in the auditorium dimmed making it harder to observe the crowd.

'Standard PDC rules. Five hundred-and-one, three sets, each the best of seven legs. Darts please.'

Rockburn lost the toss, and Reynard addressed the board. The room quietened. Reynard threw a ton-forty, and his supporters clapped and stamped on their seats.

Rockburn walked up, and replied with forty-five. There were a couple of boos. He scanned the seats.

Reynard threw tons and ton-forties, and needing one hundred and fifty-seven, checked out with a perfect triple-top, triple nineteen, double top. The room erupted, his supporters running up and down the steps at each side of the seating. Rockburn lost the next three games as he continued to survey the crowd for Hocking and Quang. He divided the spectators into sections, and when he wasn't throwing, he scanned the faces.

One set down in twenty-seven minutes. A Caiges record, boomed the commentator.

There was a short break. Reynard signed a few autographs at the edge of the stage while two bouncers with ponytails watched his back. Rockburn poured a glass of water and stared at the crowd. He held a hand to his forehead like a man at sea.

Rockburn 4 President. A placard for the underdog, for him. Holding it was Max, Flack's deputy, standing with the tattooist and the Demons. Big men in leathers and shaggy haircuts.

Reynard scored heavily in the first game of the second leg but Rockburn kept level. Redeye fluffed a double ten checkout, then a double five. Rockburn needed thirty-seven. He threw seventeen and nailed the double ten.

His face felt as hot as a stove. He drank more water and stripped to a t-shirt. His stomach was roiling. He'd felt like this before, knew something bad was going to happen. Hoped it was the darts.

He went ahead in the third game but lost. The crowd shouted and wolf-whistled. A bra was thrown onto the stage. Reynard held it up against his torso and hung it on the back of his chair. A woman at the front screamed like an orangutan.

Rockburn made an excuse and went backstage for a toilet break. He phoned and messaged Hocking, but still there was no response. Maybe the crowd was too loud to hear it ring. He washed his face in cold water and returned to the stage.

He worked his darts. He visualised scoring heavily. He scored heavily. He checked out from 150, 144, and 128, to win the second leg. One each, the decider after a twenty-minute interval.

Flack walked into his changing room. He lit up a cigar, the room instantly reeking. They both glanced at the *No Smoking* sign on the wall. The tattooist bent double, coughed violently. Slowly he straightened, yanked his belt.

'Dibble have turned up. The black woman and the Scot. They want to talk to you about the bodies at the rugby club. I told them to wait 'til after. Said there'd be a rumpus if they didn't.'

Rockburn took the cigar from Flack and took a puff. It tasted worse than he'd imagined, a nasty mix of bonfire and liquorice. He handed it back. He felt even hotter, achey, as if he was going down with something. At least if the police were present, it would be less likely for anything to happen to Hocking and the boy.

'Leave you to it,' said Flack, taking back his cigar.

Rockburn caught the door. He flapped it back and forth and propped it open. Stripped off his t-shirt and doused his upper body in cold water. He drank a glassful and returned to the stage for the deciding set.

The air in the auditorium felt like a tropical rain forest.

Reynard won the first game. Rockburn plunged his hands in the jug of iced water. Redeye's supporters jeered. Rockburn won the second game, finishing with a bullseye. His opponent clapped in slow motion. Rockburn looked out into the sea of faces.

He spotted them.

Rockburn Rocks. Holding the sign was Quang, and next to him sat Hocking. They were three rows from the back. No sign of the girl.

The third game went to the wire: Redeye needed double seven with his one remaining dart and Rockburn needed double thirteen if his opponent failed. Redeye didn't miss. At the top of the auditorium, in the row behind Hocking and Quang, people stood and shuffled around. Rockburn tried to observe. His turn to throw. A dart slipped out of his grasp. He looked up again, but people were now standing in the back rows. Everyone was standing up.

A commotion at the side, near where Flack and his boys had grouped. Security high-vis jackets were in attendance.

The match stuttered forward, the room unsettled as a pop festival. Shouting, cat-calls, jumping about. Rockburn could only think about one thing: the safety of Quang.

One set all, three legs all, the deciding game.

Rockburn opened up with a salvo of eighty-five. Reynard replied with a hundred and twenty. Rockburn took the stand, thinking *Darts Weekly* was wrong about Redeye falling apart under pressure. He should write a letter. Instead, he threw sixty, sixty, twenty. Stole a glance through the bright lights into the crowd. Quang's placard bobbed up and down. Even Hocking was on her feet.

Reynard needed seventy-three, Rockburn one hundred and nineteen. His to lose. He addressed the court. He wiped his hands, back-and-forthed the first dart. Licked the tip. He prayed to God and the Holy Ghost. He threw nineteen. The room quietened for the first time that evening. He could hear the commentator's breathing on the Tannoy.

Rockburn threw. The dart scraped in alongside the wire dividing triple twenty from triple one. The camera zoomed in for a close-up, but Rockburn knew. Triple twenty. He turned, and saw movement where Hocking and the boy were sitting. Everyone around them was standing, pushing and shoving. He couldn't see them.

One dart left.

Reynard blew him a kiss.

Rockburn swapped the dart to his left hand, wiped his fingers, swapped back. He took a breath, and threw. The dart was a good one. Spiralling slightly it flew in a near-perfect trajectory and thudded into the top of the board.

Double twenty.

The room turned upside down. Fighting broke out on the steps at the side of the seating. The commentator called for calm. Security guards climbed onto the stage and ushered the players into a wing. Elsa and Mackay appeared, followed by Flack's deputy Max. The two police officers stopped to show their warrant cards to a guard. Max lumbered across the stage.

A fire alarm sounded.

As a distraction?

Rockburn was powerless to prevent himself being caught in the melee which pushed forward to the backstairs. Like water pouring into a plughole, they all streamed down – officials, players, hangers on.

Pat the burly Irish promoter led Rockburn to his changing room. A bouncer followed, and Pat shut the door. He produced an envelope.

'Good craic tonight.'

Rockburn nodded and signed for his winnings.

The door bowled open. Max stood on the threshold, and a few metres behind him, Elsa and Mackay. Pat and the bouncer slipped out. Max slammed the door and pulled the bolt. Rockburn shoved the sofa alongside.

'Are Hocking and Quang okay?'

Max shook his head. 'No idea. Flack collapsed, coughed blood everywhere. We had to carry him out. The rest of the boys have gone with him. Bedlam when I came back in.'

'Is he okay?'

Max shrugged. 'Final station, I think.'

Rockburn phoned Hocking, but still she didn't answer. He needed to find her, and the boy, confirm they were okay, then get to the hospital. But if he stayed, he'd be arrested and unable to do anything.

The door reverberated from banging.

'Police.'

'What do you want me to do?' said Max.

'Keep them out until I've gone. Then search the building for Hocking and the young Vietnamese boy.'

231

Rockburn entered the bathroom. 'Message me soon as you've got anything.'

Flack's deputy nodded.

Rockburn shut the door. Behind him he could hear Mackay and Elsa shouting in the corridor. He opened the window and climbed out into the cold air. A gutter was dripping. He could hear the distant clatter of the alarm and the faint sound of voices.

He eased the window shut and slipped on his jacket. Checked he still had the envelope. He slalomed around a couple of temporary sheds to the edge of the car park. Supporters were thronging across. Pushing up his collar, he headed for Hocking's car.

Angry shouting erupted at the exit. A white van screeched out of the car park followed by a bunch of mopeds. A bottle smashed in the road.

Rockburn broke into a run. He stopped at Hocking's car. The tyres were flat – slashed. He ran on to the panther. The rear tyre sagged. Squatting down he found puncture marks from a knife, the tyre bouncy as a balloon. He mounted, fired her up, and wheeled round. He stopped at the exit and made enquiries with people streaming out. No one had seen or heard anything, no one knew anything. It had always been the same, would always be the same.

He rode out of the car park to the roundabout. He circled twice, the bike slewing from side to side. No sign or sound of the van or the mopeds. He slammed down his visor and gunned away, the bike sliding around like a wet fish.

Unrideable.

But he couldn't give up. Couldn't wait until the morning.

He rode to the nearest petrol station, parked by the air machine. Grabbed his tyre repair kit from under the seat. He unscrewed the valve cap from the rear tyre, removed the valve core. He attached the short, clear tube to the valve, and holding the bottle of emergency sealant upside down, injected the contents into the tyre. He removed the tube, replaced the valve core. He slotted coins into the air compressor, set it going, and pumped up the tyre. Trusted the sealant would locate the puncture and make good. A modern miracle.

The machine signalled the tyre was ready.

Not before time.

He zipped out of the garage and returned to the silvery backstreets around Caiges. Searched up and down, round and round, up and down, round and round, the search area slowly increasing. Stopped a couple of times to phone Hocking, but there was no reply.

At ten past midnight, his phone buzzed in his sleeve pocket. She was crying, her words garbled, but he knew what she was trying to say – they'd snatched Quang.

'Where are you?'

She sniffed, took a breath. 'The café in the twenty-four-hour supermarket.'

'Don't move.'

Rockburn stuffed the phone away. Pulled down his visor, revved the throttle and pulled away, the panther's back wheel spitting gravel.

32

The supermarket was the size of a football field. Rockburn parked the damaged panther in the motorcycle bay, and jogged inside.

Forty checkout tills, towering shelves of produce. Two people in the café, a member of staff doing a puzzle, and Hocking.

Rockburn hugged her, his former girlfriend feeling cold and shaky.

'They stole my phone, had to use hers.' She nodded at the woman sitting in the corner. 'Just had to get away from there.'

He bought large mugs of tea and a packet of doughnuts. Added sugar to one cup and plonked it down in front of Hocking. He sat down opposite her, opened the buns, pushed them across the table.

'Tell me.'

Gripping her mug, Hocking told him there'd been four or five of them. Young, skinny, not big, south-east Asian looking. One woman. They wore small backpacks; one carried a book and wore John Lennon glasses. They reminded her of students or radical types. They swarmed around the two of them when the darts match was drawing to a close. They showed the book to Quang, a couple of the pages, some of the pictures; Hocking couldn't really see. Ancient soldiers, maybe. Then everyone was standing up and shouting and a scuffle broke out at the end of the row. No sign of Flack or his boys. Found herself pushed down onto her seat, her arms pinioned. A dosed cloth shoved under her nose. She lost consciousness, and when she came to, Quang was gone. Her bag still lay at her feet, but her car keys and phone had been stolen.

He told her to eat something, and to drink the tea. Told her about Flack, said he wanted to call the hospital.

At the window, he phoned. The panther sat waiting. He'd liked to have changed her tyre, checked the oil. If she'd been a horse, he would have given her a bucket of water, and a net of hay. The operator came on the line, asked if he was family. Rockburn said he was a brother, waited while he was transferred to the ICU. A carrot or two.

A nurse answered. 'We're running tests, Mr Flack. Is your brother seeing a specialist?'

'I'm not sure,' said Rockburn. 'I think so.'

'What's his date of birth?'

'I can't remember. December?'

'I'm sorry, Mr Flack, you'll have to come in.'

Birthdays, anniversaries, presents, weren't his thing. Perhaps they should have been. Perhaps they still could be. Hocking's birthday was in June – or July. Quang was ten – just ten or almost eleven?

Sitting back down, he updated Hocking. He ate a couple of the doughnuts, suddenly ravenous.

Hocking sipped her tea. She pulled off a piece of bun, chewed slowly. She still looked pale.

'Why did they take Quang?'

Rockburn shook his head. He swiped through the photos on his phone to the one of the horseman. Swivelled the screen round to face her. 'Does that mean anything to you?'

'It looks a bit like one of the drawings in Richard's book.'

'Who's Richard?'

'He's a professor at the university. I met him when I was doing my MA, and we still have dinner occasionally.'

'I didn't know that.'

'I had a life before you, Rockburn.'

And after, he thought.

She tore another lump from the doughnut, jam oozing onto the packet. 'He teaches anthropology, specialises in the mythology and religions of developing countries.' She pushed the chunk into her mouth.

'Have you mentioned Quang to him?'

'I'm not sure. He did phone a couple of days ago.'

'About what?'

'You're frightening me now. Do you think he's involved?'

Rockburn shrugged. 'Do you?'

Then:

'Think, Rebecca.'

She looked up sharply. '*I'm trying.*' Behind her, a night worker with EarPods walked into the café and ordered a hot chocolate.

'What happened to the girl?'

'Her name's Sarah-Jane.'

'Do you trust her?'

'One hundred per cent. I've known S-J since school. She was with us at Caiges but had to go after an hour; had to meet her mum.'

Rockburn nodded. 'Alright, I'm sorry.' But there were so many loose ends. If he'd still been in the Job, he'd have run a check on both the professor and the girl.

Hocking spoke as if she'd been reading his mind. 'Do you think we should tell the police? I'm scared, Rockburn, scared for what they might do to Quang.'

'Makes two of us.'

*

After checking the panther's rear tyre, he gave Hocking a lift home. Said he'd sleep on the sofa. When she went upstairs, he grabbed a beer from the fridge and paced around. Opened a few cupboards in the kitchen, found an old packet of cornflakes. A relic of their time together, the best before long gone, but would have to do.

Needed to think.

He threw some imaginary arrows.

Drank the beer, ate some cornflakes. He'd won the darts, he'd won the bloody darts. He'd made the final of the North West Cup.

He replayed the last game, his last throw. Images of the crowd came back to him, a man with a native Indian headdress, three men with Redeye rubber masks, a hen night party dressed in sequins. He rewound to sitting in the reception room at Caiges, talking to Flack. The tattooist coughing – coughing badly. He rewound further to arriving at Caiges, strumming into the car park. Seeing Hocking's tiny red car, and before that, the line of mopeds with near identical registration plates.

He grabbed more cornflakes. Three reasons for similar reg plates: they were false, they'd been bought at the same time from the same place, or they were hire vehicles. He ate a solitary cornflake. If the number plates were false, they would be randomly false and completely different. He ate another cornflake, then started tapping on his phone. Still no messages. He searched the internet. There were sixteen garages and showrooms in Greater Manchester which sold mopeds. Twenty-three companies which hired mopeds. Three of the rentals operated at the airport.

The mopeds could have been bought or hired in Cheshire or Liverpool, or Glasgow, or even online. But he had to start somewhere.

He drained the beer.

Airport franchises opened early.

33

Rockburn rode to Killer Servicing in the purple haze of pre-dawn. The sliding doors were closed, secured with a meaty padlock. He was thinking about breaking in when Dave arrived at the wheel of a tow-truck.

The mechanic climbed out wearing grimy overalls, his hands already oily. He unclipped the lock and drew the doors across. Daylight streamed into the gloom; a rat scuttled out.

A red Astra occupied the left bay, the central bay was clear, and a resprayed post office van covered the pit. Dave dumped the mulch from the coffee machine in a sack, and refilled it with water. He poured in enough grounds for an autobahn truck stop and switched it on. The machine pulsed. Dave turned his baseball cap around, humming quietly to himself.

'Heard you beat Redeye.'

Rockburn nodded.

The mechanic set the panther on a stand in the middle bay and jacked it up. 'And there was a bit of a to-do.' He inspected the slashed tyre and scowled as if he'd nurtured it from a junior tread. He glanced at the labouring coffee machine. 'Help yourself.'

Dave removed the damaged tyre and found a replacement. He asked about Flack. Said he was a godhead to a lot of local people. They visited the tattooist for advice on all sorts – how to deal with stoned neighbours, or debt collectors; harassment from local kids, or from your own kids. Said there was no charge – Rockburn was a friend of Flack, and he owed Flack. Everyone owed Flack.

Rockburn said it was okay and passed over a fold of banknotes from the envelope. *Two thousand pounds*; he could afford it, and to pay a couple of bills. Even, take someone out to dinner. Dave stuffed them into a pocket and poured coffee into mugs with broken handles. He added doses of whisky from a quart bottle as Rockburn told him about the kidnap of the boy.

'To getting the fuckers,' said the mechanic, handing Rockburn a mug.

Rockburn downed the filthy fluid, readying himself for the burn, and when it came, closed his eyes and saw flashes of Quang's face amongst red and gold stars.

Time ticked as loud as a Second World War bomb.

Rockburn gunned out to the airport, and followed the signs for car hire. With its new tyre, the bike ran true as a pinball.

Repairing the panther had taken too long. He thought of Pricha Kuri at Redville, tied to the pipe and naked from the waist down. He saw Quang, cowering in a corner. He was coming, Quang.

We're coming.

The car hire section of the concourse looked busy. Passengers queued at every desk while their bored families sat on suitcases and children rampaged. A discarded ice cream melted across the floor. Two police officers wearing body armour and carrying MP5 assault rifles patrolled through. Rockburn kept his distance.

Three companies hired mopeds: Jake's Rentals, Speedy Hire, and Glitz.

He slalomed around people and luggage, pushed through

queues, and approached the counter of Speedy Hire. They were busy as a chip shop on Friday lunchtime. He waited, listening to three staff explain terms and conditions, detail petrol options, badger customers into insurance. Watched them photocopy, staple, and finally hand out keys.

A woman appeared from the back office. 'Yes, sir?' She wore a white blouse with lacy cuffs and a manager's badge. She was at least fifty, and the lines on her face said she'd seen everything. The ideal franchise manager.

'My name's Rockburn. I'm a private investigator.' He laid down a card.

The woman picked it up.

'Can you tell me if you've hired five mopeds in a single booking, last six months?'

'We haven't. Company policy is a maximum of four in one booking, my policy is two. Too much trouble otherwise: racing, tricks, stag weekends, we've seen it all.' She handed back his card. Her long fingers had perfect buffed crescents.

Rockburn nodded his thanks, and turned to go.

'Mr Rockburn.' He turned back. 'Only two other companies along here do mopeds. Glitz have the same policy as us for group bookings. But try Jake's, they hire to all sorts. They employ all sorts.'

Rockburn raised a thumb.

Jake's Rentals was the last desk. The R was missing from their sign and the tall pot plant had withered and died. A monitor was alternating between hire deals and comedy clips with histrionic laughter. There were three terminals, people queued at all of them. He hovered nearby, and when one passenger finished, stepped forward.

'Rockburn, private investigator.' He laid down a card. 'Can you tell me if you've hired five mopeds in a single booking, last six months?'

'Mike!' shouted the teller.

A thin man walked over, his shoes tip-tapping. 'Can I help you, I'm the bookings manager.'

Rockburn explained a second time, already knowing the answer would contain the words head office / policy / is there anything else. He waited, listened, picked up his card and tapped it on its sides, each time letting it fall loosely through his fingers before tapping again.

The answer began . . .

Rockburn grabbed a pen from a pot on the desk and threw it at the man's face. Picked up the pot and hurled the lot. Machine gun darts.

Giving up on the front desks, Rockburn jogged through the concourse towards the multistorey. Past the left luggage and a machine which cling-filmed your bag. He took the lift and ran across a gangway to the car hire satellite offices. Overhead signs and coloured bays signified the different companies. Jake's was on the top floor.

He climbed a broken escalator, helped a woman down with her pushchair. He ran back up, and found the cubicle for Jake's. A second attempt required stronger tactics. The door was propped open and a small, yellow-shirted man stood behind a high counter, studying a clipboard. The man looked up.

And his face fell.

'Sam Pence,' said Rockburn.

'I ain't done nothing.' Pence's face squeezed and he took a breath. 'That's the God's.'

Rockburn poured a beaker of water from the dispenser and drank it slowly. Pence was a petty criminal with form for every section of the 1968 Theft Act. There was no way Jake's would have employed him if they'd known the truth – even if they did employ all sorts. He crushed the beaker and tossed it in the basket. 'Need you to check your records, Sam.'

'And if I do, you won't tell no one?'

Rockburn shook his head. Explained for the third time.

Pence tapped one-fingered on a computer. 'We've got twenty of them hairdryers because three or four are always knackered, always going for repairs. Never done a five hire.' He fingered the wheel on the mouse. 'But someone has. Three weeks ago.'

'Customer's name?'

'Says here Ho Dong. Or Dong Ho.'

'Is there an address for where they're staying?'

Pence looked up, his lips oddly puckered. He lit a cigarette. 'They done a job with the dryers?' He snickered, suddenly in good humour.

Rockburn walked over to the water dispenser. He turned the tap so water poured out. It filled the overflow tray and cascaded down the front and onto the floor.

'Hey!'

'Do me a printout of that booking.'

Water streamed across the floor.

Behind Pence, the printer whirred. Rockburn walked round, Pence backed away, and Rockburn collected the printout, his hopes rising. Ho Dong had supplied a Vietnamese driving licence, an address of 66 Tower Road, Westgate; and a phone number ending 378.

He punched the air.

Then doublechecked the scrap of paper in his wallet with the number stored on the SIM card recovered from the canal. He wasn't mistaken. Punched the air a second time. He slotted the scrap back, pocketed the sheet, and dummied at Pence's midriff.

The old con rocked away exhaling noxious breath.

At the escalators, Rockburn doubled down and jogged back to the panther. The bomb was still ticking.

*

Ignoring the one-way signs, he exited the car park, and headed out to Westgate. The light was grey and fading and spits of rain struck his visor. Traffic was heavy.

He'd recce 66 Tower Road, check Quang was being held there, and formulate a plan. Assess the number of kidnappers, their weaponry, criminal sophistication. Snatch the boy back himself, or call Elsa and request reinforcements. Armed units in paramilitary garb, carrying shields, Glocks, and submachine guns.

The panther hummed as if she knew they'd made progress.

Rockburn hoped Quang was okay, hadn't been harmed during the kidnapping. Hoped he knew Rockburn would be searching, would hardly sleep until he was safe.

Tower Road was on the west side, and led up a steep and windy hill. He passed a church converted into a house. Said a prayer; first time for everything. He reached number 40, a large house on a right-angled corner. It didn't seem right. They were all large houses, detached with gardens. At number 60, Tower Road became Tower Lane and the numbering restarted.

He U-turned, rode back, U-turned, rode up and down. He swore under his breath, slammed the handlebars. The panther would understand, would want to share his frustration. In a pocket, his mobile rang. He stopped at a bend in the road next to a salt bin. Removed his gauntlets and extricated the phone.

'Have you found him yet?'

Hocking sounded as worried as he was. 'I had a lead at Westgate, but the address is false.' He told her about the mopeds. Said he was on his way back to the hire company.

'What if that comes to nothing?'

'I'll speak to your professor friend.' Rockburn climbed off the bike. An oil tanker drove past. 'Quang told me there were two reasons he and Mina came to the UK. One, not to spend their lives growing rice, and two, a reason I wouldn't understand.

Mina also told me the boy was special, but not why. Have you any idea?'

'Not really, no.' Hocking paused. 'Maybe he's a celebrity's hidden child, or Vietnamese royal family. But surely, we'd have heard something on the news.'

Rockburn walked over to a gate and looked across to a school field. Children were playing football, shouting and laughing. 'You must have seen Quang almost naked – was there anything that set him apart? Three nipples, or two belly buttons? Scarring, or tattoos?' As he spoke, the hairs rose on the back of his neck. 'The tattoo of a charging horseman?'

'No tattoos, no peculiar marks or scars, nothing that makes him stand out. But maybe us Westerners can't see it – whatever it is. You should talk to Richard, get the Vietnamese viewpoint.'

Rockburn looked at his watch, then across the field. 'Can you phone him, tell him it might be late.'

'He's got an office at the university library, works all hours.'

One of the boys scored a goal and his teammates crowded around and performed a complex scoring routine of hand and arm gestures.

'I've spoken to the police,' said Hocking. 'A detective called Elsa. She wants you to go into the station, said they can help find Quang.'

Rockburn turned, leant back on the gate. 'You called them?'

'I'm scared I might never see him again.'

'Did Sarah-Jane tell you to involve the police?'

Hocking's silence hung heavily. She doubted he'd find the boy and he feared she might be right.

Rockburn pocketed the phone, walked back to the panther, and mounted up. Glanced back at the school field.

Sat for a few moments staring. Images and sounds flickered in his head: the moped on the canal bridge; the whining of mopeds while he was on Elsa's barge; the moped in the yard outside his block; the line of mopeds outside Caige's. Another one somewhere . . .

An idea jump-started him.

He bumped the pannier down onto the road, and gunned back to the airport.

Pence was smoking in the doorway of Jake's Rentals. He didn't speak and seemed surprised to see Rockburn for a second time.

'They gave a false address.'

The old con threw the butt down on the shiny floor and grubbed it with a toe. 'Had no idea, honest.' He backed into the office as if away from the unfamiliar word.

Rockburn followed. 'You said mopeds are always going for repairs, so I wondered whether any of Dong's bikes needed work.'

Pence shrugged.

Rockburn pointed at the computer and waited for him to scuttle around the desk, then walked round and observed over his shoulder.

Pence scrolled through to the booking of Dong. 'Five mopeds, one to five. Moped three needed a new clutch a week into the booking. Client was offered a fifty pounds rebate if they took it to a local garage and had it fixed. They get a choice of three repair shops, we show 'em a map, and client chose that one.'

He pointed with a fingernail-chewed hand. 'King Servicing, Templeside. Everyone knows it as Killer's.'

Rockburn clapped a heavy fist on Pence's shoulder. He'd remembered seeing one there, in the middle bay next to a van. 'You'd better hope I don't have to come back a third time.'

The old con rubbed his shoulder, his face cracked in pain. 'Think my collarbone's broke.'

*

C l o s e d.

Rockburn had never seen the garage closed during the day. The sign looked peculiar – the letters separate, the script juddery, as if someone was copying.

He peered through the grimy window in the inset gate, then booted the huge sliding doors. They rocked back and forth and paint flecks showered his boots. He took off his helmet and his jacket and blew. Perspiration dripped from his nose and clouds of condensation rose from his fleece. He yanked off his headover, unzipped the fleece.

He tapped in the numbers on the sign in the window. After a short pause, the landline rang inside the garage. He tried Dave's mobile. Straight to voicemail, so he left a message.

Punched the sliding doors which rocked and rattled. Sweat was still dripping to the ground around him.

Where was Dave?

He felt that he was one step behind. The boy snatched, and now Dave missing. The mechanic's past life catching up, or for assisting Rockburn? Before speaking to the professor, he should visit Flack at the hospital. Check the big man was still where he was meant to be.

34

Rockburn approached a roundabout stationary with traffic. Fifty metres across, a grassy hummock strewn with litter.

Aware every second might count for Quang, might count for all three of them, he swerved into the oncoming lane, and slowed for a gap between the queued vehicles to appear. The panther wasn't light, but wheelies and hops depended largely on technique.

Seeing his chance, he accelerated.

In the last metres of the approach, he disengaged the clutch and squeezed the throttle Then dumped the clutch.

The panther reared.

Rockburn kept her heading straight with the front wheel raised. The tyre cleared the kerb and the back one bumped up. The bike jolted. Knew he'd be sore later. He ploughed through the grassy scrub, the wheels leaving a muddy slew. A van driver looked across at him, mouth open. At the far side, the panther crashed down. Bike and rider bruised as boxers, but still fighting.

Rockburn drummed his fingers at the nurse's station. Three nurses in dark-blue tunics consulted in low urgent voices. Behind them was a large open-plan room with six semi-curtained bed spaces. Doctors surrounded one bed, the curtains tightly drawn around another.

He'd been told to wait. Relief at Flack's presence quickly replaced by impatience and apprehension for the safety of Quang.

Hospitals were the only places which smelt worse than police stations. A cocktail of disinfectant and despair.

The nurse returned. She wore thick-framed tinted glasses which drew and rebuffed attention at the same time. Her reams of dark brown hair were fiercely constrained into a French plait. She looked vaguely like a nurse he'd met at a 999 party. The shape of her chin, her poise. But she'd been blonde.

'He's very tired but you're okay for a quick visit. Ten minutes.' She held up her fingers. She wore no rings, no jewellery at all.

'How is he?'

'We've made him as comfortable as we can.'

Rockburn followed her to the corner bedspace and waited while she slipped through the gap in the curtains. He stepped after her.

Wearing a black t-shirt showing the burning gallows insignia of a heavy metal band, Flack was sitting up in bed. Monitors and machines peered over his shoulders, tubes trailed, screens flickered. The tattooist looked lost, helpless, thirty years older.

'Ten minutes,' repeated the nurse, pointing at the clock. She glanced at Rockburn for a second too long making him wonder if she recognised him. She withdrew through the gap in the curtains. Maybe she'd dyed her hair.

'Throat cancer,' said Flack. His voice was low and croaky. 'Tests and more tests. Radioth—' He stopped, coughed. 'Radiotherapy, chemo. Front seat at the horror house.'

Rockburn grunted in solidarity.

The air was stuffy. He needed a drink – any drink.

'You ain't going to say nothing?'

Rockburn looked round at the gap in the curtains. He drew them shut, turned back. 'You sick enough for blanket baths?'

Flack cackled, stopped, wheezed. 'You got a smoke?'

'No, big man, I haven't.' He glanced at the clock.

'I've got something for you.' Flack's words rasped. He nodded at an envelope on the table. 'I found it in a corner when I was sweeping the studio. I think the Asian walk-in must have dropped it. Only a couple of kids since her.' His words faded into a coughing spasm.

Rockburn slipped on plastic gloves from a box on the side and pulled a sheet of paper out of the envelope. The printout of an airline ticket, half of it torn away. He typed the letters MAS into the search engine on his phone. Malaysian Airways. He showed Flack. 'Not a million miles from Vietnam.'

'So?'

'I'm beginning to think Mina and the boy were followed from Vietnam.'

'By Zafira?'

'No, by someone else.'

'Who?'

'I don't know,' said Rockburn, slipping the piece of paper into the envelope and pulling off the gloves. 'You up to a few more questions?'

'I ain't dead.' The tattooist lay back, closed his eyes.

'Killer's was closed earlier. Any idea why?'

Shaking his head, Flack leant to the side and coughed and spluttered.

'Do you know where Dave lives?'

Another shake of the head.

'When was the last time you spoke to someone at RCS imports?'

'Six, nine months ago.' Flack took a couple of shallow breaths. 'His name's Ezekiel – I call him Easy – imports cheap African art so is often away. Awful shit, carved giraffes and pictures with coloured dots and dashes.'

James Ellson

'What does Easy look like?'

'Fuck. Like everyone else. Fiftyish. Pot belly.'

'Well, where is he?'

'God knows, lost in the jungle.' Flack relapsed into a coughing fit.

The nurse with brown hair stepped through the curtains. 'I think he needs a rest now.' She read a couple of the machines, marked up her notes. Rockburn lingered. It *was* her.

She glanced up. 'If you don't mind.'

'Thanks for looking after him.' He walked away, thumped down the stairwell, shoved through an emergency exit into the cold air.

The only 999 evening he'd ever been to – firefighters, hospital staff, and police officers. At midnight a stag party dressed as gorillas had crashed, and the event had descended into a brawl. One nurse, a blonde who he'd chatted to about a change of career, had been hit by a broken bottle. He'd carried her out to a taxi, spent the night in A&E. A week later the mayor had written to him on headed notepaper thanking him and explaining his daughter had lost her eye. Six months later Rockburn had given evidence at court and the suspect was jailed for six years.

He phoned the mayor. A pigeon landed nearby and pecked at a waste bin. He held on. Finally, he was put through.

'How are you, sir?' He thought of the mayor's daughter, of their family Christmases and birthdays, always strained, always that one night lurking. He'd sensed the mayor had half-hoped Rockburn and his daughter would get together.

'I am as they say in this fine city, buzzin'.' The mayor was a man of, and for the people. 'Now what can I do for you, Rockburn?'

'Sorry it's like that, sir.' He picked up a stone and hurled it at the pigeon.

'It comes with the office. At least you never pretend. So?'

Rockburn explained about the murder of Mina, the murder of Zafira and his two henchmen, the kidnapped boy, and the scrutiny from his former employer. He suggested a phone call from the town hall might relieve the pressure, and let him find Quang and take him somewhere safe.

'Leave it with me,' said the mayor.

Rockburn mounted up and rode out of the car park. The pigeon waited until the last moment, then flapped away.

He parked up two streets from the block he shared with Flack and RCS Imports. He climbed the fire escape, the metal treads twanging. Unlocked his door, stepped inside. Unable to resist, he threw a volley of darts. Ton-forty. It made him think he shouldn't practise.

Eating a handful of cornflakes, he flipped up the lid of the toolbox, took what he needed. Padded down the stairs to RCS Imports.

Shoving in the last of the cereal, he stared through the tinted front door. Listened. The office was silent, appeared empty. He slipped on plastic gloves, tried the door. One central lock. He examined the mechanism. Scratch marks, slight gouges. It had been picked before. He inserted two metal sliders as far into the mechanism as possible, then tweezered and tweaked. After two minutes, he was still going and wondered if he'd have to return for a crowbar.

But it surrendered after three. He readied his torch and pushed the door open.

The hallway stank. A familiar smell to every police officer, every morgue technician, every pathologist. The smell of rotting cadavers.

Held his breath, listened, but could hear only the traffic outside. Just discernible above the street noise, he could hear the soft whir of a fan.

He crept forward.

The first room was used for storage. Packing cases, mainly empty. Some African flags, a couple of broken pictures. The legs of a carved giraffe. In the next room were a desk and an office chair. The drawers were open and lined with stationery castoffs. The shelves were bare. Nowhere to hide anything larger than a book.

At the back was a washroom with a sliding door. Inside, the fan was whirring. He slid open the door. The toilet bowl was stained, and shreds of toilet paper and cardboard tubes lay scattered on the floor. He closed the door. Adjacent was a small kitchen area with another sliding door.

Drawing it back –

the heat and smell hit him.

Gagging, he retreated a couple of steps. Fat black flies flew out. Keeping his mouth clamped shut and trying not to breathe, he stepped forward and entered the tiny space.

A loaf of white bread with spreading blue mould, an opened packet of greenish ham, and fur-covered tomatoes sat on the side. Next to them a carton of milk. He lifted and tilted, the milk curdled and lumpy. The microwave door was open, a plate of decaying food still on the turntable. A fly emerged. The heat was coming from a radiator. A box of defrosted burgers sat balanced across the vents. Bluebottles were jostling for position, the occasional one flying up and heading across to the microwave. Rockburn leant closer. Flies parted, revealing a mass of writhing white maggots.

He checked the cupboards quickly, and withdrew. Slid the door shut. The smell immediately lessened.

Someone had been spending time there, and had left in a hurry. Or left expecting to come back, but didn't. Ezekiel, the importer Flack had mentioned?

Or someone else?

Rockburn entered the final room which overlooked the backyard. Four chairs were tucked under a table. A fifth sat by the window. Rockburn glanced out through the blinds. The yard was deserted, the only vehicles Flack's three-wheeler and the burnt Kawasaki dumped underneath the fire escape. Under the chair were crisp packets and fizzy drinks bottles. A plate with crumbs. Fast food wrappers. A comic book in a foreign language.

He placed it on the table. The words and lettering were similar to the book he'd found in the bag of the Asian walk-in. He turned a couple of pages. Pictures showed ancient soldiers and villagers sparring, fighting, praying. A hardscrabble life – weren't they all.

35

Walking across the small park in front of the library, Rockburn worried about Quang, whether he'd been hurt –

The whine of a moped cut across.

He stopped, looked around, couldn't see one. A bus hissed past. Maybe he'd been mistaken – he was hearing them everywhere.

Set off again, speeded up.

As his watch beeped ten, a large dark bird took off from above the main entrance of the library and flapped away. According to legend, if the ravens left the Tower of London, it would collapse. Rockburn didn't believe in legend. He believed in the malign influence of the city. In the panther to take him to other worlds – and bring him back.

He pushed through the swing doors and showed his card. 'Rockburn, private investigator.' Not yet proud to say it. 'Professor Morley is expecting me.'

A bored security guard with a tuft of pink hair pointed up a wide set of stairs, then returned to her dogeared novel.

Rockburn read the signboard and walked up to the fourth floor. Only senior academics, Hocking had said, were lucky enough to have a study at the library, and only professors, a suite. He trekked along the corridor, pushing through three sets of doors. He passed empty rooms with chairs on the table, two people still working.

He knocked on Room 4.3.12 and waited. Wondered again about Quang. Hoped, prayed, vowed.

The door opened wide. 'Ye-es?' The professor was at least seventy, almost bald, and overweight. He wore a baggy red cardigan and slippers. Glasses perched on the end of his large Roman nose.

'Professor Morley, I'm sorry it's late. My name's Rockburn; Rebecca Hocking said you might be able to help me. She's a friend of mine.' He handed the professor a card.

'You used to be a detective,' said Morley, holding up the card. 'And now you're doing this.' He nodded. 'Come in.'

Rockburn walked inside. The anteroom held shelves of books from floor to ceiling on all four sides. A table and chairs stood in the middle. A cat litter tray and a saucer of food sat by the door.

'This is my library within the library. I call it the *Babushka* room. But come into my study.' He shuffled through an arch into a second room. A small grey kitten ran past him. 'I smuggle her in and out each day. A little bit of excitement for the old ticker.' Rockburn followed. The study was larger and held two red leather armchairs and a matching sofa. An old desk covered with books and papers and a laptop. A chunky fan heater.

'Please,' said Morley, pointing at an armchair.

Rockburn sat. The maze of rooms, the airless study, the acres of books, the learned old man, made him feel like it was judgement day. Whether he'd been true to himself, realised his potential. Whether he'd cared enough, loved enough. Whether he'd end up in heaven – astride the panther – or hell.

'Now, Mr Rockburn, would you like coffee, or maybe you'd prefer a whisky?'

'Nothing, thanks, professor. And just Rockburn.'

Morley nodded. 'Rebecca always talks highly of you.' He

walked over to a trolley loaded with drinks, poured a large whisky. He sat opposite Rockburn, set down his glass. He arched his fingers. 'So, how can I help?'

'It's a long story.'

'They're all long stories. The best ones, anyway.' He smiled, took off his glasses. Huffed on the lenses and polished them with a yellow rag. 'I'm listening.'

Rockburn described the events of the previous week, starting with the phone call from Mina and ending with the kidnap of Quang. 'Mina told me that the boy is special, and the boy alluded to a second reason to migrate to the UK in addition to a better life. What that second reason is and why he's special, I don't know. Initially, I thought they were being pursued by traffickers, possibly for more money, possibly to take back the diamonds that Mina says she obtained from a Russian man.'

The professor swirled his whisky. 'You don't believe her?'

'I think she may have stolen them.'

Morley set down his glass. 'What's your new theory?'

'Two gangs have been following them. The traffickers, in pursuit of diamonds that may or may not belong to them. *And a second gang* – from Vietnam, who've travelled to the UK to locate and kidnap the boy. Therefore, Quang must hold a value of some kind. Possibly it's a cash value to make it worth demanding a ransom. Maybe there's a wealthy or important relation Quang doesn't know about, and he's a bastard child to a Vietnamese prince. A ransom makes the most sense but would have to be an astronomic sum to compensate the risk generated by killing four people. Two murder squads have been scrambled.'

'Interesting. And if it's not cash?'

'Quang could hold a representational value.'

'Meaning?'

'A value but only to some people. Religious, mythical or something along those lines. That's my preferred hypothesis, having three times during my investigation seen the symbol of the charging horseman. Firstly, the tattoo requested by an Asian woman at the studio two floors below my flat; secondly, the burning effigy in the yard where I work; and thirdly, chalked on the ground at the rugby stadium where the three traffickers were murdered. I've tried to research the horseman but got nowhere. That's where I hoped you could help.'

The professor nodded, rocked gently in his chair. 'Anything else?'

'I'd like to show you something.' Rockburn passed Morley the clear plastic bag containing the comic book he'd found at RCS Imports. 'The bag's open but you'll need gloves.' He tossed over a pair.

The professor slipped them on and removed the book. He turned the pages, murmuring to himself.

'The artwork is very similar to a comic book in the possession of the Asian woman getting the tattoo. Pictures of an ancient people, growing rice, fighting on horseback. I took photos of that one on my mobile.' Rockburn took out his phone, tapped the screen, and passed it over.

The professor flicked through the images, handed it back.

Rockburn glanced at his watch. He hoped Quang was asleep, having a break in his nightmare.

'You like the Vietnamese boy, don't you?'

'I do,' said Rockburn, surprised at Morley's perceptiveness.

'Not having a family is my major regret in life. I have a brother whom I see at Christmas. And sometimes I catch up with a colleague or a student. Rebecca is a brightness. The life internal is rewarding but lonely.' He picked up his glass and finished the whisky.

The kitten snuck into the room keeping to the skirting board. When she was close to the professor she ran across and leapt up onto his lap. Morley began to stroke her, the kitten purring loudly.

'Let me tell you a little about my area of research – the imaginary lives of the peoples of south-east Asia and the South China Sea. Predominantly focused on Thailand, Laos, Cambodia and Vietnam. I study religions, myths, and legends and have done for almost half a century. The life internal as I said.' He took off his glasses and folded them. He set them down next to the empty whisky glass.

'The comic books and horseman symbol, Rockburn, are Vietnamese. Now, although some of Vietnam is ultra-modern and some Vietnamese have high standards of living with expensive cars and lifestyles, most of the country is poor, and the people live basic agrarian lives. The predominant religion is folk. It's not an organised system but a set of traditions devoted to the *than*. Spelt t-h-a-n but pronounced taane. *Than* can be understood as gods, but with a very wide interpretation. Heroic national figures, familial icons, events from the natural world, cosmic symbols. The emphasis is on the local and the individual. Are you familiar with Confucianism?'

'Familiar as you are with suspension bearings.'

The professor cackled. 'Worshipping or following the *than* is sometimes confused with Confucianism. But the latter is more a social philosophy, a way of behaving in a community which benefits everyone. Venerating the *than* is more personal, hence more likely to give rise to splinter-groups and sects, thinking, interpreting, and doing their own thing.'

'Like fundamentalism?' said Rockburn. The word triggered an image of the rugby stadium and the dead trafficker. Fundamentalism was Zafira's idea, and possibly his downfall.

'I thought you might say that. There are similarities in motivation and implementation, certainly.'

'And the horseman?'

'That's where it gets really interesting.'

The kitten jumped off the professor's lap and ran into the

258

anteroom. Seconds later, someone walked past. 'She's a useful early warning system.'

Nodding, Rockburn checked his watch. Ten-thirty. 'What time does the library close?'

'Midnight, we're okay for time.' The professor stood and padded across to a bookcase. He stooped, ran his fingers along a row of spines, and plucked out a book. He straightened, grimaced. 'For over a thousand years there have been four main deities in Vietnamese folk religion. Known as the four immortals. Tan Vien, a mountain god; Chu Dong Du who represents love and marriage; Lieuh Hanh, a princess; and Thanh Giong, a giant who defeated northern invaders. Giong is the one we're interested in. As legend has it, he was born in a village of the same name during the Sixth Hung King Dynasty. When he was three years old the Chinese invaded and the king appealed for heroes to fight the enemy. The baby Giong quickly matured, and wearing iron armour and riding an iron horse fought the enemy with an iron lance. When his lance broke he used a bamboo rod. The attackers were defeated, and Giong flew to heaven on his iron horse. He symbolises youthful tenacity and national solidarity.' The professor opened the book and leafed through a few pages. 'That's Giong, the iron horseman.'

Rockburn glanced at the picture of the charging rider, and nodded. 'Which I've now seen three times.'

'Not quite. Have a closer look.'

Rockburn took hold of the book and examined the colour drawing. He'd only glanced at the tattoo on the Asian woman and the effigy had been aflame. He took out his phone and checked the chalk image. He looked at the pencil drawing. He spotted one difference, then a second. 'The chalk horseman is carrying an oval shield, not a round one, and his helmet is full-face, not open.'

'There's one more.'

James Ellson

He scanned the photograph again. Then the picture. 'The chalk horseman is carrying a small dagger. You're saying they're different people, different legends, or what?'

'They are different people but the legend is the same albeit given a modern twist.'

Rockburn set the book down and stood up. He was beginning to feel Morley was teasing, treating him like a young student. 'This isn't a game, professor. A young boy's life is at risk.'

Morley sat down. 'Yes, I'm sorry. I'm tired. The images of the rider you have seen are the Second Horseman. Sometime in the last century the legend developed. Giong would have a son in the new millennium, and he like his father would help to repel a Chinese invasion. The indigenous people who adopted this new story became known as Second Horsemen.'

'Are they real differences or just mistakes in the copying of the images? A natural evolution like Chinese whispers but in artwork?'

'It doesn't matter. The Second Horsemen believe they're real differences. And they spend their lives hoping the boy will appear.'

The hairs went up on the back of Rockburn's neck. 'So you think some of these people, the Second Horsemen, think Quang is who they've been waiting for? That Quang is the Second Horseman?'

'I think that's quite possible, yes. At least some of them. Many Vietnamese are today fearful of Chinese expansionism – and the Second Horsemen think Giong's son will be the heroic figure to save them.'

'Like Jehovah's Witnesses?'

'Superficially, yes, but Jehovah's tend to be peace-loving. The Second Horsemen have fanatical elements. Research is currently being carried out. But I know of two incidents in the last ten years when Second Horsemen sects have travelled from Vietnam to find the Second Horseman.'

'Incidents?'

'One in America, one in Australia. In 2001 a young Vietnamese boy was kidnapped in Boca Raton, just north of Miami. A burning effigy of a horseman was left behind. The boy was never seen again. And in 2006 in Ferntree Gully to the east of Melbourne, another Vietnamese boy was snatched. Details are scant.' He paused. The kitten trotted back into the room. The professor picked her up and stroked her neck. 'Neither the American nor the Australian police released much information, but there have been rumours on the research forum I follow.'

'What rumours?'

'They're only rumours.'

'Professor!'

'The Second Horsemen have two theories as to how they might be saved from Chinese invasion, firstly a great victory led by the son of Giong, or secondly, sacrificing the boy so as to remove the need for a Chinese incursion in the first place.'

'You think the Vietnamese boy in Melbourne was sacrificed?'

'There is a blurry photo of a pyre and third-hand reports of an Asian boy being burnt. There is no real evidence, and the police hushed it up. However, the chatter on the forum is that it is something the sect would consider and carry out.' He set the kitten down. 'I'm sorry.'

Rockburn stood up and pulled on his leather jacket.

'You've got to understand, Rockburn, they're fanatics. They've taken a legend that has passed through tens of generations and adapted it for their modern fantasies. Everyone needs a purpose in life, and that is what the Second Horsemen see as theirs.'

'What I don't understand is why they've chosen Quang.'

'He's an only child which is unusual in the rural villages of Vietnam. And I should think one of the sect lived in the same village. Maybe they saw Quang do an unlikely thing. Or heard about it, and retold the story, but a richer version.'

Rockburn grabbed his helmet. 'Thank you so much, professor.'

Morley opened the door. 'I do hope you're in time.'

Rockburn ran down the corridor, barged through each set of swing doors and clattered down the stairs. There was no sign of the security guard with the tuft of pink hair. He pushed open the doors and ran outside.

The air was cold, the city not properly dark but deep bluey green. It smelt of the drains. A couple wearing woolly hats were walking arm in arm, their voices hushed and earnest.

He jogged over to the bicycle racks where he'd left the panther. She was waiting patiently and as he ran up, he couldn't help but admire her shiny bodywork and sleek lines.

Damn, he thought. Forgotten his gauntlets.

He jogged back to the library, suddenly concerned about the missing security guard. Maybe she was making a brew or having a pee. He pushed through the doors, and as he did so a small cat ran outside.

The professor's kitten.

It darted into the night and disappeared.

Rockburn jogged across the lobby. The guard was back at her desk, already engaged in her book.

'Forgot my gloves.'

She nodded and dipped her head to the page.

Rockburn took the stairs two at a time. Professor Morley had said the kitten was a house cat. He ran back along the fourth-floor corridor, shoving open the doors. The adjoining rooms now empty, and silent.

The academic's door stood open.

'Professor Morley?'

Rockburn stepped inside. The anteroom like the professor was heavy with learning but light with experience. Light with learning but heavy with experience, Rockburn pushed open the internal door apprehensively.

Looked arou –

the professor sat slumped in his armchair, his eyes closed.

'Sir?'

There was no answer.

Rockburn searched the room for a suspect, and satisfied, attended the professor. Morley's face was grey and already cooling. A ligature mark around his neck was all Rockburn needed to know.

Somewhere a clock chimed eleven. He remembered the fleeing bird, and for a moment wondered if the legend about the Tower of London was true.

But only for a moment.

He grabbed his gauntlets, and for the second time, ran along the corridor barging through the swing doors and clattered down the library stairs. The killer had to be nearby.

36

Rockburn ran into the lobby.

'Did anyone just come through here?'

The guard with the pink tuft looked up from her book. She shook her head. 'Not for ten, fifteen minutes. Are you okay?'

Rockburn ran to the doors. 'Professor Morley's been murdered,' he shouted over his shoulder. 'Lock the building down and call the police.' He pushed open the door and ran outside.

Sprinted over to the panther.

A moped started up, moaning like a tired child.

On the far side of the park. Three mopeds. They exited through the gate, and sped along the pavement.

Rockburn reached the panther and jammed on his helmet. He mounted up, fired the engine, and took off. On the far pavement, the mopeds bumped down onto the road, and sped away.

The shortest route was through the park. Rockburn entered through the wrought iron gate and rode across the grass, leaving a thick tyre tread. Mud spattered between his legs and up his back. At the far side he slalomed around flowerbeds and exited the park. Crashed down the kerb, skidding as he changed direction. The motorbike noise harsh as sandpaper.

Ahead of him the road was clear except for two minicabs and

a night bus. He accelerated hard to a crossroads, looked left and right, and puttered over. As he reached the far side, he saw in his peripheral vision the three faint tail-lights of the mopeds. He braked, skidded around and raced back to the junction.

Turned, took off again.

A group of teenagers piled out of a fried chicken restaurant and watched him fly past. One chucked a chip wrapper, the others looked up the road at the scuttling mopeds.

Rockburn rocketed by the swimming pool and leisure centre, then throttled back. He had two choices, either detain one of the moped riders, and force him to take Rockburn to Quang; or follow the trio back to the boy. The first involved odds of three against one and would require violence. The second was uncertain: maybe he'd lose sight of them, or they were go-betweens. He didn't think they were – the professor had described them as a tight-knit group, a sect.

He kept the panther a little way back. The three mopeds rode as an arrowhead, as if they had a command structure and a formation for riding. Black helmet at the front, red and yellow helmets behind.

The road was deserted except for a bicycle heading towards them and an ambulance in the far distance. He hugged the pavement and dropped back further. The panther's buzzing, which was usually so life-affirming, a giveaway.

Possibly already:

Yellow Helmet, riding on the left, glanced behind him and stared. He sped up, waved at his peers, and jinked into a side street. The others followed.

At the corner, Rockburn slowed and nosed around. He spotted Yellow Helmet who'd stopped on the next corner. Seeing Rockburn, the rider raced off, taking a second left from the main street.

Rockburn U-turned and headed back to the main drag.

Where horses – carrying, pulling, dragging – had once been kings of the road. If he was right, he would be able to confront the three suspects.

At the road, he slewed across and gunned back towards the university library. The three mopeds didn't show. He reached the junction they should have appeared from, and turned down it, cursing himself. No sign of them. Three mopeds had given a former detective and a superbike the slip. He stopped, ripped off his helmet.

Listened:

Heard tinny sounding engines at three o'clock, which meant they had also U-turned. He urged the panther forward again. Behind him, his helmet crashed to the ground and spun away like a tenpin bowling ball.

He flipped up the street, turned right, left, right and – there they were – turning back onto the main drag.

Rockburn gave chase, throwing the bike and his body around. He felt the engine's heat, smelt the hot rubber of the tyres, his own sweat.

At the main road, another night bus was clearing the junction and the mopeds were already two traffic lights ahead. He skid-turned into the road. Jerked the panther upright, and accelerated. The long straight road ahead was clear except for half a dozen cars and multiple sets of traffic lights.

He was gaining.

The first light turned orange, the mopeds rattling forward. The light turned red.

Rockburn had no choice. It was a test, he was sure of it. Every police pursuit sooner or later reached the same dilemma: will the police driver, constrained by law and procedure, slow and even stop at a red light. Most did. Those that didn't sometimes made headline arrests, but as often caused injury and resulted in the police driver being prosecuted. Rockburn was no longer so constrained. He checked left and right, and despite buildings preventing perfect vision, ploughed forward.

Squeezing his thighs tighter.

And tighter.

He made it.

Gained further. The lights ahead all began to change in sequence. The mopeds had been lucky, catching a repeat of the red traffic light test.

Rockburn held his breath twice more. The first time he got away with it.

He reached the next red light, and without hesitation, darted forwards.

A burgundy four-wheel drive steamed across. Rap music blaring, tinted windows, and hubcaps fitted with reverse rotation hoopla. The driver thumped the horn down, and held it there. The course of the big car set as if it were a train.

Rockburn was committed. Braking would mean a head-on collision; braking and slewing would mean a sideways collision. He accelerated, demanding every watt of power from the panther. Together, they surged ahead.

The four-wheel drive heaved across –

missing the panther's rear tyre by millimetres.

Rockburn felt the blast of wind, heard the grating rap as if it was in his EarPods. He wobbled, but kept upright, kept going. He knew he'd been lucky – had played Russian Roulette three times and won three times. He didn't look back but hared forward after the mopeds. He'd passed the red traffic light test, and Black Helmet would know they couldn't shake him that way.

The mopeds turned into a small cross-street. Bollards and raised flowerbed go-slows blocked the way. The mopeds jinked left and right and zipped on. Rockburn slowed to a halt. Dismounted. He tested the bike through the gap but it wouldn't fit. He unclipped the panniers, pushed them away, and tried again.

The panther squeezed through.

Rockburn mounted up and raced on.

The mopeds reached the junction in front of a Mercedes garage. Yellow streamers fluttered overhead and a coupe sat diagonally in the air, its underside displayed like pornography. The mopeds split up, two turning left, and one turning right.

Instinctively Rockburn followed Black Helmet and Yellow Helmet. Two darts to checkout, not one. Red Helmet was a single target and could more easily be overcome and persuaded to inform on the whereabouts of Quang. He was also the poorest rider, clipping the bollards of a go-slow and twice slithering around due to accelerating too stiffly. But Rockburn suspected Black Helmet might think that, so he rode after the two.

He slowed, rethinking his unconscious decision. Black Helmet expected him to be smart, to eschew the easy choice. It was a double bluff. He U-turned and chased after Red Helmet, still visible, and approaching a roundabout.

Red Helmet took the third exit, heading for the eastern suburbs. Rockburn weaved side to side, rethinking his rethinking. It didn't matter what he thought was the best play, only what Black Helmet thought. Had to outguess him. Maybe he couldn't follow the right moped – whoever he followed would lead him away from the boy. Or maybe all the mopeds were distractions, and were in communication with each other and with the remainder of the sect who were guarding Quang. Even if that was the most likely – they'd hired five mopeds – his only option was to pursue one or more of the three he'd followed.

Rockburn weaved wider and slower, trying to discern their level of sophistication. A Vietnamese sect, capable of multiple murders and eluding arrest in a foreign country five thousand miles from home.

He U-turned for what seemed the umpteenth time, and raced back after Black and Yellow Helmets. It might be what they wanted, or it might not. He would find out. They were a long way ahead, but he saw Yellow Helmet turn off towards the north-west gate of Little Park. Home to his jungle gym and the place he'd escaped with Quang riding in a wheelie bin. Despite its name, one of the city's largest.

At the turn off, they had disappeared. He rode to the end of the road and into the alley, hoping he wouldn't meet –

A couple of giggly lovers. He slowed and closed. Two Goths, heavily made up and thickly drunk. Laughing, they swayed into the chainmail fence next to a stack of scaffolding.

Rockburn forced the panther past and puttered forward to the gate, hoping the lazy warden might have skimped on his night round. He hadn't: a chain and fat padlock hung down. The Helmets must have hefted their mopeds over the four-foot gate. Their bikes were light and as crap as toys given away with cereal. He leant the motorbike against the fence and retraced his path.

At the stack of scaffolding, he climbed over to commandeer a plank. Hefted it up and over, climbed back. Carried the plank to the gate, and leant it against the top bar so it formed a ramp. Kicked a gash in the path so the end wouldn't move. He remounted the panther and trundled back to the start of the alley. Turned over the revs.

Shot off –

feeling in the enclosed space a heightened sense of speed. He felt like a drag racer. A stuntman.

The panther hit the plank, the plank bit into the path, the gate creaked, the plank bowed. Rockburn rode up, and over, and into the air.

Brace, brace, brace.

The two of them landed with a thump. The tyres squeaked,

the shocks squeezed tight as lion-traps. They bounced forwards.

Holding the bike upright, and hoping he hadn't damaged her, Rockburn surveyed the park. Night lamps speckled. The bars and logs of the jungle gym, Sal's trailer and the pond were all deserted. Pushing away the dark with cheap headlights, the two mopeds were three-quarters of the way across, and approaching the Lose River which formed the eastern boundary of Little Park. There were no bridges. Black and Yellow Helmets' only option was to head to the gates at the north-east or south-east corner, but maybe they didn't know that.

He barrelled after them.

The hare after the duo of tortoises. The panther was three or four times faster on a straight tarmacadam road, but only twice that across the grass. At Sal's graffiti-covered trailer he'd closed to within two hundred metres. The mopeds were fifty metres from the river and roughly midway between the two eastern gates. He had them.

Haring on, he visualised the impending confrontation. Two against one, or one fighting and one escaping. They'd committed a string of murders albeit with a noose, and Flack's walk-in had been armed with a CS canister. Martial arts, maybe. Rockburn was no black belt but could scrap as well as any.

The two moped riders reached the river, next to a dead tree which had fallen into the water.

Rockburn was fifty metres and closing. Hang on, Quang, just a little longer.

Forty metres.

Twenty metres. A moment's reflection: he'd consistently underestimated the sect. And he was doing it again. If they'd wanted to escape, why had they not turned off their headlights?

They were *luring* him.

The two riders dismounted and let their mopeds flop over to the grass. Black Helmet leading, they clambered up the roots of the tree and onto its trunk. Holding their arms out for balance they skipped across and jumped the final couple of feet to the far bank.

Rockburn skidded to a stop. As he climbed off the panther, he heard the tinny whine of mopeds. *Different* mopeds.

He scrabbled among the tree roots and climbed up to the trunk across the river. Through a small wood on the far bank, two mopeds emerged. Red Helmet and a second Black Helmet. Rockburn ran across the log, swayed, kept going.

The two new mopeds pulled up. Black and Yellow Helmets climbed aboard, and they all took off. Rockburn jumped down and gave chase.

He ran through the wood, scrub pulling at his trousers, and down a bank, and onto the road. Sprinted to the end, looked left and right. There was no sign or sound of them. Gasping for air, he kicked a wall.

And when his breathing recovered, swore black and blue.

It took him over two hours to ride back to the gate where he'd set up the ramp, climb over, replace the scaffolding plank where he'd found it, walk back to where he'd sacked the panniers and retrieve them, return to the park gate, climb over to the waiting motorbike, ride around the perimeter to a section of wire not overlooked by houses, cut a bike-sized hole, wheel the panther through, and scoot over to Killer Servicing.

At three am he pulled into Dave's open yard. There were half a dozen vehicles, cars awaiting parts, a minibus on blocks, and two rusting shells. He switched off the bike and climbed down. The panther was leaking fluid from the front forks and needed a check-up. So did he. He was filthy and spent as a match. He'd fluffed his prize line of enquiry and would have to start over as soon as Dave arrived for work.

If Dave turned up.

271

If the mechanic failed to appear, Rockburn's only remaining lead – the moped sent for repair by Jake's – would be useless, and he'd have to start a missing person enquiry. Maybe, break in to the garage, search for a home address for Dave or the spotty lad.

Rockburn washed his face at the tap, drank his fill. Then sat on a tyre and waited, his stomach growling like a rabid dog. At least the closed sign had gone from the sliding doors.

He phoned Elsa. The call went straight to voicemail, so he left a message checking she'd notified all air and seaports and major railway stations of Quang's description and details. It was possible the boy was already dead, but Rockburn didn't think so. The sect wanted the boy to worship, or sacrifice but at their leisure, in order to help repel the impending – as they saw it – Chinese invasion. More likely, Quang was being held somewhere, in the back of a van or the boot of a car, and was about to be whisked out of the country.

He phoned Hocking. Woke her up. Told her about Professor Morley before she heard it on the news. In the silence, Sarah-Jane's voice, groggy with sleep. He said he'd chased the suspects but lost them in Little Park. Promised to keep them updated, and said goodbye. At least Hocking was with someone.

Rockburn picked up a stone.

Hurling it brought back the memory of aiming at cans with Quang in the layby of Denise's burger caravan. Despite investigating dozens of cases, and meeting numerous victims and grieving families, and not even when he'd visited Pricha Kuri and her parents, had he felt a similar churn of anguish.

His heart *hurt*. Quang felt like family – his own child.

Rain pattered on the vehicle roofs. He rolled under the minibus and crashed. Dreamt of rescuing him.

Bracing the kidnappers, punching and kicking, blacking an eye, breaking a nose. Tying them up, cinching the ropes tighter and tighter. Phoning the police. Hugging the boy.

37

'Rockburn?'

He lifted his head, banged it. Lay back, opened his eyes. A couple of inches from his face was a dirt-caked exhaust line. He crawled out, feeling like he'd gone several rounds with a gypsy king.

Dave stood with his hands on hips. He took off his cap, turned it backwards. Bent down to the panther and scowled. 'You joined a circus? There's damage to the front forks and cracks in the fairing. You'll need to bring her in – and soon.' He stood up.

'Where've you been?'

'Nowhere.'

'I came here yesterday, found a closed sign.'

'Was broken into. They took the computer, God knows why. Each toolbox is worth ten times as much.'

Cupping a fist with his hand, Rockburn had a good idea why. The address he'd hoped for seemed destined to remain elusive.

'You need some breakfast, mate. We both do.' The mechanic unlocked the heavy padlock and drew back the sliding doors. They clattered the day into reality. Whistling an old war song, the spotty teenager arrived.

Rockburn felt sluggish.

Needed.

To.

Sharpen.

Up.

He laved his face in cold water from the tap. Drank a mouthful, rubbed his teeth, spat. Tamped his hair.

'Dave?'

The mechanic had disappeared inside.

Rockburn checked on the panther. She was as dirty as a trials bike. He found a rag and the jet-hose and cleaned her up. Wiped away the leaking fork fluid, checked her levels, and polished the metalwork 'til she was pretty as a centre page spread.

Feeling more awake, he entered the workshop and wandered through to the office. In the furthest bay, the teenager was already at work with a paint sprayer on a door panel. The fumes filled the garage. Tyres everywhere. His stomach rumbled like an approaching tram.

In the office, the bitter smell of coffee fought back the paint gases. Dave stood at his desk looking through paperwork and scowling. Leads for a computer, but no box.

'The break-in is probably connected to a moped you serviced recently – on behalf of Jake's Rentals. They're at the airport. Bike needed a new clutch.'

The mechanic pressed buttons on the filthy microwave, then thrust a beaker of coffee into Rockburn's hand. 'I remember it; the lad done it. He'll have finished spraying in a minute or two.' He picked up a second cup. '*Nostrovia!*'

They both drank. As good as medicine, Rockburn hoped.

The microwave pinged. Dave took out a chipped plate with steaming tubes of pastry. 'Pop-tart?'

They leant either side of a wooden counter, ate a couple each. Rockburn nodded at the plate, then at the distorted image spraying through the frosted glass.

Dave shook his head. 'He don't like 'em. Don't like much; good worker though.' They glanced over together, the small bursts of spray gun sounding like a wheezy asthmatic.

Rockburn ate another tart. Sweet or savoury, he wasn't sure. 'Is he your son?'

'Nah, not got kids. She walked out on me when I was inside, never seen reason for another one.'

Rockburn glanced at his watch. British criminals didn't get up early, but a fanatical Vietnamese sect might be different.

Taking the hint, Dave pushed open the office door, put two fingers in his mouth and whistled loud enough to wake a dead man. The boy stopped spraying, docked the gun, and limped over. A fine layer of orange paint covered his hair and clothes. He pulled down a skimpy mask which covered his mouth.

'Rockburn's interested in that moped you did the clutch. Asian lad brought it.'

The teenager nodded.

Rockburn wasn't hopeful, but asking questions was the job – former, and his new enterprise. 'Anything you can tell me about the Asian lad – maybe he arrived in a minicab, or mentioned an address, or you heard him on the phone?'

The boy shook his head.

'Anything might be helpful. Have you . . . seen him anywhere before?'

'Nah. Not before.'

Rockburn sighed.

'After?'

'Yeah, I seen him in the chinky near the pet supermarket. Seen him again at the petrol station on the corner there. He was filling up the moped. I recognised the bike from working on it, then they came out the shop, two of 'em. Same brownie. Gave me a right cold stare.'

Rockburn felt a flutter in his chest. He was back on. The sect appeared to be staying somewhere local. *Had* stayed somewhere local. If they hadn't already foxtrot-oscared, they would imminently. He nodded. 'Thanks. If you see them again, phone me.' He handed the lad a card.

Handed a second to Dave.

'Ooh, fancy,' said the mechanic, staring at the boy as he walked out into the workshop. 'Wouldn't have minded a son like that.'

'Get him a decent face mask, one that covers his eyes and with a proper ventilator. Put it on my bill.'

'You going to win the final, then? Pay off the shopkeepers?'

Rockburn zipped up his jacket. He'd forgotten about the darts. The final was supposed to be the next day. 'You still in contact with that guy?'

The mechanic downed his coffee. 'I'm in touch with a lot of peeps.'

'Usman.'

'*Him.*'

Rockburn nodded.

Dave's eyes narrowed. 'You're definitely no longer pol-ice?'

'Unfortunately not.'

'Yeah, we do his car. And send a bit of work his way every now and then – in return for a percentage. No fancy cards for him, though. Bit more cagey, doesn't take work direct.'

Rockburn took out his phone. 'I need a British passport for the Vietnamese boy I told you about – I'll send you a photo.' He tapped the screen. 'In fact, I need three,' he said on impulse. His visions of the future were varied. And sentimental nonsense, he knew that. He sent more photos.

'Is that it?'

Rockburn stood. 'Borrow a hat?'

The mechanic remained impassive for a few seconds, then broke into a wide smile. He nodded.

They shook hands, grease, oil and God knows what else transferring from one man to the other.

Grabbing a helmet from a coat stand holding half a dozen, Rockburn clomped out to the panther and mounted. He polished the wing mirrors one more time. He turned the key, stoked his favourite chorus.

Wheeled round, and headed for the pet supermarket.

38

The day was dull, grey. *Dry*. Perfect for riding the length and breadth; for a ring-road time trial; for an autobahn rip to Zermatt; a toll road blast to Spain.

Rockburn zipped the five clicks to the petrol station where the mopeds refuelled. Rode back and forth, looking for an observation post. Loitering by the air compressor would invite enquiry. No nearby café. The car park of the pet supermarket was close, but he would show out like a biker in a restaurant. He looked up at the rooftops.

Five minutes later, he looked back down. Three storeys up, he crouched on the roof of a criminal solicitors' practice which had been the bane of half his cases while a detective. The view was near-perfect. Fifty metres: a direct unobstructed line of sight to the garage forecourt where the sect had at least once filled up with fuel. It was a long shot, a throw from the auditorium at Caiges, but he had nothing else. The mopeds needed petrol and people tended to frequent the same places.

Rockburn settled back to wait. It warmed the parts to know the solicitors beneath him were aiding and abetting one of his investigations.

Ten o'clock. The forensic examination of the professor's office would be well underway, but he wasn't hopeful for a result quickly leading to Quang. Whereas the surveillance might.

Might.

A van pulled into the forecourt and two men wearing high-vis jackets climbed out. A car with a baby in the passenger seat pulled alongside. The first high-vis jacket filled up, the second walked over to pay in the shop. Rockburn could see him taking fizzy drinks from the fridge, choose chocolate bars, crisps. The woman entered. In her car, the baby started crying. The man paid, walked out of the shop, and the van drove away. The woman paid, ran back out to her car. A four-wheel drive towing a caravan manoeuvred between the pumps.

A long morning – a long day – was in prospect. Hearing a noise, he glanced behind him.

Nothing moved.

In the centre of the flat roof was a small enclosure where the internal stairs emerged. In each corner air conditioning vents wafted stale air. The fire escape he'd used to climb up from the car park was at the rear. Beyond were hundreds of similar roofs, and behind them the tower blocks of central Manchester. In their midst, a pair of red cranes rotated, lifting a huge cylindrical tube.

He turned back, clicked out his fingers.

The garage was busy, averaging a new customer every minute. A telecoms van filled up. An estate car loaded with children and suitcases. A refuse lorry covered with netting. A courier on a motorbike, but no mopeds. There was no reason for the sect to hang around – they'd snatched Quang, and had killed one of the few people who knew much about them. Perhaps even now, they were on their way to the airport, a flight home on false passports. Or a train to a port, a ferry, and a flight from Europe.

But everyone needed to sleep. Everyone ate convenience food from garages. The easiest option was to rest up and leave in the morning. It was what he wanted to believe.

A police car thrashed past on the blues and twos. It was followed by the van, the driver screaming along in second gear. Ten minutes later they drove back, in convoy, straight down the centreline. He missed it – the Job. The life.

Quiet resumed – relatively. Everything was relative. Plato, he guessed.

Two lawyers wearing suits entered the office below.

Simon had wanted to be a solicitor before he disappeared – before a moment of madness in a chip shop. Stabbed an older boy, who turned out to be a gang member of The Watts. Maybe Simon had known that, maybe he hadn't. Rockburn had assumed his brother would quickly turn up and give his side of the story.

But he hadn't, and wanted by the police and the gang, he'd stayed away – or had been unable to return. Rockburn and his grandparents had reported Simon missing, but the police hadn't been interested – as far as they were concerned, Simon had disappeared because he'd committed a serious offence. Rockburn had spoken to tens of his brother's friends and peers, monitored social media, and made enquiries with his brother's phone and email accounts, but found nothing to suggest where he was or whether he was still alive.

The incident had faded from public memory, and slowly, painfully, Rockburn had got on with his life. But there were few weeks when he didn't think about him.

Eleven o'clock. Hang in there, Quang.

Two white boys in a scruffy Ford pulled onto the forecourt. Music blared from speakers built into the boot. The driver climbed out. He wore a dirty yellow hoodie and was basketball tall. Jigging from one foot to the other, he filled up. The passenger sat with his feet on the dash and smoked and wisecracked through the open window.

The driver rocked up to the garage. He read the sign on the

cracked glass door, *With Immediate Effect: No helmets, No face coverings, Hoods down. CCTV monitoring.* He scowled and spat into the stack of barbeque fuel. He looked up and down, pulled his hood down to reveal an intricate pattern of zig-zag corn braids, and entered the shop. Rockburn recognised Mulkar, which meant the passenger was Molloy. Both were burglary nominals.

On a different day he'd have phoned it in. Wished as a young trainee detective in the crime squad he'd thought to sit up for a morning and watch a petrol station. Everyone needed petrol – and snacks. Kept repeating his new mantra.

Midday.

He needed a piss and a break. The basic rule of surveillance was that it needed at least two people. Otherwise, boredom and the necessity of human function defeated its purpose. He urinated in an old soft drink bottle and got on with it.

A moped zipped into the garage, U-turned, and halted alongside the air pump. The rider was wearing a yellow helmet.

Rockburn ran back across the roof and climbed down the metal ladder of the fire escape. He lost his footing, grabbed the rail. He slid, his hands burning. He stopped, climbed on, heart banging. He jumped the final six feet and ran along the alley to the side street. Sprinted to the end, ran into the road, cars hooting. Weaving amongst the traffic, he ran across to the garage.

Slowed to a walk.

Yellow Helmet looked about. The registration plate on the moped wasn't one Rockburn remembered, but could easily have been switched. He headed for the panther which he'd left in a parking bay.

Yellow Helmet took off his hat. The rider was black with Afro hair.

Rockburn opened and closed the panniers on the panther as if he was looking for something. It would happen, or it wouldn't. Fate. Plato again?

He clipped the panniers closed and headed back towards the roof of the solicitors' office. Waited to cross the road.

'Rockburn!'

Looking up, he spotted Elsa through the half-open window of an unmarked car pulling to the kerb. Three young constables from the crime squad sat in the vehicle with her. All three as wide as doors and itching to haul someone into the custody suite – preferably having fought with them first.

The doors opened.

Rockburn stepped into the carriageway, a car missing him by inches. He ran across the first lane, hovered on the central white line. If he was arrested, he'd never find the mopeds, never find Quang.

Two of the crime squad boys ran into the road. Rockburn launched into the opposite lane, in front of an approaching car.

The driver hit the horn and the brakes.

As the oncoming car slewed and skidded, Rockburn smelt burning rubber. He reached the pavement, glanced back at the marks on the road and the three pursuing officers.

'Rockburn!'

He ran into a side street, dinked right into a smaller one. It was flanked by overflowing green dumpsters. He pulled them out as he ran past, and heard them rolling and bumping behind him. He heard voices and swearing and car tyres screeching. He turned a corner, ran through some traffic cones, knocking them over as he passed. He jumped sideways to avoid wet tarmac, and ran on. He turned another corner.

And ran headlong into a crime squad officer.

Dropping a shoulder, the PC rugby-tackled Rockburn to the floor. He landed heavily on his side.

Winded –

but managed to kick out with his feet. One connected with his assailant's torso. The constable groaned. Rockburn tried to stand, but two more officers arrived to pin him down.

Elsa drove up and screeched to a halt, her window already down. 'Stick him in the back of the car.'

'Cuffs?'

Elsa shook her head.

Which left him a chance.

39

Rockburn and the police officers rose slowly, puffing and perspiring like Sunday footballers. The crime squad boys shared a joke. The PC wearing a denim jacket took it off and dusted it down. The other two laughed at him.

They led him over to the car, one officer controlling each of his arms. The shorter one smelt of cigarettes. One of them would have to release their grip to allow him to climb in.

The smoker let go. Rockburn put his free hand on the car roof as if he was about to duck and climb inside.

Feeling the second man's grip loosen –

He shoved back from the car and twisted his arm free. Followed up with an elbow strike. The officer staggered back swearing. His colleague reached for his baton but was too slow. Rockburn kicked him in the crotch. As the constable doubled up, Rockburn ran.

Sprinted down the street, turned the corner, past a baker's taking a delivery and entered the carpet shop next door. The bell rang.

Picking up a brochure he zig-zagged around the displays to the back of the store. His breathing slowed. He'd never been inside before and hoped it would have a rear entrance. Behind a double set of samples, he peered back towards the front door. Pulled across a swatch of heavy blue matting.

A crime squad officer ran across the front of the shop without stopping.

Rockburn pulled across another swatch of carpet. On the back was a special offer for underlay. He pulled more swatches while he observed the door and the street. The officer didn't return and no other officer appeared. Possible they'd split up at the corner, possible they were waiting there for him to reappear.

He walked deeper into the shop. Bedroom carpets, hall carpets, office carpets. Rugs – but only for floors. An area for pet-proof matting. At the back was a door with a sign: *Customer Parking*. He opened it.

It led into a short undecorated corridor with a stack of boxes of printer paper. There were two doors leading off, and at the end, the exit to the car park. He walked past the manager's office.

There was a burst of police radio chatter, and the exit door opened. Elsa stood on the threshold, flanked by the three crime squad officers. Two held batons, one a set of handcuffs.

'You going to be a pain?' Elsa sounded angry. Maybe he wouldn't be taking her to dinner with his semifinal winnings.

Rockburn shook his head. He was. Elsa the weak link – maybe he could push past her and escape through the door to the car park.

The officers advanced. Elsa telling him to put his hands on the wall, and spread his legs.

He did as he was told. One PC patted him down and the officer who he'd kicked in the groin handcuffed him in a front stack. He didn't double-lock the safety and each time Rockburn moved his hands, the cuffs tightened. Keeping his face taut, he was led outside and shoved into the back of their car. Banged his head on the roof. The crime squad were fine if you did what they said, and feisty if you didn't.

He sat in the centre of the seat like a child. He felt disappointed with the mayor, even if he was a busy man.

Elsa climbed into the driver's seat, and swivelled round to face him.

'You know I didn't do it – any of it.'

She raised her eyebrows.

Rockburn looked at his watch. 'How about a trade? Just give me twenty-four hours, you have my word I'll turn myself in.' He was sounding like a regular in the custody suite. Wheedling, whining, always wanting something, always someone else's fault.

Outside the car, the three crime squad officers were yabbering about a new girl in personnel. Behind them, two men loaded a carpet van.

'I saw Molloy and Mulkar at the garage. Look like they're on the prowl.' He relayed the registration plate.

Elsa looked unimpressed.

He tried again. 'Headley's holding his gang's firearm. It's in the shed at his uncle's allotment – on the Cowley Road towards Sheffield.' It was good intel, he knew she knew that. 'Twenty-four hours?' He raised his cuffed wrists which were already swollen and turning purple.

Elsa leant out of the car and jerked her head in Rockburn's direction.

A rear passenger door was pulled open by one of the three PCs. Rockburn shuffled along the seat and held up his handcuffs. They were unlocked, removed.

The door closed.

'Five minutes, Rockburn, then you can go. You're not under arrest, you never were.' Elsa slammed the steering wheel. Livid about something. She turned round, glared at him through the gap in the seats.

'How do you know the mayor?' Elsa smiled. Pretty when she smiled.

'Some other time.'

She passed him a bottle of water. He drank, pausing to

breathe. He definitely wouldn't be taking her to dinner, not that it had been a good idea in the first place – dating someone in the Job too claustrophobic. Nor someone who hated the Job, which is where it had gone wrong with Hocking. He took another swig of water. Maybe he should give the waitress a call. A fresh start. The panther required polishing, and he was no different.

He drained the bottle.

Through the window the officer wearing a denim jacket made a phone call. Behind him, a gangly youth carried rolls of underlay towards the carpet van.

'We have a witness who saw a chase across Little Park last night. Big motorbike involved, built a ramp, did a crazy stunt. Wouldn't happen to know anything about that, would you?'

Rockburn slid along the seat. 'Thanks for the water.'

Elsa clicked the central locking. 'We're on the same side.'

Rockburn rattled the door. Through the window the officer in the denim jacket waggled a finger.

'Listen, Rockburn. You're no longer a suspect for Mina's murder. Your bail's been cancelled. The murder team have taken a linked enquiry: Mina, Zafira and his two associates, and Professor Morley. Mackay's gone back to Glasgow – he was here on special assignment targeting Zafira and that's done with. Some of us, including the crime squad and me, have been assigned to the murder team.'

Outside the car, the officers prattled with the carpet fitters.

'Mackay sends his apologies for sending you on a wild goose chase.'

'I didn't go.'

Elsa shrugged.

'What was all that about just now: chasing me, arresting me – not arresting me? What *do* you want?'

'*Not* snippets of street crime intel, but information on the case you're investigating – what the professor told you, and what you're doing, sitting up on that petrol station.'

Rockburn fiddled with a headrest. 'You first, what have you got?'

'You're unbelievable.' Shaking her head, Elsa took a deep breath. 'The CS canister you took from one of Flack's customers – Interpol got a hit on the fingerprints. They've come back to a Vietnamese radical called Shen Nguyen. She's been banned from the US and Australia, but not from the UK. We seem to be a bit more relaxed here. She's believed to be a member of a radical sect known as the Second Horsemen.'

Rockburn nodded. Elsa had confirmed what he suspected, but nothing more. 'Flack found this when he was sweeping up.' He handed Elsa the envelope. 'Nguyen dropped it. Comes back to a Malaysian airline. You might be able to work out the members of the sect from the manifest, and whether they're booked on a return flight.'

'What makes you think they'll come by that petrol station?'

'Uh-uh, your turn. Did you get my message about a port alert?'

'For a boy we've never seen? To quote the murder team superintendent, *We're investigating a series of linked murders, not looking for Oliver Twist.* It's even crossed my mind that you've dreamt the boy up.'

'I showed you a photo.'

'Could be anyone.'

Rockburn thumped the headrest. As a Manchester detective, he'd been backed up by eight thousand police officers. As a PI, he had no one. 'Will you lend me a couple of people?'

'I'm not promising anything.'

Rockburn summarised what Morley had told him about the Second Horsemen. The Vietnamese legend of Thanh Giong the iron horseman, and his son the Second Horseman who it was hoped would appear and repel a modern Chinese invasion. The sect believed the boy was Giong's son, and wanted to return him to Vietnam, or sacrifice him to Vietnamese folk gods known as the *Than*.

'Wow. Even for you, Rockburn, that's quite a story. And you think the sect are using the mopeds to travel around on, and killing anyone in their path. How have you tracked them to the petrol station?'

Rockburn explained.

'That's all you've got?'

'Yes, and every minute I'm not watching, is a chance I'll miss them.'

'I'll feed it all back, but I know what the boss is going to say. You're clutching – far better to firm up the forensics and follow the intel.'

Rockburn shrugged. He *was* following the intel. Albeit not from Interpol, not via the official system, but it was equally valid.

'Am I free to go?'

Elsa nodded.

Rockburn shuffled along the seat. Elsa popped the door-locks and he shoved open the door. Climbed out, already feeling stiff from running and scuffling. His wrists throbbed as he walked across the car park.

He vaulted a barrier and headed back towards the petrol station. He was on his own; it was the way it was going to be, so best he got used to it.

40

Rockburn resumed his solo surveillance from the solicitors' roof. Bad-tempered traffic filled the road in both directions. The forecourt was busy. He ate half a bar of chocolate, drank a can of coke. Everyone needed snacks.

An old mini cooper entered the garage, the driver hesitant which pump to pull up against. There was an announcement over the intercom. A cashier in a fluorescent walked out of the shop. He pointed to a pump. The driver stalled, then pulled forward. The cashier filled the mini. The window pulled down to reveal a very old woman. She handed out her purse, and the cashier removed a banknote. They exchanged a few words, the cashier laughed. He washed the windscreen, and the mini kangarooed out of the garage.

Rockburn ate the remainder of the chocolate. Massaged his wrists. He felt warmed by the cashier's behaviour. Even in the city.

The mayor had also come good. Rockburn shouldn't have doubted him. He phoned a local off-licence, ordered a slab of Rat's Tail, a local craft beer. Well known the mayor liked a drink. Every popular man did.

A white van with ladders on the roof pulled out of the garage. The van involved in snatching Quang from Caiges was white.

There were a lot of them.

Another one drove in. Cars sat alongside every pump. The white van waited. Rockburn clicked out his fingers, threw a few imaginary darts. The final was in less than thirty hours. He needed to practise.

A woman emerged from the shop, climbed into her car, and drove away. The van moved up to a pump. The driver's door opened, and an Asian man wearing a hoodie slid down from the seat. He looked around. He was young, seemed nervous. A potential drive out. The van driver filled up. Screwed back the fuel cap, shut the cover. He was wearing gloves. He walked round to the back of the van, and opened the door. Two motorcycle helmets sat on the floor of the van, one yellow, one red.

Rockburn stilled. The van was similar if not identical to the one at Caiges. Adding the helmets into the mix meant it was a big coincidence, or it was *them*. Detectives didn't believe in coincidences, and this private investigator was no different. It had to be them.

The van driver spoke to someone in the back, then closed the door. He paid at the pump.

Rockburn ran across the roof, the wind ripping across him and bringing a smell of chemicals. He climbed down the ladder, sliding his hands. New burns aggravating old burns. He jumped the last six feet, stumbled, straightened, and ran down the side-street. Approaching the junction he slowed, pulled up a hood, and walked towards the traffic.

Through the stream of flitting vehicles, he could see the petrol station forecourt. The white van with the helmets in the rear was waiting to pull out.

Rockburn dashed through a gap in the traffic to the centreline. The van pulled out, drove past. Next to the driver sat the woman, Flack's walk-in customer – identified on prints by Elsa as Shen Nguyen. Definitely her. The van drove away.

Rockburn edged out into the stream of vehicles, cars swerving around him. Finally, he darted across.

Ran over to the panther. Pulled on his helmet, stuffed the gauntlets down his front. Fired her up, revved a couple of times. Then kicked in the stand, drew up his legs, and rode straight through the scrubby bush bordering the forecourt. Mud spattered all around. The motorbike climbed the short bank, and dropped down to the pavement. Two rough sleepers in a doorway held up their cans of special.

Rockburn bumped down onto the road and swung into a gap between vehicles. The white van was fifty metres ahead, caught by traffic lights.

His heart pounded like a butcher's block. Ten minutes later, Quang might be safe and Rockburn could retire with a one hundred per cent success rate. He could tour the country, playing in all the fag-end darts competitions.

The van pulled away with the traffic.

Rockburn followed, keeping his distance. At the next lights he pulled on his gauntlets. The van kept going, joined an arterial road. Joined the ring road. Ten minutes became thirty. He recalibrated. If the Second Horsemen were staying locally to the petrol station, they were heading out somewhere. A new mission, or going home? Quang hidden in a safehouse, or in the back of the van? Rockburn's only option was to keep following.

He could also phone Elsa.

But if he phoned her, and Quang wasn't in the back of the van, there were rules and regulations about extracting the whereabouts of the boy from the kidnappers. Finally, an advantage of being a PI. Maybe, he would grow to like his new role.

The van was following signs to the M6. Rockburn checked his fuel. He was good for a hundred and eighty. Two hundred if the pace was steady.

He settled half a click back on the motorway. Half a dozen

vehicles, including a supermarket wagon, between him and the van gave cover. Inclines and curves afforded the occasional view. Riding any closer to the van would risk attracting attention, further away risk losing their exit. He remained on edge. The sect might have already sacrificed the boy and be heading home. A London airport or a southern ferry terminal.

Fields passed on both sides. Every shade of green and brown. Sheep, a farmer on a quadbike, ramblers with their dogs. Rural folk so different to urban dwellers. Time to walk their pets, to appreciate a view.

In the distance, blue flashing lights. Vehicles began to slow and switch on their hazards. Rockburn wondered about a roadblock, Elsa's doing.

Little he could do.

The traffic squeezed together as it closed on the cluster of emergency vehicles. There was smoke, and an overturned car. A fire engine raced up the hard shoulder. He kept the van in his sights. The traffic funnelled into a single lane, crawled past, occupants rubbernecking. People were trapped inside the car. A second car sat facing the wrong direction, its bonnet and roof crumpled. Shattered glass covered the road.

The van crept past the accident. Not Elsa's doing.

Rockburn followed. The van resumed its middling speed, Rockburn matched it. Cat and mouse.

Big cat, and a big rider.

After a hundred and fifty miles, the van pulled into a service station near Oxford. The Second Horsemen needed fuel, and soon, so would Rockburn. The van parked at the services in the lanes marked for trailers, and next to a minibus hauling rowing eights. Rockburn pulled up fifty metres away. He pretended to check his phone. The parking was busy, hundreds of cars and few spaces. People walking to and from the services. Voices and the sweet smell of popcorn on the air.

Two of the sect climbed out from the passenger door, including Shen Nguyen. She walked round to the driver's side and said something to him through the open window. She looked about, and led off toward the glass doors of the services. The other Horseman followed, Shen Nguyen seeming to be in charge.

Rockburn could fill up with fuel, or risk doing it at the same time as the sect. That way he could take a closer look at the van.

Or he could risk a look now.

Walking a long way round, Rockburn approached the van from the rear. Music was playing inside. He closed from an oblique angle, staying out of the van's wing mirrors. At the last moment he ducked down and crept along the van's passenger side. He picked up a stone and used it to tap on the door. Squatted, tapped again.

He heard movement inside. The driver's door opened, and someone stepped out. Rockburn crept round to the rear of the van.

He could hear the driver walk around the front. The Horseman swore in a foreign language, his annoyance clear. Rockburn stood by the wheel arch so his feet wouldn't show if the driver looked underneath. He tapped the stone on the rear of the van. He could hear the driver walking along the side. Rockburn looked around but the trailer with rowing eights blocked the view.

The Horseman kept coming.

Rockburn readied. Officer safety training in the police carried the strapline, arrest and restraint. Use the minimum force to achieve the safe detention of a suspect, and if possible defuse a situation with persuasion and a warning. It was one reason British police officers were unarmed – force begot force.

The driver rounded the final corner of the van –

Rockburn hit him as hard as he could. A punch to the cheek,

a couple of knuckles raised, aiming for the back of his head for maximum force. He followed through.

The Horseman's head flew back and whacked the side of the van. His legs buckled and he sagged to the ground. He stayed down.

Definitely warming to his new role.

He dragged the body to the rowing trailer and drew back the tarpaulin. Laid the man's torso against a boat, flipped up his legs. Pulled the body straight so the Horseman lay along the bottom of the boat. He took the van keys from a pocket and pulled over the tarpaulin.

A horsebox drove past.

Rockburn looked over at the double doors of the services. A coach of pensioners was disgorging, but he couldn't see the other Horsemen.

He searched the cab of the van. In the glovebox he found maps, a pair of screwdrivers, a long crosshead and a short flathead. With its reasonable excuse, the latter was the burglar's favourite sidearm. He heard something –

Grabbed the flathead, froze.

A faint scratching emanated from the back of the van.

He walked round to the rear. Unlocked the doors and pulled them open. Travel holdalls and moped helmets cluttered the carpeted floor. He glanced back at the services, then turned and listened.

Nothing.

Then the scratching again. It came from the floor – under the carpet. He threw the holdalls out of the van and stacked the helmets on top. He pulled back the loose carpet.

There was a long panel on the floor with six shiny crosshead screws.

The sound of scratching strengthened.

'Quang?'

'He-elp.'

The cry was weak, but Rockburn recognised the voice. It sent the hairs up on the back of his neck. 'Quang, it's me. I'm here.'

He fetched the crosshead, and set to work. After he'd removed four screws he climbed back out. One of the Horsemen was waiting outside the double doors of the services. Eating from a bag of sweets. Shen Nguyen still to emerge.

Quang was gently humming.

Rockburn removed the fifth screw, but the sixth wouldn't budge. The thread was damaged. Sweat dripped off his nose. He exchanged the crosshead for the flathead, and jammed it under the opposite end of the metal panel. Levered it up. Grabbed the metal and heaved. The panel bent and twisted and sheared.

Revealed was a shallow compartment just big enough for a young boy to lie in a foetal position. A stench of urine. Quang rose up like a wakening corpse. Tears streaked his face. He clutched at Rockburn's jacket.

Rockburn pulled him out, hugged him. Told him it was all going to be okay, that he was going to take Quang somewhere safe, told him he loved him. The words tumbled out. He released the boy and climbed out of the van, glanced at the services.

They were coming, Nguyen and the second Horseman. Halfway to the van and would spot Rockburn at any second.

'Come on!' He grabbed the boy's hand and helped him climb down. The boy was stiff and sluggish. Rockburn grabbed a helmet, and together they started running.

A shout from behind.

There were tens of people in the parking area who must have been able to see what was happening. But Rockburn didn't stop, fearing they would translate it as a game, friends laughing around, or like most people, wouldn't want to get involved.

Rockburn led, his hand clamped to the boy's, half-hauling him like a tool trolley. He – they – ran pell-mell to the panther.

He fitted the helmet onto Quang's head and lifted him onto the back of the seat, but as he did so, knocked his own hat onto the ground where it skittered away. Leaving it, he climbed in front of the boy, fired the ignition and rolled the throttle. The bike leapt forward. He felt Quang clinging on, heard him scream. Rockburn pressed the horn, figuring the more people watching the better. The bike ripped through the stubby hedge between parking areas.

In his peripheral vision he could see the two sect members running. The man towards the panther, Nguyen towards the van.

Rockburn tore through another low hedge, and curved the bike round toward the services' exit. He bent forward.

'Hang on!'

He accelerated hard, the panther surging forward with a roar, as if she knew what was happening. The three of them zipped up the slip road, blasted across the carriageway and into the overtaking lane.

Rockburn drove the panther as fast as he dared. He and Quang were wild riders; bareback riders; they were the devil's horsemen. His eyes watered, and he could smell rubber and fuel, feel the boy's tight embrace. His heart thumped like a stack of speakers at a heavy-metal gig.

Slowing a fraction, he extracted the van keys from his jacket pocket and lobbed them at the central crash barrier. Then sped up, heading for the streak of tangerine sky.

41

Rockburn turned off the motorway and stopped in the entrance to a track leading to a farm. A flock of shrill black birds scoured the rutted fields on either side. He and Quang dismounted and clasped each other tight. The boy was shivering with shock. Rockburn's unprotected face was sore, dry and scoured by the wind. He sat Quang on a stile, wrapped his jacket around him, and found him a packet of nuts and raisins in one of the pockets.

Bending down by the panther, he switched the registration plate for a different one. Rocked back on his haunches, looked over at the boy chewing. Being a parent, even a pseudo-parent, was as much about providing a continuous source of snacks as anything else.

'Where w-we go-going?'

'Somewhere safe.' Via a petrol pump. The warning light had come on.

They watched the birds. Raking the soil, constantly looking round, alert for danger. As if on a prearranged signal, the birds rose and silently gusted away.

The two of them rode into the nearest town, but there was no bike shop. Rockburn puttered in and out of car parks, and at the leisure centre, took a motorcycle helmet. Arguably it was theft, but he left a fold of cash under the seat. At a petrol station on the outskirts he filled up the panther with fuel. He bought hot soup and sandwiches and fruit cake. He bought a protective jacket for the boy and gloves and newspapers. Quang put on the jacket, then sat on the kerb by the bike. He ate slowly, shaky as a probationer after a pub fight. His legs jiggered, his face contorted with anxiety.

'W–will they c–come b–back?'

'I don't know.' Rockburn paused, uncomfortable with his truth. He hoped not. 'If they do, then I'll be here.'

'Al–always?'

Again, he didn't know – he was still working out the future. But lying to kids was as bad a mistake as running out of food for them. 'Finish the soup while it's hot.'

He helped Quang pack his clothes with newspapers to ward off the chill on the bike. They filled their pockets with the fruit cake. Then they left the town, and keeping to the minor roads, blatted north. To Hocking's.

Rockburn parked at the front. Quang dismounted and ran around the back. The elasticity of youth. Rockburn climbed off, feeling like an old man. He looked up and down, but the road was clear. Wind whistled through the trees, crows circled above.

He tried to engage the bike stand, but the panther wouldn't sit still, kept wanting to topple. He wheeled it next door, and out of sight around the back. Mrs Gregory's patio was still being re-laid. Tools, and piles of flagstones, sand, bags of cement, lay all around. He glanced at the windows, but there was no sign of her.

He hopped over the fence to his childhood house and garden. Hocking was cleaning out the chickens. Kneeling by her side was Quang, asking questions about eggs and chicks. The boy started removing newspapers from under his jacket. They blew around on the grass. He explained to Hocking how they stopped him getting cold on the long ride. She glanced over at Rockburn.

'I'll put the kettle on.'

Hocking made tea and produced a packet of biscuits. She also understood the parent / pseudo-parent deal. Rockburn tried another version of the future.

The girl – Sarah-Jane, he told himself – padded downstairs and sat at the kitchen table, her legs crossed and bouncing her bare feet. She showed Quang how to dunk biscuits in his mug of tea. The boy said he'd never done that before. He laughed and ate them consecutively like a chainsmoker with cigarettes. Hocking sat at the head of the table, and wore a smile.

Rockburn kept hearing things, kept looking out. He rose, stood by the back door. A plastic container bowled across the garden and hit the chicken coop.

Sarah-Jane asked Quang if he wanted to watch a cartoon film. '*After a bath.*' The boy looked over at Rockburn. Nodding, he felt as if he'd have agreed to anything. Quang followed her out of the kitchen and up the stairs. Hocking indicated a chair, and Rockburn sat down.

They looked at each other, half-smiled. Rockburn drank some tea, closed his eyes. He needed a bath too.

A minute or two passed. Maybe more.

He opened his eyes, glanced at Hocking, who was looking at him.

'S-J's part of my life now.'

Rockburn felt the same way about the boy. Had felt that way about Hocking. For a moment or two he'd wondered, but the future wasn't written, wasn't decided. The future was uncertain as riding a motorbike across Mars.

Half an hour later, Sarah-Jane returned to the kitchen, and sat down. 'Clean, and watching the film.' She touched her scar, and murmuring to herself, took her hand away. She glanced at Hocking, at Rockburn, and waited.

The three of them sat like a council of war.

'So?' said Rockburn.

'He can stay here,' said Hocking. She glanced at the girl. 'We've talked about it – we'll look after him, see if we can adopt. He's a special boy. We both think so.' Sarah-Jane nodded. The two of them clasped hands briefly.

'He's not safe here, not for any length of time.'

An alternative was social services. But Rockburn's experience with children in care homes and adults who'd been through the system wasn't good. Through the open doorway, he could hear Quang laughing at the film.

'You could look after him,' said Hocking. 'And we would help out.'

A third option, and his instinctive preference. 'I want to, but he'll never be safe. Will always be traceable through me and what I do. No point being a private investigator if no one can get hold of me.'

'Do something else.'

Her old argument – they'd had it a hundred times. 'Investigation's all I know.'

A door banged shut. Rockburn stood and went to investigate. The closet door was closed and he could hear the boy urinating. He hovered in the front room watching the television. Cartoon chickens were meeting around a table, an annotated map in front of them. They were hatching a plan. Quang returned, still doing up his trousers. 'Hands,' said Rockburn, holding up his own. The boy about-turned, and Rockburn heard the tap run. He glanced back to the tv. The rooster held up a photo of a fox titled *Fox of Interest*. Rockburn laughed, surprised at himself. The boy returned, looking sheepish, and slumped onto the sofa. 'Okay?' said Rockburn.

Quang nodded, and Rockburn returned to his own table-top, in need of his own plan.

He sat down. 'It's an option.'

'I can't believe you're saying that,' said Hocking. 'You'd give up everything for that boy? You hardly know him.'

Rockburn twisted his empty mug one way, then the other. He listened to the blare of the tv. Outside, a vehicle drove past. 'I've known children like Quang, and what they've been through. And I've got to know him well enough. I like him, I respect him. I like spending time with him. And I hope, at least I think, he likes spending time with me.'

'We've been talking while you were out,' said Hocking. She felt for and took Sarah-Jane's hand. They smiled like the lovers they were. 'We'll move, take him with us.' The girl nodded.

'Moving to Scotland or the west country is not far enough.'

'Australia, then.'

'You'd do that?' Even as he spoke he wasn't sure. Despite only knowing Quang for less than two weeks, he'd miss him. A lot.

The two women looked at each other and nodded. 'We would,' said Hocking. 'We've both had problems here, both been a bit unsettled, wouldn't mind a fresh start.'

Outside, darkness had fallen.

The television was still squawking, and feeling premonitory, Rockburn walked into the next room to check on the boy.

42

Quang lay asleep on the sofa. Rockburn switched off the tv and sat on the seat's arm, stroking the boy's head and staring at the blank screen.

He heard a muffled sound outside – a voice, an animal cry? The darkness pressed against the window like a shutter. He carried the boy upstairs to bed. Quang woke and in a semi-doze undressed and crept under the covers. In seconds, he was asleep again.

Rockburn returned downstairs.

'Sleep on it?'

Hocking nodded, and the two women went upstairs to bed. Rockburn padded round, checking on the doors and windows. The moon appeared, and the outline of a tree reflected on the lawn from an upstairs window.

He lay on the sofa, arranged the blanket, tried to sleep. He stared at the ceiling, turned onto his side, shut his eyes. Opened them. He could hear more noises outside. Night animals shuffling about.

Throwing off the blanket, he rose, padded over to a window and surveilled the back garden. The moon had disappeared, and darkness prevailed. Hundreds of the sect could be sneaking up, and he wouldn't know. He lay down again on the sofa. Worked his way around a dartboard, invented checkouts, counted down.

The letterbox flapped –

And a receptacle of liquid crashed onto the floor. Rockburn heard the roar of an accelerated fire.

He leapt up. Smelt petrol, smoke. The sect's weapons of choice: the noose and fire-starting.

A window in the tv room smashed and a flaming object landed. He ran for the internal door. Behind him the crack and whoosh of a petrol bomb.

He hit the stairs, shouting. Ran up two at a time. Hocking and Sarah-Jane appeared in their nightwear in the hallway.

'They're here, trying to smoke us out.' He ran into Quang's room. The boy dozy as Flack after a night at the Arch. 'Get dressed.' He ran back to the hall. Downstairs, another window smashed. An explosive thump.

'We need a distraction – it's only the boy they want.' He turned to Hocking. 'Is your car sorted?' She nodded. 'Take it, no lights, blankets over cushions on the seats, drive like you've nicked it.'

'I'll do it,' said Sarah-Jane.

'We'll both go.'

'No,' said Rockburn and Sarah-Jane together. It was the first thing they'd agreed on. Smoke drifted up the stairs. Three on the panther would be a squeeze, but he was thinking ahead: they might need a second distraction. Hocking no doubt thought the car was the more dangerous alternative. 'No time to argue,' said Rockburn. He went into the bathroom and grabbed a towel. He ripped it into pieces and soaked them. Returned to the hall and handed them out. 'Hold it over your nose and mouth, now go!'

Sarah-Jane kissed Hocking on the lips, squeezed her, and disappeared down the stairs into the smoke. She was a brave woman, and Rockburn hoped she would be okay, hoped she and Hocking would work out.

He turned, ushered Hocking and the boy into the box room and shut the door. Braced it with a chair. His eyes were smarting. Hocking and Quang were coughing. Drawing a window across, he whispered his plan. Fresh air billowed inside.

Rockburn strained to hear.

Hocking held Quang's hand, and both of them stared at Rockburn. Quang remained calm, accepting of the situation, stoic. Hocking trickier to read. Scared. Scared for the boy. 'Quang has complete faith in you.'

She squeezed Rockburn's hand.

Whispered:

'Me too.'

Quang had brought them back together – but coming back together had shown they couldn't *be* together. He would get her and the boy out – or he would die trying.

'Come on, come on,' he muttered.

He wondered how the sect had found them. Tailed Rockburn in stages so they wouldn't show out. Made enquiries near to where he lived. Bribed one of his former colleagues. Done what he'd have done. It didn't matter.

Finally, the sound of a car. The squeaky garage door heaving upwards. The revving of the engine from Hocking's runaround. Shouting in a foreign language, the scrape of a car panel against the gatepost. Heavy acceleration. The sound of a second vehicle starting up.

Time to move.

Rockburn looked out of the window. Below was a small shed which bordered Mrs Gregory's garden next door. A wastepipe from the bathroom led along the bottom of the window to a vertical pipe at the corner which joined a drain abutting the shed. He gestured to Hocking.

She climbed into the opening, turned, stretched her legs down to the wastepipe. She scowled at Rockburn and shuffled sideways. She grabbed the vertical pipe and half-slid, half-climbed down to the shed roof. Rockburn gave her a thumbs up. He scanned both gardens but couldn't see anyone. Near the house they flickered with reflected light from the flames, further away, they were as black as wells. Grey smoke surged upwards.

He lifted Quang up to the window. The boy still felt bony. He lowered him so the boy's feet touched the pipe, then held his arms as he worked his feet towards the vertical pipe. He climbed down to Hocking like a monkey. Rockburn gave another thumbs up, then climbed out. He worked his feet along the pipe, and climbed down the vertical. From the shed roof he dropped down onto the half-built patio of his old neighbour.

The fire was taking hold of Hocking's house. Increasing heat, a roar of flames and exploding glass and appliances. Angry voices at the front.

Hocking helped lower Quang down to Rockburn, then climbed down to the patio. She took the boy's hand and together they waited for his next instruction.

The panther stood ready.

Hocking was shaking. 'Wh-why did you leave it here?'

Rockburn winked, trying to calm her. 'Tell you later.' He might or he might not. She'd think him daft, anthropomorphising the bike as he did. But the panther had been unhappy at the front of Hocking's, and to avoid chicken crap on the saddle, he'd reparked it at the back of her neighbour. And lucky he had.

'Only two helmets,' said Quang. Worry on his face too. Possibly thought he was going to miss out on a ride.

'I'll be fine,' said Rockburn.

The boy nodded, pulled on the smaller helmet. Hocking squeezed his shoulder, reached for the second lid. As she did, she screamed.

Quang pointed.

Rockburn wheeled round.

Two of the sect were approaching from the shadows at the side of the house. They were small, dressed in dark clothing. Men or women, he wasn't sure. But they moved silently, black bandanas with a motif around their heads. Two against one weren't the best odds, but they weren't the worst.

The Horsemen held their hands out to the sides, like people holding knitting. Except they weren't holding spools of wool, but lengths of wire.

Rockburn looked around, grabbed a rake leant against a water butt. Left by her builders, a rake for levelling gravel. He held it ready.

The two members of the Second Horsemen kept coming, from two and ten o'clock.

Quang appeared in Rockburn's peripheral vision and charged forward, yelling and wielding a plastering trowel. Months of upset and anger and grieving released in a moment of madness. Not quite the vision of the second coming, but a top effort.

Hocking ran after the boy.

Rockburn seized his chance while everyone was distracted. Surprise the best weapon in any confrontation, especially when outnumbered. He stepped to his left and holding the rake two-handed, the metal row of teeth facing downwards, he clubbed the Horseman at two o'clock. The teeth of the rake struck the attacker's head and neck and gouged down. Bone cracked and blood spurted. The Horseman crumpled and fell without a sound.

One down.

Using the minimum force necessary was the law. No leeway for private investigators, but if he was asked to account, he'd gladly argue his case.

The second attacker had confronted Quang, jerking the length of wire as the boy stabbed at him with the trowel. Behind the boy stood Hocking, urging him to run. Quang, however, stood his ground, brave as an ancient warrior, and Rockburn was tempted to believe the pseudo-religious faith assigned to him. The Horseman appeared in a quandary, working his hands back and forth, but not wanting to hurt the boy – at least, not then. Sacrificial rituals needed preparation. The Horseman dummied with the wire, and swept out a foot knocking Quang over. The attacker then advanced on Hocking.

Rockburn ran over.

Smoke from the fire next door blew across the garden. The alarm was ringing, and the chickens were shrieking in panic. Mrs Gregory's house was in danger of catching.

The welfare of his neighbour; Sarah-Jane fleeing in Hocking's car; and the whereabouts of more attackers all crossed his mind. But he had to focus. Critical incidents were about priorities and decisive action. The wider picture could come later.

The second attacker danced around Hocking's flailing arms, ignoring her screams. Jabbing left and right, the Horseman flipped the wire around her neck, pulled tight, and twisted her around to face Rockburn.

Rockburn grabbed the trowel from Quang. The shape of a flat diamond, pointed, knife-edged. The boy had chosen well.

'Let her go.'

Rockburn stood still, hands to his sides. Even if the Horseman didn't understand the words, they would understand the tone and body language. Release her, and no harm would come to them. They might also understand the pretence.

Hocking was turning pale as she struggled to breathe.

Rockburn raised the trowel, readied. He'd formed a plan of attack, but needed his former girlfriend to go limp before her assailant expected it. He stared at her, willing an understanding. When they'd been together, he'd often thought she knew what he was thinking.

The Horseman spoke.

Vietnamese words, Rockburn guessed, for *The* Second Horseman.

He shrugged.

'Boy.'

The exchange made clear. One Rockburn couldn't accept. The diamonds if he'd had them in his possession. The panther, even.

'Me,' he said, thumping his chest with his left hand. Trowel at the ready.

The Horseman shook his head.

'Boy,' he repeated.

Blood seeped down Hocking's neck from under the wire. Desperate, and hoping he'd not left it too late, Rockburn tapped his nose, pointed at her. His secret – *their* secret.

Her body sagged –

the sudden weight making the Horseman take a step back.

Rockburn darted forwards. Plunged the trowel into the Horseman's abdomen. Thrust upwards with all his strength.

Spurting blood, the Horseman buckled, and fell, releasing the wire and Hocking. She crawled away, gasping for air. *She was okay*. The Horseman lay groaning on the ground. Revealed – his bandana ripped away in the fray – as a young man. Who wasn't going to get up any time soon.

Rockburn loomed over him. Using minimum force wouldn't be straightforward to argue in court, but still possible. Two lives at stake; his own life.

'Quang's only a boy.'

The dying Horseman, only recently a teenager, stared up uncomprehendingly. Just a boy, too.

Time for the wider picture: escape.

'Come on,' shouted Rockburn.

He swung a leg over the panther, apologised under his breath for contemplating her sacrifice. He kicked up the stand, fired the engine. The noise was loud, abrasive, comforting. She forgave him. Quang clambered up and held his waist. Then Hocking, also gripping Rockburn's jacket. The air thick with smoke. The three of them coughing. Hocking squeezed forward, the seat not big enough.

Rockburn trundled the bike to the corner of the house, hoped Mrs Gregory was away. He gave the panther some revs, lined the motorbike so it was straight.

Then accelerated alongside the house. Recycling boxes and plant pots and logs knocked all over as they passed through.

Rode across the front garden, onto the drive, and shot out onto the road. Braked, turned, straightened, and accelerated hard, his two passengers squeezing up and tightening their hold on his jacket. The four of them rode away from the fire, away from the smoke, away from the crackle and pop of burning possessions.

Rockburn sensed the panther's responsibility to stay upright, Quang's excitement at the ride, Hocking's relief and worry for Sarah-Jane. Their eyes – real, virtual – all watery with emotion and the rushing air.

Riding into the night's purple blackness, the four of them felt to Rockburn as if they were one. A family.

43

They rode to Killer Servicing. And waited for Dave, huddled against a stack of tyres, Rockburn's arms around Hocking and Quang for warmth and comfort. They tried to phone Sarah-Jane, talked about her, prayed for her.

Quang slept.

After an hour, Rockburn stood up and paced around. He sat back down, Hocking pecking him on the cheek. He phoned Sarah-Jane, left another message. He tried Elsa, asked her to call back – said it was urgent. Willing the phone to ring, he stared at the vehicle wrecks, the jeep with roll bars, the old ambulance.

Dave had served eleven years for manslaughter after shooting a burglar in his own house. Setting up King Servicing had helped him rehabilitate, although most people called it Killer's. Many too thought his crime was justifiable. Rockburn believed everyone deserved a second chance – Dave, the migrants fleeing war and persecution, *him*.

When tentacles of light began creeping across the yard, the mechanic turned up on a bicycle. He rode a couple of circles to entertain the boy, the mechanic's feet flailing out to the sides like a circus clown. Finally, Dave propped the bike against a car wreck and drew the garage doors across.

'You're in luck, package for you arrived last night.'

Rockburn swung his arms, rolled his shoulders. He didn't feel lucky.

Dave wheeled out the portable heater and set it up near the entrance. Hocking and Quang warmed their hands. Dave set the coffee machine gasping and spluttering. He handed Rockburn the parcel.

'You owe me.'

Rockburn gave him the envelope from Caiges.

Dave handed out beakers of disgraceful coffee and found a packet of sweets styled like cigarettes for Quang. Rockburn and Hocking watched the boy pretend to smoke, pretend to cough. They pretended to laugh.

Then the three of them mounted up, the boy squeezed between Rockburn and Hocking. Dave waved an oily hand.

The road to the airport was fast. Too fast – they were his last moments with Quang. With Hocking. Rockburn scanned ahead, kept an eye on the mirrors, checked the laybys. There were lots of white vans, but not *the* white van.

The sect could have switched registration plates, like he'd done. They could have hired a different van, or a car. Or stolen one. A hundred and one possibilities. A thousand and one. He brooded over Sarah-Jane's whereabouts, her fate. Even if she turned up, he didn't have a passport for her. After seeing off Hocking and Quang, he would find her, send her after them.

Planes circled overhead, and one roared in towards the landing strip.

He rode up the ramp marked *Departures*. Butterflies in his stomach as if it was him starting a new life in a new country with a new identity and no friends or family to guide or help. A security guard in a yellow tabard patrolled the waiting area. Ten minutes the maximum waiting time. They dismounted.

Rockburn looked around. He hugged Quang. He hugged Hocking. The three of them hugged.

He handed Hocking her new passport and a second one for the boy – he was British now. Both stamped with six-month tourist visas. She slipped them in her shoulder bag.

'You sure you don't want me to come in, help you get your tickets online?'

Hocking shook her head. 'We'll be fine, won't we Quang?'

The boy grabbed his waist.

Rockburn ruffled Quang's hair. 'You're going to be flying to Europe, then Singapore. Then Perth. You'll see kangaroos.'

The boy nodded.

Rockburn faced Hocking. 'You'll need to find somewhere to live, buy clothes, get him into a school.' He wanted to discuss the decisions with her, the pros and cons. 'And I'll sort out the house, see if anything can be salvaged.'

'I don't care about that,' said Hocking, placing a hand on Rockburn's arm.

'I'll find her,' whispered Rockburn.

The security guard walked over.

'Are you allowed to ride three up?'

Hocking removed her hand, and Rockburn passed the guard his phone and requested a photo of the three of them. 'Our secret,' he said, the menace clear in his voice.

'Well, you need to move on,' said the security guard, trying to hand back the phone.

'Take the photo.'

The three of them hugged again, and the guard did as he was told.

Rockburn pocketed his mobile. At least he had a photo. He watched Hocking and Quang walk toward the terminal building. They held hands, and twice Quang looked back over his shoulder. Rockburn stuck his thumb up, and the boy replied in kind.

The boy was kind, was thoughtful, was funny, was mature. He *was* special. The irony no comfort.

The sliding doors of the terminal building opened –

and closed –

and they were gone.

Gone.

Rockburn looked at the third passport in the envelope from Dave's mate Usman, and glanced at the doors of the terminal. He closed the envelope and tucked it inside his jacket. One day it might come in useful.

'Move on, please sir.'

Jobsworth.

Rockburn mounted up – slowly – and ducked out into the traffic. He whipped around and between the cars, and shot down the ramp like a bobsleigh. Headed for the hospital. Before going inside to see Flack, he'd phone Elsa again, ask her to triangulate Sarah-Jane's phone.

On the motorway, hunkered down, air buffeted his helmet, and the panther rocketed past the other vehicles as if they were going backwards. He was no longer in The Job, but being a private investigator felt like it was going to be okay. His first case had produced similar feelings, seemed like a decent way to spend his time.

44

Rockburn slept like a dead man. His alarm cut into his uncon-
sciousness, unwelcome as an air-raid warning. He rose, did what
he had to. Ate a bowl of cornflakes with water, drank a mug of
black tea, threw half a dozen volleys of darts.

Elsa came round, questioned him about the fire, the two dead
men, the whereabouts of Hocking and Quang. He played dumb.
He felt numb.

'Are you arresting me?'

Elsa shook her head. 'Interview under caution – tomorrow,
after you've had a bit more time.'

Rockburn walked over to the sink, poured a glass of water.
He waited, guessed what was coming.

'We found Rebecca Hocking's car.'

The news Rockburn feared.

'A young woman, a friend of Rebecca's, according to her family.'

Rockburn set the glass down. He was sorry about the girl and
wondered if Hocking would ever forgive him. Sarah-Jane had
been brave, and selfless, and had the shapeliest legs he'd ever
seen. He poured away the water. It was a waste. The water, the
girl, everything – life itself.

*

One thing to do before the darts final at Caiges. He rode to the pawn shop, waited while Jones locked up, and gave him the thrill of his life by giving him a ride to the police station. Together, they signed for the diamonds. While Jones walked back to his shop, Rockburn rode to the other side of the city and sold them to a dealer for twenty times what the pawnbroker had advanced. At the nearest bank he paid back the loan to Jones and the rest into a PayPal account for Emma Baines. The new Hocking. The advance from the pawnbroker would serve as his commission, and cover some of his debts, and his expenses until his next case.

He hoped two dead Horsemen would be enough. That their deaths would send a message and no more would embark on a quest to find Quang. Or if they did, the boy would be safe with a different name living in a different continent.

There'd be more money, too, when he'd sold Hocking's house − after he'd sorted out the insurance and a rebuild − if he could bear to. Tomorrow's problems.

He had an hour to kill so he raced the ring road. Hunched down, man and bike as one. He was the panther, and the panther was him. They hugged the road, purred together. Clockwise to start: Stockport, Stretford, Eccles, Swinton. They kept to the overtaking lane, a steady hum enveloping them. Middleton, Ashton, Denton, Bredbury, and Stockport again. A circuit was 36.1 miles or 58.1 kilometres. He U-turned at the pyramid, all blue glass and an apex pointing to heaven. His watch showed 22 minutes and 22 seconds.

He took off a second time, accelerated until he hit the ton. The panther was still hungry for the chase of nothing but the chase itself. Bredbury, Denton, Ashton, Middleton. They avoided the worst of the potholes and lorry treads, broken glass, animal pancakes. He stole a glance or two toward the hills, to Sheffield, the Leeds chimneys. Then curved round the top, saluting Caiges, and driving on to Swinton, the wastelands of Eccles, the ganglands of Stretford.

The Stockport pyramid glinted in a rare sun. Watch check: 21 minutes, 45 seconds. Success, victory, a chequered flag. He patted the panther's fuselage as if she was a Spitfire and they'd just landed on a bumpy grassy airfield, holed and steaming. He circled the roundabout and headed north again, slower, a warm-down. To the Academy and the final countdown.

Searchlights on the roof of Caiges criss-crossed the sky, and beneath them, the Victorian building glowed in tens of spotlights. Adorned with guano-encrusted gargoyles and small smoky-glassed windows, it wouldn't have looked out of place in Gotham City. Vehicles filled the car parks. Crowds queued at the entrances, flocked around burger vans. The air was noisy with prattle, and choked with the smell of cannabis and fried onions.

No sign of his favourite programme seller. Or his godson. Hoped he would make missing Quang easier.

Rockburn parked up. He took out a couple of rags and rubbed the panther down. She was as warm as a horse back from the gallops. He huffed on the chrome and worked in some elbow grease. He checked her gauges, stood back, admired her. He took a couple of photos. One day she'd be gone, and snaps would be all he had. Snaps and memories. 21 minutes 45 seconds, a record.

A buzz rippled around the waiting queues. Mike Michaels was about to arrive. It was rumoured he had a rockstar coach with a shower and a bar.

An American-sized campervan pulled into the parking lot. *Mike Michaels, Bootle Lad* in flamboyant type on the sides and rear, and no doubt the roof too. To inform pilots and parachutists and extra-terrestrials. Except for the size of egos, the truth on darts was always disappointing. Dave Cummins owned a sweet shop; Trevor Reynard had a conviction for burgling an old people's home; the North West Cup had been running for eleven years with a three-year gap because the secretary had died and his replacement couldn't tie up his shoelaces.

The sliding door of the camper opened and Michaels stepped out. A crowd of fat, beery fans surrounded him. The Bootle lad sported an Elvis quiff and a purple sequinned top. Darts thought it was the new pop music.

Rockburn ducked down beside the panther and murmured a choice epithet, a few sweet nothings. Maybe, he'd give up darts.

His phone rang.

'Wanted to say good luck,' said Flack. He sounded far away, a distant land with white-clothed women, wine in silver goblets and lute-accompanied song. 'Win or lose, I'll still love you.' The tattooist's voice broke like Morse code.

'I'll come and see you again tomorrow.'

'Bring us –' Flack paused, breathing like a vacuum cleaner. 'Bring us some smokes.' The line cleared.

Rockburn heard a moped and leapt to his feet, scanning the car park. The noise Pavlovian. He listened, surveilled, slumped back down.

A passenger plane flew high overhead. Rockburn wondered whether Quang and Hocking had reached Singapore, their second stop on the way to Perth. He hoped Hocking would take the boy whale-watching, and sailing, and teach him to swim. And motorcycle. The plane disappeared into a bank of grey cloud. The drone faded, and then was gone. It was as if he'd daydreamed it – the plane, the boy.

He took the photo of the four of them out of his wallet. Quang, Hocking, the panther, and him. Maybe he'd get it blown up into a poster.

The car park quietened, the crowds including Michaels and his entourage all inside. Rockburn whispered goodbye to the panther and walked through a group of portacabins to the fire exit. Three or four grungy-looking teenagers stood outside. On seeing Rockburn they released shy smiles at each other and fist bumped.

'Are you going to win, Rockburn?'

'Aren't you too thin for darts?'

'Sign this, it's for my nan.'

Rockburn stopped. He signed their scraps of paper and their t-shirts; refused their cigarettes; asked the nan's name. They offered him a bag of crisps, but he said he would get grease on his fingers. They liked that, clucked like Hocking's chickens. Would make a great post, one of them said.

He left them twittering and moved to the doorway. He took a blade from his sleeve, slipped it around the frame and eased the door open. Stepped inside, let it slam. Couldn't carry a blade if he was police.

In his changing room, two good luck cards. The first from Hocking and Quang, wishing him a happy sixth birthday, and inside, a note explaining it was a lucky number in Vietnam, and was the best card the airport could offer. The second showed a picture of a horseshoe on the front; inside, a message:

Couldn't get off my shift
T
PS I don't play, but you could teach me?

Three and a half hours later, Rockburn emerged from the fire exit. He strode to the panther, cowboy boots tapping the ground. He mounted up, glanced back at the beast of Caiges. On the roof the searchlights scanned the night sky, and inside, the building throbbed with muffled music and the hubbub of a thousand people. A beast with crazy eyes.

He rode to the café in Fenwick Street where the watery-blonde waitress worked. He waited outside at the end of a row of parked motorbikes, replaying some of the match. There would be other matches – if he wanted. And he did want; he was good at darts, but he could be better. He brushed invisible dust from the panther's dials, admired her gleam.

He stared at the bus stop.

Nodded.

Tomorrow would be a new day. He'd make a statement to Elsa, visit Flack, then sit in his crib throwing darts and eating cornflakes, and wait for the phone to ring with a new investigation.

Tomorrow.

Finally, the waitress emerged. Just past midnight, a distant clock striking and striking. She saw him, took a doubletake.

She'd redone her lipstick for the journey home. She flicked her hair, smiled. Glanced up and down the row of bikes. He glanced with her. She helped herself to an unsecured helmet, and pulled it on. She fastened the chinstrap, climbed up behind him. Her breath smelt warm and sweet. She put her arms around him.

Clamped to their shiny charger, they rode out of the city, a king with his queen.

Acknowledgements

I would like to thank my wonderful editors Eve Seymour and Mary Chesshyre. Also, the brilliant cover designer Mark Ecob, and Andrew Chapman (Prepare to Publish) for typesetting and all-round publishing expertise. Thanks to Dan O'Sullivan for feedback on an early draft, and to Dan Setter for his motorbiking knowledge.

As always, I would like to thank my wife Sarah for her endless support.

If you enjoyed Rockburn, *please take a few moments to write a review. Thank you!*

You can sign up to James's mailing list at
jamesellson.com

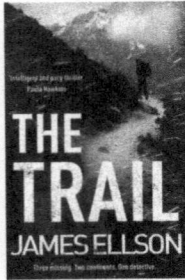

The Trail

The first book in the DCI Castle series.

**Longlisted for the Boardman Tasker Award
for mountain literature.**

A missing person enquiry leads Manchester DCI Rick Castle to Nepal.

Manchester. DCI Rick Castle is inspecting his bees when his
boss phones. A minor cannabis dealer has been reported
missing. His father's a war hero.
Rick flies to Nepal, and heads up the trail. Through villages of
staring children and fluttering prayer-flags. Brilliant blue skies,
and snow-capped mountains.
He finds a dead body.
Then a second.
Nothing in this world was ever straightforward. Nothing.
Finally, he puts himself in the firing line, and has a decision to
make. Is it the right one? The moral one?

Three missing. Two continents. One detective.

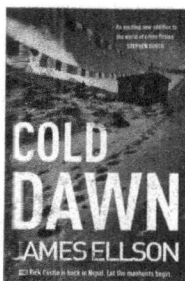

Cold Dawn

The second book in the DCI Castle series.

**Longlisted for the Boardman Tasker Award
for mountain literature.**

Against the rules, Manchester DCI Rick Castle removes a
prisoner from Strangeways and returns to Nepal.
His aim: to bring to justice his nemesis Hant Khetan, rumoured
to be the next Osama Bin Laden.
When the prisoner escapes, Rick and his small team must search
for him along the paths of the Everest foothills.
Trekking in the shadow of snow-capped mountains and
through earthquake-flattened villages,
Rick becomes increasingly desperate.
If they can't find him, Rick can't even begin . . .

DCI Rick Castle is back in Nepal. Let the manhunts begin.

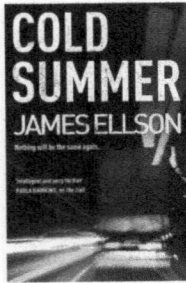

Cold Summer

The third book in the DCI Castle series, and the final part of the Nepal trilogy.

A race against time as DCI Castle hunts for two wanted suspects before they kill each other.

Manchester, England, the European migration crisis rampant...
On the site of a disused supermarket, the hidden compartment
of an articulated lorry is being unloaded. At the same time,
a prisoner escapes from Strangeways.
Are the two things connected?
DI Rick Castle, recently demoted but inspirational,
starts to investigate . . .

Nothing will be the same again.

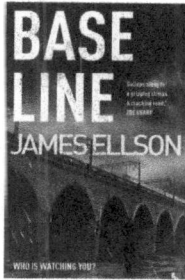

Base Line

The fourth book in the DCI Castle series.

A routine case leads to a Russian cell operating in Manchester.

Investigating a tyre blowout on a school minibus is not what
DCI Rick Castle had envisaged in his new job in charge of
Special Investigations at South Manchester. He'd prefer to be
making headway on a cold case murder, and following up leads
from his recent press conference.

Then drugs are found in his car, and he's arrested.

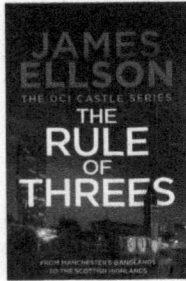

The Rule of Threes

Out June 2026.

The fifth book in the DCI Castle series.

A protected witness who's been given a new identity has gone missing. The original case involved William Redman and his South Manchester organised crime group. DCI Castle travels to a remote part of Scotland to make enquiries, and makes an arrest, but discovers he is also being targeted.

Are the two things linked?

Is Redman involved?

Rick is pushed to his limit, but is it enough?